The Black Stiletto

Endings & Beginnings

ALSO BY THE AUTHOR

The Black Stiletto Series
The Black Stiletto
The Black Stiletto: Black & White
The Black Stiletto: Stars & Stripes
The Black Stiletto: Secrets & Lies

Novels
Evil Hours
Face Blind
Tom Clancy's Splinter Cell (as David Michaels)
Tom Clancy's Splinter Cell: Operation Barracuda (as David Michaels)
Sweetie's Diamonds
A Hard Day's Death
Metal Gear Solid (based on the videogame)
Metal Gear Solid 2: Sons of Liberty (based on the videogame)
Dark Side of the Morgue
Hunt Through Napoleon's Web (as Gabriel Hunt)
Homefront: The Voice of Freedom (cowritten with John Milius)
Torment
Artifact of Evil
Hitman: Damnation

James Bond Novels
Zero Minus Ten
Tomorrow Never Dies (based on the screenplay)
The Facts of Death
High Time to Kill
The World Is Not Enough (based on the screenplay)
Doubleshot
Never Dream of Dying
The Man with the Red Tattoo
Die Another Day (based on the screenplay)
The Union Trilogy (anthology)
Choice of Weapons (anthology)

Nonfiction
The James Bond Bedside Companion
Jethro Tull: Pocket Essential
Thrillers: 100 Must-Reads; Ian Fleming's *From Russia, with Love* (contributing essayist)
Tied In: The Business, History, and Craft of Media Tie-In Writing (contributor)

The Black Stiletto

Endings & Beginnings

The Fifth Diary—1962

A Novel

Raymond Benson

Oceanview Publishing

Longboat Key, Florida

For Marion Givercer and Boots Benson

ACKNOWLEDGMENTS

The author wishes to thank the following individuals for their help: Ronald Bennett, Dan Duling, Tony and Tori Eldridge, Susan Hayes, James McMahon, Pam Stack, Grace Stewart, Pat and Bob Gussin, and everyone at Oceanview Publishing, Peter Miller, and my family, Randi and Max.

AUTHOR'S NOTE

While every attempt has been made to ensure the accuracy of Los Angeles and Odessa in 1962, Flickers nightclub and the Bartlett Ranch are fictitious.

The
Black
Stiletto

Endings &
Beginnings

I
Martin
The Present

Ever since I revealed my mother's secret to my daughter, much of the anxiety I experienced in the last year had settled down. The same thing happened when I first told Maggie that my mother, her patient, was the Black Stiletto. I felt somewhat relieved that I didn't have to deal with the burden of that explosive information alone. Now that Gina also knew, it was even better. I just hoped my nineteen-year-old could keep quiet about it. So far, so good, even though she completely immersed herself in the history of the Black Stiletto to a disturbing degree.

Gina was still reading the diaries—she finished number three already and started the fourth—and she was studying all the ephemera my mother left behind in that secret closet in the basement of our old house in Arlington Heights. I gave her a copy of the key to the safety deposit box at the bank where I keep that old stuff. Gina also looked up vintage *New York Times* and *Los Angeles Times* articles from the fifties and sixties on the Stiletto. The more she found out, the more fascinated she became about Judy Cooper, the girl from West Texas who ran away from home to New York City and became a masked vigilante.

My daughter couldn't believe I hadn't tried to contact my uncles in Odessa, Texas—my mom's brothers, John and Frankie. My response to that was I wouldn't know what to say to them, and I wasn't sure they knew the truth about their sister Judy. Gina proclaimed her determination to find out if they were still alive. I warned her not to attract attention to ourselves, and she agreed.

Never a fast reader, I was just beginning to read the fifth and last diary. Besides, I had to admit it still bugged me to find out stuff about my mother that I never knew. The truth about the identity of my father, for example. For my entire life, and I'm forty-nine, I thought my dad was one of the first casualties of the Vietnam War. I never knew him. I never knew what he looked like, because Mom possessed no photographs of him. None.

Richard Talbot. Right.

Then I learned in my mother's fourth diary that my father, I was pretty sure, was an Irish-Italian gangster in Los Angeles named Leo Kelly, and that he screwed over my mother pretty badly. Cruelly. I didn't know if he was still alive. It was no wonder she completely shut any memories of him out of her life, and mine as well. Still, she had lied to me. I was sure she did it to "protect" me, as Uncle Thomas insisted. She didn't want the bad guys in California to come after her or me. So Judy Cooper changed her name to Judy Talbot and moved to the Midwest to live in obscurity. She got hold of an obscene amount of money somehow, and that's what we lived off of. I was an idiot not to have been even remotely curious about where Mom's money came from.

I supposed I'd find out in the fifth diary.

Complicating matters was the fact that *someone* in Texas, probably Odessa, was looking for my mother and damned near found her. I was in New York checking out Gina's new life as a Krav Maga student and teacher—after she dropped out of Juilliard—and thanks to something stupid I did, a couple of hired killers put a bullet through my neck. I was lucky. The vagus nerve was severed, but otherwise the round missed my spinal cord and carotid. Now, a month after surgery, the wound was healing nicely and my voice was better. I still sounded like I was talking through sandpaper, though.

Gina—my amazing warrior—put both men in the hospital.

One would never walk again. We still don't know how all the legal repercussions of that incident would be resolved.

That worried me. It was only a matter of time.

As if on cue, the phone rang. It was Uncle Thomas, who was first my mother's lawyer and now mine and Gina's. He asked if I could come by his office to discuss the case after I got off work.

I looked at the clock on my office wall and saw that it wouldn't be unreasonable to slip out. Tax season was over—at least the crunch was—so I could leave Wegel, Stern, and Talbot, Inc., where I worked as a CPA. I owned the place now too, for Sam Wegel handed me the business when he found out he had cancer. Sam still worked three days a week, but I usually had the place to myself, except for the presence of Shirley and another assistant named Pat whom we'd recently hired.

It was time for another heart-to-heart with the man who wasn't any true relation but whom I've known since I was a child.

"Well, if it isn't Martin Talbot," Janie greeted me warmly. She was Thomas Avery's secretary, and she'd been working for the guy as long as I could remember. I gave her the obligatory hug, and asked if he was available.

"He's with someone, but they should be finished in a jiffy. Would you like some coffee while you're waiting?"

I heartily accepted. Just as I put the cup to my lips, Uncle Thomas's door opened and there he was with his client, an elderly man I didn't know. Thomas was perhaps a couple of years older than my mother, I thought. He'd always been a close friend to our little family of two, which was why I called him an uncle. He greeted me with a smile, although he'd lately worn a sheepish, guilty look on his face when he saw me. After I confronted him a couple of months ago and forced him to tell me the truth about my mom, he finally relented and admitted that he had known all along that she was the Stiletto.

"Hello, Martin," he said after seeing his client to the door. I stood and we shook hands. "Let's go inside."

He closed the door as I sat across from his desk. It had been just a little over a year since I received the lovely news, right here in this office, that my now-dying mother was once the ultra-famous Black Stiletto. I was slow on the uptake; it had taken me this long to suspect some complicity on the part of Uncle Thomas in her fantastic tale. It was time for him to come clean.

"How's our Judy doing?" Thomas asked.

"No change, Uncle Thomas. She stays at a perpetual level of pure hell. It's so hard to watch."

"God, I know." He pondered that silently for a few seconds, and then asked, "How's Gina doing?"

"She's fine. She's really interested in the Black Stiletto now. Wants to know everything about her." I shook my head. "I'm not sure what I think about that."

"Does she know that I know?"

"I don't think so. She hasn't said anything. But I think she should know, don't you?"

Thomas shrugged. "I suppose that's up to you if you want to tell her. I don't mind. I have to tell you, though, there's something we need to discuss."

"That's why I'm here."

"First of all, the case as it stands in New York. We'll know in a week whether or not Gina will face any charges for what happened to your two attackers, but the DA has admitted that his inclination is to chalk it up to self-defense, and both Gina—and you—will walk away. No one's complained on the bad guys' side, so it's practically a done deal. I think you can rest easy about that."

"That's great news. I didn't see how they could accuse Gina of anything, considering what those guys did."

"And they've also been charged for the murder of that woman who said she was the Black Stiletto."

"Betty Dinkins."

"Right."

"So, they're not going anywhere." I was referring to Bernard

"Bernie" Childers, the man with the broken neck, and William "Stark" Simon, who was still in jail without bail. "Have you found out anything more about them?"

Uncle Thomas sighed heavily. "That's what I wanted to talk to you about. I didn't say anything when we first heard the men were from Odessa, Texas, but in light of what I've discovered, it's my duty to tell you that I think your mother is in grave danger. You and Gina, too, I suspect."

That sent a lightning bolt of renewed anxiety through my chest. "What did you find out?"

"Officially, they're employees of Bartlett Supply Company, a large outfit that services the oil industry. There're a lot of oil wells around Odessa."

"I know."

"Well, the fact that this Bartlett Supply Company comes into the picture has me worried."

"Why?"

"I used to know some people there."

"What?" I was getting angry. "Uncle Thomas, I know you know a lot more about my mom—and *everything*—than you've told me. So why don't you just tell me everything and we'll go from there."

He looked at me with a pained expression. "Martin, back when I first met your mother, in 1962, she came here from Odessa, Texas. Not Los Angeles. I had a cousin in Odessa then, and he hooked up your mother and me."

"What was she doing in Odessa?"

Uncle Thomas wrinkled his brow. "You haven't read the last diary?"

"I'm just starting it. I'm a slow reader. So, what was she doing in Odessa?"

"Arranging to disappear so she could hide for the next fifty years. Christ, Martin, you make it difficult for me. I promised your mother I wouldn't talk about it until after you'd read the diaries. *All* of them. I have to honor her wishes. So read the goddamned diary, Martin! Then I can talk to you."

He slapped the top of his desk. I could see he was very upset, his face turned bright red. A guy his age—I didn't want him to have a heart attack or anything.

"Hey, Uncle Thomas, take it easy, it's okay. I'll read it. But why is my mother in grave danger? You can't very well tell me *that* and not say why."

"I can say this much. My cousin's name was Skipper Gorman."

The name rang a bell. Then Thomas provided the other clue.

"Skipper had a brother—also my cousin—in Los Angeles. His name was Barry Gorman."

Holy shit! That was the guy my mother befriended and worked for when she moved to the West Coast. An unofficial private detective who worked for the DA. They weren't lovers; at least they weren't in the fourth diary. I also remembered Skipper being mentioned.

"Oh boy," was all I could manage to say.

"You know who they are?"

"From the last diary."

"Have you come across the mention of someone named Ricky Bartlett?"

That set off a mental alarm too. He was the cowboy dude that my mother once saw at a mobster meeting. The whole damned story was knee deep in mobster shit.

"Yeah. There wasn't much about him though."

"Ricky Bartlett was a big man in organized crime in Odessa back then."

"My mom called it the Dixie Mafia."

"Right. That's what they called it in the sixties and seventies."

"Bartlett Supply Company. Am I to assume—?"

Thomas nodded. "Ricky Bartlett owned it. It was the family business, and a successful one. Bartlett lived like a king on a ranch outside of Odessa. He had cops and judges in his pocket. Oddly, he was very charitable. He put on a rodeo weekend event every year to raise money for various causes. So he was actually well liked in town, except by the people who were afraid of him."

"Was he after my mom?"

"He was. He wanted her head. He thought she'd stolen money from him. A lot of money. Over a million dollars."

"Did she?"

"That's something I *don't* know, Martin. Skipper down in Odessa handled her money arrangements before she came up here. He was an accountant; he worked as an investment guy. She did have that amount with her when she arrived, though, and I helped her place it in accounts so she could live off of it for decades. It was my job to see that she wasn't found by Bartlett's people, or, for that matter, Vincent DeAngelo's people. You know who *he* is, right?"

"Yeah. He's the Big Daddy of 'em all, according to my mother's historical treatise. So the fact that Bernie and Stark worked for Bartlett Supply Company, that means Bartlett is still looking for Mom?"

"Bartlett died sometime in the early eighties. DeAngelo died in prison in the late sixties."

"So who would care now? Why would anyone still be after her?"

"I think the answer has to do with that million dollars," Thomas said.

"Geez." It didn't sound good. "All of Mom's money is gone. So are you telling me the Bartlett family is still involved in West Texas crime?"

"You realize that if you hadn't called attention to yourself in New York, Mr. Childers and Mr. Simon wouldn't have found you? They'd been sent by whoever currently hires them for dirty work. They were there to check on Mrs. Dinkins's story that she was the Black Stiletto. They quickly figured out she wasn't the real Stiletto. I imagine they tortured Ms. Dinkins for the truth before killing her, and then found that letter you wrote to her. Either they or their boss thought you must know something about the Black Stiletto, since you interfered with their plans."

"I know, I know. I'm an idiot. I shouldn't have done it."

"What's done is done. The thing is, I believe those two men

were on a mission to murder the Black Stiletto if they found her. That means, since they failed, whoever's behind it will send more troops—and you and Gina are the next viable leads."

"Damn you, Uncle Thomas!" I probably yelled it a bit too loud. The man flinched. "You've lied to me. All this time."

"I haven't lied to you, Martin." He looked crushed that I'd accuse him that way.

"Well, you haven't completely told me the truth."

"I'm sorry. I played it the way I thought your mother wanted me to."

"I know, but still—" There were actually tears in his eyes. "All right, I'm sorry I yelled. So what are you saying we should do?"

He got hold of himself. "For the first seven years or so that your mother was here with you, I made her move around, not stay in one place too long. Ricky Bartlett's dogs were sniffing around, but eventually the heat disappeared. After two years of no activity, I allowed your mother to permanently move into that house here in town where you grew up. I thought it was safe then. And it was. We never heard a peep out of Bartlett or DeAngelo or anyone."

"So you're still—connected? Is your cousin still alive?"

"No, Skipper died back then, helping your mother. And I'm not 'connected,' as you call it. Not anymore. That was a long time ago. I did some shady things back then, one of which was to help your mother and you disappear."

The concept of possessing a million dollars blew my mind. "Didn't my mom work sometimes? I thought I remembered her working as a waitress."

"Yes, she tried a few jobs, but mostly she lived off the money. The first few years while you both moved around, she didn't work. It was only after you moved into your house on Chestnut that she started trying a few jobs. Yeah, she was a waitress for a while, but I think that was just so she could do something. She called herself a 'consultant' on her income tax forms, but she didn't consult on anything. Your mother worked at odd jobs that paid only cash, and not for very long.

Mostly, she wanted to stay out of the public eye." He chuckled a little. "I'm pretty sure people that knew her thought she was odd. A recluse."

"She read a lot, I know that, and she pounded on that punching bag in the basement quite a bit," I said.

"She was very protective of you, Martin. Probably overprotective."

That made *me* smile. "It's probably why I'm so *nebbish*."

We were quiet for a moment. I wasn't as ticked off anymore, but I *was* a little scared. "So what do we do?"

Uncle Thomas didn't hesitate with an answer. He said, "I think you should consider moving your mother out of the nursing home and hiding her somewhere safe."

When I walked into Woodlands, the nursing home where my mom lived—although "lived" was probably too generous a description of her existence there—I actually thought I didn't need to take Uncle Thomas's suggestion seriously because it was doubtful my mother would survive much longer.

Alzheimer's had really done a number on her. It hit her hard and the symptoms came quickly and mercilessly. Her decline in the past year was what most patients experienced in three. Maggie thought the rapid onset of the final stages were due to my mother's heightened senses that drew her to become the Black Stiletto in the first place. When my mother entered puberty, she could suddenly see and hear better, and she had an uncanny knack for sensing danger and penetrating lies. Her brain definitely had something to do with it, and that was the organ that Alzheimer's targeted.

In the last month, especially, Mom got pretty bad. I had to arrange for a hospice service to oversee her care. A feisty black woman in her thirties, Virginia Hawkins, was assigned to my mother, and she was great. Mom seemed to like her too, although it was difficult to tell what Mom thought. Mom needed everything done for her now. She couldn't walk anymore; she had to be in a wheelchair. Her everyday bathroom chores had to be assisted. She had to be spoon-fed.

Maggie—Dr. Margaret McDaniel—said it wasn't going to be much longer. My mom was in the final stage. It was possible she could die any day, or she could live another month or two. My mother's body was shutting down. Her brain didn't know how to operate the machine anymore.

It was all very, very sad.

I went into Mom's room and found her asleep. It was already after dinner, and she usually went to bed pretty early. No one else was there. Maggie was at her house—our house, although I still kept my own—and would expect me there for dinner soon. I just wanted to stop in, since it was on the way to Deerfield.

At least Mom looked peaceful. Her breathing was deep and steady.

"Can you hear me, Mom?" I asked softly.

She didn't stir. I stared at the shape of her frail body under the covers and still marveled that the woman lying before me had once been the Black Stiletto. Unbelievable. Totally crazy, and yet incredibly awesome.

"Leo Kelly," I said. No response. "Why didn't you just tell me the truth? I know he hurt you badly, and he was a mobster and a killer, but he was my father, wasn't he? The math works out, except you were pretty late, by almost a month. Unless there's another man in the picture at the very beginning of sixty-two, he has to be Kelly. Or was he Barry Gorman? I guess you really want me to read those goddamned diaries to find out. Why? Why, Mom? It's like you're making a game out of it."

Actually, that would have been just like her. She liked games. I couldn't tell you how many times we played Monopoly together, just the two of us, when I was a kid.

I thought I should shut up before I really *did* wake her. But then something else in my gut boiled to the surface. "I'm afraid for Gina, Mom. She knows all about you now, and I'm scared she's kind of like you. Actually, she's a *lot* like you. I don't want her to turn *into* you, if you know what I mean. But you know something? I think *you* wanted her to. You saved all that stuff for her, not me."

Mom's expression changed and she snorted in her sleep. And then she *smiled*. Had she heard me? She hadn't woken up. What was I doing? Why was I talking to her like that? I was nuts, no question about it.

"Aw, gee, Mom," I muttered. I knew I couldn't let anything happen to her. Nothing violent, that is. It was my duty to protect her. I needed to find out what was going on in Odessa, Texas, and try to avert trouble if it was coming.

I leaned over and kissed her cheek. "Goodnight, Mom. I'll see you tomorrow."

When I left the room, I pulled out my cell phone and called Maggie.

"Hi, honey," she answered.

"Hi, I'm at Woodlands."

"I figured. Dinner's almost ready. When will you be here?"

"I'm leaving now. Say, do you still have that private investigator's phone number? You know, the one you had on your refrigerator?"

"Bill Ryan?"

"Yeah."

"His card is still on the fridge."

"I think I want to hire him to take a little trip to Texas."

"Oh, Martin, do you really want to do that?"

"Yeah. And you're not going to like this either, but I want you to start thinking about how we can move my mother out of Woodlands and hide her for a while."

2
Judy's Diary
1962

Leo had some kind of nerve last night. He actually showed up at my apartment and banged on the door. Called out loudly for me to answer it and disturbed my neighbors. The woman down the hall yelled for him to shut up.

I stayed quiet. Pretended I wasn't home.

After a while, he left.

Good riddance.

Today they're going to put Maria DeAngelo—I mean Maria *Kelly*—in the ground.

The funeral is this afternoon. In Las Vegas, of course. There's a lot of press coverage of the event, and police will be present. After all, this was a top mobster's daughter who'd been gunned down.

It's taken me a week to come out of my shell. I've done nothing but stay cooped up in my apartment. I called in sick to Flickers. I told Charlie I had the flu. I think he knew better, but he cut me some slack. He knew I took the breakup with Leo pretty hard.

I suppose I've been in shock over what happened at the New Year's Eve party. The image of that Black Stiletto *imposter* robbing Maria of that beautiful diamond necklace and then shooting her at point-blank range—it will haunt me forever. And Leo, the supreme bastard, just stood there with his mouth open, playing the innocent, bereaved husband. And it looks like they all believed him, too. The "Stiletto" had also knocked out a servant in the wine cellar, through which the underground passage went from the gazebo to the house. What a charade.

But to me, it's pretty clear. The imposter was Christina Kelly. And she was in cahoots with her brother, Leo, to steal the diamond and bump off his new wife.

The police never called me to give a statement. After all, I was a witness. The only witness, I think. Everybody at the party was focused on the fireworks. It was just me, Leo, Maria, and the phony Black Stiletto. I'm sure Leo never mentioned that I was there. He wouldn't have wanted my presence at that party known by his father-in-law, the great and powerful Vincent DeAngelo. So, by official accounts, I *wasn't* there.

The news was full of the murder. "Black Stiletto Slays Vegas Socialite" was how most papers described the crime. Inferences that Maria Kelly was the daughter of a mafia boss were practically non-existent. The press did say that DeAngelo was a "successful businessman" with holdings in Vegas properties. He was quoted as saying the Black Stiletto "will be a dead woman," so he must believe Leo's story. Leo himself was cited in a Vegas paper, claiming he was "devastated" at the loss of his wife of less than a week. "It all happened so fast," he said. "We were watching the fireworks, and suddenly there was the Black Stiletto."

Right.

Was the imposter Christina? Moments after the shooting, after I had melted away from the scene and strode back to the house, I saw her emerge from the back door. She acted suitably thrown by the news when I told her what had happened. I suppose I can't be totally sure, but my intuition tells me it's so. I don't know how she pulled it off. Boy, would I like to get proof that I'm right. Then I'd give it to Vincent DeAngelo and show him what a slimy, murdering son-in-law he has. That would show Leo. His life wouldn't be worth a nickel.

In the meantime, the Stiletto is wanted by the cops. Same old story. It never ends, does it?

I've had one conversation with Barry about it on the phone, as the Stiletto, of course. I told him that the phony was probably Christina and that Leo was behind the robbery and murder. Barry's response was what seems logical: "It would be suicide for Leo to do something like that." I know, it would be madness on Leo's part. Still, my gut instincts have never failed me yet. Barry said the police don't know what to think about this new development and that the DA has put on hold any further "projects" with me. He said he was sorry, but he'd work on changing that. Great. Now I don't have that extra income. I said I'd like to string up Leo Kelly by the neck. Barry doesn't know *Judy Cooper's* reason for my vitriol, so he laughed and said, "Don't get too hasty, Stiletto, we need Kelly alive if we ever make a case against DeAngelo."

That's all I feel like writing today, dear diary. I'm not in the best of spirits.

JANUARY 9, 1962

It's early morning, four o'clock, and I just got home.

The Black Stiletto—the *real* one—just paid a little visit to Leo Kelly and scared the crap out of him, I hope.

I decided to go back to work on the night I last wrote. Charlie and everyone else at the club were glad to see me. Even though the place reminded me of Leo, it felt good to be around people again. It took my mind off of my troubles. So I worked again last night, the 8th. Everything was going great, and then Leo showed up around midnight.

A singer named Dore Alpert was just finishing his set. I was enjoying his music, too. He was a handsome guy who also played trumpet with his band. I thought his trumpet playing was better than his singing. Alpert told the audience that he was about to record an album, and for the occasion he was going to drop the name "Dore" and use his real first name, which is Herb.

Some folks were already starting to leave since it was the witching hour, so I stood at my post at reception and said good night to the guests. Or, good evening to late arrivals who just wanted to sit at the bar.

I swear I felt my internal danger radar tingle just before it happened, and then Leo walked in. I could tell he was drunk. He stank of booze and he had that belligerent tone of voice that he got when he'd been drinking too much.

"You *are* here," he said, a little out of breath. "Someone told me you came back to work. I've been trying to talk to you."

I practically growled at him. "Leo, go away. I can't talk to you here. I'm working!" I was pretty angry that he'd shown his face. Like I said, the *nerve!*

He got close and put both hands on my upper arms. "Judy, please just give me a minute! I can explain everything!"

I roughly shook him off and stepped back. "I don't want to hear anything you have to say."

"Judy, I love *you*. I've always loved you and only you. That marriage to Maria—it was a sham! It was something her father ordered me to do."

"Oh, he *ordered* you to marry his daughter?"

"Yes! It was a goddamned business arrangement."

"I don't believe you!" My voice had risen enough that Gary gave me a warning glare from behind the bar. I brought my rage down to a harsh whisper. "Go away, Leo. Don't ever call me again."

"Damn it, Judy, it can be like it was before. I'll—I'll move out of the house in Vegas and come back here. We can—"

"Shut up, Leo!" Again, I was too loud. Charlie would come running pretty soon, so I moved in close and spoke very softly. "Listen to me, Leo. If you try and contact me again, I will tell Vincent

DeAngelo and Sal Casazza and everyone that knows you that it was you and *Christina* that stole Maria's diamond and killed her. That was Christina in that Black Stiletto outfit, wasn't it?"

He jerked and blinked his eyes rapidly as if I'd punched him in face. Dear diary, it was difficult to read his reaction. On the one hand, he could have been surprised that I knew the truth; on the other, it could simply have been disbelief that I'd accuse him of such a thing.

"No!" he spat. "Are you insane? Christina?"

"Come on, Leo. Don't lie to me."

"Do you think I'd be crazy enough to do that to my own wife? To Vincent DeAngelo's daughter?"

"I think you and your sister are capable of anything."

"Well, it's a lie!"

Again, I tried to read his face, but he was too drunk. I couldn't get a reliable sense of whether or not he was telling the truth.

Frustrated, I shouted at him. "Get out of here, Leo, and *don't call me*! Don't come to the apartment. Forget I exist, all right? I never want to see you again!"

"Judy!"

That voice was Charlie's. He stood behind me with his hands on his hips.

"Oh, hi, Uncle Charlie," Leo managed to slur.

"Get out of here, Leo," my boss snapped. "Now."

"But Uncle Charlie—"

"*Now*, Leo! Or do I have to have you thrown out?"

That shut Leo up. A hangdog expression formed on his face. He gazed at me with pain in his eyes, and then he turned and left.

I started crying. Charlie came up to me and put his arm around me. "Stop it," he said, and not pleasantly. "Either you're back at work or you're not. Get hold of yourself."

"I'm sorry, Charlie," I sobbed. "I didn't know he'd show up like that."

"I know. If he wasn't my nephew, I'd have him banned from the

club. But you gotta admit he's had a rough week. His wife and all—"
Just like everyone else, Charlie believed the official story of what
happened that night. "Is this going to be a problem?" he asked me.

"No. I'm sorry."

"Okay. Go to the ladies' room and fix your face. Then get back
out here. Alpert's set is almost done. Then you can go home."

I nodded and did what I was told. The rest of the night went all
right, but I was careful to check the employee parking lot behind
Flickers to make sure Leo wasn't waiting beside my Sunliner. He
wasn't, so I drove home and stewed about what had happened. I
was hopping mad.

I decided that the real Black Stiletto needed to take a look around
Leo and Christina's house. Maybe I'd find evidence that she was
the phony. And if either one of them were home, then the Stiletto
would have to lay down the law.

Even though it was one in the morning, I put on the outfit and
trench coat over it, got my backpack and mask, and went down
to my car. It took me only twenty minutes to drive to their house
on Woodruff. It appeared that no one was home. No cars in the
driveway. No lights on in the house.

Good, I thought.

I drove a block away and parked.

3
Judy's Diary
1962

I put on my mask and backpack, and then slipped out of the car. Running up the street to the house, I was careful to keep to the shadows. It was a residential neighborhood, so that was pretty easy to do. As I snuck up the drive to the side of the house and the door to the old lower-level bedroom where I lived for the first month I was in LA, I thought, *what the heck am I doing?* I had no plan. If I encountered Leo or Christina, I didn't know what I'd do. I hoped I could control my anger at him. I looked at the wooden stairs leading up over my head to the door to Christina's floor. I wondered if I should direct my rage at *her.* She deserved a good whupping for trying to impersonate *me.*

The lock pick worked easily on the door. I bet Leo never changed the lock after I moved out, but I left my key with him when I did. As I entered the place again, I felt a chill. The bedroom hadn't changed a bit. I guess Leo hadn't talked any other young, innocent, unsuspecting female newcomers into staying with him recently, ha ha.

The house was dark, so I unhooked the flashlight from my belt and flicked it on. The batteries were running low and the beam was dim. I made a mental note to buy new ones. I went up the steps to the ground floor—the living room and kitchen. The plan was to go up the staircase to Christina's room and start looking around for a Black Stiletto costume, but just as I was halfway up, I heard a car pull into the drive outside. I quickly darted back and looked out the kitchen window. It was Leo's Karmann Ghia. He got out and started moving toward the front door.

I slipped over to the bar where he kept all of his alcohol. I grabbed a glass, poured a bit of whisky into it, and stood with my back to the door. I heard him come in, and then the lights flicked on.

He audibly drew in his breath when he saw me, and then he blurted it out: "Jesus! You scared the shit out of me, Christina! What the hell? Why are you in that getup again? I thought I told you to burn it."

I turned around and smiled at him. With the mask on, I didn't think he'd recognize me as Judy Cooper. No one ever does.

Dear diary, you should have seen his jaw drop when he realized I wasn't his sister!

He reached inside his jacket, so I charged him and tackled him to the floor. He kept fumbling for a gun, but I twisted his wrist hard until he yelped. I grabbed the pistol and tossed it across the room. He was obviously now carrying a weapon on him at all times. That figures.

I stood so he could sit up. He stared at me wide eyed, rubbing his hand. He was scared, no question about it.

"Well, well," I said. "Now I have confirmation that it was Christina Kelly who impersonated me at Vincent DeAngelo's New Year's Eve party. And I heard it right from the horse's mouth."

"You, uh, you don't know—I . . . I was talking about her Halloween costume."

I rolled my eyes. "Don't make me laugh, Mr. Kelly. I know a liar when I see one." It was true, too. He had sobered up some since I last saw him, but his flimsy attempt at falsehood was apparent to me.

"I thought it was time that you and I meet, face-to-face, or rather, face-to-mask." He started to stand up, but I drew my knife and pointed it at him. "Nuh uh. Stay sitting. That way you're closer to the other creatures of your kind—worms and rats." He resigned himself to it, brought his knees up, and wrapped his arms around them. "That's good."

I walked around behind him and then squatted so I could place the stiletto's blade against his neck, just beneath his quivering chin. I held it there for several seconds, allowing him to relish the sharpness of the cold-steel edge.

"Now, this is what's going to happen," I finally said. "I'm going to clear my name. And I'm going to make you and your sister pay for what you did. The police are already on to you and your involvement in the mob. They know you're working for DeAngelo and Casazza. They're just waiting for you to slip up, and then they're going to come down so hard on you, you won't know what hit you."

"They don't have anything on me."

"No? What did you do with that big ol' diamond you took?"

Leo reacted angrily to that. "I didn't take the damned diamond!"

"No, your sister did."

"That's a lie."

I knew it wasn't. It was all over his face. The truth was in the sweat oozing out of his pores.

"I'll bet you know where it is," I said.

"I do not!" Another lie.

Dear diary, I really wanted to slit his throat. Suddenly, the memory of Douglas Bates, lying bloody and dead on the floor of his trailer home in Odessa, Texas, flooded my brain. My handiwork. I had rid the world of an evil, disgusting man. The urge to do the same to Leo was powerful. For a moment, I thought I was going to do it. I didn't even want to warn him or say another word. I just wanted to dig into the bastard. There's a myth that you see red before an act of violence. That was never the case for me, but I swear this time the crimson color flooded my eyes. Part of me was screaming, *Do it! Do it!*

I'm not sure what stopped me. I *didn't* do it. I've killed before, and as gratifying as it was to get rid of Douglas, the other deaths attributed to me were done in self-defense or were accidents. I was not a murderer. And, like Barry said, Leo was an important material witness against DeAngelo if the cops could get some credible physical evidence that linked him to the mob's crimes. Leo deserved to go on trial for Maria's killing and become the target of his father-in-law's wrath.

So I brought the point of the knife up and jabbed him lightly on the right cheek, enough to prick him and cause a little blood to drip.

"Ow!" he cried.

I stood away from him and sheathed the knife. Leo looked at me with a combination of hatred and humiliation in his eyes.

"What would your father-in-law say if he knew you and Christina were responsible for murdering his daughter? What if he knew your dark secret?"

He started to protest again, but I held up my hand. "Shut up. I don't want to hear you speak. It was a rhetorical question. One I just want you to think about. You'll never know when Mr. DeAngelo will start hearing the rumors. The innuendos that Leo had his wife of six days killed. What will happen to Leo?" I shook my head and went, "Tsk, tsk, tsk."

After a moment, he looked at me with a straight face. "They're going to kill you, you know."

To tell the truth, dear diary, the seriousness in his face scared me a little. There was no question the mob wanted me out of the picture.

"There's a contract out on you," Leo said. "A big one."

My temporary fear dissipated, and I almost laughed at the irony. I hadn't been in Los Angeles a year, and already the mob wanted to kill me.

Leo attempted some bravura, saying, "If you show up any place where there are people who work for DeAngelo or Casazza, they'll shoot first and ask questions never."

"But right now, you're the one on the floor," I said. It was time to leave, so I strode around him, stopped, leaned in closer, and said, "Anything happens to me, and you can be sure DeAngelo will know about you."

I let that sink into his sweaty face, and then I quickly turned and shot out the front door. I figured I'd have to come back another time to search for the Stiletto costume, if Christina was stupid enough to hold on to it. Although Leo's admission was enough for me to confirm their guilt, the police would need the costume to prove it in court. Unfortunately, if Leo had told his sister to burn the clothing, then she probably did. I was probably out of luck on that one.

As soon as I hit the darkness of the night, I ran. I kept to the shadows and made it to the end of the block before I stopped to look back. Leo wasn't there. He didn't have the gumption to leave the house and chase me.

I got in my car, removed the mask and backpack, and drove home.

Did I accomplish anything? Not really. But it sure felt good seeing Leo nearly wet his pants.

4
Leo
The Past

Why did I have the feeling that the shit was going to hit the fan at any time?

Damn Christina. Damn the Black Stiletto. Damn Judy Cooper. Damn DeAngelo. Damn Maria, may she rest in peace.

It's strange. As soon as we were married, I wanted to get rid of her; but now that she was gone, I wouldn't mind having her back. I missed her. I *did* love her in so many ways. She was likely the most beautiful woman I'd ever gone to bed with, and that was saying a lot.

I didn't miss her mouth, though. She was already turning into a shrew on our wedding night. I was in bed, naked, and she was in the bathroom. I saw the box with the diamond in it, so I took the necklace and got back in bed with it. I held the jewel, gazed through it, felt its polished sides and fine edges. It was heavier than it looked. It was a thing of great beauty. And great wealth.

And then Maria came out of the bathroom, also naked, and saw me holding the diamond. "Put that back!" she ordered.

"What? I'm just looking at it. It's beautiful."

She climbed on the bed and aggressively snatched it out of my hands. "My father gave me that."

"Maria. I was there, remember? What's the problem?"

She just pouted. "I don't know. I'm sorry. I just suddenly got possessive. I wanted it to be all mine."

"It *is* all yours, honey. I'm sorry, just put it away."

"No, you can hold it. You *are* my husband now."

She had shattered the mood. "No," I shook my head. "It's all right. I don't need to. I saw enough of it. Put it away."

Only when she'd placed it in a locked safe in the bedroom did I ask her, "You're planning to wear it to the New Year's party, aren't you?"

"I wouldn't be dressed without it." Then she climbed back in bed and attempted to make up for being a bitch.

Well, now she was gone, and I had the diamond. It was in a safe hiding place at my office, right there in plain sight on my desk. I always said I'd only put an object of great beauty in my mother's Chinese jewel box. Only my gold key or a sledgehammer could open it.

And now I was afraid that goddamned diamond would be the death of me and my sister.

At the moment, everything was cool. DeAngelo and everyone else believed my story. Luckily it was backed up by the servant Christina clobbered in the wine cellar. Someone in the house saw her in costume, too, so there was plenty of evidence that the Black Stiletto was at the party. The only one who smelled something fishy was Paulie. Maria's brother never liked me. He was against me joining the family and getting involved in his father's business. That night, after it happened, he kept asking me questions, like, "Why didn't you do something? Didn't you have a gun?" I explained that I wasn't carrying at the New Year's Eve party. "Why didn't you jump her? Call for help?" The idiot didn't understand that the Stiletto's appearance was a surprise and that it happened so quickly no one could have responded.

It was such a risky goddamned thing to do. It was like betting the farm on red. Either it would work or it wouldn't.

At home, Christina practiced the quick change a million times. Then we made sure Christina was allowed to spend the night at the ranch over New Year's Eve so she wouldn't have to stay in a hotel or drive back to LA.

Since she wasn't in the bridal party at the wedding, she took the time on Christmas to explore the DeAngelo house and figure out how the job would go down while I was saying my "I dos," and everyone was outside. She mapped out her route from a bathroom in the house, down the stairs to the basement, through the wine cellar, into the tunnel, and up to the gazebo—and back—so that she could do it quickly and stealthily. By the time everyone had reacted to the murd—to Maria's death—Christina had already changed back to her civilian dress and was outside again. She claimed no one saw her. I never knew exactly where she'd put the costume, but she said it was in her overnight handbag that was stored near the bathroom.

But she wasn't supposed to kill Maria. That was never part of the plan. The diamond was what we were after. It was meant to be just a robbery.

When my sister shot my wife, I was stunned. It wasn't difficult to play the shocked, grieving husband and son-in-law. I completely forgot Judy was standing nearby. She slipped away during the chaos that quickly spread over the backyard. My God, the wailing and screaming that went on—Maria's mother and father were beside themselves. Vince swore a blood oath on the Black Stiletto. And I was both dumbfounded and very, very angry at my sister. Christina told me later that's why she'd done it. She wanted my shock to be genuine. And she said she knew I didn't really want to be married to "the bitch" anyway. "Now we have the diamond and it's just you and me again, Leo," she told me.

I bawled her out. I lost my temper with my sister. That rarely happened, because Christina had always meant everything to me. She fought back, though, telling me that everything that had happened was for my own good. "You think you're the tough one, Leo," she said, "but I'm the one who sticks my neck out for you." She reminded me of how she took the rap for the bank job we did a while back. The twelve months she served in jail had been for me. Luckily, DeAngelo pulled some strings for her since he was best friends with our father. Otherwise, she'd be in jail fifteen years or more.

My guilt over that ended the fight. All I could say was, "Just make sure you burn the costume. Get rid of the evidence."

"Why?" she asked. "I could impersonate her again and do some more damage to DeAngelo's operations. Maybe to DeAngelo himself."

I told her to forget that.

My sister had always been protective of me, but at that moment I knew she was actually *jealous* of anyone who tried to take me away from her. She wanted me to herself. She never liked my seeing Judy. Or any other dame. It was okay with her when I played the field and had a different gal every weekend, as long as it wasn't serious. That was not a threat. She did the same thing. Christina went to bed with whomever she wanted and never made a commitment to anyone. She expected me to do the same. She wanted us to be a team forever.

Now that it was done, though, truth be told, I didn't miss Maria as much as I should have. Christina was right. I was still hung up on Judy, no question about that. I guessed I'd burned that bridge. She wouldn't talk to me. Uncle Charlie was pissed at me, so I couldn't show my face at Flickers on nights that Judy was working. That whole thing ended very badly, and I regretted it.

The problem now was fencing the diamond. I had a guy in place, all the way across country in New York, but I had to wait. If that diamond showed up on the black market too soon, the odds were that it could be traced back to me. I had to wait months. Maybe a whole year. It would probably be fenced overseas for my protection. In the meantime, Christina and I had to sit tight and play everything out. I was going to be a part of DeAngelo's family and business. As soon as the "mourning period" was over, Vince wanted me to learn how to manage the Sandstone Casino. I told him I already had my warehouse business. He asked me what I'd rather do. "Let your sister run Kelly Warehousing. You come work for me," he said. I explained that I didn't want to give up my father's business. He was disappointed. Then I told him I'd spend some time at the casino as soon as I was "over" the tragedy that had occurred. He accepted that. I also told him I'd be moving back to my house in Hollywood. He said that when I was in Vegas, though, it was fine for me to stay in what would have been Maria's and my bedroom, or in a room at Sandstone's hotel. He really treated me like a favored son-in-law now, so that kind of made what we did a lot worse. I had to properly mourn Maria and pretend everything was hunky-dory with the family. It would be difficult.

At least the counterfeiting operation was going well. The Heathens and Los Serpientes had settled their differences, and things were more or less back to normal in the gunrunning and phony dough business.

Now if only the real Black Stiletto would step in front of a bus. My God, last week when I found her in my house, I nearly had a heart attack. What she had to say made me very nervous. If Vince—or anyone, really—heard suggestions that Christina and I were responsible for what happened to Maria, we'd be dead. When I told my sister that the real Stiletto had been in our house, she became furious. "Let her show up when I'm here!" she snarled. Actually, a battle between my sister and the Black Stiletto would be pretty interesting. I bet Christina could take her. We discussed the possibility of maybe luring the Stiletto somewhere. Christina could jump her and get rid of her. Then we'd be heroes with Vince and the rest of 'em. We really *would* bring DeAngelo the Stiletto's head.

"Did you get rid of the costume?" I asked her again. She wouldn't answer me. She went out to see her new boyfriend, yet another Heathen biker scumbag. I really don't like those guys. It seemed as if Christina wanted to screw each and every one of them. She was attracted to bad boys in a big way.

This morning, however, Christina brought up something she described as another risky project, but she thought we could pull it off.

"*We?*"

She just grinned.

I'd spent three nights at the casino, going through stuff with the current manager, a guy named Stefano, and getting a tutorial on how things ran. I learned how the floor worked, how money was handled, and what security procedures were in place. I told Christina about that, and she asked about the physical transfer of money from place to place. When did it happen? How? What days and times did the armored car deliver money to the bank, or vice versa?

"What are you thinking, Christina?" I demanded, crossing my arms like a stern parent. Of course I knew, and the idea terrified me.

"It's going to be a while before we see any money from the diamond, right?" My sister wiggled her eyebrows at me. "Maybe in the meantime the Black Stiletto could rob the casino."

5
Gina
THE PRESENT

I've read the first four diaries that Grandma Judy wrote about her life as the Black Stiletto. Oh my freakin' *God*, it was so unbelievable! The Black Stiletto! It took me quite some time to get my head around that one. I was so impressed and, frankly, quite in awe of her. I'd go to the bank and sit in the private room with the contents of the safety deposit box, and I couldn't help touching the clothes, feeling the edge of the stiletto, and even trying on the mask! Now I understand why my dad was so freaked out lately. It all made sense now. I was dying to get my hands on the fifth diary, but Dad has it and he is the slowest reader in the world. I can't believe it took him a year just to read those first four. I read them in two days! He told me reading them made him very uncomfortable and gave him anxiety attacks. Still, how could he not want to know the entire story?

I haven't returned to New York. I've been staying in Buffalo Grove, going back and forth between Dad's house and Mom's place, where she lived with my new stepfather Ross. They have an extra car I can use, which is helpful. I am glad my mom is happy; Ross is a good guy and I like him. Usually, I camp out at Dad's house because it is empty most of the time. He normally stays over at Maggie's. I keep telling him he should marry her. She is cool. Very doctor-like, but still cool. I like the way she treats my grandma.

Grandma Judy is getting worse. It breaks my heart to watch it.

Dad is handling it badly. I don't know what will happen to him when Grandma finally goes, but we all have to grow up and eventually go on living without our parents, right? Hopefully, that is a long way off for *me*—Mom and Dad are healthy and only in their late forties. Dad turns fifty this year. At any rate, I try to visit Grandma every day. I'm not sure she knows me anymore. It used to be that I was the only person she seemed to recognize and could communicate with. Sometimes there was a spark in her eyes when she saw me, but it was hard to say what she thought. She didn't talk much. The words just weren't there for her. I could see her struggle to find them, but, more often than not, she simply said things that might be appropriate responses but were actually placeholders for what she really wanted to impart. Alzheimer's is truly horrible.

Josh calls me every day. I miss him, but I can't go back to Manhattan now. There is too much of a mystery to solve. He keeps telling me the program guy can't wait too long or they might find someone else. I've tried to make Josh understand that I have to deal with serious family issues right now. Dad doesn't want me to tell Josh about Grandma being the Black Stiletto, at least not yet. I don't blame him. At first, I wanted to shout it out to the entire world, but now I realize how it could place Grandma—and us—in jeopardy. There are bad guys out there still looking for Grandma Judy. Dad and I encountered two of them in New York. I put one in the hospital and the other in jail, thanks to Josh's training. Still, I want to get back and stay with the program, so I continue to work out at Buffalo Grove Fitness Center—I joined temporarily—and practice all my moves. Mr. Page would just have to wait. He told Josh I was the most promising candidate for the program, so if he was serious about it, then he wouldn't go to someone else before I return.

The rest of my time is spent researching stuff in Odessa, Texas. After reading the diaries, I wanted to find out more. First of all, I was dying to know if my great uncles were still alive—John and Frankie Cooper. The online white pages weren't the best. There were several John Coopers listed in Odessa, and I called each and every one. None of them were related to Judy Cooper. There were no Frank Coopers in the directory either. Of course, these days, people often don't use landlines. Everyone has cell phones and those aren't listed.

Uncle Thomas—Grandma's lawyer—found out some things for us. Thankfully I wouldn't be facing any charges stemming from the assault in the hotel room in New York. The police determined that I acted in self-defense against "Bernie" Childers and "Stark" Simon, and they are also being charged for the murder of a woman who claimed to be the Black Stiletto. What was disconcerting was the fact that they were from Odessa, and were employees of Bartlett Supply Company. I read in the fourth diary about Ricky Bartlett, who was a big shot in what they called the Dixie Mafia back in the sixties.

So I Googled him. Articles on the Internet were sketchy from that period, but there was a lot about Bartlett Supply Company today. It is apparently a longtime firm in Odessa. The supply company once belonged to Ricky Bartlett. There was a Bartlett Ranch in Odessa, but I learned that Ricky Bartlett died in a fire in 1983. Wow. Apparently, it was alleged foul play, but arson was never proven. A Bartlett company employee named Dallas Haines was questioned and released.

There were some links to his obituary from the *Odessa American* newspaper, so I clicked on them. Bartlett was survived by his wife but no children. I didn't know if she was still alive or not. If the ranch was still there, then maybe she was, too. The obit said Bartlett was a "well-loved" member of the community. He was wealthy and gave a lot of money to charity and organized an annual rodeo for that purpose. His oil well supply business was inherited from his father and was very successful, and he also dealt in livestock.

I continued to look at various links about him and dug up another article from the newspaper that claimed he was "suspected" of being involved in organized crime and had been arrested twice—once in the '70s and once in 1981—on racketeering charges. The first one was dropped and nothing ever happened. The arrest in 1981, though, actually went to trial. He was acquitted on all counts. Apparently, there was some kind of raid on Bartlett Supply Company's warehouse in town. The FBI was involved because it was speculated that the local police were in Bartlett's pocket. Smuggled weapons and drugs were confiscated in the building. Others went to prison, but Bartlett claimed not to knowing anything about it. Likely story. Unfortunately, I couldn't find anything else about it online.

I figured I needed to go to Odessa myself to find out more, probably visit the public library and look up old newspapers. Maybe search for people who knew Bartlett. When I mentioned that to Dad, he said, "Absolutely not!" But I was a big girl and I could take care of myself. He told me that he and Maggie sent a private investigator named Bill Ryan to Odessa to see if he could find out who sent Bernie and Stark to New York, because *they* weren't talking. Ryan didn't know about Grandma, only that the two men attacked Dad and me.

Maybe if I went to Odessa and took care of whatever or whoever it was that was behind it, Mr. Page would consider my absence an extracurricular part of my training. I'd have to ask Josh. But I also needed to convince my loving boyfriend that something amazing was going on in my life and that I would share it with him when I could.

6
Judy's Diary
1962

JANUARY 22, 1962

Yesterday was Sunday and Barry invited me out to his place in Laurel Canyon for a barbecue. He also wanted to talk to me. I figured it was about the police not wanting to work with me anymore because of my alleged murder of Maria Kelly. So I drove into the hills beyond North Hollywood and to the boondocks. There's something romantic and magical about Barry's home on the mountain. It's as if he's a Gold Rush pioneer living in a log cabin far away from civilization, with only the sky for company. I sometimes envy that he can escape the hustle and bustle of Los Angeles and become a hermit if he wants. Of course, he has a car and a dirt road that leads back down to the modern world. The situation is ideal. The area is starting to attract movie stars and musicians, so, technically, he's not alone. Barry thinks in five years the place will be swarming with residents. I wonder if there are other houses perched above canyons that might be for sale or rent.

Just before arriving at the house, I put on my mask. It was chilly in the hills, so my leather outfit was warm and comfy.

Barry gave me a big hug. It was the first time we'd seen each other since before the New Year. He reeked of tobacco, like he always did, but I have to admit I missed him. But before we went inside,

I stood for a moment to gaze at the expansive city to the south. A brownish haze hung over the metropolis. I'd never noticed it when I was there.

"What is that?" I asked him.

"What, the smog?"

"*That's* smog?"

"Yeah. You live in LA. Haven't you seen smog before?"

"You know, I guess I haven't. I've heard about it, but boy, I can see it now. The last time I was here, I didn't see it."

"Some days are worse than others. Today just happens to be one of the bad ones. It's from all the exhaust that comes out of cars, you know. I can't imagine what it's going to be like ten years from now."

"Gosh, people won't be able to breathe." He lit a cigarette and offered me one. "No, thanks, I still don't smoke, Barry."

"Oh, right, I forgot." He coughed, turned away, and covered his mouth with his fist.

"Sounds like the smog's getting to you already. Or maybe it's those things you inhale. They can't be good for you."

He waved me off and said, "Come inside. Want a beer?"

In the past when I've visited, we'd sit on his porch outside. It really was nippy, being January and all. It was like the equator compared to New York in winter, so we lounged in his small living room in front of the fireplace. He jokingly said we could roast marshmallows if I wanted, and I almost took him up on it. It's a cute place, although it's obvious a man lives there. It's kind of messy and needs a good cleaning. There are two bedrooms. I asked him what the other one was for, and he shrugged. "You never know when you might have overnight guests," he said. It was also his office, but Barry said he rarely worked in it unless he needed to make phone calls. He pointed to his head. "My office is right here in my skull."

It looked like Barry had already been nursing a tumbler of Wild Turkey, for the open bottle and the glass sat on the coffee table. As we sat with our beers, Barry said, "DeAngelo is still telling the press that the Black Stiletto killed his daughter and stole a precious diamond necklace he'd given to her for Christmas."

"What else is new?"

"The underworld is gunning for you. Have you been out as the Stiletto since New Year's?"

I didn't tell him about my visit with Leo. "No."

"You might want to lay low, although I have a job for you if you want it."

"You mean the DA still wants to work with me?"

He shrugged. "I think I've done a good job convincing Bill that it wasn't you." Barry looked at me sideways. "It wasn't, was it?"

"Barry! No!"

"All right, I just wanted to hear it from you in the flesh." He got up and opened the back door. "Come out here with me; I gotta light the grill."

We took our beers outside. I'd never been behind his house. I hadn't realized how close it was to the edge of the cliff. There was enough space for his car to drive around the house, and sure enough, the Ford Fairlane was sitting right there. A sizable shed stood about twenty feet from the back and to the side of the cabin.

"What's in there?"

"Oh, that's a garage. And a toolshed. I can keep my car in it if I want, in case there's a hurricane."

I laughed. "Right."

He opened an ancient-looking grill and dumped coals from a bag into it. Then he took a can of lighter fluid that sat on a little table next to the grill, squirted the stuff on the coals, and used a match to light them. I wandered to the edge of the cliff and gazed down. I noticed several life-size, people-shaped cardboard stands on a ledge, maybe thirty feet below. Caricatures of gangsters were painted on the stands—they held guns that pointed straight ahead. The stands were full of holes.

"What are those?" I asked.

"You found my buddies?"

"Uh, I guess."

He joined me at the cliff edge. "That's my shooting range. I use 'em for target practice. I got 'em when I was a cop." He pointed to some rocks that resembled steps. "I go down to that ledge there and practice my aim. Do you shoot?"

"I don't have a gun."

"That's what I thought. Come inside while the coals get hot. I want to show you something."

I followed him back into the house. While I waited in the living room, he went into his bedroom for a minute, and then returned with a small wooden box. He set it on the coffee table in front of me and said, "Merry Christmas. Sorry it's late."

"What?" I laughed and picked it up. "What's this all about?"

"Open it."

I did. Inside was a handgun.

"That's a Smith & Wesson thirty-eight Special from World War Two."

"Really?" I picked it up. It was heavier than I thought it would be. It looked as if it had seen a lot of action.

"It's the Victory Model issued to US forces. Thirty-eight caliber." He then produced a smaller box from behind his back and set it down. "And here are some cartridges to get you started. They're a hundred and fifty-eight grain, full-steel jacketed, copper flash-coated bullets."

"I have no idea what you're talking about."

He laughed. "Yeah, but with my help you'll be an expert in no time."

"Barry, I can't let you give this to me. Where did you get it?"

He shrugged. "I got it for a good price. I want you to have it. Really. I'll teach you how to use it."

"It's a revolver, right?"

He laughed again. "You really don't know anything about guns, do you?"

"I told you!"

"Yes, it's a revolver. It holds six rounds. Come on. Let's go back outside and down to the range. I'll give you your first lesson."

"What about dinner?"

"Those coals have to get hot. Come on."

Well, dear diary, Barry suddenly became a pro instructor. He showed me how to handle the gun safely, and how to load and unload it. He told me to squeeze the trigger, not "pull" it. I should make sure to focus on the front sight post when I aim the gun, not on the target, and that to shoot straight I should imagine I'm pulling that front sight back through the notch in the rear sight.

He showed me the best way to grip the gun to control recoil, that's so I can get the sights back on target quickly for more shots. He said that's important because it's not like in the movies where one shot ends the fight. He told me, "Ammo is cheap. Life is expensive," and, "Anything worth shooting is worth shooting twice—or more." Even experts can't do the stuff you see in movies and TV where they shoot the gun out of the bad guy's hand, or just shoot to wound. I'm supposed to aim for the center of the shape I'm shooting at to get the best chance of hitting it. It was scary at first, but by the time we'd finished, I was having fun. My aim got better with each shot. I shot eighteen rounds altogether, and my aim got better toward the end. On number fifteen, I hit the bull's-eye, which was drawn dead center on the chest of the "gangster." He said the next things to learn are the proper way to draw the gun and bring it onto the target, how to keep both eyes open while shooting so I can pick up other movements, and how best to transition among multiple targets.

Gee, I think I learned a *lot* in that first lesson!

By then, the coals were plenty hot. Barry grilled steaks while I chopped up and made a salad in his kitchen. I have to say it felt really weird being in my Black Stiletto outfit and participating in such a domestic scene! I was very tempted to remove my mask and reveal myself to Barry. I trust him now, and I need someone like Freddie in LA, but I guess I just wasn't ready yet. Maybe next time.

Dinner was fabulous, and it was over the meal that he told me what he had in mind for a Stiletto job.

"We have a new lead on the counterfeit money operation," he said. "The police detectives believe the fake dough is picked up wherever it's being printed, which they still don't know, but they suspect it's taken to a distribution center that they *do* know. It's an auto-repair shop in Santa Monica, and it's owned by the Heathens."

"Those motorcycle clubs sure like auto-repair shops, don't they?"

"Yeah, those places are their public livelihoods. One thing you can say about those bastards is that they're good mechanics. If they weren't criminals, I'd probably take my old Fairlane to one of their shops for service."

"I think you need to *replace* your old Fairlane. It looks like it's going to fall apart on you!"

"Shut up. I love my car. Yeah, it's beat up and looks like a turd— excuse my language—but it still runs fine, thank you very much."

That made me laugh. "You don't have to apologize for saying dirty words. Believe me, I'm used to it. At the gym where I exercise, I'm the only woman."

He raised his eyebrows. "As the Black Stiletto?"

I laughed again. "No, silly, as myself. My real self."

"And who would that be?"

I wagged a finger at him. "Maybe someday I'll tell you, Barry, but not right now. Anyway, tell me more about the Heathens' shop."

"I'll give you the address. Basically we just need some intelligence on the place. Is there funny money there or not? Are any of DeAngelo's men involved? Sal Casazza and his team?" He nodded at the Smith & Wesson on the table. "You probably shouldn't use that until you're a little better at it, but I got it for you because I'm worried about you. Having a price on your head is no fun."

"I had a price on my head in New York, and I lived through it. And Barry, I'm the Black *Stiletto*, not the Black *Revolver*. I seriously doubt I'll carry that thing around. It's illegal, isn't it?"

"That it is. Technically, I'm not supposed to be in possession of a firearm, either, being an ex-con and all. It's a good thing I have friends in high places. But you're right, you don't want to get arrested holding an unregistered handgun."

"Is it stolen?"

"No. It belonged to the father of a guy I know. The father was killed at Anzio. My friend needed the money, so he sold it to me. Please take it."

I put the box and ammunition in my backpack, stood, and kissed Barry on the cheek. "Thank you, Barry."

Dear diary, I probably stayed too long at his house. I didn't want to drink too much since I had to drive home in the dark, and I hate doing that in the hills. There are no street lights in that neck of the woods. I left around 9:00 after thanking him for the lovely dinner and again for the Christmas gift, if one can call a weapon a present.

Barry's not a bad-looking guy. He's a decade older than me, but that's never been a problem in the past. I wish he didn't always smell like cigarettes. With a little better hygiene on his part, I might be attracted to him. Maybe I already am. I suppose at first he was a father figure to me, like Freddie. Now I'm beginning to think of him as my best friend.

Is it possible to be friends *and* lovers?

I think I need to push that thought right out of my mind. I'm still upset about Leo, and I wouldn't want to rush into a "rebound" relationship. That's always a mistake.

But I must say I had a good time last night, and Barry made me feel better than I had in weeks.

JANUARY 26, 1962

It's around two in the morning and I just got to my apartment from the little outing to Santa Monica to check out the Heathens' auto shop. *Well.* That turned out to be not such a good idea. The thing is, I went alone, without Barry or police backup. Apparently DA McKesson had second thoughts about paying me while the "investigation into Maria Kelly's murder was still underway." I talked to Barry about it yesterday, and he told me the news. I have to admit I was disappointed. Barry apologized and said he'd do everything he could to convince him otherwise. But it also made me madder at Leo for putting me in that mess. I wanted to do something about it.

Last night I wasn't working at Flickers, so I decided to go out as the Stiletto and just have a look-see at the auto shop. Stay at a distance and just see if anything was going on. Fully equipped, I got in my car. Although it was nearly 11:00, there was still a lot of traffic on the streets. I took Santa Monica Boulevard to Wilshire Boulevard, and then I followed that east to my destination, near 26th Street, on the north side of the road. It was called "Diablo Auto Shop," which I thought was weird. Los Serpientes were their mortal enemies, and yet the Heathens named one of their garages in Spanish.

Diablo wasn't open for business at such a late hour, but there was certainly some activity going on. The lot was fully illuminated and there were several Heathens clad in their signature black leather jackets standing around, smoking cigarettes, and drinking beer out of cans. As I drove past the place, I debated whether I should stop and get a closer look.

It wasn't much of a debate. A couple of blocks farther south, I made a U-turn at an intersection and got on Wilshire going north. I parked as soon as I could, and made sure no one could see me before I left my car. It wasn't easy staying in the shadows, for Wilshire is a brightly lit, busy street. Unlike New York, though, most people in LA drive rather than walk, so I didn't encounter anyone on the sidewalk. Directly across from the shop, on my side of Wilshire, was a dark office building. Perfect. It afforded me a place to crouch and observe from beneath its awning.

Something was definitely happening at Diablo. A meeting, perhaps. Lights shone through windows, indicating men were in the customer waiting room or in the back offices. I counted six Heathens standing out in front of an open garage bay door. Three of them had girlfriends. More than six motorcycles were lined up in the lot, though. Loud music came from the open bay—and believe it or not, it was Elvis singing "Jailhouse Rock" on the radio. That gave me confidence. Probably *over*-confidence.

I studied the scene in front of me, trying to figure out if I could get closer. The property sat in the middle of a block, and a wire fence surrounded the perimeter just like all the other auto shops I've visited in the last year, complete with the barbed wire coiled on top. The one driveway was the only way in or out. Their lot was full of the usual junky cars and motorcycles that were awaiting repairs or for their owners to pick them up. A sidewalk stretched along Wilshire, and parked cars sat in spots up to and leading south from Diablo's driveway.

Then I saw it. I couldn't believe it.

Leo's Karmann Ghia. It was parked on the street three spots south of the shop. I knew it was his, I'd recognize it anywhere. Coincidence? I doubted it!

He wasn't in sight though. The big shots were all inside.

I dug my camera out of the backpack. The last time I'd tried to use it I didn't have film! Luckily, I'd bought some and loaded it a couple of weeks ago. I snapped a couple of shots of the scene, making sure I got Leo's car in the frame. That wouldn't prove anything though. I needed to get *him* in the photo.

Movement. A door opened, and a man I recognized came out of the shop and approached the loitering Heathens. Big, bald, with a swastika tattoo on his arm. Doug Bryson. The leader of the Heathens. I snapped the camera again, but I feared I was too far away to get a clear picture of anyone's face. I needed to get closer, and that wasn't going to be easy. The place was lit up like a birthday cake for a ninety-year-old. They'd see anyone approach, dressed in black or not.

Wilshire was a boulevard, so the road was divided by a median that was lined with some palm trees and grassy patches. I thought perhaps I could cross my side of Wilshire, stop at the median, and use a tree for cover. It was risky. The median was well lit, and the headlights from traffic going both ways wouldn't make it much of a hiding place.

In hindsight, it was a stupid idea.

I darted across my side of Wilshire as soon as there was a lull in the traffic. As I reached the median, I hit the ground and laid flat on the grass behind a palm tree. Miraculously, the Heathens didn't notice me. They were too busy gabbing and smoking and drinking. I dared to crouch on my haunches, peer around the tree trunk, and take more pictures of the gang.

Then three more men emerged from the shop—Paulie DeAngelo, Maria's weasel-like brother; Ricky Bartlett, the cowboy gangster from Texas; and Leo. *Oh my God*, I thought. A perfect opportunity to prove that Leo's involved with DeAngelo's organization. A photo of the four of them, standing together right there on the auto shop lot—the big boss's son, the man who was at the top of the food chain of the Dixie Mafia in the south, the leader of the Heathens, and that lying, murderous bastard, Leo Kelly. Once again, dear diary, I was tempted to pull out the handgun Barry gave me—it was still in my backpack!—and take a shot at the creep. But that wasn't my style. I wanted to take him down properly so he'd rot in prison. And besides, I'd fired the gun only once before. I wasn't good enough to hit him!

A photo would do the trick, though. I raised the camera and aimed to get all of four of them in the frame—and just as I was about to snap the picture, the driver of a car, its headlights practically on top of me, honked his horn. He'd seen me as he drove south on Wilshire. Reflexively, I snapped the picture anyway, but the noise from the horn attracted the gang's attention.

One of the Heathens pointed at me. "Hey!" he shouted. "Look!"

I didn't waste any time waiting for them to say, "It's the Black Stiletto, let's get her!" I bolted from my position and was forced to run south along the median. The northbound traffic was so thick

I couldn't cross back to the side of Wilshire where I'd started. All I could do was display myself on a busy boulevard that was fully illuminated by streetlamps.

Two of the Heathens gave chase. They ran out into the street, dodged oncoming traffic—horns blared—and poured on the juice. But I was leaner and faster. Although they were young, strong guys, they also had a little too much weight on their bellies. There was no way they could catch me. On foot.

As a lull in northbound traffic appeared ahead of me, I heard the loud, unmistakable roar of motorcycles behind me. I had to get off the boulevard or the morning headlines would read BLACK STILETTO SLAIN IN SANTA MONICA. So I took the chance to dash just before that traffic lull. Horns honked and I had to zigzag a bit, but I made it. At least the Heathens would have to go down to the light and make a U-turn in order to reach me. Or so I thought. Actually, they rode their bikes just past me and then turned and *jumped the median*. They hit the northbound side of the boulevard directly in front of a couple of cars. Tires screamed as those drivers slammed on the brakes to avoid hitting the motorcycles, but they were rear-ended by vehicles behind them.

I didn't stop. There was a street perpendicular to Wilshire just ahead of me, more residential and a little darker, so I cut across a parking lot to reach it.

And then, oh Lord, I heard gunshots. The bastards were shooting at me!

Instead of running down the street, I veered right and zipped in between two townhomes. A wooden fence prevented me from going farther, but it was easy to jump and climb over it. That led me to the paved alley behind the buildings—and it was very dark. I could just make out garbage cans and carports in back of other townhouses along the street. Should I run? Stay put? I could still hear the motorcycles, and they were moving. They were going around the block so they could enter the alley, too.

What did I do?

I crouched in someone's carport, reached into my backpack, and removed my brand-new handgun. It was unloaded, so I had to take the time to also grab the box of shells. I was so nervous my hands were shaking. Then I saw three headlights round the corner at the end of the alley. They were coming. I opened the cylinder and started to shove cartridges in the slots—but I dropped some. The engines grew louder. The headlights illuminated the entire alley.

They were almost upon me just as I finished loading.

I stepped out in front of the oncoming headlights, raised my arms with the revolver in both hands just like Barry had taught me, pointed it just above the bikers' heads, and started shooting. Dear diary, I didn't know what the heck I was doing. I didn't want to kill anyone, just scare them. I squeezed the trigger, once, twice, three times. Then three more times.

I didn't hit anything, but the three motorcycles slid on the pavement as they braked. One bike fell on its side and toppled its rider; he got to his feet quickly. Then one guy fired back at me. He missed, but I felt the heat of the bullet as it went past.

I stuck the gun in my belt, turned, and ran from the three Heathens. They hustled to get back on their bikes, and that's when I heard police sirens. The bikers revved their engines and took off after me—but a police car, with its red and blue lights flashing, pulled into the alley in front of me, about fifty yards away. The headlights bore down on me, but I swerved sideways in between two buildings, leaving the cop car facing the three Heathens. I didn't stick around to see what happened. I leaped over another fence, found myself back on whatever street I was on before, and kept running.

A few seconds later, I spotted a three-story apartment building with a fire escape. It reminded me of my New York days, so I rushed to it, and climbed the stairs all the way to the top floor. Then I jumped from the landing and caught the eave of the roof with both hands, performed a pull-up, threw my leg over, and rolled onto the surface.

I took a moment to catch my breath. Now there were several

police sirens, most likely lured by the gunshots. Wilshire Blvd.'s lights were in the distance, but I couldn't see what was going on. Maybe they were arresting everyone. Perhaps Leo would get thrown in the tank with Paulie DeAngelo and the other men.

An hour passed. I stayed on that roof the whole time and waited for things to settle down. Twice a cop car drove down the street I was on. Eventually, the streets became quiet. Once I thought it was safe, I descended and made my way back to my car. I got in, removed my mask and backpack, and drove along Wilshire to Diablo Auto Shop. It was dark and no one was in front. Leo's Karmann Ghia was gone.

Now that I'm home, I can't wait to give Barry the film in my camera and see how my spying turned out. Maybe the DA will reinstate me.

Fingers crossed!

7
Judy's Diary
1962

It's Sunday and there's nothing to do, dear diary, so here I am. I
was going to go to the gym and beat the tar out of a speed bag, but
I didn't feel so good. I threw up again this morning. I've thrown
up a couple of times this past week, right when I got up. After a
while I felt fine, but no one likes to throw up. I wonder if I have
some kind of bug.

A lot has happened in the last two weeks. First of all, Barry developed my film—we met at our old stomping grounds, Boardner's—and
I called him two days later to find out the results. Paulie DeAngelo
and Doug Bryson are recognizable in the one group shot I took. The
other two guys—Leo and the fellow from Texas—were blurry. The
DA used it to escalate some indictments against a list of names they've
been compiling. So I was paid for my efforts after all. However, the
DA told Barry he's not to hire me again until the DA says it's okay.

Last week the police struck in Los Angeles and Las Vegas. It
was all over the news. Doug Bryson and several Heathens were
arrested, along with a bunch of Los Serpientes. I'd like to see how
they all got along in *that* holding cell! Other small-time crooks in
the "Sal Casazza Organization" were busted, too, but I found out
later that both Casazza and Paulie DeAngelo were brought in for

questioning and held for twenty-four hours before high-powered lawyers got them out. They haven't been charged with anything yet. There simply isn't enough evidence. However, the motorcycle club members are in trouble. They'd been caught with illegal guns *and* counterfeit money. Two gun storehouses were found, but the cops still don't know where the fake dollars are being made. No one's talking.

I was interested to learn that Leo's office was searched. The police produced a warrant, and they were specifically looking for "contraband," as Barry put it. It's a good thing I have a contact that's privy to what the police are up to, or I'd never know this stuff. For a former disgraced police officer and ex-con, Barry sure has friends in high places.

Nothing was found at Leo's. But now he knows they're on to him.

As for me and the gun Barry gave me, I don't think I want to carry it as the Stiletto. I took the box and the shells out of my backpack this morning and put them in a dresser drawer.

Yuck, I don't feel good. I'm depressed too. I might write to Freddie and tell him I'm thinking of coming back to New York. Ever since New Year's, that's been on my mind more than I've admitted to myself.

FEBRUARY 15, 1962

Yesterday was Valentine's Day and I didn't have a valentine.

Well, I guess Barry made up for it. I didn't have to work at the club, so he bought me a couple of drinks at Boardner's. We met there last night just for fun since I can't work for him anymore. It was after ten o'clock when I showed up, because first I wanted to watch Jackie Kennedy give a tour of the White House on television. That was *neat*! She is so classy and beautiful.

Anyway, the bartenders and waitresses at Boardner's all know me and respect my privacy as the Stiletto. We have our own little table in the back. Sure, some customers do double-takes when they see me. So far they've kept their distance. Once or twice someone says, "Are you the real Black Stiletto?" Most of the time, though, they probably think I'm just a kook that dresses up like her.

After we had our drinks, Barry suggested we go for a ride. He said there's a building in the Wholesale District that has come to his attention. "Want to check it out together?" he asked. I thought, *why not?* So we went and got in his Ford Fairlane—Holy Moses, it *really* smelled like cigarettes!—and he drove to the area just south of downtown. When we were on Alameda, I noted that we passed 7th Street, which is where Leo's office is located. But Barry turned on Wholesale Street and rolled slowly past a warehouse that was completely dark. It was three stories high, like most warehouses, with windows lining the top.

"Looks like nobody's home," I said.

Barry pulled over to the curb and cut the engine. "I wonder," he replied. "It's a wild hunch, really. It may not mean anything. A police informant that frequents this part of town reported something suspicious the other night. He saw a truck pull up to the loading dock of this building and watched men load bundles into the back. The thing is, he thought it was an empty, unused building too. As soon as the truck left, the place went dark. Sometimes there're cars parked in back all day long. The cops checked it out. It's owned by a company called A-1 Outriggers, but it appears they don't use it. The police chalked the lead up to a big zero. I got curious, though. Public records show that the building is leased by Kelly Warehousing Enterprises."

"Aha!"

"The odd thing is that A-1's corporate headquarters is in the Cayman Islands!"

"That's weird."

He shrugged. "I just wanted your opinion. Do you see anything?"

"You want me to get out and take a look around?"

"Do you mind?"

"Not at all."

I got out of the car and sprinted to the building. Its small parking lot was empty. The main front door was locked and dark. I went around to the back. The rolling steel door on the loading dock was shut tight. No lights on in the windows. There wasn't any easy access to the roof without a fireman's ladder. I could always try my rope and pulley throw, the way I got into that warehouse at the Port of Los Angeles last summer. Before I did that, I thought I'd check with Barry. I went back to his car and got in.

"I'd have to get up to the roof and maybe try to get in through one of those windows at the top, but none of them are open," I reported.

"Nah, don't bother. I'm probably wrong and it's nothing. The informant most likely gave us the wrong address."

He started the engine and began to pull away from the curb—but another car was on the street and it drove past us.

It was a blue-and-white Corvette. I recognized it.

"That's Christina Kelly!"

Then, heavens above, she pulled into the driveway of the dark warehouse and drove around to the back. Barry whistled. He immediately pulled back into the parking place and shut off the car.

"What do you want to do?" I asked.

"Wait a minute. Let's see if she stays."

We waited less than sixty seconds before the Corvette appeared again. The headlights aimed right at us, so we ducked down. I guess she didn't notice that ours was the same car that was pulling out when she arrived. The light beams wiped across our windows and then we raised our heads. The Corvette had gone on to the end of the street.

"What the hell was she doing here?" Barry asked.

"She wasn't here long enough to park and get out of the car. She just circled the building."

"Maybe she was checking to see if anyone else was in back."

"You think?"

"Should we follow her?"

"You're the one driving."

So Barry pulled out and tailed the Corvette. He's an expert at it. I'm pretty sure she never knew we were behind her, so we followed her into Hollywood. At first I thought she was going home, but then she went all the way to—surprise, surprise—Flickers nightclub. We watched her leave the car with the valet and enter the building. I pointed to a Karmann Ghia that was parked on the street. "That's Leo Kelly's car," I said.

"What should we do?" he asked.

I was in my outfit and couldn't very well remove my mask and become Judy Cooper in front of Barry. "Park the car and go inside. See who's in there. I'll stay here."

"You sure?"

"Yeah. Go ahead."

He parked the Fairlane and got out. I rolled down the window and waited as Barry went to the front door of the club and went inside. About ten minutes later, he returned.

He said, "I told them I wanted to see if a friend of mine was in the club, so they let me take a look without having to pay the cover."

"What did you see?"

"I saw Leo Kelly and his sister. They were sitting together at a table, watching the act, having drinks. The waitress had just taken Christina's order. I looked around and saw Sal Casazza and some of his goons sitting at another table. Not once did Kelly or his sister look at Casazza. I was tempted to stay—Frankie Avalon was singing on stage."

"Oh, yeah, they got him for Valentine's Day."

Barry looked at me sideways. "How'd you know that?"

Oops. "Oh, I sometimes check out live music in my civilian persona," I lied.

"I see." He smiled as if he knew something.

"What?"

"Nothing. What do we do now?"

"I guess you take me back to Boardner's. Nothing we can do while they're in the club, right?"

"I guess not."

So he dropped me off and we said goodbye for the evening. After I saw his taillights disappear, I made my way to my own car, which was parked a block away.

As I drove home, I thought about what I'd seen. Perhaps that warehouse deserved a closer look.

FEBRUARY 17, 1962

Oh my God, Christina's done it again. At least I *think* she has.

It was in the paper this morning, but I found out about it at Flickers last night. BLACK STILETTO STRIKES ARMORED CAR. It happened in Vegas yesterday afternoon in broad daylight. A Brink's armored car carrying cash from the Sandstone Casino to the bank was robbed by a woman wearing a Black Stiletto costume. She had a handgun and she *shot* one of the guards! He didn't die though. She got away with thousands of dollars—the paper doesn't say how much.

As soon as I heard, I called Barry. He confirmed that it occurred right outside the casino as the guards were finishing loading the truck with the bags of money. I assured him that she wasn't me, and he believed me. She had an accomplice, a man who wore a mask of Dracula. When I fought those bank robbers last September, *they* wore monster masks too. Could they be the same people? And if Christina is the woman in the Black Stiletto costume, does that mean she was one of the bank robbers, the one who wore the Bride of Frankenstein mask?

Was *Leo* her accomplice? I understand he's often seen at the Sandstone Casino. Daddy-in-law must be trying to get him into the family business. Would he be crazy enough to first steal Maria's diamond necklace and *kill* her, and then rob her father's casino? It doesn't make sense. Maybe I'm completely wrong about them, but I don't think I am.

Now the police *really* want to catch the "Black Stiletto." And so do I.

8
Leo
The Past

I swear, if Christina wasn't my sister, I'd kill her.

She actually went and did it. Of all the insane, crazy things she's done in her life, robbing the Sandstone Casino takes the cake.

Even though I'd revealed everything I knew about the security procedures they implemented at the place, I didn't want anything to do with the job. I valued my neck too much. She told me if I just got her the details on how they moved the cash, then I'd get a piece of the action. So, against my better judgment, I studied how the financial side of the casino worked. Every two days, a Brink's truck came and two armed men picked up bags of money from the office. It was never more than what two men could carry. A third man was the driver, and he always stayed with the truck. One of the armed guards then rode up front in the passenger seat, and other man sat in the back with the dough. It happened at three o'clock sharp on Monday, Wednesday, and Friday. Once the money was safely in the armored car, they drove it to the bank, which was only two blocks away. Seemed like a foolproof method.

Christina didn't warn me she was going to do it. In fact, at the time I was in LA at my office, so there was no way anyone could suspect me of being involved. My crazy sister got her latest Heathen squeeze to be her driver and co-robber. The guy double-parked across the street from the casino, exactly parallel to the Brink's truck. He wore one of the monster masks that we used in the bank job last year. As soon as the two guards emerged from the front door of the casino, the Heathen tore the car around with a U-turn and parked next to the truck, blocking traffic. Christina—dressed as the Black Stiletto—and the other guy jumped out with weapons in hand and surprise attacked the guards. Christina shot one of them in the leg just to show them they meant business, and then she shouted for them to drop their guns. As soon as they did, Dracula picked up the money bags—$62,000 worth, I might add—and hauled them to the trunk of the idling car. It took him two short trips. Christina kept her gun on the two men and the driver, who had gotten out of the truck to help his colleagues. They were powerless, though. One of them was on the ground, bleeding like a son of a bitch. It happened so fast that all the witnesses were frozen in place, and there were a lot of them too. As soon as Dracula shut the trunk, he whistled for Christina, and the "Black Stiletto" joined him in the car. They took off and disappeared. The police arrived within two minutes, followed by an ambulance for the wounded guard.

Christina told me they went straight from the casino to a house with an empty garage that was only a minute away. The place belonged to the Heathen's mother. They then transferred the money bags to Christina's Corvette, and drove back to LA without the costumes. She said the car they used for the holdup was a stolen junker that came from a Heathens' auto shop and could never be traced to anyone. Her accomplice moved it to a different street, wiped the steering wheel for fingerprints, and abandoned it.

For a woman, Christina has some set of balls.

Apparently, I was going to get ten grand just for supplying the intel.

Needless to say, Vince DeAngelo was *pissed off.* He swore once again that he would hunt down the Black Stiletto and mount her head on a stake. The way things were going lately, it was another bad blow to the business. After the police raided the warehouses and auto shops last week, DeAngelo and Casazza had to do some reshuffling of personnel. Paulie nearly got pinched, but Vince's lawyer quickly did his magic and got the kid out. I wouldn't have minded if Paulie had been sent to San Quentin for the rest of his life, but that wasn't to be. Casazza was also spared the long arm of the law. Cops wanted to talk to Vince, but he refused. He challenged them to come up with a subpoena or warrant or something, otherwise he had nothing to say. So far they've left him alone. Paulie and his dad had a huge argument, from what I've been told. Paulie hated me. Ever since New Year's, he's had his evil eye on me. He still thought it was my fault his sister was killed—although it was because he believed I didn't do enough to stop the "Black Stiletto," not because I was in on the job. Paulie objected to his father giving me so much responsibility now. When I'm at the ranch, he won't talk to me and leaves.

It scared the crap out of me when the cops came to my office with a search warrant. All it said was that they were looking for "illegal contraband." I suspect that meant they wanted counterfeit money or maybe guns. The Black Stiletto was right—they *were* on to me. I had to be extra careful and watch my step. At least they still didn't know about the A-1 warehouse. I've temporarily halted production of bills until things blew over. It had been going so well, too. Ricky down in Texas was very pleased with the quality of Mookie's counterfeits. The operation was just becoming extremely profitable when the raids went down. I promised Ricky that things would get back to normal soon when it was safe to do so.

I've learned a lot about the casino business, but I had to keep a handle on the warehousing company too. Luckily I had some employees who could take care of things when I was away. Christina did her part—when she was there. Half of the time she didn't show up when she was supposed to. I talked to her about it, and all she said was, "So fire me." I was afraid she was moving back into a life of dangerous crime and she would end up back in prison. Or dead.

I hadn't seen her since Valentine's Day. Even though we lived in the same house, we were like ships passing in the night. She was always out late with her Heathen boyfriends, and she slept during the day. I was spending more time in Vegas, and that drive back and forth from LA was starting to wear on me.

At Flickers, Christina was all charm and beauty, as usual. She gave me no indication of her plans for the 16th, but she did say something that bothered me. She noted that Sal Casazza was there with Shrimp and Mario; they sat in their usual spot with their backs against the wall. Frankie Avalon was on stage doing his shtick. Christina leaned in to me and whispered, "What would happen to Sal's territory if he was to disappear?"

"What do you mean?" I asked.

"You know. Say he got pinched and sent to jail. Or something. What would happen?"

"I guess Vince would appoint someone to take his place. Probably Paulie."

"You, maybe?"

"I doubt it. I don't have that kind of experience."

"But you're doing such a great job managing the, um, money project."

"What are you getting at, Christina?"

She took a sip of her drink and shook her head. "Nothing. Forget it. Just daydreaming."

I didn't think any more of it until now. What *was* she thinking about doing?

Sometimes I wished I could just leave LA and go someplace where I wouldn't have to worry about anything. Maybe convince Judy to go with me to a tropical island. *That* wasn't going to happen though. Uncle Charlie banned me from the club on the nights Judy was working. My name was Mud to her.

I guess I didn't blame her, but she would regret it someday.

9
Martin
THE PRESENT

I had to be on a panel at a silly income tax presentation at the Arlington Heights Memorial Library after work one evening, and by the time I got out it was nearly nine o'clock. At least I was paid a hundred and fifty bucks. I thought I'd stop at Trader Joe's to pick up some of the wine Maggie and I like, so I did and then started home, traveling north on Arlington Heights Road. Uncle Thomas's office was on that street, and as I passed it, I noticed the lights were on. I knew Thomas liked to work late, but it was unusual for him to be there after nine. It had been a week since I'd spoken to him, so I decided to stop and stick my head in. I pulled the BMW into the small parking lot behind the building, got out, and went to the front door. It was unlocked, so I opened it and went in. Janie's desk was empty, and Thomas's door was closed.

"Uncle Thomas?" I called.

No answer. Strange. Had he stepped out for a minute? Surely he wouldn't leave the office unlocked. Perhaps he hadn't heard me.

"Uncle Thomas?"

Then I saw a woman's shoe on the carpet by Janie's desk. A single pump. I closed the door and moved to Janie's desk. The other shoe wasn't under it.

I'd once thought maybe Thomas and Janie had something going on a long time ago, but Thomas eventually got married. He was a widower now, and I was pretty sure Janie was divorced or was also a widow. Were they behind his closed door? I certainly didn't want to interrupt them if they were doing something that adults were entitled to do in private. But that didn't make much sense. Maybe I was wrong, but I didn't think Thomas or Janie were the types to do that at the office.

In fact, I was sure they weren't. A very strange feeling passed over me. I couldn't explain it, but I knew something was terribly wrong.

I went to Thomas's door and knocked. "Uncle Thomas?"

Nothing.

That apprehension I felt began to veer toward a full-blown anxiety attack. Whether or not it was a hereditary premonition—much like the kind my mom used to have—I had no idea. Somehow, though, I knew what was behind that door.

I opened it anyway, and I was pretty sure I screamed when I saw the gruesome tableau.

"Hello."

"Maggie, it's me. Oh my God, Maggie, listen, you have to get Mom out of Woodlands *now*, I'm going to call Gina and have her meet you there, it's got to be done fast, we have to figure out somewhere safe to take her, please, you have to do this right *now*—"

"Whoa, Martin, slow down! Martin!"

"—there's someone who wants to kill her, I'm waiting for the police now, you have to—"

"*Martin!*"

She was right. I was babbling like a maniac. But I was also scared to death and probably in shock. The first thing I did was phone the police. They were on the way, and I'd been told to wait for them. Maggie was the second person I called. She was at the house. It was essential that something be done quickly. There was no telling where the killers were. *Oh my God*, they probably had my address! I had to get hold of Gina!

"I have to call Gina! Just get Mom out of the nursing home and move her somewhere safe!"

"Martin, will you tell me what's going on?"

"Uncle Thomas and Janie are *dead*! *Murdered*! Go now! I have to warn Gina!"

I hung up and dialed Gina's cell. Oh Christ, it went to voice mail. Was she home or at the gym?

"Gina, don't go home!" I blurted after the beep. "Go to Woodlands and help Maggie get your grandmother out of the nursing home! Do it now! Call me back!"

My phone chirped—it was Maggie calling me, so I disconnected and answered hers. "What?"

"Martin, you have to tell me more. For God's sake, where are you?"

"I'm at Uncle Thomas's office. I saw his lights were on when I was driving home from the presentation, so I stopped. Oh, Maggie, I can't believe it, it's horrible. I think . . . I think they were *tortured* before they were killed."

"Thomas *and* Janie?"

"Yes! They're both lying on the floor in Thomas's office. Their hands are tied behind their backs and there's blood and—oh, Jesus, it's *got* to be connected to Mom, don't you think?"

I heard the police sirens.

"All right, I'm going," she said. "Did you get hold of Gina?"

"No! I left a voice mail. I think she's at the gym. I have to go, the police are here."

Three of Arlington Heights's best entered the front door with guns drawn. I held up my hands and shouted, "I'm the one who called nine-one-one!" At that moment, my cell rang. The device was in my right hand, above my head. I glanced up and saw that it was Gina. "Can I answer this? It's my daughter!"

One of the cops nodded. "You can put your hands down." They went into the inner office as I huddled close to the front door. I didn't want them hearing what I had to say.

"Dad?"

"Gina, where are you?"

"I just got out of the locker room at the gym."

"Don't go to my house. It could be dangerous. Go to Woodlands and meet Maggie there. We have to get Mom out. They're in town, Gina, they killed Uncle Thomas and Janie!"

"Oh my God!"

"I have to go, the police are here and I have to talk to them. Just go now!"

Detective Mike Scott appeared to be a veteran with the force—he had gray hair and was wearing plainclothes. He arrived forty minutes after the first officers arrived on the scene. After spending another half hour in Thomas's inner office, he sat me down in the outer one to interview me and take a statement. I think a dozen cops and EMTs had gone in and out of the place. So far they hadn't removed the corpses. There was still a lot of crime-scene processing to be done. I certainly couldn't look in there again. My anxiety level had shot through the ceiling. The wound in my neck started hurting again. I needed either a heavy dose of clonazepam or a very strong drink. Detective Scott had to say, "Try to calm down, Mr. Talbot," a million times.

I told him everything that had happened that evening—where I'd been, why I stopped in, my entire history with the "deceased." Thomas Avery was my mother's lawyer and I'd known him since I was a child. I had come to talk to him about Gina's legal case, and recited the epic drama of how Gina and I had been attacked in New York.

"And you think what happened here tonight is related to that?" Scott asked.

"It's what I suspect. Listen, I have to go see about my daughter and mother."

"Just a few more questions, Mr. Talbot, and then I can release you. I will need you to come to the station tomorrow, though, for more questioning."

That disturbed me. "Come on, I'm not a suspect, am I?"

He looked at me sharply, and said, "Not at this point, but we have to be very thorough. Now tell me more about these men in New York."

So I repeated everything I'd said to the NYPD. As with them, I left out the part about me writing the cease-and-desist letter to Betty Dinkins, which was what led Bernie and Stark to me in the first place. Of course, I didn't mention that my mother was the Black Stiletto. Scott told me to not go anywhere, and then he went outside to his car to make some calls on his radio. Thirty minutes later, he returned to say that he sent the Buffalo Grove police by my house. It had been broken into and the place was ransacked. Hearing that *really* made my heart palpitate. If I didn't take some meds soon, I'd be a basket case. It was just as I feared—the killer or killers had most likely traced me and Gina to her lawyer—Thomas. And my poor Uncle Thomas and his secretary were tortured to find out more about me, Gina, and my mother. God, what all did Thomas say? Did he give up The Secret?

"Do you really think the break-in is related to this? That whoever killed Mr. Avery and Ms. Watson is after you?" Scott asked.

"Yes."

"And you're convinced it's all a big misunderstanding on the part of the perpetrators? They think you're someone else?"

"They think my *mother* is someone else. I think. I really don't know!"

Scott stared at me a long time, as if he was attempting to discern whether or not I was lying. I wasn't, but, well, I hadn't told him the entire truth. It was just too dangerous for Mom to do so.

It was nearly midnight when he let me go. Detective Scott had Maggie's and my contact numbers, and we would arrange a time tomorrow to meet at my house to go through it and determine what, if anything, was missing. In the meantime, the Arlington Heights police was coordinating an investigation with the Buffalo Grove cops to see if they could find clues at both crime scenes that might point to the same suspect. At any rate, I couldn't leave town. I promised to call him in the morning, and then I drove to Maggie's as fast as legally possible.

10
Judy's Diary
1962

FEBRUARY 24, 1962

Damn, damn, damn, damn, damn.

I haven't had a period since before Christmas. How could I have not realized that before now?

Is that the reason for the morning sickness? For three weeks, very often I'd throw up when I awoke. That's passed, but when I didn't have a period this month, it made me realize I didn't have one *last* month.

Oh my God, am I pregnant?

I'm afraid to go to the doctor. I don't know what to do. If it's true, the worst part about it is that Leo is the father. I have to work tonight. How am I going to concentrate? Damn, damn, damn, damn, damn.

FEBRUARY 28, 1962

I still haven't gone to the doctor. I'm too scared. I wish there was someone I could talk to. I wish Lucy was around. She'd know what to do.

Imagine that. The Black Stiletto can break into dark warehouses and fight armed men, but she's too much of a chicken to go to the doctor and find out if she's pregnant or not.

How am I going to explain to Barry that the Black Stiletto can't come out and play anymore? "Sorry, Barry, I've gained some weight and my outfit doesn't fit."

Maybe I'm not pregnant. I keep telling myself that. I've heard of girls who miss periods sometimes.

I never have.

The best thing for me to do is pick up the telephone and make an appointment with a doctor. The problem is that I don't know any doctors. I haven't been to the doctor since I got to LA. Maybe I can ask Helena who she sees. She's probably the best friend I have at Flickers. I'll see her tonight. I can confide in her.

In order to get my mind off of it, I went out as the Stiletto last night. I'm doing stuff on my own, without Barry, because ever since the casino robbery, the DA won't have anything to do with me. Whoever was impersonating me shot a *guard*, and the police consider that the same as one of theirs. Barry is even under a lot of pressure to reveal how he and I contact each other. He tells them the truth—I call him. He doesn't know how to get in touch with me. Barry warned me that I should stay away from his house for a while. The cops really want to catch me.

You know me, dear diary, something like that just makes me want to get out there and show them I'm innocent. I want to catch Christina—and I firmly believe that she's the one doing this—and turn her in. If Leo—the father of my maybe baby—is part of the package, then so be it. I've had it. I'm furious at both of them.

Since Barry and I saw Christina drive around that closed warehouse, I took the time to see it again—as a civilian. I went once, two days ago, during the day, when it was just an ugly old building built in the early part of this century. There was room in the rear to park five cars, plus the space for a truck to back up to the loading dock. Three cars were sitting in the lot. I didn't recognize them. Parking on the street can be difficult sometimes, so it was possible that the people who owned the vehicles were just taking advantage of unused free spaces. Still, it didn't feel right, because the building looked like no one was inside. I stopped the car and got out. The front door was steel. No window. No identifying signage, just the street number. I tried the knob. It was locked.

I returned after dark the same day. Two of the cars were gone, but one was still there. It was a turquoise-and-white Edsel. The lot was dark and there wasn't a sliver of light coming from any of the windows that I could see.

Yesterday, the lot was empty during the day, but last night around 10:00 I went back as the Stiletto. I parked down the street and made my way to the warehouse on foot. Unlike most streets in LA, the Wholesale District is pretty dark at night, which was good for me. Sure enough, the Edsel was parked in back. If only I could catch someone getting in or out of the car.

I went to the front door and this time tried several lock picks before I finally got it open. It creaked loudly, which I certainly didn't wish to happen. I froze and listened. Dead silence. So I stepped inside. A heavy whiff of "musty, dusty, and old" hit my nose and I almost sneezed. I held the door open to usher in light and beheld a big empty space. Zero. One big three-story box of a building with nothing inside. The concrete floor was bare. To tell the truth, I was stunned. It wasn't what I expected. I didn't know *what* I expected, but not that.

I made sure the door locked when I returned outside, and then I went around back again so I could look more closely at the loading dock. My flashlight revealed numerous skid marks on the surface; they looked like small tire tracks. Could they simply be signs of old usage from whenever the building was actually a working warehouse? Surely at one time it was. On the other hand, it's also possible the marks were made recently. The place had been used for *something* not long ago, but it was empty now. Why does A-1 Outriggers own it? What is A-1 Outriggers?

There was nothing else to do, and I didn't particularly want to sit somewhere cold and wait for Mr. Turquoise Edsel to show up, whenever that might be. So I started back to my car. But when I made it to the front of the building and prepared to dart up the shadowy street, I heard an odd noise. *Very* odd.

It was the loud creaking sound of the warehouse front door opening.

I whirled around and saw a man leaving the building and then locking the door! *Where the heck did he come from?*

Once again I froze in place, which was fortunately near a clump of hedges belonging to the property next door. In my black outfit, I blended into the gray shapes. He didn't see me.

The guy looked like a college professor. Not that I ever went to college, but he's what I *imagine* a professor resembling. In that dim light, he appeared to be in his late thirties or forties. He was tall and thin, wore glasses, a jacket, and a hat. He'd loosened a tie, and he carried a *lunch pail and thermos.*

He walked to the back of the building, opened his car, and put the pail and thermos inside. Then, instead of getting in the driver's seat and leaving, he walked back to the front of the warehouse and off the property to the sidewalk. I'd been prepared to rush up the street, get to my car, and follow him, but I could now tail him on foot, which was a *lot* better for me. I stayed a good forty to fifty feet behind him; he never knew I was there as he walked to Alameda Street. When I reached the corner, I was careful not to advance farther. Alameda is a fairly busy street in LA, even at that time of night. There was some traffic, so I didn't dart out. Staying put, I watched the man cross the street at the next intersection and enter a dive bar on the opposite corner. It had no name, just two neon signs in the window that read BEER and COCKTAILS.

The guy acted like he'd just gotten off work and was stopping for a drink on his way home!

Where did he come from?

I sprinted back to my Sunliner and drove around the block so I could park on Alameda and watch the bar. There was a parking place catty-corner and across the street that provided me a good view. He didn't seem the type to be a drunk. By watching him walk, I got a chance to better observe him. My perception was that he was not a dangerous person. He looked like an ordinary Joe.

Exactly twenty-two minutes after he'd gone in, Ordinary Joe came out of the bar. He crossed Alameda and started heading toward me. I ducked in my seat until he went past. He was on the way back to his car behind the warehouse, I was sure of it, and I was in the perfect position to just turn onto the street as soon as he pulled out of the lot.

That's exactly what happened.

I waited until I saw his headlights sweep across the road as he left the warehouse. I turned my car and tailed him, staying as close to him as I safely could. I doubted he'd realize anyone was following him. He just didn't seem the *type* to even have to *worry* about someone following him.

He turned west on Sunset and took me to the Silver Lake neighborhood, which wasn't terribly far from the Wholesale District. Eventually, he veered into a side street that went up a hill. Near the top, he parked in the driveway of a modest house. A light was on in a window, but the rest of the place was dark.

The man went to a side door and used a key to get inside. He was obviously home, and I was willing to bet he lived there with his family. I sensed there were indeed at least a wife and most likely children asleep in their bedrooms.

I went home. I was and am still very puzzled by all this. After I wrote it down, dear diary, I realized it doesn't make a bit of sense.

Where did that guy come from?

March 5, 1962

I finally went to the doctor this morning. Helena came through and gave me the name of her doctor. His name is Dr. Bernard. He asked to hear about my symptoms, nodded, and ordered me to pee in a cup.

I was told to go home and that they'd call later that afternoon with the results.

Dear diary, I'm going to have a baby.

I've been pregnant for 67 days. A little over two months. I'm confused, angry, and frightened.

Damn Leo.

11

Judy's Diary

1962

MARCH 13, 1962

I'm making myself nuts. I don't know how I feel about being pregnant. Even the word itself sends shivers down my spine. Of all the dangers on the streets that I've faced in the past few years, nothing scares me like this.

What am I going to do with a baby?

If only Leo wasn't the father, I might be able to have a more positive attitude about it. I just don't want to have *his* child. He doesn't deserve to have offspring. And yet, strangely, I have a compulsion to tell him the news. In fact, I feel an *obligation* to do so, but I don't know what I expect him to do about it. I don't want his support. I don't want his money. I don't want him around. I don't want him to be the damned *father*!

Helena at Flickers asked me how my doctor appointment went. I didn't answer, but when she saw my face, she guessed correctly. I whispered to her not to tell anyone. She asked me who the father was and I wouldn't say. Then she hit the bull's-eye.

"Oh my God, is it *Leo*?" Everyone at Flickers knew I was seeing him for a while.

I shook my head and lied. "I don't want to talk about it," I told her.

Then she sidled up to me and spoke quietly. "If you don't want it, I know where you can, um, take care of it."

She was talking about an abortion. At first I didn't think that was possible, but Helena says there are some doctors in LA who will do it discreetly. I've heard horror stories of women who died from having that procedure done by unqualified physicians. Nevertheless, I asked her to write down the information for me, and she did. Helena said I'd need to make an appointment for something else and then tell him what I wanted when I saw him. I could mention that she referred me. Apparently, Helena has done it and she's still alive, so I guess this guy must know what he's doing.

That was two days ago.

I'm sitting here now in my apartment, looking at that piece of paper. A doctor's name, address, and phone number. Should I call?

No. I can't do it, dear diary. I can't kill my baby.

Since I found out, my emotions have alternated between shock, anger, fright, and…wonder. I wonder what he or she will be like. I wonder what his or her name will be. I wonder if I could be a good mother. I wonder if I can love the child even though I hate the father.

I wonder—I wonder—

March 14, 1962

This morning I called Kelly Warehousing Enterprises to find out if Leo was in his office. Lo and behold, he was. Lately he's apparently been spending a lot of time in Las Vegas, but his secretary said he was coming in after lunch.

As I drove to the Wholesale District, my stomach was in knots. I didn't want to see him again. I was afraid Christina would be there too, and I didn't want to see her either. But I couldn't sleep last night. I kept thinking that if I did *anything*, I should let the father of my baby know about the situation. I can't explain it. Common sense would dictate that I just go away and never tell him. What good was it going to do to let him know? I have no idea. There was no reason for me to feel guilty about it. He didn't *need* to know. And yet, I felt it was my duty. I could march into his office, tell him the news, and *then* never see him again. The dilemma would be off my conscience. Then the baby would become *my* concern and mine alone.

I arrived at his building a little after two o'clock. I have to work tonight, so I wanted to be done quickly and back here to have dinner and relax a bit before going to Flickers. When I entered the Kelly outer office on the second floor, a woman at one of the two secretary desks greeted me. She appeared to be in her forties and was probably who I spoke to on the phone. At the other desk sat Christina. She was dressed conservatively, in a business dress, and held a phone receiver to her ear. Looking gorgeous, as usual. Her eyes widened when she saw me walk in; I imagine she might have tried to stop me, but she didn't interrupt her conversation. I spoke to the other lady, told her my name, and said I wanted to see Leo. She buzzed him on a little machine. His voice came out of a little speaker. "What is it, Evelyn?"

"Judy Cooper is here to see you."

There was a moment's pause. "My God," he said. The machine switched off and suddenly the door to his private office swung open.

"Judy!"

"Hello, Leo."

"Come in!"

Christina shot eye daggers at me as I walked in between the two desks.

Leo closed the door behind me and made a move to embrace me. "You look absolutely beautiful, Judy, you're—glowing!"

Isn't that what people say about women who are pregnant? I held up my hands and moved away from him. "Don't touch me, Leo," I said.

"Judy, what—this is a surprise. I didn't expect—I didn't think you wanted to talk to me."

"I don't. I don't want to see you or talk to you or hear your name."

He kind of laughed. "Then what are you doing here?"

"I have something I need to tell you."

"Oh?"

"It's important."

"All right. Should I sit down?"

"You might want to."

He blinked a couple of times. "All right. How about a drink first?"

That actually sounded good. My nerves were live wires. The butterflies in my stomach were threatening to fly out of my throat. I didn't see any booze, though. "What do you have?"

He grinned and removed his set of keys from his pocket. He picked one out and displayed it. "*Voilà*. The magic key."

Hanging off the ring next to the one he held was another key that was shiny gold. He'd shown that to me before. It opened the Chinese jewel box he kept on his desk. He went to a liquor cabinet on the opposite side of the room from his desk. He unlocked and opened it, revealing several different bottles of booze, along with glasses. "Ta-da!" he said.

"Just a small one, please."

"Whisky?"

"Sure."

"I don't have any ice. Neat okay?"

"Yes."

His back was to me when he poured the drinks. I glanced at his desk and, sure enough, the pretty ornate jewel box was still there. I remembered that it was his mother's, and that he said he would keep only objects of great value inside. The last time I was there, it was empty. I don't know what made me think of doing it, but I faced him, and with my hand behind my back, I picked up the box. I shook it lightly.

Something was inside. I felt it bounce around the velvet inner lining.

Was it the *diamond*? The one the "Black Stiletto" stole from Maria? Was that possible?

I set it down as he turned and brought me the glass. He clinked his against mine, and said, "Cheers. It's good to see you, Judy." We both downed the drinks in one swallow. The burn felt great. "I've missed you. It's been—difficult."

I handed him my glass and went to the window without responding. The view from the second floor included the small parking lot and part of 7th Street.

"What did you want to talk to me about?" he asked.

My gaze remained on the sunshine outside. "You want to sit down?"

"Not really."

"All right." I turned and looked him in the eye. "I'm going to have a baby."

I swear his face changed expressions three or four times in the space of a few seconds. Surprise, confusion, fright—and then he smiled. "You mean—it's *mine?*"

"There was nobody else, Leo."

He laughed and waved his arms in the air. "Judy! That's fabulous news! That's incredible! Ha ha!" He approached me, arms outstretched, but I held up a hand.

"Stop."

"Judy, please. Let me congratulate you. Let me congratulate *us.*"

"Leo, there is no *us.* There's only me and the baby. I just felt you should know. It was only right that I tell you."

"Well, of course. Judy, don't you see, this changes everything! We can get *married!*"

"No."

"Judy, I love you! This settles it, doesn't it? I mean, you . . . you *have* to marry me, don't you? I *want* you to."

"No, Leo, I don't have to marry you. I don't want to marry you. I never want to *see* you again. I have no intention of getting married. I'm not even sure I'm going to have this baby."

He wrinkled his brow. "Judy. No, you can't—I can't allow you to—do *that.*"

"I can do whatever I want."

"It's illegal. And it's…it's *immoral*."

I said I wasn't sure. "If I have the baby, I will raise it myself."

He went back to the liquor cabinet with the two glasses. "Hold on, hold on…I need another." With his drink refilled, he turned, and said, "You understand I have a strong Catholic background?"

"So?"

"So I *must* marry you. I can't have a child out of wedlock."

"I'm the one having the child out of wedlock. Not you."

"But it's *my* child!"

"That doesn't matter."

"Yes it does! And I sure as hell won't let you kill it. *That's* not going to happen!"

"Oh, Mr. Decency here. You, Leo Kelly, have qualms about *murder*? Come on, Leo. You're a criminal. A liar, a thief, and a killer. How dare you question *my* morals!"

"Judy, I forbid you to end your pregnancy, and I cannot allow you to have my baby and raise it as a bastard! We're getting married!"

I wanted to slap him. "*No!*" It was a mistake to go to his office after all. I was very upset. "I'm leaving. Now you know, and I've fulfilled my obligation to tell you." I stormed past him and went to the door. "Don't try to contact me. Don't call me. Don't come to Flickers when I'm there. Frankly, Leo, hell can freeze over before I'll ever let you have anything to do with this baby. Goodbye." I opened the door and found Christina standing there. Had she been listening with her ear to the foggy-glass window?

"Judy!" Leo called. "Wait!"

I started out and Christina tried to stop me. "What's going on?" she demanded.

I roughly pushed her arms away. "Don't touch me, Christina!" I snapped, and kept moving to the front door. Before the siblings could do anything else, I was in the hallway and running to the stairs. I fled to my car with tears streaming down my cheeks. I couldn't help it. The fight had brought out emotions I didn't think I had. That has been happening a lot lately. Perhaps it's part of being pregnant.

Now I'm home, dear diary. I have a few hours before work. I'm hungry and tired. That's a component of being pregnant as well. Eating for two. Sleeping for two. I have to take care of myself. I have to think about the baby.

That is, *if* I'm going to keep it.

12

Leo

THE PAST

All I wanted to do was get drunk.

After the big fight with Judy, followed by the big fight with my sister, I sure didn't feel like doing anything else. I couldn't go to Flickers, though, because Judy was working tonight. Maybe I'd just sit at home and polish off a bottle of something all by myself. Sounded pretty great to me.

What a day.

First Judy hit me with her incredible news. Wow. I was going to be a father. Unbelievable. I bet it's a boy. It would have to be. My son. I never thought I would say those words. My son. Has a nice ring to it.

Unfortunately, his mother wouldn't have anything to do with me. Bitch.

I would marry her, though, if she'd only say yes. In fact, I was intent on marrying her. I was going to pull out all the stops. I wouldn't leave her alone until she agreed to the wedding. Damned if I was going to let her have my son out of wedlock. That was not going to happen. And another thing—she had better not abort my son. If she did that, I would kill her. I would use everything in my power to wipe that girl off the face of the earth.

Christina thought I was out of my mind. She never liked Judy and claimed Judy never liked her. That was probably true. Other women found it difficult to like Christina. I guessed she threatened them somehow. Christina did just fine with men, but I didn't think she'd ever had a single female friend.

I told my sister I was going to marry Judy and we were going to raise the baby together. Christina scoffed. She said I need to forget about Judy, let her have the kid by herself, and then be rid of them both. We had a fight. Lately we've been having lots of tiffs. When I accused her of doing a reckless thing—robbing the casino—she actually told me to "go screw yourself." My own sister! I wanted to hit her. She couldn't talk to her big brother like that. But I didn't do anything. I just yelled back. It became a shouting match. She walked out of the office. Evelyn sat at her desk with her mouth open. I told her to go home for the day and forget about what she'd seen and heard.

Starting tomorrow, if my hangover wasn't too bad, I am going to start putting the pressure on Miss Judy Cooper. She was going to marry me.

Or else.

13
Gina
The Present

Dad's phone call was very alarming. I was just about to go back to his house from the gym, when I noticed I had a voice mail message on my cell. After hearing his panicked words, I called him back and learned that my lawyer, Uncle Thomas—whom I've known all my life—and his secretary had been murdered by persons unknown. I couldn't go back to the house, even though all my stuff was there. Dad's address was most likely known to the killers. And I had to help Maggie get Grandma Judy out of the nursing home. Immediately.

I drove to Woodlands. Visiting hours were over and the front glass doors were locked. You had to use an intercom to gain entrance and I didn't want to do that. Instead, I phoned Maggie's cell. She answered and confirmed that she had just arrived. Duh, I recognized her Hyundai in the parking lot. I stood at the front and waited—she came and opened the door for me.

"We have to be quiet," she said. "What we're doing is highly irregular, to say the least."

I followed her past the reception station, where a lone black man wearing an orderly outfit sat reading a magazine. He didn't look at us.

"Thank you, George," Maggie said.

"No problem, Doctor."

We walked down the long hall toward the dementia unit, where the Alzheimer's patients lived. "What did you tell him?" I asked.

"Nothing. Just that I was letting in a resident's family member."

She punched in the code to get into the unit and we went inside. The patients were in their rooms, hopefully, asleep. A couple of nurses sat at the station in the common area. Apparently, it wasn't unusual to see one of the doctors there late at night. One nurse glanced up and asked, "Everything all right, Dr. McDaniel?"

"Absolutely, thanks."

We went through the space and into the corridor where the patient rooms were located. The doors were all ajar so that nurses could peek inside during nightly rounds, just like in a hospital. Grandma's room was near the end of the hall, close to the emergency exit. We both entered and found Grandma Judy sound asleep in her bed. Luckily, she didn't share the room with anyone else. Maggie turned on a desk lamp so as not to startle my grandma with the bright overhead light. She didn't wake up.

"What do I do?" I asked.

"Look in the closet for a suitcase. Start packing her clothes. I'll see if I can wake her."

Maggie went to the bed and gently tried to rouse Grandma. It wasn't difficult. Grandma rarely slept through the night. To her it might have been morning. I found a suitcase and began throwing clothing into it.

"Judy?" Maggie spoke softly. "We're going for a ride. Won't that be fun?"

"What?"

"Look who's here, your granddaughter Gina."

I moved closer and blew her a kiss. "Hi, Grandma!"

"What?"

It turned out Grandma needed her disposable underwear changed—I learned a while back that it was bad form to call them "adult diapers" to preserve the dignity of the patient. It was the first time I ever had to do that, and I appreciated even more what a hard and underpaid job it was to care for the elderly. Maggie and I did it together. We didn't bother dressing Grandma in street clothes—we left her in her nightgown.

She couldn't walk, and we couldn't attract attention by putting her in a wheelchair.

"We'll have to carry her outside to the car," Maggie said. "Can you do it?"

I couldn't believe what was happening. Maggie grabbed the packed suitcase, along with what toiletries were in the bathroom. I put one arm behind my grandmother's back, the other under her knees, and then picked her up and held her in my arms like a baby. You know that famous sculpture of Mary holding the dead Jesus? That's what I felt like.

"Oh!" Grandma said when I lifted her off the bed. She was so light and frail. I don't think she weighed more than a hundred pounds.

"Isn't this fun?" I asked her.

"Ohh!"

I was sure it wasn't fun at all and I hated doing it. Grandma was frightened. She didn't know what was happening.

Maggie led the way. First, she looked out into the corridor to make sure the coast was clear—and sharply held up a hand to stop me. She stepped out, slightly closing the door behind her. I moved back into the room, still holding Grandma Judy in my arms. I heard a male voice say, "Oh, hi, Dr. McDaniel."

"Hello, Johnny," Maggie answered. He was another one of the orderlies. "Things pretty quiet tonight?"

"Yes, ma'am. Even Mr. McGregor went to bed without a fuss. I think that's a first."

"That's good. He's getting used to his new home. It sometimes takes a while."

"How's Miss Judy?"

"I was just checking on her. I thought I heard her moaning, but I think she was just dreaming."

"What are you doing here so late?"

"I had some paperwork to catch up on. I'm about to leave now."

"Okay, Doctor, see you tomorrow."

I heard her walk away with Johnny. What was I supposed to do? Put Grandma back in bed? I stood there, smiling and making kissy faces at her.

"Ohhh!" she said again, staring at me.

"Shh, we're going to sneak out. This will be fun, Grandma! It'll be just like high school!"

A minute later, Maggie returned. She whispered, "I had to walk him down to the nurse's station so he wouldn't get suspicious. I think it's okay now." She made another peek into the hall and then gestured for me to follow her. She moved to the emergency exit. Something had to be disengaged to prevent an alarm from going off, but I didn't see how she did it. Maggie held the door open and I stepped outside with my grandmother.

Although it was late spring, the air was brisk. I carried Grandma to the parking lot. "Let's use my car," Maggie said. She unlocked it, and I placed Grandma in the front passenger seat. The poor woman clutched my arms tightly. She was understandably agitated; her eyes were wide with fear. I don't know how long it had been since she'd ridden in a car.

"Ohhh!" The word had become more of a terrified whimper.

"It's all right, Grandma. Dr. McDaniel is taking you for a ride."

I looked back at Maggie and whispered, "Where are we going?"

"My house."

"She's taking you to her house! Aren't you lucky? Won't that be an adventure? I'm coming too, in my car. I'll be right behind you."

And that was how Dr. Maggie McDaniel and I abducted my grandmother from the nursing home.

We put Grandma Judy in one of Maggie's spare bedrooms. She was wide awake, scared to death, and shaking. I felt so sorry for her. At that moment it was very difficult for me to see her as the Black

Stiletto. Of course, it was unbelievable *anyway*, but my grandmother seemed particularly vulnerable as Maggie and I tried to make her comfortable. She started crying. I didn't know what to do. Maggie spoke encouragingly to her, and then I simply started singing "Love Me Tender." I didn't know all the words, but I did my best. And, gosh, it worked! Grandma's eyes widened when she heard the music and calmed down a little.

"Do you have any Elvis CDs?" I asked Maggie.

"I think I do. I'll go look." She left the room, and I continued singing, starting over from the top. A few minutes later, she returned with an old boom box and the *Elvis—30 #1 Hits* CD.

"I thought I'd bought this when it came out some years ago," she said. The opening track was "Heartbreak Hotel," which of course was too loud and raucous! Maggie quickly studied the track listing on the back of the CD and switched it to "Love Me Tender." And that did the trick. Grandma's rapid breathing slowed and she seemed to relax. She actually smiled. I hadn't seen her do that since I'd come back from New York.

Dad walked into the house sometime after midnight. He was pale, shaken, and not himself. The first thing he did was ask about his mother. I explained that she was in a spare room and had finally fallen asleep. Maggie gave him a pill to take, which he insisted on washing down with a shot of whisky. She chastised him for that, but he angrily snapped at her, "*I'm* the one who found them! *I'm* the one who'll have to live with the images of their battered, bloody bodies!" That upset Maggie, but a few moments later, Dad apologized to her. He then went to look in on Grandma, satisfied himself that she was all right, and then collapsed into a chair in the kitchen.

None of us could go to bed. We were too wired and freaked out. Dad grilled me about what might be at his house that could give away our presence at Maggie's place. I didn't think there was anything. More importantly, he wanted to know if I'd left anything to do with the Black Stiletto. I didn't think I had. My laptop was there, but unless someone had the smarts to study browser history and such, I didn't think they would know I'd been doing research on her. Maggie was worried about her job and if she would get in trouble for taking Grandma out of the nursing home. Dad tried to convince her that if there were any problems, she could easily explain that her actions were in the interest of Grandma's safety. Maggie said the best thing would be for her to go in tomorrow and explain to the brass exactly what was going on. Dad told her to do what she thought was best.

I wanted to go to Dad's home and see what the killers had done, but he said we had to wait until daytime, when the police could accompany us. He was also afraid whoever had done it might be watching the house, and he didn't want to take the chance that they'd follow us back to Maggie's.

Maggie pulled out the sofa bed in the living room and said I could sleep there, but I didn't think that was going to happen any time soon. Instead, I asked her if I could use the computer in a little room she used as an office. She and Dad went upstairs in an attempt to go to bed, while I browsed the Internet.

So far there wasn't anything online about Uncle Thomas and Janie. I went to the *Odessa American* site—I had subscribed—and started to scan the recent papers. I had got in the habit of doing that the past few days. A headline on today's issue—well, yesterday's—caught my attention. ILLINOIS MAN FOUND SLAIN. When I read it, my blood froze. I printed the article, took it upstairs, and quietly knocked on Maggie's bedroom door.

"Dad? Maggie? Are you still awake?"

"What is it, honey?" Dad answered.

"I have something you need to see."

"Come in, Gina," Maggie said.

Dad was in bed, but the lights on the nightstands were still on. Maggie was in her bathroom removing makeup and getting ready for a restless sleep.

"This is from yesterday's Odessa paper," I said, handing it to Dad. "It says an Illinois man from Northbrook was found murdered in the oil fields outside of town. His name was William Ryan."

Maggie gasped. "Bill?"

Dad's brow furrowed as he read it. "Oh my God. Body found… identified as William Ryan—*a licensed private investigator in the State of Illinois*—oh, Christ—the body was bound and gagged—it doesn't say how he died, only that the corpse was 'several days old.' Oh, Jesus, I think I need another pill."

Maggie sat on the bed and read the article. "Oh, no," was all she could say. "We sent him there."

"What are we going to do?" Dad asked, rhetorically.

I answered him. It was something I'd been thinking about anyway. "I'm going to Odessa. I'll get to the bottom of this."

"What? No way, Gina."

"You can't stop me, Dad." I was angry. I didn't want our lives to be what it had become that night. I'd had enough.

"We have to let the police handle this," he said.

"No. I'm going to book a flight right now. Look, it's the only way, Dad. You don't want the police knowing about Grandma, do you? We have to take care of this *ourselves!*"

"Then I'm going with you," Dad said.

"*That* I won't allow," Maggie said. "You're in no condition to go to Texas and, besides, your mother needs you here. The police would think it awfully suspicious if you disappeared tomorrow, and they ordered you not to leave town. You have an appointment with that detective, don't you? Be reasonable, Martin."

I stood and declared my intentions. "Dad, you have to trust me. I'm more prepared for something like this than you think. I won't do anything stupid. I'm going to find out who's behind all this, and I'll do my best to stop it. Tomorrow I'll get my things from the house—if they're still there—and fly out later in the day."

The look on Dad's face told me that although he didn't like it, he agreed it was the best course of action we could take.

14
Judy's Diary
1962

MARCH 15, 1962

Dear diary, it's the first night in my new home.

That's right, I've moved out of the apartment on Franklin and now, for the time being, I live with Barry in his house in Laurel Canyon.

It's a long story. I was up all night and it was actually very traumatic.

When I got home from Flickers, it was a half hour after midnight. I had just trudged into my apartment, dead tired, and was about to tear off my clothes and jump into bed—when there was a knock at the door.

"Judy! Open up, I gotta talk to you!"

Leo. He must have been sitting in his car on the street, waiting for me to come home.

He sounded very drunk. "Open up, Judy!" He had that tortured child whine in his voice that I can't stand.

"*Go away, Leo!*" I whispered loudly, next to my door. "*Go away or I'll call the police!*"

"Judy!"

By that point my neighbors probably wanted to hang me, so I opened the darned door and let him in. He grabbed hold of me, pathetically sobbing against my chest. I shut the door and stood there with the blubbering bastard. "Judy, I love you, please marry me, please, please, please."

He got on his knees and *begged* me to marry him, which, quite frankly, disgusted me. I pointed at the door and said, "Leo, I mean it. You're drunk. We're not getting married. Get out, now. I'm calling the police!" I strode to the kitchen to the phone, picked it up, and started to dial the number.

Leo stepped over and slugged me in the face. I didn't see it coming. I wasn't able to anticipate the blow like I usually can; those senses of mine were already at their peak due to his very presence. There's a limit to what I can detect. I fell, dear diary, the bastard knocked me to the floor. I dropped the phone before I'd finished dialing.

He squatted next to me and pointed, jabbing the air as he spoke. I'd never seen him so out of it. His eyes were bloodshot, he was trembling with rage, and he stank of booze. "You better not kill our baby. You better not. You wouldn't. I know. I know you better than that. I don't think you would or could do it." Despite the slurring words, he managed to speak in complete sentences. I actually wanted to hear his threats before I clobbered the heck out of him. I was very near giving away my Stiletto abilities.

"What I *bet* you do is run off," he continued. "You're gonna run off with my son. I'm not gonna let you do that, Judy. I'm not gonna let—" He ran out of breath and suddenly seemed as if he realized what he was doing. He looked confused. When his eyes returned to me and saw the red welt forming on my left cheek, he said, "Oh, God, Judy, I'm sorry." He reached for me, and I knocked his arms away. His mood swings between remorse and monster were abrupt. I quickly scooted back from him so I could stand.

Before he could react, I ran to my bedroom and shut the door. There was no lock on it, but it gave me the one or two extra seconds it would take for him to come through it. I leaped for the dresser, pulled the drawer, and grabbed the box containing my Smith & Wesson. Leo burst open the door at that moment, just as I was opening the box. I lifted the handgun out and pointed it at Leo. It wasn't loaded, but he didn't know that. His eyes bulged and his body jerked, a reaction slightly delayed due to his intoxication.

"Leave, Leo. Now."

"Judy."

"*Now!*"

He held up his hands, but he glared at me with intense venom. "All right. All right. But if you run off with my son, I'll find you. I promise you that. I'll find you, and I'll kill you both." Then he turned and left.

It all became clear to me. If there was one thing I was sure of, it's that Leo meant it. He would do it. He would hound me for the rest of my life until I shared his child with him. I had four options: One—well, marrying Leo was out of the question. Two—the prospect of terminating my pregnancy didn't appeal to me at all, although it was probably the most sensible thing to do. I understand why some girls do it. Or three—I could have the baby and be an unwed mother. I suppose there is some shame that comes along with that. I'd have to live with the reactions, mostly negative, of anyone the two of us came into contact with. My child and I would be shunned. Not only that, we'd have to contend with the presence of Leo in the same city. *Dad.* He would always be in my life, and I don't want him there. Ever.

Which left me with only one other thing I could do. Just what he was afraid I would do.

Run.

Hole up somewhere and have the baby and keep away from Leo. Leave town.

As I sat on my bed attempting to control my emotions—I was quite shaken by what had just occurred—I heard police sirens grow louder outside. The cops pulled up to my building, and I had a pretty good idea why they were there.

I hid the gun.

They came and I let them in the apartment. I told them my ex-boyfriend hit me and threatened me, and that he was drunk and attempting to drive. I said to look for a Karmann Ghia traveling on the wrong side of the road. Sergeant Leggett was very nice and concerned about me. He wanted me to go to the hospital to check out my face—it was fine, the sting on the skin hurt more than my jaw—and he took down Leo's name. I gave them his Woodruff address.

Did I want to press charges?

At first, I did. Then I realized I'd have to see him again, go to court, and live in a nightmare. I told them no and that I was sorry.

After they'd gone, I sat on my bed, still pondering what to do. I couldn't stay in the apartment. Not after that. There was no telling what Leo would do. A crummy lock on the door wouldn't keep him out. I needed somewhere to stay while I figured out where I was going to go to keep out of Leo's reach. A hotel wouldn't work—he'd have ways of tracking me down in the city.

There was only one place I could think of, so I made the decision and started packing everything I owned. I can't remember the number of trips down to my car, loaded with bundles of *stuff* in my arms. In the middle of the night. Clothes, shoes, my records and record player, the television—which was so heavy I almost died—most of my kitchenware, all my bathroom items. It was a lot, but in the grand scheme of things, I really don't think it is. I've always lived sparingly. In my room above the East Side Gym, I had only the bare essentials. I spread out a little more here in the apartment and acquired more things, but everything fit in my car. I doubt another girl my age living alone could do that.

I wrote a note to the landlord, saying I was moving out, and that anything I left behind he could keep or sell or give to the next tenant. There may have been a security deposit refund for me, but I didn't give him a forwarding address. I put the letter and the key in an envelope and used one of my last postage stamps.

I split. I dropped the letter in the mailbox downstairs. Then I got in my car and drove, still in the dark of night, out to Barry's. I figured it was time to do what I had to do. I trusted him. I liked him. I knew he was my best friend in LA.

He was about to find out the identity of the Black Stiletto.

The drive was scary. It felt like my car was the only one in the world, traveling on pitch-black, winding, hilly dirt roads with just the beams of my headlights illuminating what was in front of me. I saw a pair of wolves at one point. Their eyes glowed like yellow light bulbs in their heads. It was creepy. I had to drive slowly because the turns were treacherous. I didn't want to end up at the bottom of a canyon, even though that's one way Leo would never find me, ha ha.

I did finally make it to Barry's cabin just as the sun started to peer over the horizon. Although it was dawn, I imagined he was sound asleep. He was in for a rude awakening. I parked in front and lightly tapped the horn. That was surely a better way to wake him than me banging the door and scaring him to death. I wasn't dressed as the Stiletto, so I put on just the mask and waited a moment before getting out.

A light came on inside, and I went to the door. It opened, and there he was in boxer shorts and an undershirt. His hair was sticking up and he didn't look happy. I might have laughed if I hadn't been so desperate.

"What the hell?" he asked.

"Barry. I'm sorry to wake you. I need your help. Can I come in?"

He rubbed his eyes and nodded. "Sure, honey." He held the door for me, and I moved past him. He noted my jeans and sweatshirt. "Hey, I like your new costume. Very casual."

"Hush. I've had a terrible night."

He closed the door and followed me in. "What's going on?"

"Sit down, Barry. Are you awake? I need to talk serious."

He yawned and sat on the big couch. I took the comfy chair on the other side of the coffee table. "I'm as awake as I can be at—" He looked at the clock on the wall. "—five-thirty-eight in the morning."

"Sorry. I really am. But I need—I need a place to stay for a few days. Would it be all right with you if I take that extra room until I can figure out where I can go?"

He leaned forward. "What's happened? Are you in trouble?"

"Sort of. Well, the Stiletto isn't. But *I* am." With that, I removed my mask and revealed my real face to him. "Hi, Barry. My name is Judy Cooper. Leo Kelly is threatening me, and I need to hide from him. I think I have to leave California, Barry. That is, Judy Cooper needs to get away from him."

Barry stared at me for a few seconds and then he smiled. "I've known you were the Black Stiletto for months. For nearly as long as we've been working together."

That shocked me. At first I didn't believe him, but I sensed that he was telling the truth. "Really?"

"I'm an investigator. Not a licensed one, but I know everything a real PI does. I found out who you are pretty soon after we met."

I wasn't sure if that made me angry or not. "And you didn't tell me?"

"I figured it'd be better for our working relationship to play dumb until you decided to tell me yourself."

I laughed a little. "Gee whiz, and I thought I was so clever." Then I felt a rush of anxiety. "God, does anyone else know?"

He shook his head. "Not from me. I'm pretty sure no one does. The DA wanted me to find out who you really are, but I told him the Stiletto was very protective of her 'secret identity,' just like Batman and Superman. Oh, and it's fine for you to stay here. I'd love for you to. It would mean a great deal to me."

I breathed a sigh of relief. "Thank you."

"But I don't think you need to leave LA."

"I do."

"Why?"

With a big sigh I told him the truth. "I'm going to have Leo's baby." That made his eyebrows rise. "Yeah, yeah, I know, it's disgraceful."

"No, no, it's not that, it's just, well, that's quite a development."

"Tell me about it. Anyway, Leo wants me to marry him, which I don't want to do, and if I have the baby 'out of wedlock,' as he puts it, he'll kill us. The man is insane."

"He's got a Napoleon complex," Barry said. "A short guy like him, he wants to be in control. He wants to be the commander of the ship, and he wants ownership of you. When I was on the force, we used to see that kind of character all the time. They make the most interesting criminals."

I'd never thought of Leo that way, but it fit. "Now you know why I have to get away. I can't let Leo lay his hands on my baby when I have it."

"You know, Stiletto, I knew you were seeing him, and I started to worry about you once we figured out he was in the mob. But I wasn't supposed to know you in your personal life."

"That's all right. I'm glad you were concerned."

He smiled again.

"What's funny?"

"Nothing," he said. "It's just that the Black Stiletto is pregnant. What a headline that would make!"

That made us both laugh.

"How far along are you?"

"Not quite three months. I just found out for sure a week and a half ago. It's crazy, isn't it?"

"You *want* to have it, Judy? Is it all right to call you Judy now?"

"Yeah, you can call me Judy. And, yes, I want to have it. For a while I was considering—an alternative—but I'm about ninety percent sure that I'm not going to do that."

He nodded and smiled again. "Well. Let's get your stuff out of the car. I'm afraid I didn't have the maid make up your bed with clean sheets."

I laughed again and then gave him a hug when we stood. "Thank you, Barry."

"You're welcome, Stiletto." I shot a frown at him. He grinned and added, "I mean, Judy."

15
Judy's Diary
1962

MARCH 18, 1962

I'm settling in at the cabin. Being out in the country makes such a difference to my state of mind. I like the calming effect it has on me. I feel 100% less anxiety being here.

Just about all my stuff fit in the single bedroom, although my television is useless. Barry has one, but the aerial on his roof picks up only one channel since he's so far out in the boondocks. Luckily, it's CBS, so I can still watch *The Twilight Zone!* But there are other shows I'll have to miss. He didn't have a record player, though, so I set mine up in the living room. As for the TV, maybe I can sell it at the flea market.

After I moved in, I think I slept for nearly twenty-four hours. Yesterday, I phoned Flickers and told Charlie I had to quit. I was honest and said I had to get away from Leo. He understood, but he was sorry to see me go. Another girl could fill in my shifts this week until he found a permanent replacement. I think he was another one of those older men who fall in love with me, ha ha. He asked what my forwarding address was, and I said I'd let him know. But I wasn't going to do that. Too risky.

We put my Sunliner in Barry's garage. He didn't mind leaving his Fairlane outside in back or front of the house. Driving my car in Hollywood would be a gamble. There was always the chance I'd run into Leo. But considering there are millions of people in LA, the odds were pretty good that he would never spot my car unless he was staking out the places I might go—like Flickers, for instance. But I will never go back to the club, I'm sorry to say. It was a fun job, and even though Leo pulled strings for me to get it, it was Charlie who made it a good experience.

Barry thinks I should trade in the car for a different one, especially if I'm going to continue being the Black Stiletto, that is, until my pregnancy dictates that I *can't*. Already the pants are getting tight. He found out the identity of the guy I followed home from the spooky warehouse. His name is Hugh Costa, and he's a former printer, as in printing presses. His current employment is unknown, but he supports a wife and two kids. No arrest record. The fact that he's a former printer automatically makes him a suspect in the counterfeiting racket. It would be interesting to solve the mystery of that empty warehouse.

Last night, Barry and I sat in his living room and drank whisky. I have a feeling that might become a ritual, although I don't know what effect booze has on an unborn baby. I should probably try to tone down the drinking. Anyway, I revealed that I want to leave the state and go somewhere far away. Barry mentioned his brother again, Skipper, who was down in Odessa, Texas. My old stomping grounds. Skipper is an investment expert, and he tends to do work for some shady characters. It was some of the doings with Skipper that got Barry sent to prison. But, apparently, Barry and Skipper are still close.

"I love my brother," he said. "I can't help it. He's a lovable guy."

"If he works for shady characters, does he know Ricky Bartlett?" I asked.

"He does. I asked him. Skipper is Ricky Bartlett's investment advisor. He's going to give us some good information about where Bartlett's money is coming from. I just hope he doesn't get in trouble."

Barry said Skipper could help me "disappear." He had a talent for finding ways to change someone's identity and integrate the person into a community with little chance that he or she would be found. "I can do that, too, mostly the ID stuff," he said, a little sheepishly. "At least I know where it can be done. So if you want to change your name, which I advise you to do, then I can help you."

I asked him how much it would cost, so I guess that meant I accepted the notion that I was going to change my name. He said I should keep my first name—Judy—because that's what I instinctively respond to. Just the last name has to be different.

And if I wanted, Barry said he could ask Skipper to find me somewhere safe to live in the country. I told him to wait on that, and he was happy with that response. "You can live here as long as you want, Judy," Barry said. "Leo doesn't know me. Not very many of those guys in the underworld know me. The ones that do certainly don't know where I live. You're safe here." He spread his arms and indicated the space. "You can live with the baby here. There's plenty of room."

I thought about it, and said, "I might do that for a while. I want to pay rent though."

"Don't be silly."

"I mean it. I'm going to pay you something fair. I insist. Don't argue with me."

"Fine, fine." He held up his hands in surrender.

"And I'll need to be able to see my doctor," I said.

Barry frowned. "I don't think that'll be safe. I tell you what, though. I know some people at Linda Vista Hospital. What if I can set you up with a *fantastic* doctor and it'll all be on the QT?"

I shrugged. I wasn't particularly fond of Dr. Bernard, so I said okay.

Barry lit a cigarette and rubbed his chin as he smoked. He was thinking about something. "What is it?" I asked.

"You'll need a birth certificate for your baby. My doctor pal can arrange that too. But you know, the plan will work a lot better if you're married."

I looked at him sideways. "Is that a proposal?"

He swallowed hard and furrowed his brow. "Why not? We like each other a lot, don't we? I mean…maybe…maybe we could enjoy being together."

It was so sweet, dear diary. *He* had a crush on me, too. I sort of suspected it throughout the past year. "Oh, Barry," I said. "I'm afraid not. We're friends, right? We're friends for life, not husband and wife."

He took a second and then chuckled. "You're a poet and don't know it. Sure, Judy, I can live with that. You're right. Still, it would be wise for you to be married. Being an unwed mother will call more attention to you in the system. How about being a widow? Your husband is dead. We can fake that."

"You want me to invent a fictional husband?"

"It happens all the time when people change identities."

I didn't know if he was joking or not.

"Just think about it," he said.

MARCH 20, 1962

Ever since Barry brought up the phony husband idea, nothing else has been on my mind. In fact, it's been fun creating scenarios that never happened. I was swept off my feet in New York one day, married quickly, and then the guy bravely sacrificed himself defending my honor against a bunch of ruffians. Or he was a prince from Arabia and I married him, but then he was killed in battle against the infidels in the desert. Or he was an FBI agent, someone like my old friend John Richardson, who got in the way of a bad guy's bullet. Sure, some of it was kind of morbid, but I had to be a widow, right?

Today in the paper there was an article about Kennedy and the country of South Vietnam. Actually, it's been in the news a lot lately. Everyone is afraid Vietnam is going to be another Korea. The north part is Communist and the south is fighting to stay democratic.

It's been going on for a few years, and America has been sending men there to "advise" the South Vietnamese, but everyone knows these soldiers get caught in battles. There have been casualties. It's getting worse too.

Barry said the truth about our "military advisors" is classified. Therefore, it would be really difficult for anyone to find out anything about a particular soldier in Vietnam. What if my "husband" was one of the men who have already died there? Maybe he was blown up by a bomb and his body couldn't be sent home.

That's the fiction I'm leaning toward. It would work. Barry approved.

Now the dead husband needed a name.

Last night on *Shock Theater* they showed *The Wolf Man*, starring Lon Chaney Jr. I had never seen it before. Barry and I watched it together. It was a lot of fun, one of the best monster movies I've ever seen. The Wolf Man's name when he was a normal human was Lawrence Talbot. Seeing the movie reminded me of the bank robbery last September. The bandits wore monster masks and one of them was the Wolf Man. The guy might have been Leo, but I'm not certain. But come to think of it, Leo is kind of like the Wolf Man—he turns into a beast sometimes, ha ha!

"What's your middle name, Barry?" I asked him.

"Barrington. That's why I'm called Barry."

"That's your middle name?"

"Yep."

"Then what's your first name?"

"Richard."

"Why don't you use that?"

" 'Cause people would call me 'Dick' and I hate that."

I thought about it. "Okay, I have a name for my dead husband."

"Yeah?"

"Richard Talbot."

"That's not bad." I thought so too.

Barry said he'd get to work on getting the change started. I'll need a new Social Security number and card, a new driver's license, and some other records. I didn't ask questions. I just told him to go ahead.

That means my name will be Judy Talbot from now on.

16
Martin
The Present

I thought I was going mad. Everything in our world had gone topsy-turvy.

Gina and I met Detective Scott and two other policemen this morning at my house in Buffalo Grove to see what kind of damage the burglars and suspected killers had done. As it turned out, it didn't appear that anything was missing, but, man, the place had been overturned. All the files in my home office had been emptied and scattered all over. My bedroom had been ransacked. Gina's things in the guest room had also been rifled through, but again, nothing was gone.

"What were they looking for?" Scott asked.

"I imagine they were trying to find my mother," I answered, which was the truth.

In an attempt to add some humor to the situation, Gina added, "In the filing cabinets or my suitcase?"

I didn't think it was funny and neither did the detective. When he asked why they were searching for her, that was when I started to fudge. "I don't know," I kept saying, and I was sure he didn't believe me. I insisted my mother's past was a mystery to me; that she had lived in New York and Los Angeles and was originally from Odessa, Texas, but that was all I knew. Scott bluntly asked if my mother was involved in any kind of criminal activity when she was younger, and I denied knowing anything about that. I came clean that we had moved Mom out of the Woodlands nursing home for her own protection and that she was now at Maggie's house.

It turned out that a gunman went to Woodlands earlier this morning and demanded to see Judy Talbot. According to a staff member by the name of Marissa, the man showed her his gun, which he kept in a jacket pocket, and threatened her to show him to my mother's room. Marissa later claimed that the man had promised to shoot her if she indicated to other staff members that she was in trouble. They marched into the dementia unit as if she was leading a visitor to a patient. However, they found my mother's room empty. Marissa was shocked and insisted that she had no idea where my mom could be. She asked at the nurse's desk and was told Mom had been "moved." Apparently Maggie had left word with the higher-ups that she had authorized Mom's transfer to another location, but poor Marissa didn't know about it. Frustrated, the gunman left without harming her—and then the police were notified.

He was described as a large, imposing man in his fifties with gray-brown hair and a scar on his left cheek. He wore jeans, a blue denim shirt, and a brown windbreaker. Not much to go on.

That meant the Riverwoods police were now involved in the case. So far, Uncle Thomas's murder investigation included the suburbs of Arlington Heights, Buffalo Grove, and Riverwoods. How long would it be before the killer figured out my mother was hiding in Deerfield?

I suddenly thought of Sam at my office. While we were still going through my house, I phoned him at Wegel, Stern, and Talbot, to make sure *he* was all right. Thank goodness, Shirley answered the phone and put me on to him.

"Some shady-looking guy came in here looking for you," he said. "Wouldn't give his name. I told him you were on vacation and hadn't been in for days." I told Sam he'd said the right thing and filled him in on what was going on. "Then you *are* on vacation, and that's that," he said. "Don't come back to the office until this is all done. I'm feeling pretty good, so I'll take care of everything." Then I put him on the phone with Detective Scott, who asked a few questions and promised to send a patrolman over to get a statement. Apparently, the visitor's description matched that of the gunman from Woodlands. There was no doubt about it—the man wanted *me*. Thank God the guy didn't hurt Sam or Shirley or anyone at Woodlands.

After I was satisfied that nothing important was taken from my house, I took some things I needed—clothes, toiletries, and a few files from the office—and Gina packed up her stuff. Detective Scott advised us not to return to the house until he knew more. I informed him that we were staying at Maggie's, and he said he would stop by sometime soon to talk to us further. In the meantime, we were to keep our whereabouts quiet.

I went back to Maggie's and Gina had to run some errands before going to the airport. She had booked a flight to Odessa, something we purposefully neglected to tell Detective Scott. By late afternoon, she met us back at Maggie's, I followed her to her mother's house so she could leave the car she'd borrowed, and then I drove her to O'Hare. Carol was under the impression she was returning to New York. We both hated to keep her in the dark about what was going on, but neither of us wanted Ross or my ex getting hurt either.

"Don't worry about me, Dad," Gina said as we hugged at the terminal curbside.

"How can I not?" I answered. "Please, I want daily phone reports. Promise?"

"Yes. Just keep Grandma safe, all right?"

"I'll do my best."

"And try to keep calm. No more anxiety attacks!"

"Ha ha. You just keep your head straight," I said.

As I drove back to Deerfield, a thousand possible scenarios went through my head—none of them good. I had to admit I was a born pessimist.

Tonight at dinner, Maggie said, "You didn't sleep a wink last night." I admitted it was the truth. I felt like shit and my neck wound hurt. "I have to go to work tomorrow, you know. Virginia will be here at ten o'clock. She'll help you out."

"Okay." Virginia was the hospice worker we had secured. She was a godsend. "Can she keep a secret?"

"We can't worry about that. I've told her we had to move your mother for 'legal' reasons. Probably best not to scare Virginia with stories of killers who are looking for us."

"What do you think about moving Mom somewhere *really* out of the way? A hotel or something? I'm afraid that whoever this guy is, he'll eventually figure out you and I are a couple, and he'll trace us here to your house."

"I've thought of that too," Maggie said. "My parents have a summer house on the lake in Wisconsin. I've told you about it."

"Yeah, but I've never been there. Where is it, exactly?"

"Pleasant Prairie. It's south of Kenosha, just over the Illinois border. It's a lovely, isolated house on Lake Shore Drive, facing Lake Michigan. We could go there. I'll take off from work. The other doctors can handle my practice, and we can get someone to cover for me at Woodlands. What do you say?"

I thought about it for maybe ten seconds, and then said, "Let's do it."

17
Judy's Diary
1962

MARCH 26, 1962

Today I went to see Barry's friend, Dr. Abernathy. He's associated with Linda Vista Community Hospital, which is located near downtown LA. It's uncomfortably close to the Wholesale District, but I guess I have to take what I can get. Dr. Abernathy's private office is on Wabash Avenue, and that's where I went to see him for "stomach trouble." He knew all about the situation though, Barry had prepped him. He's very nice and I like him a lot. I reckon he's in his late forties or early fifties. There's gray in his hair and he wears glasses. He called me "Mrs. Talbot" when he walked into the examination room. A nurse accompanied him, and for all I knew, to her I really was Mrs. Richard Talbot.

After examining me and asking all kinds of embarrassing questions about when the baby was conceived and when I last had my period, he told me that everything looked great. My baby and I were exactly where we should be at around three months. He thinks my due date will be between September 20 and 28. But it could be earlier too, that happens to many women. It's also possible the baby might be late too, but that's rarer.

Anyway, I can continue whatever I do for "exercise"—I didn't tell him I like to climb ropes and break into warehouses—and be sure to eat well and get plenty of rest. He wants to see me again in two months unless I have any problems.

In the meantime, I've spent the last week getting used to my new home and laying low. The only time I've ventured off the mountain was to go to the doctor. I'm sure by now Leo has figured out I'm not in my old apartment any more. I hope he's going crazy wondering where I am. Of course, I could be flattering myself and he's not thinking about me at all. But I doubt it. I really am afraid he will do everything he can to find me. I worry that Barry isn't as isolated as he thinks. With him being an ex-con and an informant, as well as having lots of contacts in the underworld, I would think he'd be well known.

Every day I've gone down the canyon steps and practiced shooting my gun at Barry's targets. I think I'm getting to be a better aim, but I'm not sure I really enjoy it. At first, holding the gun in my hands gave me a feeling of power, but something Barry said has haunted me. "Respect the weapon. It's dangerous." Maybe the fact that it's a machine that human beings invented to kill other human beings with is what bothers me. I use a stiletto, and I suppose you can say the same thing about it, but a knife is used for so many other purposes. A gun exists only to hurt or kill. Still, I want to be knowledgeable about it. Being able to fire a pistol is a skill every girl should have, ha ha.

April 2, 1962

I did a crazy thing last night.

I played an April Fool's joke on Leo. A big one.

I stole his diamond. At least I think it's the diamond that's inside his mother's Chinese jewel box. I have the box, anyway.

Yesterday was Sunday, so Leo's office and the other businesses in his building were closed. During the day there're usually a few people around, even on the weekend, but at night—the building is more often than not empty and deserted.

The Black Stiletto drove into town. Barry was out; I wasn't sure where he was. He continues to do his detective work without me. I suddenly felt cooped up at the cabin and decided to take the car for a drive. I dressed in my outfit—ugh, it's getting tight; I'm gaining weight fast—with the trench coat on top, and took off down the mountain and into the city. The weather was beautiful, but the winding roads were dark and just as treacherous as always. At one point, somebody was behind me and wanted to go faster. I wasn't about to let him push me into speeding on such dangerous paths. He honked his horn, and all I could see in my rearview mirror were his headlights. Finally, at one point in a long stretch of road that angled for a long, straight drop, he passed me, kicking up gravel and dirt. Bastard. I was very tempted to put on my mask and chase the guy, but I had better things to do.

Once I got to the Wholesale District, I circled 7th Street a couple of times to make sure I didn't see Leo's or Christina's cars. Finally, I parked up the block, donned the mask and backpack, and made my way in the shadows to the building. A light above the door was troublesome, for it illuminated the entire space. Anyone driving by could see me attempting to break into the front door. I had no choice but to take my stiletto, reach up, and stab the light bulb from beneath the lamp covering. It shattered and I was plunged into darkness. The building's maintenance man surely will wonder how it happened, for I planned to leave no other trace that I'd made a visit.

The door opened easily with a lock pick. The entry and hallways were dark. I stopped and listened carefully to make sure no one was walking about. Feeling safe, I went up the stairs to the second floor and down the corridor to Kelly Warehousing Enterprises. Another lock pick got me through the main door, and then I was in the secretaries' outer office.

With flashlight in hand, I paused at Christina's desk and took a look around. All I could find was paperwork pertaining to the warehouse business. There was nothing unusual in her desk drawers. I didn't know what I expected to find. Surely, she didn't keep her Black Stiletto costume at the office!

Picking Leo's door was trickier; it took me three tries, but I finally got it open. Once inside, I went to the desk and picked up the jewel box. I shook it again and heard the object knock about the inside. I tried a lock pick on the little hole but it wouldn't work. I opted for another size. And another. Nothing opened the darned thing. Leo was right. It could only be opened by that blasted gold key he keeps on his key ring. Unless I try the sledgehammer method, which could damage the gem.

So I put the jewel box itself in my backpack, and wrote a note on the pad that was on his desk.

It said—"April Fool's!"—and I signed it "The Black Stiletto."

I left the note where the box had been, and then I rummaged through the desk drawers. Interestingly, I found a handgun and a box of rounds. It wasn't like mine. It said "Browning" on the side and it didn't have a cylinder for shells. A semi-automatic. Barry told me all about them. I can't believe I knew so little about guns until he started teaching me. I put it back in the drawer, although I probably should have taken it and the ammunition and thrown them in the ocean.

As I left the building, I thought about what I'd done, and I'm still thinking about it. Am I a thief? Have I done something terribly wrong?

No. I justified my actions by reminding myself how awful Leo is, and what he did to obtain the diamond. My guts tell me it's inside the box. That big, beautiful diamond necklace. And if it isn't, then it must be something else valuable. If Leo was going to put only something of great beauty in the box, then it had to be something that meant a lot to him. Maybe by "borrowing" it and giving him a heck of a fright, I could gain a little bit of satisfaction in tormenting him. And if I end up never giving it back, I will find a way to open the box and discover its contents. If it's valuable, then it was most likely obtained illegally and therefore it was fair game.

Maybe it would help me support my son or daughter.

APRIL 3, 1962

Oh my God, the phony Black Stiletto has struck again, and this time it's pretty serious.

Sal Casazza was gunned down on a street in Hollywood. It was in all the papers.

Apparently he was getting in his car, which was parked in front of a convenience store. The manager told police that Casazza had come in to buy cigars. After he left, the man heard shots outside. He went to the door and saw the Black Stiletto, holding a gun with both hands. It was pointed at Casazza, who had slumped against his car. The "Stiletto" ran and had disappeared into the night by the time the police and an ambulance arrived.

Casazza is dead.

And now I'm being blamed for that too.

18
Leo
The Past

I was going to kill my sister for what she did.

If I thought I had a death sentence with the casino stickup, what in God's name did I have now? What would Vince DeAngelo do to me when he found out Christina stole his money, killed his friend and lieutenant, *and* murdered his daughter?

I didn't know my sister anymore. She was a different person. During the past three months she went through some kind of mental and emotional change. Something was wrong. I couldn't say she was particularly *sick*, because I'd never seen her happier. It was as if every minute of her waking hours was a thrill. She'd become so reckless and unpredictable. Her performance at the office was erratic. Some days she was her normal self, and other days she was—weird. Very agitated and overexcited, for no reason. On those days she couldn't concentrate on the work and spent the time having a one-way conversation with Evelyn. At home she'd taken to lighting candles. I don't know why. She put candles all over the house and she lit them when she was home. When I asked her about them, Christina said she thought candles were beautiful. That was something new. I was worried. *Very* worried.

Poor Sal Casazza. I never liked the guy much, but she didn't need to kill him. What made me feel the shittiest was that Christina thought she did it for *me*.

When I confronted her this morning in our kitchen, her response was, "Leo, you silly fool, with Casazza out of the way, and with Paulie and his father fighting, you've got an opening to slip in. Go tell Daddy-in-law that you want the job. He'll give it to you."

I blew my top. "Are you mad? Christina, I can't believe this! That's never gonna happen—"

"Calm down, you're getting hysterical."

"*Calm down?* Christina, you're out of control!"

The fight abruptly stopped. That hurt her. I knew if there was one thing in which Christina took great pride, it was control. She glared at me with such fierce antagonism, for a moment I really thought she was going to hurt me. Instead, though, she stepped forward, lifted a hand, and lightly pinched my chin. Her eyes burned holes through mine as she spoke softly, "Leo, you may be my older brother, but I know *exactly* what I'm doing. I'm in *perfect* control." Then she dug her thumbnail into my skin *hard*. I jumped back.

"Ouch. Christina! Jesus!"

Then she laughed. If she'd been anyone else, I would've torn into her. Man or woman. I'd always held my own in a fight if it got physical, and I'd have no problem rearranging a girl's face if she sassed me the way Christina had. But I couldn't do it. Not to my baby sister. So I picked up a plate from the counter and threw it across the room. It shattered noisily.

Christina just furrowed her brow, and said, "Oooh, tough guy. *You're* going to clean that up, you know."

I took a deep breath, and said, "Christina, I love you, but you can't do this anymore. You can't be the Black Stiletto again. It's too dangerous! This thing with Casazza, it's the last straw."

She held up her hands, and actually said, "I know. You can stop whining. Everything you say is true. I'm risking both our necks. The Black Stiletto will lie low for a while."

"Christina, you said you'd burn that costume. Why didn't you?"

"Because I thought it would come in handy again, and it has!"

"Well, you have to get rid of it now!"

She pointed a finger at me. "Listen, Leo. You want to know another reason why I did this?"

"What."

"So you'll stop pining away for Judy! You need to start focusing on what's at stake here. You've got a real chance to advance in the—" She wasn't sure what to call it. "—organization. And all you've been doing is pulling your hair out over that stupid girl. So she's gone. You can't find her. Leo, she *left town*. She didn't want you for a husband *or* her baby's father, so get over it."

Lately, her train of thought was like that. She'd jump from one topic to another without totally resolving the first matter. "What's that have to do with you burning that costume?"

"I just *said*. I did these things for *you*. For *us*. It's always been you and me, Leo, and it always will be." She folded her arms over her chest and leaned forward. "Listen to me, Leo. You have a chance to form a stronger alliance with Ricky without DeAngelo."

"No, I don't."

"Yes, you do," she said. "Ricky told me."

I looked at her. Since when was she talking to Ricky Bartlett? "What?"

She shrugged. "Ricky and I are friendly."

The connotations of her sentence made my mind reel.

With that, she blew out a candle she had burning in the kitchen, and then walked out the side door to her car. Before she left, though, she announced, "Oh, I'm not coming in to work today. Evelyn can handle everything without me." Before I could protest, she got in the Corvette and drove off.

My sister and one of the most powerful men in the Dixie Mafia?

She was right. If Christina formed a relationship with Bartlett, I would be favorably linked to his outfit just for being her brother.

That made me pause.

Also, unfortunately, Christina was correct on the other thing, too. I *had* been going a little nuts over Judy. When I found out she'd moved out of her apartment and quit her job at Flickers, I panicked.

She went and did exactly what I thought she might. The bitch ran off, with *my* son inside of her. Uncle Charlie didn't know where she was. He claimed she didn't leave a forwarding address. I didn't know if he was lying to me because he was mad about the way I treated her or if he was really telling the truth.

I didn't have a clue where to look for her. She probably left the city, maybe even the state. She could be anywhere, a needle in a million haystacks.

Okay, so now I wanted to kill *three* women—my sister, the real Black Stiletto, *and* Judy Cooper!

The phone rang and I answered it. Luchino Battilana, DeAngelo's *consigliore*, was on the line.

"The boss wants to see you," he said.

"How soon? I have to go to my office today."

"I'm just telling you what he said. He told me to call you. How soon can you get here?"

"Look, Luchino, tell him I'll be there later tonight. I have to go attend to some warehousing business, and then I'll head out this afternoon. I should be in Vegas around seven or eight, all right?"

That would have to do. Luchino hung up.

As I drove to the Wholesale District, I wondered what the hell Vince wanted. The blowup with Paulie changed things. The last time Vince and I saw each other, I'd told him I needed to spend more time in LA, taking care of not only my company, but getting the counterfeit operation up and running again. The Heathens and Los Serpientes were grumbling awfully loud that we haven't supplied them with any funny money to sell for a couple of months. I figured it was time. The heat had died down. The guys that got arrested weren't squealing, and a lot of them were released on technicalities. Byron was still in jail, though, but the Heathens were operating just fine without him.

It was a Thursday, and I hadn't been in the office since last Friday. Sal's death caused some fires I had to put out. Shrimp and Mario were beside themselves. They were ready to go out on the street and start gunning down cops. Some of the bozos in Sal's crew tried to assert some authority overnight, but Vince sent Rico Mancini to head up an emergency meeting. He said Vince was going to appoint the new head of what he called the "LA branch." There were a lot of unhappy mobsters that night, but I did get the go-ahead to start up the funny money machine again.

Paulie got pissed off that his daddy didn't automatically appoint him in charge of Casazza's territory. He accused his father of favoring *me* over him, his own son. They weren't speaking to each other. It was kind of funny, actually. That put Vince in a *terrible* mood.

My office building was a beehive on a workday. All the other businesses were typically abuzz with activity. Last I looked there were sixteen different companies that had offices in the three-story building. I went in Kelly Warehousing Enterprises and found Evelyn holding down the fort. She'd known since last Friday I wouldn't be in until today, and was fine with that, but I could tell she was peeved that Christina hadn't come in. She'd been left alone, running my firm. Maybe I don't pay her enough.

"Hello, Mr. Kelly," she said, handing me a pile of telephone messages and the mail. "Here you go. And don't forget your appointment with Mr. Branson at four o'clock."

He was a warehouse client. "Please call him and reschedule. I have to leave early today." I didn't wait to see her response—I unlocked my office door and went inside. I dropped the mail and messages on the desk; most likely bills, but there would also be a few warehouse lease payments.

The fight with Christina and the summons to Vegas unnerved me. Even though it wasn't noon yet, I went to the liquor cabinet, unlocked it, and pulled out a bottle of whisky. I poured a tumbler full, shut the cabinet, and took the glass back to the desk.

Nursing the whisky, I sat and stared out the window at the bright sunshine. I didn't feel like working. I dreaded going to Vegas. I wanted to punch Christina. I wanted to murder Judy. *Work* was just not on my mind.

Eventually, though, I stopped daydreaming and turned to everything that was on my desk.

My heart stopped.

In the spot where my mother's Chinese jewel box always sat, there was, instead, a note.

When I read it, I swore so loudly that I'm sure everyone in the building heard me.

19
Judy's Diary
1962

APRIL 8, 1962

I'm in the hospital, dear diary, and I thought maybe I could write an entry but I feel too weak.

APRIL 10, 1962

I think I'm out of danger now, but I'm still in the hospital. When Barry asked me what I wanted him to bring from home, the first thing I thought of was my diary. I hope no nurses or doctors find it when I'm asleep and take a peek.

Barry saved my life. He also saved my baby's life. I owe everything to him. My poor baby went through a tough time the last few days.

It hurts to sit up; I'm going to do this another time.

APRIL 15, 1962

I've been in Linda Vista Hospital for over a week. Even though the gunshot wound was not as serious as it could have been, it was still life threatening.

That's right, dear diary, I was shot. Christina Kelly shot me in the lower left abdomen. The bullet did what the doctor calls a through-and-through, right next to the baby. According to Dr. Abernathy, the round barely missed the abdominal cavity and my spleen. It did, however, nick my large intestine, and that had to be "resected." I apparently lost a lot of blood and I had to have a transfusion. My poor baby went into distress for a short time, but everything calmed down after Dr. Abernathy performed the operation. It was a good thing I was unconscious during the crisis. I'm not sure how I would have handled it. Somehow it was all kept quiet from the police. Barry and his inner circle of under-the-table dealmakers were able to keep it hush-hush that a pregnant woman with a gunshot wound had been admitted. My name was still Judy Talbot, and it was actually a good thing that I was already in the hospital records. Normally the cops would be alerted when someone came to the emergency room in such a condition. I asked Barry if Dr. Abernathy knew about me, and he said no. The doctor thinks I'm one of Barry's informants, and maybe even believes Barry and I are more than friends.

I'm still bandaged up, but I will have yet another ugly scar on my body, matching the one on my left shoulder.

I was in and out of reality for the first three or four days, but now I'm pretty lucid and ready to get the heck out of here. The doc says that after I'm released to go home, I can't have any physical activity for at least a month. In fact, I've been sentenced to bed rest.

Ugh. I'll go stir crazy.

APRIL 19, 1962

I'm waiting for Barry to get here and pick me up. I'm finally being discharged. I would have written sooner but I was a little depressed. Feeling sorry for myself. Same old story, how I get sometimes. I felt as if I'd been defeated. I wondered if being the Black Stiletto was a thing of the past for me. Did I have to give her up for good? Did almost getting killed knock some sense into me? Or did it make the whole compulsion worse? I really want to get back at

Christina and Leo, but that's going to be impossible for quite some time. The conflicting emotions and mind racing got me down.

I'm better now though. At least my wound is healing well. Dr. Abernathy is surprised that I got better so fast. I attribute that to my heightened senses, or whatever it is that happened to me when I was an adolescent—and I'm not going to call them superpowers because they're not. But they're what make me the Black Stiletto. Superpowers, ha ha, big deal. They didn't stop me from almost dying.

I remember everything that happened up to the gunshot. It was Friday night, April 6.

During those first few days after April Fool's, I tried to get that darned jewel box open. I showed it to Barry and he tried some more sophisticated lock picks, but to no avail. I simply had to get that gold key off Leo's keychain. It was also bugging me that I never finished the task of searching Leo and Christina's house for her Black Stiletto costume or any other evidence that might tie her to the crimes. The papers continue to perpetuate the myth that the Black Stiletto killed Sal Casazza and Maria Kelly, and that I'm a "dangerous criminal." It had to stop.

I knew it wouldn't be long before I wouldn't be able to wear my outfit—it was already so tight; maneuvering in it was a struggle. It was "now or never." I decided to go and take a look at the house. If he or Christina were home, I'd split. But if they weren't—I told Barry my plans. He tried to talk me out of it because he wasn't able to tag along and back me up. He was on another job and had to meet an informant somewhere in Hollywood. I told him not to worry about me, that I'd be *fine*.

Barry's here. I'll write more later.

LATER

I'm home in the cabin on the mountain, lying in bed. My wound is very sore, but otherwise I feel all right. Staying in bed when I don't particularly feel sick is very annoying. It's going to get old fast. But the doc says I have to stay down, no matter what. Barry's been charged with enforcing the rule. He's arming me with some books. He got me *The Agony and the Ecstasy* and *The Carpetbaggers*, both of which I want to read anyway. He also moved the TV into my room. Strangely, the reception was much better!

My car is hidden in Barry's garage. He and a trusted friend found it. Barry drove it up the mountain while his friend followed in the Fairlane. Barry said the guy wouldn't think anything of it.

Back to the night of April 6. I drove the Sunliner to Woodruff Avenue and saw that the Kelly house was dark and silent. No cars sat in the drive. Leo and Christina weren't home. I found a parking spot around a corner and a block away. The odds of Leo spotting my car on the street were miniscule. I left it there, I was completely dressed as the Black Stiletto. The residential neighborhood had plenty of trees, providing enough shadows for me to travel through as I made my way back to the house. Getting in the side door to my old basement room was as simple as sticking the lock pick in the keyhole.

Nothing had changed since the last time I was there. The house was dark, so I grabbed the flashlight from my belt and went up the stairs to the ground floor. But when I emerged from the top step, I bumped into a card table that was inexplicably set up in the way. There was a pile of playing cards on it. It appeared as if they'd been playing Go Fish or something. I thought maybe the table had been in the middle of the room when they were playing, and they had simply moved it out of the way, in front of the stairs. Leo or Christina rarely needed to go downstairs to the basement.

I was definitely alone in the place, so I went up to Christina's lair on the second floor. Her bedroom door was closed. Just to be diligent, I listened with my ear to it before opening it.

Even during those weeks when I lived in the house, I never saw Christina's room. This was my first time, and I almost laughed at how messy it was. Clothes were lying all over the floor and bed. Underwear, jeans, tops, and shoes. She also had a lot of candlesticks with partly burned candles in them. Weird. I wanted to turn on the light, but it would be seen outside. The flashlight beam had to do.

I searched through her closet, her dresser drawers, under the bed, between the mattresses, and in other nooks and crannies, but I didn't find anything of interest. For a half hour I scoured the space, careful not to move anything out of place. Frustrated, I stood in the middle of the room and asked myself what I was missing. If she still had the costume, it could be stored at another location, which was possible. Otherwise it had to be in the room somewhere.

A headboard on the bed consisted of a cubbyhole bookshelf and a place to put knickknacks and an alarm clock. A reading lamp sat on top. The piece of furniture was about a foot deep, which meant it was presumably hollow beneath the shelf. I moved to the side of the bed and examined the headboard more closely. I stuck my hand between the wall and the back of the headboard and felt the plywood. On a whim, I pushed it laterally, and it *slid* open, like a cabinet door.

The Black Stiletto costume was stuffed inside, along with a handgun and ammunition.

It wasn't difficult to move the bed, with the headboard, away from the wall a few inches. I then removed the camera from my backpack and took some photos with the flash on. I captured the bed, the headboard, and what I could see of the back hiding place. Then I took pictures of the costume and gun.

When I was finished, I put everything back where it had been. I considered stealing the costume, but then I couldn't prove it came from Christina's room, despite my photos. I thought the pictures might provide Barry with the means to persuade the cops to get a search warrant. One of the mistakes I made, though, was putting the camera in my jacket pocket instead of safely in the backpack.

A pair of car headlights shot through the window and swept across the room. I dared to peek and saw Leo's Karmann Ghia pulling into the drive. Oh my God, I didn't want him to catch me there. I bolted from Christina's room, shut the door, and practically flew down the stairs. The front door was opening just as I made it to the basement level bedroom. I plastered my back to the wall and fought to catch my breath as I listened. I heard him walk into the living room above me. He turned on the lights, illuminating the staircase and basement.

There was a long silence, and it made me very nervous. I considered attacking him, like the time I threatened him in his house just after New Year's. I figured he had to have known about the missing jewel box by now. It would have been gratifying to rub it in. Then Leo sighed loudly and I heard him go into the kitchen. He opened the fridge. For the next few minutes he ate or drank something. I was starting to sweat, hoping like heck that he'd go to his bedroom or something. Just as I made up my mind to confront him, the phone rang. He picked it up and I heard his side of the conversation.

"Hello. Yeah, hi. No, I haven't found it. I just got back from Vegas. Vince wanted to see me. I spent the night and most of today at the ranch. No, it was nothing. It was about reorganizing the LA business. I guess I should be flattered he asked me to join the discussion. Yeah, Shrimp and Mario were there. Oh, come on. Look, Christina, I'm sorry, but I had to go to Vegas! And how am I supposed to *find* the goddamned diamond? The goddamned Black Stiletto has it, Christina. Unless we find her, we'll never get it back. Look, come home. We have to talk about this. How long will you be? Okay. I'm going to take a shower. Yeah, I'll be here, I'm not going anywhere. I'm dead tired. Yeah, bye."

He hung up and I heard him shuffle around above my head, and then he went to his bedroom.

Then the idea struck me—if he was going to take a shower, that meant he had to take his pants off. And inside the pants pocket was the key ring.

I waited a few minutes and then crept up the stairs to the ground floor. The sound of the shower running floated from his open bedroom door. I slipped around the card table and flattened against the wall beside the entrance to his inner sanctum. I listened for movement and there was none. He was in the shower stall. Perfect. I went into the room. His clothes were thrown on the bed. I picked up his pants and rifled his pockets. Found the key ring. The gold key was there along with all his others. I forced it off the ring and pocketed it, and then I put the ring back in the pants pocket.

My senses started tingling. Something was out of whack. A creak of the closet door beside me. I turned, and a *figure* appeared.

Leo, in his boxer shorts, pointed a gun at me. "Hands up, bitch!" he snarled.

I had no choice but to comply. He had tricked me. "Surprised I'm not all wet and naked?"

"Don't flatter yourself," I replied. My heart pounded rapidly.

"I built a house of cards on that table in the living room. Ever since you broke into my office, I put it there. Anyone coming in through the basement would knock it over. I knew someone had been in or was still in the house."

I didn't say anything.

"Where's my jewel box?" he snapped.

"If you shoot me, you'll never see it again."

"I want it back."

"I'm sure you do."

"What are you doing with my pants? Looking for something? Want to take money from my wallet? Rob me?" That told me he hadn't seen me take the key.

"Here, why don't you put them on?" I abruptly threw them in his face and bolted out the door. His gun went off, but he blindly shot a hole in his bedroom wall. I ran like the dickens to the front door and fumbled with the doorknob as Leo came running after me. I flung open the door just as he took another potshot at me and missed.

By then I was outside, running across his lawn to the street. And that's when the blue-and-white Corvette pulled in to the drive. Christina. Great, perfect timing.

Leo shouted, "Get her, Christina! Stop her!"

I had to run toward her car to get where I was going, so I shot past the tail end of it and kept running down the street. I heard the car door open behind me. And then the camera fell out of my jacket pocket and rattled as it bounced on the pavement.

Agh! Another mistake—I made a near-fatal decision to stop and retrieve it. I turned and at first I couldn't see the camera due to the darkness. I wasted another second or two looking for it as Christina ran toward me. Finally—there it was. I went to pick it up and—*blam*. Christina shot me. I felt a terrible burning sensation in my left lower side. Oh my God, it hurt, dear diary. The next thing I knew I was lying on the street in pain.

And then—a miracle. I heard tires squeal on the street as a car screeched to a halt beside me. I heard a man shout, "Back off!" and there was another gunshot. Then another. And another. I didn't know what was going on.

Then *Barry* leaned over me. "Can you stand?"

All I could do was groan.

He picked me up as if I was a child and literally *threw* me in the back seat of his Fairlane, jumped into the driver's seat, and took off. I think Christina may have fired her gun again at him, but I'm not sure. Barry told me later that I said three words before passing out—"Save the baby."

Everything went black for a long time.

When I woke up, I was in my hospital room. I'd been unconscious an entire day.

If Barry hadn't shown up—

He told me that he'd been worried about me, so he cut his meeting short and drove by Leo's house just to check on things. How lucky was that? He drove me to Linda Vista Hospital as I bled all over the back of his car.

I lost the camera with the incriminating photos, but I escaped with the gold key and the lives of me and my child.

Once again, I owe Barry so much.

20
Gina
THE PRESENT

I changed planes in Dallas, Texas, and arrived in Odessa after sundown. Although I couldn't see much, I was immediately struck by the feeling of desolation and emptiness. Everything was so *flat*. The night sky was full of stars; I'd never seen such a clear one-hundred-and-eighty degree view of the heavens. I rented a car at Midland International Airport, which was located between the "twin" cities of Midland and Odessa, and drove along Interstate 20 until I came to the hotel that I'd booked—the La Quinta Inn. It was on the east edge of town, by the highway. The sun had gone down by then, so I didn't do anything else but check in and go to my room. I figured the suitcase I'd checked was safe. It contained some things I felt I needed to have near me on my mission, and I doubted they would have gotten through carry-on security.

The next morning I went to the Ector County Public Library, which sat in the old downtown area. Driving around the city was a strange experience. It was odd to think that my grandmother—the legendary Black Stiletto—came from the place. Surrounding the city was nothing but desert, mesquite, and oil wells. In fact, the air *smelled* like petroleum. The streets were ridiculously wide, the sun was very bright, and the buildings were so low to the ground. Everything else reeked of a place out of time, stuck somewhere between the nineteen fifties and, well, maybe a decade ago. After having grown up in the

Chicago suburbs and living in New York for a while, I really felt like a fish out of water. Odessa had a population of over a hundred thousand people, but it felt very much like a small town. The only thing I really knew about Odessa was that it was somewhat famous for a high school football team that Hollywood made a movie and television show about. I never watched it.

At the library, I had access to old newspapers. Using an index, I looked up "Judy Cooper" and found nothing. I then tried "John Cooper" and found dozens of entries. The only way I could determine the articles were about my great uncle was to look them up and read them. But after scanning through a dozen, I realized there were just too many to wade through and there were more important things to look up. I did, however, attempt to locate "Frank Cooper" and found out something very disturbing.

In the paper dated December 14, 1962, there was a piece about a man named Frank Cooper who was murdered in his home on Beechwood Street. Apparently, there had been a break-in and he was killed during a robbery gone bad, or so the police thought. The obituary, which appeared in the paper a day later, said that Cooper owned a hardware store on the east side of town. He was survived by a wife, Sarah, and a daughter, Angela. Was that my great uncle? I continued to follow that story, but references to Frank Cooper disappeared after a couple of months. The case was never solved.

I made copies of all the relevant articles.

Then I turned my attention to Ricky Bartlett. There were *tons* of articles about him throughout the years, beginning in the late nineteen fifties. It was going to take days plow through them. Instead, I concentrated on the early eighties, around the time he was killed in a suspicious fire.

It happened in 1983. Bartlett had an office at his supply company building, which was located on Andrews Highway, where all the oil well businesses had operations. Apparently, a fire broke out there one night while he was working late. Investigators found a forklift parked in front of the office door, indicating that someone had intentionally trapped Bartlett inside. As I'd read before, an employee, Dallas Haines, age twenty-seven, was detained and questioned, but he was never arrested. The case was classified as arson, but apparently it was never solved. While Bartlett's obituary didn't mention it, other Op-Ed pieces speculated that Bartlett's "death" had something to do with the big bust that occurred in 1981, in which illegal drugs and weapons were found hidden at the supply company warehouse. Bartlett and several of his high-ranking employees were arrested for smuggling and racketeering. Bartlett was acquitted in the subsequent trial—he obviously had some very good lawyers—but others went to prison.

The county sheriff, who was the arresting officer at the time, was a man named Ralph McCambridge. I wondered if he might still be alive and if I could talk to him. One of the librarians appeared to be in her fifties or sixties, so I asked if she knew him.

"Oh, yes, I remember Sheriff McCambridge," she told me. "He's retired now. I imagine he's in the phone directory. Shall I look him up for you?"

"Yes, please."

Turned out the county sheriff's office gave her his mobile number, no questions asked! After I had it in hand, I went back to my research. I was there all day except for a lunch break—I went to a fast-food Mexican joint called Taco Villa that was surprisingly good. Mid-afternoon my own cell rang. The librarian shot me a stern look, so I took the phone outside as I answered it. Josh was calling from New York.

"How's the 'burbs?" he asked.

"Fine, but actually, I'm in Odessa, Texas."

"*What?*"

I told him the whole story because I hadn't had a chance to call him—the murder of Uncle Thomas, the break-in at my dad's house, moving my grandmother out of the nursing home, and why I was at that moment in the Ector County Public Library.

"Why didn't you call me?" he demanded. He was pretty angry.

"Gina, this doesn't sound good at all. You should let the police handle this! And Mr. Page really wants you back here."

If only I could tell him about Grandma Judy and why we had to discreetly investigate the problem, but I just couldn't yet. I tried to explain that there was something in my grandmother's past that my *family* didn't know, and I was looking into it. It sounded lame, but it was the best I could do.

"Do you want me to come down there?" he asked, now genuinely concerned.

"No. But I wonder if Mr. Page might consider my 'work' here part of the training? Really, Josh, it'll be good experience. I think it fits right in with the program's intentions. Don't you?"

"I have no idea." He was silent for a moment, but then he said, "I'll talk to him. But, look, this sounds pretty shady. After what happened to you and your father in New York, it's pretty clear these people are not very nice. I don't want you getting hurt."

"You know I can take care of myself," I said.

"Not against bullets."

It was my turn to get a little curt. "Well, tough shit, Josh. I'm doing this and I'm afraid you and Mr. Page can't stop me. This is a family matter, and my family is very important."

"Okay, okay, I understand. I want you calling me, though. Every day."

"You sound like my dad."

"Well, he's right. You're still young and you're very green."

"I know."

"You have a tendency for impulsiveness."

"I know."

"You act without thinking."

"I *know*, Josh. I'll follow the training we've been doing."

"The only time you're not supposed to think first is when you're actively in the throes of *retzev*. Krav Maga only works when—"

"Josh, please don't treat me like I'm a beginner."

"All right. I'm sorry."

We ended the call on a sour note, but I didn't care. Our relationship was solid. I had other things to worry about at the moment.

Back at the newspapers, I looked up the name Dallas Haines in the index and found a few more entries, especially in the late eighties. In 1988, he went on trial for second-degree murder. He had killed another man in a fight outside a bar, but Haines got a lesser conviction of manslaughter. Nevertheless, he was sentenced to fifteen years in prison. There were no further mentions of him in the papers, but I assumed he was out now, unless he'd died there or committed other crimes. If he was twenty-seven in '83, then he'd be fifty-six or fifty-seven now.

It was nearly dinnertime when I finished for the day. Before going to find food, I made a call to Ralph McCambridge. It took me by surprise when a man answered.

"Um, I'm looking for former sheriff Ralph McCambridge?"

"You got him."

"Oh, hi. You don't know me. My name is Gina Talbot, and I'm visiting Odessa from Illinois."

"Uh-huh?"

"Well, I'm doing some research on some things that happened in Odessa when you were sheriff, and I wondered if you might be willing to meet me for coffee?"

"What kind of things?" He had a very pronounced Texas drawl, much more than my grandmother had.

"I'd rather not say over the phone, but it involves Ricky Bartlett. You may remember, he—"

"I certainly know who Ricky Bartlett was. What's this about, Miss, uh, Talbot, was it?"

"Yes, sir. I'd really rather meet in person to talk about it."

"I'm kinda busy. If you can't tell me on the phone, then I don't think I can see you."

I went for broke. "Well, my family is in danger and I think someone here in Odessa is behind it. And whoever it is, they're somehow associated with Ricky Bartlett in the past. That's all I know."

The man was silent for a moment. "Mr. McCambridge?"

"I'm still here. When did you want to meet?"

"As soon as whenever's convenient for you."

"How about tomorrow morning? You want to meet at the Starbucks?"

"That'd be great. Um, where is it?"

"Where are you?" I told him where I was staying.

"Well, there's one on Forty-Second Street, just west of Grandview. You know how to get there?"

"I'll find it. I have a GPS in my phone."

We set a time for eleven in the morning and I thanked him. I couldn't tell how nice he was going to be. He sounded a little gruff, but I couldn't worry about that. If he was willing to help me, then fine. I could handle a billy goat.

After dinner at Rosa's Café and Tortilla Factory—Tex-Mex food again!—which was located near the University of Texas–Permian Basin, I went back to the hotel with a list of Cooper phone numbers and spent an hour calling all of them. There was no luck finding anyone related to a John or Frank Cooper who had lived in Odessa in the 1950s. The hardware store mentioned in that obituary no longer existed and, besides, I wasn't positive the Frank Cooper that was murdered in 1962 was my grandma's brother. The only lead I could follow was the address on Beechwood Street that was reported in the article about the robbery-homicide at Cooper's home.

I thought that perhaps tomorrow, after meeting with Mr. McCambridge, I'd go find that house and see if anyone living there now might know anything.

21
Judy's Diary
1962

Barry sold his Fairlane for $600 and bought a slightly used 1961 Buick Electra 225. It's a pretty brown. He did it because Christina—and possibly Leo—had seen the Fairlane when he picked me up. He didn't want to take the chance that they also caught the license plate number and ventured to track him down. He also recommended that I do the same thing. I told him I love my Sunliner, but he's probably right. If I'm going to stick around Los Angeles, at least until the baby is born, then I may need a different car. I replied that if he finds any good deals, I'd consider it.

He doesn't think Christina actually saw his face. He was wearing a baseball cap and she was twenty to thirty feet away when he dumped me in the backseat. And it was dark. The entire pickup took less than thirty seconds, so the odds of her identifying him were slim. Still, he didn't want to take the risk. He planned to lay low for a while. The DA asked him recently if he'd heard from the Black Stiletto; Barry lied and said no. He doesn't want anyone to know that I live in his cabin now. Even Dr. Abernathy isn't aware of where I am.

We talked a lot about what I saw and heard at Leo's house.

I don't think Christina would know I found her Stiletto costume. Even though I knocked over Leo's stupid house of cards and gave away my presence, I was extremely careful to cover my tracks, especially in Christina's room. If only I still had my camera. There's no question that Leo and Christina have it. Would they develop the film? If so, then Christina *will* know I found the costume. Drat. Then she'll either get rid of it or hide it somewhere else.

So, basically I really screwed up that mission.

However, I have the diamond.

Wow.

The gold key opened the jewel box like a charm.

Barry nearly choked when he saw it. I lay in bed and he sat in a chair beside me as we took turns holding it up to the light, feeling the cold surfaces, touching the finely cut edges and points. I've never seen anything like it.

"How much do you think it's worth?" I asked him.

"I have no idea."

"Do you think we could sell it?"

"I have no idea."

"Was it stolen to begin with?"

"I have no idea."

I laughed. "I like you 'cause you're so smart, Barry."

"Do you really want to sell it?"

"Well, I don't think I could get away with wearing it. I think the money would be much more practical. Although it *is* beautiful."

"Let me talk to Skipper. He might know a fence or two."

"Don't give away too much about it. This has to be our secret."

"I know. Leave it to me, darling."

"Oh, I'm your darling, now?"

"You've always been my darling." With that, he leaned over and kissed me on the cheek. I'm sure I blushed. When he left the room, I continued to play with the diamond.

I don't know why, but I think my future is somehow tied to it.

MAY 15, 1962

I haven't written much because there was nothing to say. What was I going to write? *Today I stayed in bed. Tomorrow I plan on staying in bed some more. Maybe the day after that I'll stay in bed.* Ha ha. Well, now I no longer have to do that. Barry drove me to see Dr. Abernathy this morning and he said I'm doing very well. I no longer need 24-hour bed rest. The wound looks great, but more importantly, the baby is doing fine. He or she has a strong heartbeat. I'm now approximately five months pregnant. My belly is huge, and it's going to keep growing. None of my clothes fit me. Barry promised to take me shopping for maternity stuff tomorrow. He's funny. He acts like he's the father in this whole situation. He looks after me, makes sure I eat right, and chastises me if he thinks I'm doing too much physical activity. One thing is for sure—the Black Stiletto is taking a hiatus. That's something I can't do for a while.

There's been nothing in the news about the *other* Black Stiletto. I guess Christina figured it was too risky for her to appear in public again. I can't fathom why she would rob Vincent DeAngelo's casino and kill Sal Casazza. If she got caught, it would only jeopardize Leo's business with the mob. As for shooting Maria Kelly, well, maybe I can understand that. She was jealous of Maria. Leo and Christina have a very strange relationship for a brother and sister. There's something abnormal about it. I don't want to think that maybe it's a physical one, but I wouldn't put it past them. She was always very possessive of him. I think that's why she hated *me* so much.

Barry said there was a big bust the other day in New Mexico. A caravan of Heathens was caught running guns and counterfeit money. Los Serpientes was involved too. Everyone was arrested, but no one was talking. The highway patrol in New Mexico believes the goods came from "organized crime outfits" in Los Angeles. At any rate, Barry thinks this means that DeAngelo's machine is up and running again without Sal Casazza. The distribution is spreading throughout the south—no doubt thanks to the Dixie Mafia, which is obviously in bed with DeAngelo. Is Leo in charge now? Is he able to manage his warehouse business and live a life of crime at the same time? Apparently so. At least *I* believe he's heavily involved. I've seen it with my own eyes.

And I still want to take him and his sister down.

In the meantime, I'll continue to rest, watch TV, read books, listen to my records, and go down to Barry's target range in the canyon to practice shooting my gun.

Not a bad life, but I'm getting restless.

It was my idea originally to set up the counterfeiting operation and Vince DeAngelo trusted me to run with it. It helped that I had a recently vacated warehouse on my hands that I knew was in disrepair, so my dummy company, A-1 Outriggers, could lease it, spend money on some exclusive renovations, and stay hidden from the public. It had worked, but internal politics and bad blood between the Heathens and Los Serpientes, along with the goddamned Black Stiletto's interference—the *real* one—mucked up everything. The gun-running business, which I had nothing to do with, got in trouble. After the big arrest in Texas, things got ugly. Heathens pointed fingers at Serpents, and vice versa. Then fingers became guns.

What was supposed to happen was that the Heathens would deliver the guns—and some of my funny money—to a drop point in western New Mexico, near Albuquerque. From there, Los Serpientes would transport the goods to Odessa, where Ricky Bartlett and his gang would happily receive them. DeAngelo had already been paid up front, so no money exchanged hands. What Bartlett and the Dixie Mafia did with the merchandise after that was none of our business. They took it over for their own distribution across the southern United States.

After Christina killed Casazza, I thought there was a chance that DeAngelo might appoint me in charge of the LA branch, but the old man sure enough made Paulie boss after all. Unfortunately, on the first run that Paulie set up, things didn't go well. At the New Mexico rendezvous, the Heathens and Los Serpientes first got into a verbal and then a physical fight. Someone pulled a gun. Somebody else drew one too. Shots were fired. A man was killed. More shots. More killed. And so on.

The police hit the scene of carnage with full force, as they had already been monitoring the movements of the two motorcycle clubs. The bikers who were wounded or unhurt were arrested. The merchandise was confiscated. All clues pointed back to Casazza's territory. DeAngelo now owed Bartlett a lot of dough. Not good.

Paulie really screwed up. DeAngelo kicked him out of the ranch house in Vegas. Now Paulie was dying to make it up to his daddy, but there's no question that Vince wasn't happy. His network was falling apart.

Christina thought it was the best time for me to assert some leadership and grab some power.

That's why I'm going to meet with Ricky Bartlett on my own.

After checking on Hugh and his boys in the warehouse, I went outside for some fresh air and a cigarette.

I kept thinking about the night the Black Stiletto was in the house. What had she seen? As she fled, she dropped her camera. Christina retrieved it, but the thing was damaged and we couldn't roll the film. We had to force open the camera, and by then the film was ruined. We'll never know what was on it. Probably nothing. It didn't appear that anything in the house was disturbed except my card deck burglar detector.

Still, I was worried. What did she know? And, more importantly, was she still alive? Christina swore she clipped her good. It was amazing how that guy appeared from nowhere to pick her up. But how was he going to save her? Take the Black Stiletto to a hospital? Well, we checked all the nearby hospitals. There were some gunshot victims admitted that night, and some of them were women, but none of them could possibly have been the Stiletto. Damn it, if she was dead, it would be even harder to get the diamond back. She had it somewhere, and I will do everything I can to find it.

As for my ex-girlfriend, she was long gone. Right now finding the Stiletto was more important to me than searching for Judy. But I wasn't going to give up. My son wasn't going to be born without me.

And to hell with Judy.

23
Judy's Diary
1962

JUNE 11, 1962

Ugh, I'm nearly six months pregnant. I'm uncomfortable all the time. Having the extra weight feels alien and *weird*. I think my body is so used to being fit that it's fighting the process! My physical activity is decreasing and that frustrates me. I just can't go too long without some kind of exercise routine. Much of the time when I went out as the Stiletto in New York, it was just that—a workout. I miss living in and around the gym. I miss the Manhattan streets. I miss Freddie.

I keep wondering what I'll name the baby. Barry teases me by saying that if it's a boy I'll probably name him Elvis. I wouldn't do that to the poor child, ha ha. It'll be bad enough having *me* as a mother! Of course, I don't know that. I may be a very good mother. My heightened sensitivity to feelings indicates that I'm changing my attitude about the whole thing. It's strange, but I'm already treating the unborn baby inside me as another person. I talk to him/her. I silently think, *what would he/she like for dinner tonight?* And then I pick up something I sense the two of us would enjoy. When I put on a record, I'm thinking, *Listen to this, little one, it's a great song!*

So, in many ways, I'm excited about having a baby. Whereas before I hated the idea and dreaded what I'll have to sacrifice—now I'm looking forward to it. I keep telling myself that even though Leo may be the father, I'm the mother. The fact that I had to change my name and invent a fictitious dead husband will help me keep the truth about Leo from my child. Daddy was a soldier in Vietnam, and he died. End of story. The reason I don't keep photographs of the man is because of grief. I can't bear to see his face: it depresses me. He didn't have any brothers or sisters, so there are no uncles or aunts. His parents are dead, so no grandparents. I'll have to nip in the bud any conversations concerning the subject of "who and where is Daddy?"

Barry and I have become good friends. I really enjoy his company. I think he's very sweet on me, but he does his best to hide it. I don't encourage him. I want to remain friends. He gave me a new camera. It's a Kodak Pony IV, and it's much more sophisticated than my old Brownie. It's a little heavier too, but it will be easier to use and will take better pictures. That was really nice of Barry. He blushed when I gave him a big hug to thank him.

We've talked a lot about the diamond. I told him that if his brother Skipper can really fence the gem for a lot of money, then I'd split it with him and Skipper. According to the newspapers, the "stolen" diamond is over 130 carats and worth at least 3.5 million dollars! A fence might not get that much for it, but close to it.

I'm getting restless. I think I might go for a drive. It's a nice day out.

LATER

I'm still puzzled by that building.

Dressed in a new flowery cotton maternity dress, I took the risk of driving the Sunliner down the mountain and into Hollywood. I had to move back the seat in my car so my belly could fit! Barry was out doing his job somewhere, and it was the middle of the afternoon. I drove with the top down. The sunshine and breeze on my face felt fabulous. I wore sunglasses; my black hair trailed in the wind behind me as I sped through the streets. Maybe I looked like a movie star. I wasn't worried about running into Leo or Christina. It wouldn't have been pretty if it had happened though.

Being a Monday, the Wholesale District was buzzing with activity. Trucks and vans were all over the streets. First I drove by Leo's office building. I didn't see his Karmann Ghia, but that didn't mean he wasn't in. Sometimes Boone drove him in the Lincoln. The more important he gets in DeAngelo's organization, the necessity for a bodyguard increases. Christina's Corvette wasn't in the lot either.

I then drove to the street where A-1 Outriggers was located and couldn't find street parking. The building's own lot, however, had plenty of open spaces. Many of the ones closest to the driveway and sidewalk were taken—probably by people who worked in other buildings and couldn't find a closer spot on the street. It was an empty, vacant warehouse, so why not? I pulled in there too, and parked.

Then I got out and *waddled* to the back of the building and the loading dock. Surprise, surprise, Hugh Costa's Edsel was parked next to three other vehicles I didn't recognize. One was a blue Ford pickup truck, another was a white van, and the third was a brown-and-tan Bonneville. I wrote down the license plate numbers on a little pad I had in my purse.

So where were the drivers? Where was Hugh Costa?

I went around to the front of the building and approached the door. It was locked, of course. Lock picking it wouldn't be a good idea in broad daylight, so I just put my ear to the door and listened carefully.

I'm not completely positive, but I thought I heard the faint sound of running machinery. It was impossible to determine if the noise came from the building or not. But it couldn't be! I saw the empty floor with my own eyes. There was nothing from the floor to the ceiling, three stories high. So where was the machinery?

As I left the site in my car, I couldn't help thinking that the solution to the puzzle was right in front of my face, but I wasn't seeing it. If I wasn't so darned *pregnant*, the Black Stiletto could try exploring the place again. Maybe I didn't spend enough time when I was there before. Perhaps there's an underground secret lair beneath the warehouse, and that's where all the counterfeit money is being printed. Ha ha, that sounds like something you'd see in one of those old crime movies starring Dan Duryea or Sterling Hayden.

I guess I have a vivid imagination!

24
Martin
The Present

Pleasant Prairie, Wisconsin, was a sleepy village just south of another snoozing town called Kenosha. It was directly across the border between Illinois and Wisconsin, not far from Gurnee and the Six Flags Great America amusement park. Maggie said that her parents—who were now gone—had the little house on Lake Shore Drive in the South Carol Beach section of the village since the sixties, but after they passed away the cabin went into neglect. Maggie's younger sister, Felicia, lived in London—I'd never met her—and she rarely came back to the States, so care of the Carol Beach house was Maggie's responsibility. She hadn't done much but pay the real estate taxes.

We took Mom there this morning. Once again, she went into a fit of anxiety at being moved in a car. Alzheimer's patients do not like change. We had disrupted her environment twice in a few days and it was extremely detrimental to her well-being. She cried and muttered and moaned for the forty-five-minute drive up I-94. However, when we reached the cabin, she suddenly calmed down. We could hear the lake lapping on the shore—Lake Michigan seemed more like an *ocean* than a lake—and Mom became entranced by it. Maggie had managed to borrow a wheelchair from Woodlands, so we placed Mom in that before going into the house. We wheeled her along the little path through the trees until we came to the beach—and, lo and behold, the vast expanse of the water took my Mom's breath away. She simply said, "Oh, oh, oh," shaking her head at its beauty. The weather was perfect. Birds flew in the sky. Children and their parents frolicked in the sand. Dogs chased each other and barked. It was a little piece of paradise.

"Maggie, why the hell have we not come up here before?" I asked. I was also impressed.

"You haven't seen the house yet," she answered. "I think we're going to have to spend all day cleaning it."

It did look like my image of a country cabin. The wood house was located on a bend in the road, so it was the only structure in sight. Unlike the more well-known Lakeshore Drive in Chicago, this Lake Shore Drive was a near-private, barely-two-lane paved road that separated a row of houses from a row of trees, and beyond that, the lake. From Maggie's place, it felt as if we were alone and isolated. Other residences were around curves in the road on both sides, just out of sight, but couldn't be seen due to the trees that surrounded the cabin.

When she unlocked the front door, a musty, dusty smell that screamed dilapidation hit us in our faces. But we wheeled Mom inside anyway, and took stock of the situation. All three of us sneezed within a minute of each other.

Actually, it wasn't bad at all. The front living room adjoined a kitchen that had a small area with a dining table for four. A couch, two chairs, and a coffee table occupied the main space. There was no television; instead a lovely brick fireplace dominated one wall and a couple of shelves were well stocked with old books and board game boxes.

"Is there a telephone?" I asked.

"Nope," Maggie answered. "My parents wanted to get away from civilization when we came out here. Felicia and I were little. How's your cell phone reception?"

I checked it. "Good."

"Me too. We'll have to rely on that."

The two bedrooms were furnished and even had sheets and blankets on the beds. "We'll have to wash the linens before we get in them," Maggie said. "Last time I was here, there was a Laundromat in town not far away. There's no air conditioning. It'll be hot. We have a couple of fans though."

My mother gazed at the cabin's interior with wonder in her eyes. She had no idea where she was or why, of course, but there was indeed a tranquil atmosphere about the place.

"How do you like it, Mom?" I asked. "You're on vacation!"

"That's nice," she said. Standard auto-response, but I think she meant it.

It wasn't going to be easy. I'd never had the privilege of performing the real *work* of taking care of my mother. The people that worked at nursing homes were *saints*.

Mom couldn't go to the bathroom by herself anymore. She was unable to walk. Her mind wouldn't let her remember how. She had to be spoon-fed. The woman once known as the Black Stiletto couldn't hold a fork or knife or even a cup of water. She still had the ability, however, to suck through a straw.

After a full day of playing orderly, I was about to go nuts. Not only was it difficult, it was *disturbing*. Maggie went out to buy some groceries and cleaning supplies, and when she returned, she found a basket case sitting in the living room. Tears ran down my face.

"Martin, are you all right?"

"What do you think?"

"Oh, Martin." She put down the bags and sat beside me. "I know it's hard. How's she doing?"

"She's asleep now. I think we need to get a CD player and some of her music. That's something you forgot from Woodlands. You think you can go by there and get her boom box?"

"Sure, tomorrow."

"I just . . . I just don't think I can handle this. I mean, maybe if

I was Mom's *daughter* I could do it, but it's just too weird for her son to be changing her diap—her disposable underwear. Can't we call Virginia? She could come here and work for us full time."

"Do you think that's wise, Martin? It would be another person who knows where we are."

"She's trustworthy. Don't you think? If we tell her Mom's in danger, she would respect that. Remember that scene in *The Godfather* when Al Pacino goes to the hospital and orders the nurse to help him move Marlon Brando to another room because people are coming to kill him? It's like that. Virginia can handle it."

Maggie made a face, but eventually nodded. "All right. I'll call her tomorrow too. For now, let's get some dinner started."

As the evening progressed into night, my anxiety grew worse. I'd had it under control for so long, but the recent events had certainly exacerbated my condition. The only thing I could do was take my meds and attempt to relax. It was strange that the anxiety irritated my neck wound too, although Maggie thought that was a psychological reaction. I wished we had a television. The books in the shelves didn't interest me. I decided I'd go back to Illinois and hit the public library in Wheeling and find a couple of good thrillers to read.

Thrillers. Who was I kidding? I could write my own!

I also realized that I was never much of an outdoors type. I detested camping, and my temporary foray into Boy Scouts when I was a kid was a disaster. Being in the cabin at the edge of the lake was like going camping. No A/C, no TV, no Internet. Thank God for cell phones.

Even though it was beautiful and peaceful where we were, being cooped up would give me the heebie-jeebies before long.

My mother's health was also a big concern. Even with Maggie around, I was worried that Mom wouldn't get the care she desperately needed. She had declined terribly. As much as I hated to admit it, I feared the end was near. The specter of death was hovering over her. I could feel it.

In some ways it was unthinkable. But on the other hand, well, my mom would be free of the terrible vise the disease had on her mind and body.

If only we weren't hiding from a completely different kind of phantom.

25
Judy's Diary
1962

JUNE 28, 1962

I'm listening to Elvis's new album, *Pot Luck*, as I write this. It's pretty good, but there aren't any hit songs. I thought "Good Luck Charm" would be on it, but it's not. "Kiss Me Quick" could be a single. I don't know. I'm probably going to listen to *Blue Hawaii* more than this one. There're some better records out there. I like "I Can't Stop Loving You" by Ray Charles, and "Soldier Boy" by the Shirelles is dreamy.

Physically, I'm doing well, I just get tired sooner than I used to, and my belly is growing like the Blob. I get hungry a lot and I have cravings for bananas. I'm definitely past six months, and I'm in for the long haul. September can't come soon enough.

I've seen some movies I liked. We go down to Hollywood to different theaters. *The Music Man* and *Lolita* just opened. I enjoyed *The Music Man*, especially Robert Preston. I loved the book *Lolita*, but the movie was different. I don't think they could have made a faithful version of the book, it was too scandalous. The actress they cast as Lolita was too old for the part, but I guess they had to do that. A couple of weeks ago, Barry wanted to see *The Man Who Shot Liberty Valance*. That was fun; Jimmy Stewart and John Wayne were in it. The best movie I've seen recently is *Jules and Jim*. One of those French foreign films with subtitles, it's a love story between a woman and *two* men at the same time!

I took Barry's advice and traded in my Sunliner for a used Ford Falcon Futura. It's only a year old and has 15,000 miles on it. It's a light-blue color, with two doors and bucket seats. It's smaller than the Sunliner and doesn't have the convertible top, but I think it's going to be less conspicuous on the street. It only cost me $1,000 with the trade. Barry knew a guy who knew a guy who wanted a Sunliner and was willing to do a good swap. Driving the Futura makes me feel safer when I'm out and about. I can't stay cooped up in the cabin *all* the time.

The crime scene has been quiet. Since I have a different car, I've driven to the Wholesale District several times to do some surveillance of A-1 Outriggers. During the day, when lots of people and cars are everywhere. When I can park across the street, sit in the car, and watch the building. See who comes in or out.

I've learned a few things. The best time to observe something is in the morning, around 9:00. That's when Hugh Costa arrives and parks in back of the building. He has a brand-new car too! It's a shiny white Chrysler Valiant. Could it be that he's making more money? Anyway, after he parks, he walks to the front and uses a key to get in the door. Within fifteen minutes, the pickup truck and van usually arrive—not together—and park. The drivers also go to the front of the building and through the door. I've taken photos of them with my new camera, but I'm across the street and the faces won't be too legible. Like Costa, they look like ordinary guys going to work. One of them also carried a lunch pail and thermos.

The men usually leave between 6:00 and 7:00. Sometimes Costa stays a little longer. I've watched him occasionally walk alone to the bar on Alameda. After one or two drinks, he walks back to the warehouse, gets in his car, and drives home.

Once, Christina's Corvette was parked in back. I never saw her leave though.

Another time, Leo's Lincoln—complete with Boone, the

driver—pulled in the warehouse lot. I ducked a little lower in my seat, just to make sure I wasn't seen. The car sat there in front of the building with the motor running. A moment later, Leo emerged from the front door, got in the Lincoln, and it drove away.

That convinced me that whatever was going on in the warehouse happened underground.

I followed Costa home a few times just to see if he went anywhere else. Last night he stopped at a liquor store. I guess the guy likes his after-work booze. Since it was a public place, I parked and went in the store at the same time. It might have looked funny for a pregnant girl to enter a liquor store, but I could have been buying for my husband, right? In fact, that's what I said when the clerk asked if he could help. I said, "My husband wants some Wild Turkey." Barry likes it, so it won't go to waste.

Hugh Costa was in there buying two bottles of whisky. The clerk grabbed a bottle of Wild Turkey, so I stood right next to Costa as he paid for his booze first. I noticed that there were dark splotchy spots on his hands and fingers. Ink stains.

Obviously, he was still in the printing business.

He was the man doing the actual machine work, I was sure of it. Now I just had to get the proof that they were operating out of that seemingly empty building.

July 5, 1962

Last night Barry and I sat on his front porch and watched different sets of fireworks from a distance. We saw at least three spots over the city where people were shooting displays. I'm sure there were more. The night sky was clear and all the stars were out. I've never seen so many stars in all my life. It was beautiful.

Barry smoked cigarettes and drank Wild Turkey until he passed out. I don't drink anymore; Dr. Abernathy says it's bad for the baby.

I made sure Barry got in his bed all right, but I was too wide awake to go to sleep. Usually, I'm dead tired at night, but for some reason I felt like my mind wouldn't shut off. So instead of tossing and turning until dawn, I got up and drove my car down the dark mountain and into the city. It was nearly 3:00 in the morning. Once again, it was as if I was the only person on that lonely road in the canyon. In Hollywood, of course, there were still cars on the streets. The Wholesale District, however, was silent and still. It was my chance to get inside A-1 Outriggers.

There was no way I could wear my Stiletto outfit anymore. I dressed in a dark sweatshirt and sweatpants, brought along the backpack and knife, and wore my mask once I got out of the car. I felt like I was wearing Black Stiletto pajamas, ha ha. This time I parked in back of the warehouse. No one was there. I got inside the building by using the same size lock pick that was successful before. This time I used my flashlight to carefully go over the entire space.

For one thing, there *is* some kind of trapdoor in the floor. I thought the entire floor was made of cement, but I was wrong. Abutting the bottom of the loading dock security gate is a rectangular section that measures the width of the opening by ten feet or so. By stomping on it with my boot, I could tell that it wasn't solid underneath. The controls for operating the loading dock door were on the left side of the opening. Next to it was a metal panel that opened like a fuse box. There was a keyhole and a couple of buttons. I tried lock picking it, but I was unsuccessful. It had to be the way the floor panel was opened. I bet it's hinged on one side and drops down like a trapdoor. I took pictures.

There was also a bag of trash sitting on the floor by the loading dock, waiting for someone to take it outside to be dumped. I went through what was there—mostly food garbage, wrappers, paper sacks, coffee cups, and emptied ashtrays—yuck. But I also found a couple of dollar bills—both twenties—in which the ink was smeared.

Rejects of counterfeit bills.

I took photos and stuck them in my backpack to show Barry. Even though I was frustrated that I couldn't open the floor section, I left the warehouse with some vital evidence, and I made it home without incident.

26
Judy's Diary
1962

I look, and feel, like a hippopotamus.

I've got less energy now to go out and spy on the warehouse. All I do is sit at home, read books, watch TV, shoot the gun in the canyon target range, and occasionally drive into Hollywood to see a movie. I saw *That Touch of Mink*, *The Road to Hong Kong*, and *Mr. Hobbs Takes a Vacation*. Televisions shows are in summer reruns, so I'm catching up on some of episodes I missed—*The Twilight Zone*, *Gunsmoke*, and *The Dick Van Dyke Show*, mostly. I got the new 45 by Elvis—"She's Not You"—and it makes up for my disappointment with *Pot Luck*. Am I growing tired of Elvis? Not a chance! He still makes my heart soar. I'm not thrilled with most of the other popular music I hear on the radio. I haven't listened to my jazz records in a while, so I bought a Miles Davis album called *Someday My Prince Will Come*. Barry doesn't like jazz. He likes to hear people sing.

Barry was unable to convince the DA to investigate Hugh Costa. The police are following other leads. Apparently Barry is on the outs with his buddy in City Hall. The DA accused Barry of knowing where the Black Stiletto is hiding and not revealing it. The man now doubts Barry's story that I had nothing to do with Maria Kelly's murder, the theft of her diamond necklace, the robbery at Sandstone Casino, or the killing of Sal Casazza. The phony Black Stiletto hasn't appeared again, so DA McKesson thinks maybe Barry was wrong about the whole thing. They got into a big argument the other day and Barry walked out. He called a couple of his friends in LAPD and they gave him the brush-off too. The fact of the matter is that lately he hasn't come up with anything solid that produces arrests and convictions. The problem is he doesn't have the *real* Black Stiletto doing the work for him! The progress we made last year was because of everything I did to help him. Now Barry is starting to run low on cash, so he can't pay his informers and contacts in the underworld. I've offered to loan him some of my money, but I've got to be careful too. Without my job at Flickers, all I have is my savings, and that's not a whole lot now. After the baby is born, I will have to think about what I can do for money. Maybe Barry's brother can fence the diamond and we'll all be rich, but that's going to take some time. Barry has Skipper working on it already, but Skipper needs to see the gem before anything can really be done.

We've learned that Paulie might have been running things in LA for his father, but maybe not anymore. After the big bust in New Mexico, there could be some reshuffling of management. Paulie left the ranch house and is hiding out in LA somewhere and no one knows how to reach him. Sounds like he's just as spoiled as his sister was.

This morning I asked Barry how much he knew about Hugh Costa. He tossed me a file folder with a few notes inside. There was nothing in it I didn't already know, but I did see a phone number for his house in Silver Lake, so I thought, *what the heck*. It was Sunday. He'd be home.

I called him. The wife answered and I asked, "Is Hugh there?"

I'm sure she was very surprised to hear a girl's voice asking for her husband. "Who's calling?"

"A friend from work," I answered.

She hesitated, but then said, "Hold on." After a moment, he came on the line. "Hello?"

"Hugh?"

"Yeah?"

"Hello there."

"Who is this?"

"This is the Black Stiletto."

Silence. "What?"

"You heard me."

"Is this some kind of a joke? Who is this?"

"It's no joke, Hugh. This is the Black Stiletto, and I've been watching you."

He hung up. I immediately dialed the number again. This time *he* picked up. "Hello?"

"Don't hang up on me, Hugh, that's not nice."

"*Who is this?*"

"I told you. I'm the Black Stiletto. And I know all about A-1 Outriggers, that warehouse where you go every day."

That got him. After a pause, he asked, "What do you want?"

"First of all, I don't want you to tell anyone I called you. Do you understand?"

"Uh, sure."

"Second, I just want you to know I'm watching you. You look like you have a nice family, a nice house there in Silver Lake, and a brand-new car."

I could just picture him sweating on the phone with his wife staring at him, wondering who the heck he was talking to.

"Yeah?" His voice shook a bit.

"It would be a shame if you went to jail and lost all that."

"What do you want?"

"Nothing. Just think about it. I'll call again sometime." Then I hung up.

Dear diary, I have no idea if that accomplished anything, but I thought if I could find a weak link in Leo's organization and exploit it, then maybe I can get the evidence I need to clear my name, put Barry back in good graces with his bosses, and get Leo and Christina arrested.

It's worth a try.

27
Gina
THE PRESENT

Mr. McCambridge was late to our appointment at Starbucks. I sat with a cup of coffee and my laptop for fifteen minutes past the specified time. I thought, *that figures*. On the phone he hadn't sounded like he wanted to meet with me. But just as I was about to give up and leave, a tall, broad-shouldered man with gray hair came into the place. He was dressed in cowboy boots, jeans, and a plaid shirt with the sleeves rolled up. The guy was obviously pushing seventy, but he was very fit and looked like he could take on anyone in a bar brawl. The man scanned the customers and then his eyes settled on me. I gave him a little wave; he nodded and strode toward me.

"Are you Miss Talbot?" he asked in that distinctive drawl.

"Yes." I stood and held out my hand. "Call me Gina. Thanks for coming, Mr. McCambridge." He shook my hand. "Can I get you anything?"

"Cup of coffee?"

"Tall, grande, or venti?" He looked at me like I was crazy. "Small, medium, or large?"

"Medium."

After that business was taken care of, we both sat with coffee cups in front of us. I asked, "How long were you sheriff, Mr. McCambridge?"

"You're a mighty pretty girl, Miss Talbot."

I felt myself blush. "Thank you. Like I said on the phone—"

"You say you're from Chicago?"

"That's right."

"Been there a couple of times. Too cold."

"It can be. Anyway, how long were you sheriff, Mr. McCambridge?"

"Sixteen years. Nineteen-eighty to Nineteen-ninety-six."

I thought he'd say what he did afterwards, but he didn't offer the information. "Tell me about this assault you claim happened in New York."

"It did happen, Mr. McCambridge. Two men from Odessa assaulted my father and me. They tortured my dad and he was shot in the throat. Luckily, the bullet missed his spine and vocal cords, but he's going to have permanent damage to some nerves."

"And *you* put them in the hospital?"

"I take self-defense lessons. One of them is paralyzed. The other is in jail. William Simon and Bernard Childers. They went by nicknames—Stark and Bernie. Do you know them?"

He stared at me a moment and then nodded. "I know Stark and Bernie. They're low-life criminals who've been in and out of jail a few times."

"And do you know about that private investigator from Chicago who was found dead in the oil fields recently? Bill Ryan?"

He nodded again. "What do you know about that?"

"It was in the papers. He was down here working for my family."

"Is that so? I think the local police would like to know that."

"I'd rather they not know yet."

He squinted at me as if to ask, *what's your game?*

"Tell me the whole story, would you?" he asked. "You've got my attention."

So I did, although I didn't mention anything about the Black Stiletto. I repeated what Dad had been telling the police in Illinois— that the men had mistaken him for someone else, but now someone was in Chicago looking for us and had already killed my lawyer.

Dad was hiding, and I was in Odessa trying to figure out what was going on.

"Why aren't the police looking into this?" McCambridge asked. "Or the FBI?"

"That's a good question." I couldn't tell him the whole truth, so I said, "The police refuse to do anything until they have more proof that there's an Odessa connection. They still haven't found out who's responsible for the murders in Chicago. The investigation is still under way. I came here on my own."

"You're playing detective?"

"I guess you could say that."

"That's a very dangerous thing to do, young lady."

"Maybe it is. I don't care, my family's in danger."

"Who else knows you're here?"

"No one except my family." Then I added, "And my boyfriend." McCambridge rubbed his chin as if he was considering what to do with me. "I know Mr. Childers and Mr. Simon are—or were— employees of Bartlett Supply Company. That's why I think they're associated with Ricky Bartlett's old criminal enterprises. Does the Dixie Mafia still exist, Mr. McCambridge?"

He raised his eyebrows, and he grunted. "I haven't heard that term in a long time, Miss Talbot. But to answer your question, yeah, there's still an organized crime network in Texas and other southern states. Just like anywhere else. And you're right, Ricky Bartlett was probably involved in it back then, but we couldn't prove it. I arrested him in 1981, but he got off. I knew Ricky pretty well. You might even say we were friends. Everyone knew Ricky. He was well liked in this town. It was embarrassing for me to arrest him. When he got off, my career took a bit of a hit. I almost didn't get reelected, but I did."

"It was all about drug smuggling, wasn't it?"

"Yeah, that and guns. We put away some folks we had evidence against, but not Ricky. His hands were squeaky clean. He had a knack for staying that way."

"What can you tell me about his death? I understand he died in a fire and that you thought it might be arson?"

"You're well informed, young lady. You been doing homework?"

"Something like that."

"Yeah, there was a fire at his company out on Andrews Highway. Someone barricaded him in his office, so it was obviously murder. We never caught anyone for the deed, though. Bartlett was in debt up to his eyeballs because of what happened in eighty-one. He had a lot of enemies by that time, even though he was something of what you might call royalty in Odessa. There were a number of people who might've been behind it. Even the FBI couldn't figure it out." He shrugged. "There were some that thought his wife was behind it."

"Oh, please tell me about his wife. I can't find too much about her in the Odessa papers."

"She's pretty much a recluse."

"She's still alive?" I asked.

"Sure is. She's seventy-nine now. Still lives out at the Bartlett Ranch."

"Wow. What's her name?"

"She always went by 'Mrs. B.' That's what everyone called her then and still do today. Mrs. B. She and Ricky got married in the late seventies. The thing is, there was a bit of a scandal back then, right before Ricky was killed. There were rumors that Ricky and Mrs. B. were headed for a divorce. The town gossip was that she was having an affair with a feller a lot younger than she was, a kid that worked at Bartlett Supply. She was in her late forties at the time, and he was in his twenties." McCambridge chuckled a little.

I put two and two together. "Was his name Dallas Haines?"

Again, McCambridge's eyebrows went up. "You are *definitely* well informed, young lady. How'd you know that?"

I smiled. "I'm a good detective, I guess. Tell me about him."

"He still works for Mrs. B., and you can take the inference of that as you wish."

"So he's in his fifties or so, right?"

"Uh-huh. Pretty tough guy, too. He was in prison for a while for manslaughter."

"I knew that, too. Did Mrs. B. remarry? Does she still run the Bartlett business?"

"No and yes. After Ricky's death, she became the recluse she remains today. No one ever saw her unless you were part of her circle and visited her at the ranch. She never left it. She inherited Ricky's businesses, all of them. They were already rich, but she became even wealthier. She had a good business sense and operated everything from the ranch and still does. Employs a few men and a cook and maid that stay out there with her. No one sees her—and I'll be honest, I'm a part of that circle of acquaintances. I've known her a long time. I've given her legal advice and such."

"Is she still a criminal?"

McCambridge paused and said, "I never said she was one. I got out of the law enforcement business after I was sheriff. I will say most folks are scared of her and think she's a little crazy. She fought off some lawsuits here and there, there are some who think she screwed them out of money and what have you. But Bartlett Supply Company is still going strong. She still owns it, but doesn't manage it. Mrs. B. turned that over to another firm that runs that business. She sold the cattle business a long time ago."

My thoughts were growing clearer by the second. I simply had to ask him straight out. "Mr. McCambridge, could Mrs. Bartlett possibly be behind my family's problems?"

He held out his hands. "Why? What connection would she have with you or your father? She's just a crazy old lady, Miss Talbot. Rich and powerful, yeah, but she keeps to herself."

"Do you think I'd be able to talk to her?"

"No." He said it forcefully and with conviction, and then he looked at his watch. He stood and said, "Miss Talbot, I have to go. If I may be blunt, I suggest you run along home to Chicago. You're not gonna find out anything here, and if you go sticking your nose into Mrs. B.'s business, you might be opening up a big ol' can of snakes."

Wow. He meant it too, but there was something he wasn't

telling me. I could read it all over his face. "Well, I don't know, Mr. McCambridge, I still want to dig around a little bit. It's a free country, as they say."

"Yeah, it sure is." He gave me a little smile.

"Look, we have each other's cell phone numbers," I said. "If I have any more questions, can I call you?"

"I don't see why not. Where are you staying?"

I told him, and then I held out my hand. He shook it again, and then left.

As I packed my laptop and finished my coffee, I kept thinking how a lot of these mysteries might be revealed in my grandmother's fifth diary. Dad had better hurry and finish the damned thing so I could read it. The next time I called him I planned to pester him about it.

There was no question in my mind though. Some of my grandma's secrets were still buried in Odessa.

28
Judy's Diary
1962

It's late afternoon on Sunday, and I just got home from a weekend in San Luis Obispo!

It was on a *whim*, I swear, that Barry and I decided to drive up the coast just to have a change of scenery for a little while. That was Friday. It was around 11:00 in the morning and we were having breakfast. Early rising has gone out the window for both of us. We both sleep late and live like we're *married*, ha ha, except in separate rooms. And I have to say that after this weekend, I feel more romantically inclined toward Barry. He really is a sweet guy, but there's also a toughness about him that appeals to me. Nothing has happened, dear diary, except we kissed a couple of times and we slept *in the same bed*. It was a big king-size bed at the Madonna Inn, a fancy new hotel in San Luis Obispo. I'm too *pregnant* to do anything in bed but sleep!

Traveling was a risk, I suppose, of me going into labor early. It's still a month and a half until my due date, so I thought I was all right to go. My motherly instinct—which has been getting stronger every month—told me that my bun in the oven wasn't finished cooking yet.

The drive was gorgeous. Barry was behind the wheel of his new Buick Electra the whole time, and I just sat in the passenger seat and marveled at the landscapes around us. It isn't the most comfortable thing, being pregnant and all, but I was too enchanted by the scenery to care. We took Highway 1 along the coast. The ocean looked so massive and marvelous. I got to thinking how small we are as humans next to that horizon of water. It's like outer space. Kennedy says we'll put a man on the moon in the next decade. It seems like it's been easier for us to put a man in space than deep in the ocean.

We went through Santa Barbara, where we stopped and had a bite to eat. I asked Barry where we were going to stay, and he said he'd phoned ahead and made reservations for us at the Bates Motel, ha ha. I almost hit him. Then he fessed up and said we have reservations at a "nice hotel." The road moved away from the coastline around an air force base that we passed. Next came Santa Maria and Arroyo Grande, both lovely towns. Compared to Los Angeles, these California coastal communities make you feel like you're in a completely different state. The mountains and forests surrounded us and I no longer felt the "buzz" of LA close by.

We arrived in San Luis Obispo just after dinnertime. When I saw the Madonna Inn, I gasped. The design was so pretty, kind of European. Barry said it was made to look like it might be a Swiss chalet. He really had called ahead to see if a room was available and we were in luck—there had just been a cancellation. He handled the bags and we checked in as "Mr. and Mrs. Barry Gorman." I felt a little scandalous doing that. Then, when I saw our room, I was really embarrassed. There was only the one bed. I thought there were going to be two.

"They didn't have a room with two beds. I took this because it was the only one available," Barry said. "If you'd rather find someplace else—"

"No, no," I said. "If you can stand me taking up most of the bed like a beached whale, then I think I can manage. Just don't snore too loud."

"Do I snore?"

"I've heard you in the other room at home."

"Well, no offense, but you do too."

I was appalled. "Really?" He shrugged and smiled. Then I asked, "How are you affording this?"

"Don't worry," he said. "I got it." I offered to pitch in, I still had money, but he wouldn't let me. He said he'd been saving up some money to get a baby gift when the day arrives and also do something to celebrate. He figured a little vacation would take care of the latter, and it was easier to do it *before* I had a babe in arms.

We had a nice dinner in the rustic Copper Café, but after that I was tired and ready to hit the sack! I told him I probably wouldn't be any fun, that I couldn't really do much sightseeing. He said he didn't care.

That night I dressed in some really dumpy pajamas and got in bed before he did. He wore man pajamas that looked suspiciously new; I'd never seen them before. We didn't talk about it, but I'm sure we both took it for granted that nothing was going to happen. I was eight months pregnant! And our relationship hadn't really progressed that far yet, if that's what we are having.

I lay on my side facing away from him. Before turning out the lamp, he leaned over me and kissed my cheek. "Good night, Judy," he said. I turned my head to face him, we looked at each other for a moment, and then I let him kiss me on the lips. It felt lovely. Then I said good night and he turned off the light.

In the morning, I asked him if he had any trouble sleeping next to me, and he replied that he hadn't. I slept very well.

We took a walk through the town, which was quaint and full of character. The "twins," Bishop Peak and Cerro San Luis, hovered over the village like benevolent gods. I loved the atmosphere. It wasn't too hot; the temperature was in the seventies. The only thing that kind of turned my stomach was an alley in the downtown area where people had stuck wads of chewing gum on the rock walls.

Apparently that was a popular thing to do in town, and the practice had just started in the last couple of years. We went in shops but didn't buy anything, and eventually I got hungry and tired.

I had a nap in the afternoon and then we went to dinner in the hotel's Gold Rush Restaurant.

Nighttime was a repeat of the previous one. A kiss on the cheek, a kiss on the lips, and then out with the light. That time I didn't fall asleep immediately, but Barry did. He started snoring lightly, but I didn't mind. I thought about what it might be like if he and I really do end up becoming lovers someday. Could he be a father to my baby? Would that be a good thing? Maybe, dear diary. I'm starting to lean that way.

After breakfast this morning, we hit the road back to LA. Once again, just looking at the ocean and forests and mountains, all the while listening to the car radio, was heaven.

At some point during the trip, I thought about that phone call I'd made to Hugh Costa. I wondered if the Black Stiletto should make one to Leo too. Tell him he's being watched. Make him paranoid. Maybe do the same thing to Christina. And perhaps… it's possible… I could lead them into a trap.

LATER

Oh my God, we just heard on the news that Marilyn Monroe is dead of a drug overdose. She was found in her home in Brentwood this morning. They don't say, or know, if it was an accident or if she committed suicide. I can't believe it. She was only 36. All of Hollywood will be in mourning for her. She was such a glamorous movie star. I don't know if those rumors about her having an affair with President Kennedy are true or not, but it seems like yesterday that the television broadcasted her singing "Happy Birthday" to him with that sexy voice in front of all those people in New York. Gosh, that was three months ago!

Things aren't going to be the same in this town.

AUGUST 13, 1962

I phoned Leo at his office today. I didn't know if he'd be there, but I called and I'm sure it was Evelyn, the secretary, who answered. My voice is always a little different when I'm in my Stiletto persona, so I'm confident she didn't recognize me as Judy Cooper.

"Is Leo Kelly in today?"

"Yes, ma'am, he is. Who may I ask is calling?"

"Tell him it's Janet Leigh."

I think she believed me, for Evelyn said, "Yes, Miss Leigh, I'll alert him!"

In five seconds, Leo was on the line. "This is Leo Kelly."

"This is the Black Stiletto." I could detect the disappointment on the other end. He didn't say anything. "Sorry, did you really want to talk to Janet Leigh?"

"Is this really you?"

"Of course, don't I sound like me?"

"Yes. What do you *want?*"

"Shouldn't the question be, what do you want? I bet you want your diamond back, don't you?"

"You're damned right."

"Hmm, what are you willing to do for it?"

"What?"

"Come on, Leo. What are you willing to do for the diamond?"

"I'm willing to hunt you down and kill you."

I made a tsk-tsk sound. "Leo, that's not very nice. I was hoping you might buy me flowers or something. Maybe take me to dinner."

"*What?*"

I used the sexiest voice I could muster. "What if I said I was willing to meet you somewhere private so we could get to know each other better?"

His demeanor changed. "Are you serious?"

"I've heard what a ladies' man you are, Leo. It's made me kind of—curious."

"Well, let's get together then," he said. "We can talk about it."

"Talk? That's what we'd do? *Talk?*" I laughed.

The taunting was getting to him. "What are you getting at? Quit playing games."

"I never play games with my love life, Leo Kelly. Maybe I'll call back another day and you'll be in a more receptive mood."

"Wait! I can be—" But by then I'd hung up. Golly, the phone call had got my adrenaline going. That was *fun*. I think I know how to torment him.

When I told Barry what I'd done, he said he'd go take a look at A-1 Outriggers to see what kind of activity was going on. I decided to ride with him, so we drove to the Wholesale District together. We were surprised that no cars were parked in back, and it was a workday. Costa's Chrysler was nowhere in sight. We chalked it up to the counterfeiters taking a day off. I hoped Costa hadn't blabbed about me calling him. I didn't want them to move the operation to another hideout. I asked Barry to try and find out how to get me in touch with Paulie DeAngelo.

"What for?" he asked.

"I'm not sure yet. I've got a plan developing but it's still early," I told him, and that was the truth. I do have an idea.

AUGUST 20, 1962

Barry and I have driven by the warehouse three more times since I last made a diary entry. There's still no one parking in the back, and now I know why.

I phoned Hugh Costa today at home. He picked up.

"This is the Black Stiletto," I said, using my sexy come-hither voice.

He was quiet a moment. "What do you want?"

"Have you told anyone that I called you?"

"No. You said—"

"I know. Why haven't you been going to the warehouse lately, Hugh?"

"Work has stopped temporarily."

"Why?"

He caught himself. "I'm not saying anything. I don't know who you are, really."

"You want me to show up at your house and prove I'm the real deal? Say hello to your wife and kids too?"

"No! Please don't."

"Then you'll have to believe me."

"Sorry. I have to go."

"Hugh, don't hang up. I know you're printing counterfeit money. You're going to have to start cooperating with me, or soon *everyone* will know you're printing counterfeit money."

"Wh . . . what do you want?"

"Why has the work stopped?"

He brought his voice down to a whisper. "A plate broke. We're waiting on another one to be made."

That sounded plausible. "Who makes it?"

"Some guy in New York."

"What's his name?"

This time Costa *really* whispered. "Samberg. Mookie Samberg."

That was useful information. "Okay, I'll call again soon," I promised, and then hung up.

Since my first call to Leo, I've also phoned *him* twice. I kept the conversations short and playful. I teased, taunted, and flirted with him. I can tell he's getting intrigued now. He's still defiant and would probably shoot me if he saw me, but I think I've got him hooked. He wants to see where our conversations are going.

I also talked to Christina once. I had tried calling Leo at the office, but was told he wasn't in. So I phoned his house—and she answered.

"Hello, Christina, this is the Black Stiletto."

It took her a couple of seconds, and then she growled, "You bitch! Leave my brother alone!"

"Oh, he told you I've been talking to him?"

"Of course. He tells me everything. I'm going to kill you. I'm going to break your kneecaps!"

"My kneecaps? Oh, my, such tough words from such a pretty mouth."

"Shut up, damn you!"

"You both want the diamond back, don't you?"

"You bet we do!"

"How come you haven't put on that phony costume and blamed some more crimes on me?"

"Shut up, bitch!"

"Christina, you call me a bitch again and I'll ram that word down your throat."

"*Come on!*" she challenged, which was just what I wanted her to do.

"You think you can take me?"

"You bet I can. I'll meet you anytime, anyplace."

"I'll keep that in mind. I just might take you up on it." Then I hung up. That worked. I wanted to get her so mad that she would do something very reckless.

Did she tell Leo I called? Probably. I wish I could have been a fly on the wall at the Kelly dinner table that night!

Barry's been unsuccessful trying to get Paulie DeAngelo's phone number. No one knows where he is.

In the meantime, I wait for B-Day, as Barry calls it, ha ha.

29
Leo
The Past

Of all the rotten luck. Just when I got the funny money operation up and running again, one of the goddamned plates broke. Miles dropped it and it shattered. Hugh tried to salvage what he could, but there was a visible fracture line in the printing. I had to call Mookie in New York and pay to have a new plate made. Although Mookie was the best counterfeiter around, he wasn't the fastest. So that was going to cost me time and money. Then, to top it off, Mookie went and got himself hit by a bus in Manhattan. That sounded like a "dog ate my homework" story, but it was true. The damned fool wasn't looking and he stepped right out in front. The bus clipped him but didn't kill him. He was in the hospital and should be out soon, but his hands were damaged. It might be a month or more before he was able to work again.

So, we were on hold, which was unfortunate. I started talking to Ricky Bartlett about the possibility of us doing business together. He and DeAngelo were on the outs. Ricky blamed Paulie for that shipment that was busted. DeAngelo hadn't returned Ricky's money. He kept saying that Bartlett would be reimbursed with interest, but that bunch down in Texas wasn't happy. For guys who were supposed to be laid-back cowboys, they sure were impatient.

One good thing about the hiatus was that the Black Stiletto couldn't do anything. But what kind of game was she playing? The phone calls, the flirting, the weirdness of it all. She was being down-right friendly and acted like she wanted to see me again. I didn't know—our last couple of face-to-face encounters didn't turn out so well. She was after something, and sooner or later she was going to have to get around to telling me what it was. She seemed amenable to a deal. I'd get my diamond back, and she'd get—what? I don't know yet. At least she hinted at an arrangement.

One thing was for sure. The Black Stiletto was sexy. Over the phone, her voice was intoxicating. She put images in my head that I couldn't get rid of. I found that I didn't want her to hang up, but she always kept the conversations short.

Christina just wanted to kill her. Ever since my sister talked to the Masked One, she's been howling for blood. The Stiletto practically challenged her to a one-on-one fight, and Christina was chomping at the bit. That rage she kept bottled up was starting to ooze. There could be trouble. I'd have to keep an eye on her. She still had that goddamned costume and refused to get rid of it.

I was taking a more sensible approach to the phone calls. The Stiletto was smart, and apparently she liked to be dramatic. I wanted to see where these talks went. If I could get her to agree to meet me on my terms, I could catch her. If I delivered her to DeAngelo, I'd be rewarded beyond my wildest dreams. Vince would replace his son, Paulie, with me, and *I'd* save the old man's outfit.

Every now and then I thought about Judy. I figured she was going to have that baby soon. I had men trying to trace her move-ments when she moved out of her apartment, but it was as if she simply vanished. There was no trail. I was convinced she left town, fled the state, and lived some place where she thought she was safe.

But I'd find her, eventually.

30
Judy's Diary
1962

Today Barry and I went to see *Kid Galahad*, the new Elvis movie. It was entertaining, but I didn't believe for a moment that Elvis was a boxer. He was supposedly trained by real boxers, but *I* could have done a better job of showing him the ropes. Aside from that outing, I've been staying at home. It's just too much effort to try to go out. I've stopped driving anywhere unless it's a quick trip down the mountain to Laurel Canyon Blvd. to pick up some milk and eggs. And bananas.

Barry is arranging to get the birth certificate for the baby. He's asked me for a boy's and a girl's name—for whichever gender pops out!—so he can go ahead. I can't decide. I asked him how soon he needs to know, and he shrugged. "The sooner the better, but I suppose you don't have to decide until you're actually looking into his or her eyes." Gosh, I can't imagine doing that. It's going to be soon too. My due date is a month away, and there's always the possibility it could be early. Dr. Abernathy saw me after we got back from San Luis Obispo, and everything is going the way it's supposed to. He says I'm "very healthy."

One thing Barry told me about the birth certificate doesn't make me too happy, but I have to live with it. "Judy," he said, "the purpose of this is to keep Leo from ever knowing about your baby."

"That's right."

"Then it's best if the date on the certificate is not the actual birth date."

"Huh?"

"Leo could have connections at all the hospitals. He might monitor single-mom births around the time of your due date. If your child's official birthday is a month later than his real date, it only helps to hide the kid's identity."

"So if he's born on September 26, say, he would have to grow up believing his birthday was *October* 26?"

"I'm afraid so."

That makes me wonder how *I'd* feel if I found out that the day I thought was my birthday all my life suddenly wasn't. Dear diary, it's another lie I'll have to tell my child. I feel bad about it, because I was already prepared to lie to him about his father.

I just have to keep telling myself that it's for his own good. It'll keep him safe.

Gosh, I find that when I talk about him, I'm starting to refer to him as a *him*. Could he really be a boy? My instinct tells me it's so, but I must keep an open mind. I'll love a boy *or* a girl. At any rate, he's been kicking me a bunch lately. I think he's using my womb as a punching bag. I guess he takes after me, ha ha.

In the past couple of weeks, I've called Hugh Costa twice but was unable to reach him. The wife answered, so I hung up. Boy, I bet she's suspicious of what mild-mannered hubby is up to!

I've also talked to Christina once and Leo twice. When Christina answered and I told her who I was, she started cursing at me with four-letter words I won't write. I told her she had a potty mouth and she got even madder.

"When are you going to meet me someplace so we can settle this?" she snarled.

"What, pistols at dawn?"

"Whatever you want. Guns, knives, baseball bats…or our bare hands. I'll wipe the floor with you. I'll make sure you never open your eyes again, bitch. I am going to kill you. I'll break your kneecaps. I mean it. You will be dead."

The girl was serious. If that wasn't a threat, I don't know what is. "Why are you so obsessed with my kneecaps?" I asked.

"Because getting them smashed *hurts like hell*, and that's what I'm going to do to you! So when are we going to have at it?"

"In due time," I said, "you'll get your chance."

Then she called me a coward, and that really made my hackles rise. Pregnant or not, it made me want to drive to Hollywood that instant and beat the holy crap out of her. But she had a point. Why didn't I put my money where my mouth was? I controlled myself and said, "Be patient, honey. You'll get your chance. I'm out of town." I thought fast. "I'm in New York, calling you long distance. I can't believe I'm spending the money to do that, but I just love hearing how mad you get when I call."

"Well, get back here! *I'm going to break your kneecaps!*"

"I have personal business to take care of first, honey. I'll be back in LA in—" I had to think—I have the baby in September, I'll have to wait at least a month and maybe more, before I could really do anything—"November. So you'll just have to wait until then."

She hung up in frustration.

As for Leo, I've been wrapping him around my finger. He's getting to where I think he'll do anything I say. It's actually fun. When I get past the immediate revulsion I feel just by hearing his voice, I enjoy the role-playing. I've actually got him with his tongue hanging out, and in the end it will be his undoing.

"Those times we met at my house, let's forget them," he said. "I want to meet you again. Properly, this time. No fighting. Start over. What do you say?"

"So you and your sister can ambush me and kill me?"

"No! I'll keep Christina away. Just you and me. We can meet at a hotel. Or anywhere you say."

"A *hotel*? What do you have in mind, Leo?"

"Stop teasing me! All I can think about is that lithe, muscular body of yours. That tight little outfit you wear. Your long, incredible legs. Those curves, oh my God, those *curves*! I want to take you in my arms and make mad, Mexican, bone-crushing *love* to you!"

"Oh my!" was all I could say to that. He made me blush! But I also knew what a rotten person he was. It was all bluff and smarmy bravado. He wanted to "have" me only because I'm taller. It would satisfy his Napoleon complex.

"What do you say, Stiletto? Are you woman enough for me?"

"Ha. I think the question should be the other way around—are you *man* enough for me?"

"You bet I am." Then his voice dropped to a whisper. "Listen. You and me, we could make a deal. Be partners. Let's sell the diamond together and split the money. I know someone who can fence it."

"And I'm supposed to trust *you*?"

"Sure!"

"What if I've already sold it?"

I heard him gasp. "You haven't!"

"No, I haven't. Just wanted to scare you."

"Please, how about if I buy it back from you? I'll give you twenty-five grand for it."

"Don't make me laugh, Leo. It's worth six or seven times more than that."

"Fifty grand."

"Don't be an idiot."

"A *hundred* grand."

"You're embarrassing yourself. As soon as you start talking *real* money, then maybe I'll listen. In the meantime, just keep dreaming about my legs and curves. Who knows, maybe someday there really will come a time when you'll get to touch them. Goodbye, Leo."

"Don't hang up!"

But I already had.

Gosh, it feels good to do that! Here I am, pregnant as all get-out, on the other end of a phone line, and I'm manipulating my two biggest enemies into frenzy. I want Christina to be so crazed that she will do *anything* to get a shot at me. And I want Leo so confused and desperate and *horny*, ha ha, that he'll walk right into my trap.

It's just too bad I can't set it until after the baby is born.

Hurry up, little one. I'm tired of waiting!

SEPTEMBER 6, 1962

Well, I made it through Labor Day without anything happening, ha ha!

I'm ready though. I feel like I'm going to explode. I feel him kicking and squirming, as if he can't wait to breathe fresh air too. I've already packed an overnight bag to take to the hospital when my water breaks. Of course, it's probably not going to happen for another two to three weeks. In the meantime, I just lie around and pretend I'm a sea lion.

I haven't made phone calls to Leo, Christina, or Hugh recently. I've been letting them stew for a while. I dreamed about Leo last night though. It started out with me as myself—Judy Cooper—and we were in his house on Woodruff. I think I was using his bathroom or something, for I remember walking into the bedroom without clothes on. I wasn't pregnant. He was fully dressed and sat on his bed. The diamond was in his hands. He caressed it, gently feeling its edges, admiring its beauty. Without looking at me, he said, "Judy, I'm so glad I found you." Only then did he take my hand and pull me onto him. As we laid back and started kissing, I thought I heard Elvis music, but I couldn't make out what song it was. I even asked Leo if it was a new song; I recognized it, but I didn't recognize it— dreams are so weird in their logic. Then, with him clothed and me naked, I suddenly felt ashamed. The anger and hurt I felt against Leo came rushing back to me and I started beating on him. I don't know what happened to the diamond.

At that point I became the Black Stiletto. I was masked and in full regalia, slugging at his face until it became blurry. It was like a photo of his face, but out of focus. Then—as I clamped my hands around his neck to strangle him, the face cleared up and he was—*Douglas Bates*, my cruel stepfather who raped me and killed my mother with neglect. It frightened me, and I jumped back from his body with a start. But then, he was Leo again, sitting on the bed like he was at the beginning of the dream. This time, though, he wasn't holding the diamond in his hands.

He was holding a baby.

That's when I woke up. I was in a sweat and my heart was pounding a mile a minute. I had to get out of bed and get a glass of milk to calm me down.

I'm not one to attempt to interpret dreams, but it convinced me even more that I must keep my son or daughter away from him—forever.

31
Martin
The Present

Mom was sinking rapidly, no question about it.

When she was distressed and unable to express the problem verbally, she'd simply cry. The rest of the time she was practically comatose. She'd just lie in bed and stare at the ceiling, or if we propped her up in a chair, she'd focus on the wall. A couple of times a day we took her outside in the wheelchair to look at the lake. Unlike that first day, now the lovely view did nothing for her.

Her muscle control was worse than ever. Whenever we tried to change her disposable underwear, or clothes, or comb her hair or brush her teeth—at first she'd struggle a little and fight us. But then she'd weaken and become limp and let us do whatever it was we wanted.

She just seemed so sad. As if she knew exactly that her mind had left her and there was nothing she—or we—could do about it.

Was she giving up?

Virginia came up to the cabin today after Maggie contacted her. She was a little weirded out by the fact that we had my mother in an isolated house in Wisconsin without proper medical attention other than Maggie's expertise and my floundering uselessness. We told her the truth—someone wanted to kill my mother.

"Why in the world would someone want to do that?" Virginia asked.

"It's from something that happened a long time ago, before I was born," I told her.

Virginia was African American, probably in her forties, was good at her job, and had a no-nonsense attitude. She looked at me sideways, and I suspected she didn't quite believe me. It was obvious she disapproved. "Hmf," she said.

"Virginia, you can't tell anyone we're here," I said. "Please. We're paying you extra."

"I ain't saying a word," she answered, holding up her hands in defeat. Then she got to work. Unfortunately, her time was not completely ours. She had other patients and could spend only a few hours every other day with us. It would have to do.

Once Virginia was ensconced at the house, both Maggie and I left her alone with Mom so we could take care of some things back in Illinois. It was a bit of a risk to run by our respective houses and places of employment, but it had to be done. Additionally, Detective Scott had left several voice messages on mine and Maggie's phones, so I waited until I was in Buffalo Grove to call him back.

"Mr. Talbot, where have you been?" he asked.

"Hiding."

"I specifically asked you not to leave town. I must say your actions are highly suspicious. I understand you've taken your mother out of Dr. McDaniel's home. Are you sure that's wise?" he asked.

"We have some help. We're managing. What have you found out?"

"We're expecting some forensics results later today. Mr. Talbot, I have to say I think you know more about all this than you're telling me. It's connected to your mother, and you're her son. You need to come clean. We can help you."

"Thanks, Detective Scott, but there's really nothing I can tell you. I'm just as clueless as you are." Yeah, right. "I just want to protect my mother."

"At least tell me where you are. That's something I think I should know."

Against my better judgment, I revealed the location of the beach house. He thanked me and asked me to be more diligent in returning his calls. I promised I would.

While I was in my neck of the woods, I thought about all of Mom's stuff in the safety deposit box at the bank. There was that gun—the Smith & Wesson that Barry Gorman had given her. She'd left that with her costume and other ephemera. I knew nothing about guns, but I wondered if I should have one out at the house for protection. I'd never fired one in my life, but what could be so difficult, right? You loaded it, you aimed it, and you pulled the trigger. Easy.

So I went to the bank, took out the box, and brought it into a private room, opened it—and almost had a heart attack.

The revolver was there, along with the ammunition, along with most of the other stuff. Shaking, I picked up the weapon and ammo and put them in the briefcase I use for work. It has a combination lock on it.

What freaked me out was that the costume was missing. The boots, jacket, trousers, belt, knife, and mask.

And there was only one explanation.

Gina had them.

32
Judy's Diary
1962

SEPTEMBER 13, 1962

Dear diary, I'm the mother of a baby boy!

I wanted to quickly jot down what's happened before they bring him back to me for nursing. It's nearly midnight and I need some sleep.

I went into labor yesterday afternoon, on the 12th. That seems like a lifetime ago. My water broke as I was standing in the kitchen fixing myself a sandwich. I made a bit of a mess, but the kitchen floor is all linoleum, so it was easy to clean up. Barry wasn't there. In fact, I didn't know where he was. His car wasn't outside.

Trying not to panic, I phoned Dr. Abernathy's office and got through to a nurse. I told her I thought my water broke, and she said to come to the hospital. She assured me I probably had several hours before the contractions would start, so that gave me some time.

Where was Barry? He didn't have an office where I could call him. I wasn't about to drive myself to Linda Vista Hospital.

I finished my sandwich and drank some water. I made sure I had everything I needed in my overnight bag.

I waited. Watched some TV. And waited.

After an hour, I decided that I *was* about to drive myself to Linda Vista Hospital. Cursing my roommate, I left him a note, threw the bag in my Futura, got in the car, and started the drive down the mountain. The good part was that it was a clear, sunny day. The bad part was that I suddenly didn't feel too well. My abdomen was starting to cramp. It wasn't terrible at first, just a low-level ache that lasted for a while and then stopped. I'd already forgotten about it when it happened again. When it occurred a third time, I knew what was going on.

I was at least an hour away from the hospital.

I made the mistake of putting my foot on the gas a little too hard. The car sped down the winding dirt road. On one side was a mountain. On the other side, for most of the way, was a drop with no guardrail. Barry lived in the boondocks. I must have taken a curve too fast, for the car skidded sideways and made a horrible screeching noise on the rocks and dirt. It scared the bejesus out of me. I slammed on the brakes and the car ground to a halt—inches away from the cliff edge. Oh my God, I thought, I already almost killed my baby before he had a chance to be born.

For several minutes, I sat sweating in the car, frightened and not thinking straight. It was a terrible sensation. I really did almost panic—but then, I swear this happened—I heard Soichiro's voice. A memory jarred in my head. A lesson he had taught me years ago in New York. *Relax and breathe.* That's what I did. I closed my eyes and thought about Soichiro, how he had been an instrumental part of my life. His words, echoing in the recesses of my brain, soothed me.

In five minutes, I was ready to go. I backed away from the edge and returned to the road. I took it easy the rest of the way down. When I got to Hollywood, the contractions had started again.

Eventually, I made it to the hospital. Dr. Abernathy had previously arranged for "Judy Talbot" to be admitted, so there was no problem there. After I signed some papers, an orderly took my bag and asked if I wanted a wheelchair. To tell the truth, that sounded good, so I nodded. He fetched it, and then he wheeled me to the elevator. Once I was in the room, a nurse had me undress and put on one of those weird open-back gowns. She examined me, and then a doctor whose name I can't remember—I'd never met him—came in and said he was working for Dr. Abernathy. He examined me too, and he announced that I was in labor. Thanks a lot, Doc, I think I knew that. I was in an irritable mood. Everything was annoying me. I was irked at Barry for not being home, I was mad about having to drive on that dangerous road, and I thought the nurses and hospital staff asked a lot of stupid questions.

The contractions got pretty strong around 7:00. Did it hurt? *Hell, yes*, it hurt, but I must admit it wasn't as bad as I expected. I'd heard horror stories about how it's the worst pain imaginable. But I kept up Soichiro's directive—*relax and breathe*—and I didn't become tense. That kept my body loose and flexible, I guess.

By midnight, the contractions were coming one right after the other. Dr. Abernathy finally showed up. He pressed on my big belly—which hurt like the dickens—and took a look down there. He said it was time. I'd been in labor for about six hours. They got me on a gurney and rolled me into the delivery room. A nurse kept telling me to breathe, but I was already doing it. I almost snapped at her to shut up.

The doctor asked me if I wanted any medication to ease the pain. I told him I didn't. I wanted to experience birth naturally, no matter how badly it hurt. He did give me something in the IV that took the edge off. When the moment finally came, there was a tremendous surge of pain as I pushed, pushed, pushed—and then there was a sudden pop and a feeling of intense relief down there. I was a bit stunned and wasn't sure what had just happened for a few seconds. But the disorientation went away as soon as I heard my son cry.

He was born at 12:33 a.m. on Thursday, September 13, 1962.

The nurse cleaned him up and placed him in my arms. She asked if I had a name for him, and I replied, "Not yet."

He was so darling. So tiny. A little tuft of brown hair. Brownish-green eyes like mine, but not as dark. I couldn't tell if he looked like me or Leo—he was just a newborn baby. He weighed seven pounds, three ounces.

Dr. Abernathy congratulated me and left the room. The nurse asked if I wanted to try nursing, so I did. It didn't work. He wouldn't do it. The poor thing couldn't figure out how. I put my nipple right up to his little mouth and he'd just slobber on it. After twenty minutes, the nurse took him and said we'd try again later. I didn't want to let him go, but she said they needed to do some tests, take a blood sample, and that kind of thing. And I needed to rest. Yes, I was exhausted. So they rolled me back to my room, and I fell asleep.

I woke up around four in the morning and they brought him in to me for another try at nursing. This time I pinched a little milk out so that it was on my nipple when his mouth touched it—and the taste got him interested. Centuries-old instinct kicked in and he started sucking. It was an odd but comforting sensation.

The nurse said I had a male visitor outside. He'd arrived at the hospital a couple of hours earlier. At first I feared it was Leo, but, of course, it was Barry. He'd found my note and came in to apologize for not being at home. He was out on a job for the first time in a while, gathering some information about a recent bust of some Los Serpientes who were caught with illegal guns.

Around dawn, Barry was asleep in the guest chair in my room. The staff must have thought he was the father, so they let him stay. I kept thinking about a name for my son, but I couldn't decide. "Elvis" was definitely out!

It was around the time they brought my breakfast—which was pretty bad, I must say—that I heard a radio playing down the hall. I think it was at the nurses' station. Every song was something I knew, and it put me in a marvelously happy mood. After I finished my meal, they brought my boy in for another feeding. It seemed like he couldn't get enough! Barry woke up to admire him, but then he left the room when I started to nurse. As I was doing so, I started singing along with some of the songs on the radio. The baby seemed to respond. His eyes looked up at me with interest, never releasing his mouth from my nipple. I heard Dean Martin sing "Ain't That a Kick in the Head" and I suddenly thought—Martin. Martin Talbot. Why not?

When Barry came back in the room, I told him my decision.

"That's a good name. What about his middle name?"

I had no idea. I almost said, "Barry," but hesitated. Maybe it was best not to name him after anyone I really knew. For some reason, the movie *The Man Who Shot Liberty Valance* popped into my head, and I thought of James Stewart and John Wayne. I considered "Martin Stewart Talbot" and "Martin Wayne Talbot," and I liked the sound of the latter.

So, my son became Martin Wayne Talbot.

The rest of the day was more of the same. Dr. Abernathy came in to say Martin was perfectly healthy and that I was looking good. He said I could go home tomorrow. They circumcised Martin this afternoon, but he should be all right to come with me. The thought of doing that to his little wee-wee sent shivers down my back, but I guess all boy babies go through it these days.

I picked up my diary just after the last feeding, and here I am. It's been a long day!

I'm a mother! Unbelievable.

Before they took him away for the night—well, until he wanted to nurse again—I gave Martin a gentle hug, kissed his forehead, and said, "Little Man Martin, as soon as I complete some unfinished business, I promise I'm going to change my life and be a good mom to you."

And I mean that, dear diary.

33
Judy's Diary
1962

SEPTEMBER 17, 1962

Martin and I have been home for a few days now, and I have to begin a regimen to regain my strength and lose weight. If the Black Stiletto is going to wage all-out war on Leo and Christina Kelly, then I've got to be in shape. I felt pretty weak when I got home, and Dr. Abernathy told me I need to take it easy for at least a month. I asked him about exercising, and he told me to start small and just do a little bit at a time. I'm thinking about getting a speed bag to install in my room at the cabin. Punching on that thing will be good therapy for body *and* mind.

Barry bought a secondhand crib while I was in the hospital. He put it in my room, and it was there when Martin and I got home. That was *so* thoughtful of him! It's got little colored wooden balls on posts that are on top of springs around the sides, so when the baby's able to stand, he can play with them.

Little Man Martin is a doll, but he's a fussy baby. He's what they call "colicky," which means he cries nonstop for a couple of hours for no reason that I can see. He nurses fine and gets plenty of nourishment. I had to bring him in to Dr. Abernathy, who referred me to a pediatrician from now on. I'm taking Martin to see him tomorrow to see what's going on. I've heard that it's often caused by trapped gas or some intestinal problem. I hope it's something simple.

The crying really gets to me and sometimes it happens in the middle of the night. He keeps me awake and leaves me exhausted the next day. Barry went out and bought earplugs for himself, and I can't blame him. I guess he's bitten off more than he can chew by inviting me and my newborn to live with him!

Oh, Martin's crying now. I better go tend to him.

SEPTEMBER 18, 1962

Today Barry drove me to the pediatrician's office, which is located on the same street as Dr. Abernathy's. His name is Dr. Perlman and looks like he came right out of a Norman Rockwell painting. He's old with white hair and acts like a kindly grandfather. The funny part is that he has several little toy animals safety pinned to his white lab coat. He also has a bicycle horn attached to his belt. When I asked him what it's for, he *honked* it and replied that it amuses the little kids. Sure enough, when he honked it in front of Martin, my little one's eyes got real big. Of course, he didn't cry when we were at the doctor's.

We talked about what I eat and drink so he could rule out stuff that might be in my milk that's causing Martin to cry. Dr. Perlman examined him and couldn't determine that there was anything physically wrong. Finally, the doctor said there wasn't much I could do except let Martin cry it out so that he gets tired and falls asleep. However, the doc said it's best to hold him upright to my shoulder to do this, not put the baby on his back in his crib except when he's supposed to sleep. He also recommended swinging the baby with small jiggling movements—about an inch back and forth—while always supporting his head and neck. Another thing I could try was giving him a pacifier.

I'm supposed to bring Martin back in a week. After the visit, we stopped at a drugstore, and I bought a pacifier and some baby toys to hang above the crib.

One thing I've found out is that music helps. Last night, during a crying spell, I put on one of my Miles Davis records. That seemed to soothe Martin enough that he went to sleep. During the day, he seems to like Elvis Presley.

I guess he takes after his mom.

September 25, 1962

I phoned Costa this evening. He was home, and I heard kids arguing in the background.

"Sounds like this isn't a good time," I said.

"Uh, no, *Ralph*. I don't know when those items are going to come in."

Aha. The wife was in front of him. "You can't talk freely."

"That's right," Costa answered and then called away from the phone, "Honey, could you quiet them down, this is work—"

"Okay, just listen. Pretty soon we're going to meet in person. When we do, don't be frightened. I'm not going to hurt you. I just want to talk. All right?"

"Uh, sure, uh—"

"And you're not to tell *anyone* about it, especially your employers."

"Oh, no, sir, not at all, sir—"

"Good. I'll be in touch, Hugh. I'd like you to be able to keep that nice home and family. Stick with me and I'll make sure you don't go to jail."

"Uh, I, uh—"

"So long, Hugh."

"Wait! What did you mean? That—what you said—about—"

"Jail?"

"Yes, sir."

"Something's going down soon, Hugh. That's all I can say." Then

I hung up. I'm sure that left him all shook up. Barry asked me the other day why I keep calling Hugh, Leo, and Christina, and to tell the truth, I don't know. I'm confident that I have a plan, but I'm not totally sure how it's going to work out.

OCTOBER 17, 1962

Wow, a month has gone by. Sorry, dear diary. Being a mother is a full-time job.

Martin celebrated his one-month birthday on the 13th. Barry and I had cake! He went out to the store and bought a small birthday cake with "Martin" written in frosting on top. He also presented me with Martin's new official birth certificate. DOB: October 13, 1962. According to the piece of paper, Martin *isn't* a month old. Today, he'd be the ripe age of four days! It will be strange not celebrating the real September birthday. Maybe I can think of something special to do with Martin on every September 13 and call it the "Month Before Your Birthday Day" or something dumb like that.

His colic is better. Gosh, when I got Elvis's new record, "Return to Sender," and played it the first time, Martin was in one of his howling moods. He wasn't interested in his pacifier, which usually did a surprisingly good job settling him. The music, however, immediately caught his attention and he shut up. He hasn't smiled yet, and I understand that doesn't happen until 2 to 3 months. But I think if he'd known how to smile then, he would have.

Since then, and it's only been a few days, the crying spells have cut down to maybe a third in number and length! So I play a lot of Elvis, along with everything else I own. He does respond to jazz, which is interesting. Maybe it's that plaintive, soulful melancholy that, in a way, is very soothing. Heck, what do I know? I'm just glad he's a happier baby.

Dr. Perlman suggested starting to switch from breast milk to the bottle. I buy Similac, a powder that you mix. Martin really likes it. It seems to have helped the colicky symptoms too. So now I breastfeed once a day and use the bottle the other times.

Barry and I knew we needed to find a babysitter; someone who can come here and be with Martin when Barry and I go out. Pretty soon it will be time for the Black Stiletto to appear in public again. Barry said he'd work on finding someone we can trust, and he did. She's a Mexican woman named Rosa. She and her husband run a taco truck at Kirkwood and Laurel Canyon Drive, near the country store. She doesn't speak English well, but she seems good with Martin, and he likes her too. So I guess Rosa will work out. Tonight is her second time to watch him.

Yesterday I tried on my outfit. It's still too tight, so I put on a black shirt and pants. With the mask, the backpack, and belt, Costa won't know the difference. I *have* lost a good deal of weight. I intensified my exercise routine in increments over the past month, but I need to do more. I wasn't supposed to resume normal physical activity for 5 to 6 weeks. Well, I'm getting restless and I need to go out. I'll be careful. I'm just going to meet Hugh and talk in a car.

On a recent reconnaissance of A-1 Outriggers warehouse, we learned that they were back in action. Costa's car was parked in back, along with the others. So tonight Barry's going to back up the Black Stiletto when she goes to meet the crooked printer in person.

34
Judy's Diary
1962

October 18, 1962

Barry parked near the warehouse where we could see the building and lot. Shortly after 7:00, the pickup and van left. The sun was nearly down, so it was fairly dark. I got out of the car and ran across the street, slipped to the side of the warehouse, and moved with my back against the wall toward the rear. Costa's Chrysler was still there. After making sure no one else was about, I sprinted to the car and checked the doors. Unlocked. I opened the back door and reclined in the backseat.

After fifteen minutes went by, I started to wonder if the guy was going to show up. I didn't want to stay there all night—although the car still had that nice new-car smell. He eventually appeared at 8:05. The guy got in the car, threw his lunch pail and thermos on the passenger seat, and lit a cigarette. Just as he was about to start the car, I made my presence known. Costa screamed in fright.

"Take it easy, Hugh," I said. I started massaging his shoulders from the backseat. "I told you not to be frightened when we met."

"How was I supposed to know you were here? You would've scared *anyone!*"

"Sorry, Hugh. Just relax, okay? This won't take long. I just want to have a chat."

He kept looking in the rearview mirror at me. "Are you really her?"

"What do you think?"

He shrugged. "If you say so."

"I'm the real deal. Not like that phony that killed Sal Casazza and Maria Kelly. That wasn't me, all right?"

"I don't know nothing about that."

"I don't know *anything* about that. If you say you don't know nothing, that means you know *something*." He couldn't reply to that one, ha ha. "So let's get down to business," I said.

"What do you want?" I could tell he was very nervous. "Information. I want to know how the counterfeit operation works. And I want to know the secret of this building."

"I want immunity."

I tsk-tsk'd him. "That's not up to me, Hugh. That's the DA's call. However, if you cooperate with me, then maybe I can influence his decision."

"They'll kill me if they knew I was talking to you."

"I can help protect you. Just don't tell anyone. There will be a big bust coming up, and I'll do my best to make sure you're spared. We want the big shots. So who's really in charge here?"

"Leo Kelly. He set up the operation, paid for the renovation on the building, got the equipment, and hired me and the other guys. He *was* working for Sal Casazza, but since Casazza's dead, Kelly took it over as boss."

"But isn't it Vincent DeAngelo who's the big boss, the guy who's really in charge?"

"I don't know. Maybe. All I know is that Leo gives the orders."

"Tell me about the building."

"Leo spent some money to build a trapdoor in the floor. It's right at the back of the warehouse, next to the loading dock door." That confirmed what I'd seen before. "You open it with a key and it's operated by an electric motor that uses counterbalanced springs, kind of like a garage door opener. Three sides of that section of the floor drop, but the fourth side stays connected." He demonstrated by flattening his hands and holding them horizontal, side by side. He then pivoted his right hand down to form a right angle to the left. "There's a ladder connected to the inner wall and we use that to get to the basement, or the dropped section of the floor acts as a ramp so we can move equipment and goods in and out of the loading dock."

"So that's where the printing press is, the basement?"

"Yeah. Everything's there. The paper, the press, and all the tools we need. The fumes from the press are expelled through a clever ventilation system that connects to the roof. We get oxygen that way too."

"Doesn't sound very safe, Hugh." He shrugged. It was his job. "Is there anything else about it I should know?"

"I don't know. Oh, there's an underground passage that leads to the building next door. Leo's company owns that warehouse too."

"Really?"

"Leo had that installed when he did the renovations. For an easy way out in case there was trouble."

That was interesting. "Now, tell me about the process."

Another shrug. "There are usually two or three of us working. I'm the foreman because I have the most printing experience. We print the money every couple of weeks. The rest of the time we spend cleaning the presses and plates. The plates have to be perfect. I told you we had to wait for a new one to come from New York, right?"

"Yeah. That's all taken care of?"

"Uh-huh. It took a while, but Samberg came through."

"The guy that makes them."

"Yeah, he lives in New York."

"Have you met him?"

"A couple of times. He came here at the beginning to make sure everything was printing properly."

"Do you have any awareness of what's going on in the warehouse above you when you're down there? Would you know if someone entered the building?"

"Yeah. Leo set up a speaker system. Switch it on and we can hear everything that happens on the ground floor. Also, every time the front door or the loading dock opens, we're alerted. Usually, though, anyone that comes is authorized to be there."

"What about outside? Do you hear what's going on?"

"Nah. It's like we're in a bunker."

"So you'd have no clue that a hundred policemen were outside, trying to get in?"

He actually laughed. "You're trying to scare me." Then he shrugged. "I guess if it was that bad, it wouldn't matter if we heard them outside or not."

"Do you know Christina Kelly?"

"Sure."

"What's her part in all this?"

He shrugged again. "She comes and checks on things. I guess she works for her brother."

"Okay, what happens to the counterfeit money?"

"These guys on motorcycles come and pick it up. A motorcycle gang."

"The Heathens?"

"Yeah, them. They come with their bikes and a truck or van. They pick up the phony cash, which is sealed in separate stacks, just like the banks do it. Where they take the money, I don't know. To distribution points. I know nothing about that. I just do my job, and don't ask questions."

"They pay you well?"

He nodded. "More money than I've ever made in my life."

"Well, Hugh, that's not going to last much longer, so you better start putting some away for a rainy day."

"Is there anything else?"

"Yeah. What do you know about the guns?"

I saw Costa's eyes grow wide in the rearview mirror and he turned his head to look at me.

"*That* I know nothing about! I swear. I know DeAngelo and

Casazza were importing guns from overseas, and maybe DeAngelo still is, but that's a whole other area I have nothing to do with. Really."

"All right, I believe you." And I did.

"You know I can't testify in court, right? I'd be a dead man for sure."

"Don't sweat it. We'll work out something. Now, one last thing."

"What?"

"Do you know Ricky Bartlett?"

"Who?"

"A Texan. Ricky Bartlett."

"No, I don't know him."

"What about Paulie DeAngelo?"

"He comes around sometimes. He doesn't have much to do with the operation."

"So you know him?"

"I've met him."

"I need to discreetly contact him."

Hugh turned his head to look at me. "I don't know how to do that."

"Surely someone knows how to get hold of him?"

Hugh shrugged. "I don't know."

"Well, that's your next assignment. I want to know how to reach Paulie DeAngelo without anyone knowing it. Can you do that?"

"That's going to be really hard."

"Then I leave it to you to figure out a way to get the number. And there's one other thing."

"What?"

"I want a copy of the key that opens that trapdoor in the floor."

"Oh, Jesus, I can't do that."

"Yes, you can. Just take it to a hardware store and get a copy made."

"Please, don't make me do that."

"Next time I see you, you better have it." With that, I got out of the car, stood by the driver's side, and leaned in the window to deliver a last message to Costa. "Remember, Hugh, don't say anything to anyone about this. I'd hate to give you up to the cops. I guess your wife wonders who the heck is calling you at home, huh?"

"She sure is. You gotta stop doing that. She thinks I'm fooling around or something."

"But you're not the type to do that, are you, Hugh?"

"No! I really—"

"You're a family man, right? You don't want to lose your family and go to jail, right?"

"Right!"

"Then we've got a deal?" I held out my gloved hand. He hesitated, and then he finally shook it. "I'll see you again soon, Hugh. Have a good evening."

I took off toward the street and hid in the shadows until he drove out of the lot and disappeared. I then made my way back to Barry's car and got in. I filled him in on what I learned as we drove back to the cabin. I divested myself of my mask and other Stiletto gear before going inside. Martin was sound asleep and Rosa was watching television—something she and her husband didn't have at home. I paid her more than we'd promised, and she was very grateful. Barry ran her home while I sat next to Martin's crib and sang a slow version of "Return to Sender" to his angelic face.

But I'd never return him!

OCTOBER 22, 1962

Oh my God, I'm scared. The Soviets are installing nuclear missiles in Cuba.

Barry and I watched President Kennedy on TV tonight. He announced the news with a very grim face. Apparently he's trying to talk to Khrushchev about it but isn't getting anywhere.

Is there going to be a war? A *nuclear* war?

Everything that everyone's been talking about the last couple of years is coming true.

I fear for our country. I fear for my son.

I don't think I can write any more tonight.

OCTOBER 29, 1962

Whew.

It's over. I think. At least for now it is. I haven't been able to write a word for the past few days. I refused to leave the cabin and stayed glued to the television for any news about what was going on in Cuba. The other day there was almost a confrontation between our navy and a Soviet cargo vessel. But I learned this morning that yesterday Khrushchev agreed to remove the missiles. Kennedy called his bluff. I don't know if he made some kind of deal with the Soviets, or what. I'm not sure anyone knows what went on through those "hot lines" they have in Washington. Whatever happened, the Russians backed down.

I am so relieved. To celebrate, I gave Martin ice cream for breakfast, ha ha.

35
Leo
THE PAST

It'd been a hell of a couple of months. Throughout most of it I was either frustrated, pissed off, or at my wit's end.

The plate breaking at the beginning of August was the beginning of it all, but it looks like that's been taken care of. I flew back from New York with the new plate in my luggage. Mookie came through, and he was all right too. Turned out he wasn't as injured by the bus as they first thought. So he got it done and now everything is back up and running at the warehouse. We were resuming distribution, and that was a good thing. I'm supposed to go to the Netherlands and France in November. I'll be meeting with some organizations there that could distribute the funny money in Europe. American money was the king over there. So after two months of headaches, that part of my life was finally back on track.

Then there were all the phone calls from the Black Stiletto. And then there weren't. But then she called again. There was a period in which she didn't call at all and I thought she'd gone away. Christina said she was in New York. I actually missed talking to her! She was such a tease. She was a goddamned sexy vixen, but she was also my sworn enemy. *She had my diamond!* And I wanted it back. I even offered a million dollars for it the last time we spoke. The profit I'd make on fencing it would be at least three or four million, so it wouldn't be a terrible price to pay. I was willing to do it. But she refused. She wanted something else, and I hadn't figured out what it was yet.

In the meantime, she called Christina every now and then and pushed all of my sister's buttons. She got Christina so riled up that I thought my sister might go out in the street and shoot up the town just to let off steam. Instead, she always went to the range and practiced with targets. That seemed to settle her down. Then she'd come home and light candles. I was concerned that Christina was going through something, because she just didn't act like she used to. She was so reckless and brazen lately. Even though she acted like she was having the most *marvelous* time being alive, I thought she was angry and bitter about her life. I was afraid the Black Stiletto was going to talk her into some kind of duel.

I wanted to catch the goddamned bitch. I kept imagining that moment when I delivered the Stiletto's head to Vince, and got my diamond back too. If only she'd succumb to my charms. I was giving it everything I had. She sounded so *interested*.

I had a feeling it was going to happen, and soon.

36
Judy's Diary
1962

NOVEMBER 4, 1962

It's my birthday! I'm 25 years old. Wow. It's hard to believe. In many ways I feel like I'm still that 14-year-old girl who ran away from home in 1952, and in other ways it seems I've already lived a lifetime. I've fallen in and out of love, I've had my heart broken, I've experienced joy, and tasted revenge, I've been shot twice, stabbed, beaten, and I've ended the criminal careers of a whole lot of bad guys. And I've had a child, and pretty soon he'll be 1 month old. Well, 2 months old, really. I'm still not used to the deception. Will anyone notice? He definitely *looks* like a 2-month-old, not a 1-month-old. I tell myself babies change so much in the first six months of their lives, and after he's 7 or 8 months old, the one month difference won't matter.

Barry grilled steaks outside and we had cake and ice cream. Martin loved the ice cream. It got all over his face and he was a sticky mess. Barry got me flowers and black pearl earrings. He didn't have to get me anything, but he did. Freddie probably would have sent me something, but we've been out of touch since I moved to the cabin. No one really knows where I am. So this year my birthday was just for our little family.

And speaking of family, Barry is more the daddy than ever. And, dear diary, I've slept with him. Three times. The first time was Halloween night! We drank a little bit—actually more than a little bit—since I was no longer pregnant and could enjoy a drink or two again. After Martin was in his crib, I told Barry I could go join the costume parade down Hollywood Boulevard dressed as the Black Stiletto and no one would care or notice. He agreed and figured there would be several Black Stilettos there. I teased him and said I was going to put on my outfit anyway, since it was Halloween. I must have been feeling awfully frisky, because I took my clothes off, very slowly, in front of him. I suppose I was craving the intimacy; I initiated it. In just my underwear, I went to him, sat on his lap, and kissed him on the mouth. It didn't take him long to respond!

I reckoned it had been enough time since I'd given birth. I still felt like the Grand Canyon down there, but Dr. Abernathy said I could resume "sexual activity" after six weeks, and it had been almost seven.

So now we sleep together—and I do mean sleep—in Barry's bed, and Martin has the crib in my bedroom. We've "done it" twice and that's all. I'll probably use my own bed more often than I use Barry's. He and I haven't talked about what's going on between us. I admit I'm not in love with him, but I do care for him. He's my best friend right now, and the fact that he's a man just made one thing lead to another.

I'm exercising more and am almost back to my weight before I got pregnant. There's still milk in my breasts, but most of the extra flab in my belly and waist is gone. I'm proud of myself! After I stop nursing, which I think I will do after Christmas, then I can lose the rest of that extra little bit of me. Nevertheless, I'm much closer to being in Stiletto shape again.

I've also made progress on Barry's shooting range. For someone who doesn't like guns, I'm getting to be a pretty good shot. I hit the bull's-eyes on the targets about 90% of the time.

As for Leo and Christina, I hope I'm making them sweat by not talking to them. I've spoken to Hugh, though, on the phone.

He hates it when I call his house. I told him I'd gladly explain to his wife that I wasn't his mistress, ha ha. He didn't think that was funny. I wasn't too happy that he hadn't found out how to reach Paulie, but he did say that Leo's going to Europe for the first half of November. Apparently, Leo is trying to set up some overseas distribution deals for the counterfeit money.

With Leo gone, there isn't much I can do. I think I'll be better prepared and in top notch shape in a month. That's my goal, anyway.

Sometime the first week of December, there will be a Day of Reckoning!

NOVEMBER 17, 1962

It's nearly midnight and I just got back to the cabin. This time I went to A-1 Outriggers alone to meet with Hugh. Barry stayed home with Martin. I honestly didn't think it would be a big deal. I'd meet with Hugh and leave. I didn't expect trouble, but that's what I got.

Two months after Martin's birth I was miraculously able to get into my outfit without it feeling too tight. I was back to my normal weight and strength, and it felt invigorating to put on the leather pants and jacket again. It took a lot of willpower not to speed down the mountain and into the city.

It was already dark when I arrived in the Wholesale District. I parked the car on the street, donned my mask, and moved in the shadows to the warehouse. The other guys had already left, but Hugh's Chrysler was still in back. This time, though, his car was locked. I considered using a lock pick to get inside, but I didn't want to scare him too badly. I simply sat on the hood and waited. Eventually, he came walking around the side of the building from the front.

"Good evening, Hugh," I said sweetly.

"Oh," he said, not very enthusiastically. "Hi."

"How are you? It's been a while."

He just unlocked the car and got inside without saying anything.

I jumped off the hood, knocked on the passenger window, and he unlocked the door so I could slip in. "No time for chitchat, Hugh? I'm fine, thanks for asking."

"Christ." He shook his head at the absurdity of the situation.

I laughed. "Hey, at least I didn't break into your car and scare you to death when you got in."

"Yeah, thank you for that." He lit a cigarette and offered me one.

"No, thanks. So, what's going on? How's the funny money business?"

He shrugged. "Just like always."

"Is Leo back from Europe?"

"Yeah."

"And did he get some distributors?"

"I have no idea. He doesn't share that stuff with me."

"You're just the printer?"

"That's right."

"Do you have my key?"

"Yeah." He dug into his pocket, pulled out and handed me a strange metal key with a lot of grooves in it.

"This will open the trapdoor?"

"Just turn the key in the slot and push the button. That's all there is to it."

"Thank you, sir. Any luck with Paulie DeAngelo?"

"As a matter of fact—" Hugh looked around nervously and dropped his voice to a whisper, even though there wasn't a soul in sight. "A fellow owed me a favor. I don't know how he got it, but I have Paulie's phone number where he can be reached. I can't guarantee he's the one who'll answer it." He dug his wallet out of his trouser pocket, opened it, and removed a piece of paper. "He's staying somewhere in Venice Beach now. No one's supposed to know though."

I took the slip and stuck it and the key in the pouch on my belt. "You don't know where?"

"No. Sorry."

"That's okay. Do you know what he's up to?"

"Not a clue."

"You don't know much, do you, Hugh?"

"Hey, I got you the phone number and the key. Listen, I have to—"

Before he could finish the sentence, a pair of headlights panned across the lot. A car pulled in from the street and drove alongside the building toward us. It was too late for me to hide—whoever was driving would have already seen me. I really didn't want Hugh to be caught with me, for his sake, but it couldn't be helped. Then, when the headlights weren't in my eyes and the car parked next to Hugh's Chrysler on the passenger side, I saw whose vehicle it was.

Christina's Corvette.

"Tell her you were just leaving and I surprised you," I said to Hugh in a low voice. "It's the truth." I then burst out the car door, jumped on top of the Chrysler and bolted over it, landing on my feet by the driver's side of the Corvette. I drew my stiletto, pulled open the door, and held the blade against Christina's neck before she could reach into her purse and grab a weapon. Sure enough, I spied the butt of a handgun sticking out of it.

"Hold it, don't move," I growled. "Keep your hands on the wheel." She actually complied.

"What are you doing here, bitch?" she spat.

"I could ask you the same thing. I've had my eye on this building for a long time. Why don't you step out of the car and keep your hands raised?"

I kept the knife at her throat but stepped back so she could get out. Once she was standing, I moved away, but kept the stiletto in hand.

"I didn't know she was here, Christina!" Hugh pleaded, as he got out of his car. "I finished work and came back here and—"

"Shut up!" Christina snapped. "Don't say another word." She looked at me, and said, "This is an empty building."

I really didn't want her to know that I was aware of the warehouse's secrets. "It sure looks that way. So why are you and this nobody here?"

"I don't have to answer your questions."

"It's pretty strange that I found this guy parked in back of an empty and unused building, and then you show up too. Pretty suspicious, if you ask me."

She just rolled her eyes, and then said, "Kelly Enterprises owns this building and leases it to a tenant. I have every right to be here." Christina tried to stare me down, but after five seconds, she said, "So you're back in town. It's about time. Are we were going to meet someplace and settle our differences? You ready for me to bust your kneecaps?"

"You'll get your chance, but not tonight, sweetheart." Then I made a mistake. I sheathed the knife. She took that opportunity to scream like a banshee and leap forward. The woman slammed into my body and pushed me against the side of her car. It took me completely by surprise. She then started pummeling my face, chest, and stomach like a pro. I blocked her blows the best I could, but then she kicked my shin hard, obviously aiming for my knee. *That* hurt, and it woke me up. My honed reflexes ignited and I caught her right wrist in midair with my left hand. She tried to hit me with her left, but I blocked her with my right forearm, and punched her on the chin. Then I kneed her in the abdomen, causing her to break away and step back. My shin was crying in pain, and only then did I see that she was wearing pointed-toe boots. I was lucky she didn't break my tibia.

So I went on the offensive. I pushed myself off the car and delivered a perfect *ushiro-geri*—back kick—to her face. It felt *so good* to do it too; it'd been a long time since I've seen any action. Right then and there, I knew the Black Stiletto was back.

My blow stunned her. She shook her head and looked at me in confusion, as if to say, "How did you do that?" A trickle of blood appeared at the corner of her mouth. Then her expression changed and she cried out in anger. The next couple of minutes were a flurry of punches, kicks, and shoves. I think it's the first time I ever fought another girl. One of the first things that went through my head was that I shouldn't hit her too hard. My *karate* or *wushu* blows could be *fatal* if they struck the right—or wrong—spot. However, I quickly learned that Christina knew what she was doing. She probably didn't have the training I've had, but she'd obviously picked up a lot of technique in prison or on the street. She may have kicked like a woman, but she could certainly hit like a man.

Dear diary, we had at it right there in the dark parking lot behind the warehouse, and she really was serious about trying to break my kneecaps—her every kick was an attempt to hit them. Poor Hugh just stood there and watched, probably too scared to do anything. What Christina didn't know about hand-to-hand combat she made up for with sheer determination and a heavy dose of rage. And that was her downfall; Soichiro taught me those many moons ago that anger was a bad thing. It blinds you. I was therefore able to anticipate and block many of her blows and connect several of mine. She got in some good ones, though, and I have the bruises to prove it.

As we fought, I became aware that this was going to ruin my plan to catch her and Leo. It was too early for the Black Stiletto and Christina to "settle our differences," as she'd put it. I had to end it fast and get the heck out of there. So I waited for the perfect opening and delivered a powerful *tobi-geri*—jump kick—and slammed my boot into her nose. I'm sure I broke it. She went down and was out for the count.

I quickly went to her to make sure she was alive. Blood poured from her nostrils like a water faucet. Yep, I'd broken her nose. She groaned, so I left her there and went to Hugh. He was in shock. "Just keep to your story," I warned him, and then I turned and ran off the lot. I was long gone in my car by the time Christina was up and on her feet. I bet she had to go to the emergency room and get treatment. She wasn't going to be so pretty anymore. I didn't really mean to do it, but serves her right. I suppose, if anything, now she'll want to get even with me more than ever.

And that plays right into my plan.

37
Gina
The Present

After the strange meeting with Mr. McCambridge, I used my GPS to find the house on Beechwood that was mentioned in the newspaper article about the break-in and murder of the man who might be my great Uncle Frank. The neighborhood appeared to be old—well, old as in perhaps dating from the 1950s or so. The structures were brick ranch houses, nothing over one story.

There was a Toyota Camry parked in the driveway, so someone was home. I figured I was wasting my time. Whoever lived there would probably think I was crazy trying to find out something about a family that lived in the house fifty years earlier. But I had nothing to lose.

When I rang the doorbell, it was answered by a heavyset woman wearing a simple housedress. Although she was behind a front screen door, she appeared to be around Dad's or Maggie's age. She had a pretty—and friendly—face.

"Yes?" she asked.

"Oh, hi, I'm sorry to bother you, but I'm trying to find some people who used to live in this house a long time ago. I just took a chance to see if you might know anything about them."

"I beg your pardon?"

"Sorry, maybe I'm not making myself clear. My name is Gina Talbot, and I'm trying to track down the family of the man who was my great uncle. His name was Frank Cooper. He and his family lived in this house in the early six—"

Her expression changed so dramatically that I stopped speaking. The woman's mouth fell open and her eyes widened. She took a breath and said, "Frank Cooper was my father."

That answer rendered me speechless. It was my turn to drop a jaw. We stared at each other for a few seconds until I blurted, "Really?"

"Yes!" She opened the screen door. "What did you say your name was?"

"Gina Talbot. My father is Martin Talbot. His mother is Judy Cooper, your father's sister. I guess that makes me your—second cousin?"

"Are you *serious*? No way!"

"If I got the right family, then yes, I'm perfectly serious!"

"You better come in. Please."

So I did.

What an amazing two hours I spent with Angela Sandlin. It was true. Angela was Frank and Sarah Cooper's daughter, born in 1960. She was only two years old when my great uncle was killed. She and her husband inherited the house after her mother passed away; since it was paid for, they moved in.

I learned a great deal about my grandmother's family from her. We sat in the kitchen and had coffee. She was *very* nice. I liked her a lot. I tried to call Dad from there, but I got his voice mail. All I said was, "Dad, you're not going to believe this, but I'm sitting with your cousin, Angela, Frankie's daughter! Call me back if you get this soon."

Angela was Frank and Sarah's only child. The Coopers married in 1959. Uncle Frank owned a hardware store until he died. My Aunt Sarah sold it shortly afterward. She worked in a department store called Dunlap's. I was sorry to hear that she developed cancer and passed away in 2002. Angela was married to Delbert Sandlin, who worked during the day at Chevron Oil Company in downtown

Odessa. I didn't quite understand what he did, but it had something to do with geology. She and Delbert had two children, both grown now—Frank, who was twenty-seven and living in Austin, and Jane, twenty-three, who was in med school in Dallas. Angela also told me about my other great uncle, John. He was killed in a helicopter accident at an army base in California the same year Angela was born. That was sobering to hear.

I told her all about Dad and Grandma—leaving out the Big Secret, of course—and how Grandma had Alzheimer's and all that. Angela asked what I was doing in Odessa, so I just said I was trying to track down the family tree. The subject eventually got around to what happened in 1962.

"I was too young to remember anything about it," Angela said. "My mother had taken me to a doctor's appointment—I had an earache or something—and when we got home, the house was in shambles. It had been torn apart, and my father was lying on the living room floor, dead from a gunshot wound. His wallet was gone, and some of Mom's jewelry was missing. The police said it was a robbery gone wrong, pure and simple. They never caught who did it."

"Gosh, I'm so sorry."

Angela shrugged. "I never knew him, not really. I can't even picture his face except from photographs. Hey, since you're here, I'd like to ask you, well, tell you something. I probably shouldn't say this, but, you know, Mom always said your grandmother Judy was a crazy woman. I'm sorry, Gina, but it's what I've grown up to believe. I thought you should know that, and I feel bad telling you."

"Oh my God, why would she say that?"

"Because, apparently, she never communicated with my father. The story went that she ran away from home when she was just a teenager, went to New York City, and never contacted her family again, except right before my dad was killed."

I didn't want to argue with her, but I said, "What you say is true, she did run away, but it was because their stepfather abused her. Did your father ever tell your mom that?"

"I don't know. I don't think so."

"She did live in New York. She came back, though, in 1958 and saw your dad. I know that from reading one of my grandma's diaries."

"My mother never mentioned that either. That was before they were married, of course. The only time my mom met her was when your grandmother visited here, in this very house, the day before my dad was killed. My mom, well, she sometimes thought your grandmother may have had something to do with that. She and my dad apparently thought his sister was in some kind of trouble with the law, and she brought that mess with her when she came to visit."

Angela looked at me for some kind of confirmation, but I stayed as stoic as possible. "I'm shocked, I don't know anything about that," I said. "I don't think that could possibly be true."

"Then why didn't she try to get back in touch? We never heard from her again. Did she even know my dad had been murdered?"

"No, I don't think so. Angela, all I can tell you is that my grandmother was a very free spirit. She *was* abused by her stepfather. She was raped. And he was also responsible for my great-grandmother's death—your grandmother's. The woman died of a broken heart and mistreatment from that awful man. I think my grandma's memories of Odessa were very painful to her. It wasn't because she didn't love her brothers or mother. Unfortunately, she can't defend herself now. She's probably going to die soon."

"Well, who knows when it comes to families, right? Maybe Mom's views on that time were warped. I would have liked to have known your grandmother. I never had an aunt. Or an uncle either, for that matter."

We got quiet after that, but then she perked up and tried to alleviate the awkward situation. "You want to see some pictures and stuff?"

"Yes! Show me everything!"

We spent the next hour going through some of her scrapbooks. There were pictures of my Uncle Frank and Aunt Sarah when they were married, photos of Angela when she was a baby—and oh, my God, there was a picture of Grandma Judy sitting with her brother Frankie in the very house we were in. And she was holding a baby.

"That was the day she came to visit, the day before the robber killed my dad," Angela explained. I had seen very few photographs of Grandma Judy when she was young. She was *beautiful*. Long, dark hair. Kind eyes. The picture was black-and-white, but you could tell how radiant she was. And the *baby*!

"Is that my dad she's holding?" I asked.

"I think so. That was December 1962, would that be right?"

"Yeah." Amazing. Dad needed to see that.

Angela showed me around the house and pointed out an antique pendulum clock on the wall. She said it was a genuine Westminster and had belonged to her grandmother—my great-grandmother. Apparently, it was the only thing that had survived from Uncle Frank and Grandma Judy's childhood home. It was gorgeous, and it still worked. "I keep thinking I might sell it," Angela said. "It really has no sentimental value for me. It's probably worth a little." I agreed. "My mom told me my dad always thought there was something special about it." She shrugged.

My cousin asked if I wanted to stay for dinner, but truth be told, I started feeling uncomfortable. The things she'd said about Grandma Judy had hurt, and I didn't think I wanted to stay much longer. It was great to meet her and get to know her, but I made an excuse about having another appointment. She wanted me to come back and meet Delbert when he was home, so I promised I'd call her again before I left town. We exchanged numbers, and I also said I'd have Dad contact her as soon as I got in touch with him. We weren't going to disappear from her life this time!

As I went to find a place to have supper, I couldn't help speculating about my Uncle Frank's death. Was Angela correct about my Grandma having something to do with it?

Dad had better finish that freakin' fifth diary!

I'd seen a place this morning that made my mouth water—the

Texas Roadhouse, on Grandview. I'm normally not a big meat person because I try to eat healthy, and I'd *already* had two Tex-Mex meals, but being in Texas made me hunger for barbecue. It was a chain, but they served pulled pork and "Fall-Off-The-Bones Ribs," and it was all yummy. I reached Dad while I was sitting in the booth, alone, digesting my food.

The first thing he did, of course, was yell at me for taking the Black Stiletto costume with me to Texas. "Why in the world would you do that?" he ranted. "It's valuable! What did you think you were going to do with it?"

"I don't know!" I answered truthfully. "I can't explain it, Dad, it was just an *urge* that came over me. Something told me to bring it with me. I just wanted it close to me, that's all. It's like Grandma is here, looking over my shoulder. She's *with* me." That really was why I did it. I couldn't explain it in words. I needed Grandma's vibes at my side while I uncovered all her secrets in Odessa. "I'll be very careful with it, I promise. It's safe in my suitcase at the hotel."

"Well, I have her gun here," Dad admitted. "It's in my briefcase, sitting on the coffee table. That gives *me* some comfort."

That surprised me. "Do you know how to use it?"

"I think I can figure it out. I managed to load it without any problems."

I started to laugh, but I resisted. Instead, I told him all about my progress and how I'd spent the day with his cousin. He'd heard my message and was very impressed I'd managed to accomplish so much in a short time. I suggested that he call Angela, but he hemmed and hawed. Finally, I pushed him to finish the fifth diary. He claimed he'd been trying. "I'm over halfway through," he said, "but, hey, I've been taking care of my dying mother, hiding from bad guys, and trying to keep sane. Reading about the Black Stiletto only makes me even more crazed, and I'm sleep-deprived enough as it is."

I really did laugh when he said that.

"I'm serious!" he said, but he laughed too. We ended the call on a good note. It was dark outside when I finished at the restaurant, so I drove back to La Quinta Inn for the night. I thought I'd phone Josh once I got back to my room.

The door to my room faced outside, motel-style. I parked in front, got out, locked the car, and pulled the key card from my purse. Slipped it in the slot, opened the door, and saw that my suitcase and other belongings had been gone through and thrown around the room.

A lightning bolt of terror went up my spine when I realized the Black Stiletto clothing was nowhere in sight.

38
Judy's Diary
1962

NOVEMBER 25, 1962

Martin had his first Thanksgiving on Thursday. Barry and I worked together to roast a turkey and prepare a lavish dinner for the two of us. Martin had his usual Similac and some oatmeal that he likes. I've been buying Gerber's baby food in those new little glass jars too, and he likes most of that. He doesn't care for strained peas for some reason. Spits 'em right out. Anyway, Barry and I had fun and drank a bottle of red wine with the meal.

Rosa came over to babysit yesterday so Barry and I could go see the new Elvis movie, *Girls! Girls! Girls!* It was a lot better than his last one. I haven't got the record yet, but I plan to do so the next time I'm in Hollywood.

The time is rapidly approaching for the showdown between Leo, Christina, and me. I've picked December 1st as the date. It's a Sunday, so things should be pretty quiet in the Wholesale District. Barry has told DA McKesson about the plan and he has agreed, reluctantly, to supply the necessary backup force. Barry will act as liaison to the police, but the cops will be led by an officer in their ranks. They're just waiting for final confirmation. I'm glad Barry and his DA buddy have more or less made up.

Just before Thanksgiving, I went to see Luis at the gym. He was very surprised to see me. He hadn't seen me for months.

"Judy! Where you been?" he asked in broken English.

"Sorry, Luis. I had a baby."

"Bambino? Really?"

"Yeah. Baby boy."

"You should bring him in. Start training him early!"

I laughed. "Listen, has anyone been looking for me?"

He told me that a short white guy that looked like Paul Newman had been asking about me, but that was earlier in the year. Leo. He knew I liked to work out at the gym, so it must have been one of the first places he tried looking for me.

"What did you tell him?"

"The truth! I hadn't seen you!"

"Good. Listen, I need to borrow some equipment."

"Sure, Judy, whatever you want."

I knew Luis owned a couple sets of portable boxing ring materials—inflatable "poles" that you could attach ropes to. They allowed you to set up a ring anywhere. I told him I'd have the stuff back to him soon, but he waved me off. "Forget it, Judy. You can keep it. That's old and I need to replace it."

I thanked him and left. Next, I tried to make all the various calls I needed to make to set everything in motion.

First, I phoned Hugh Costa. His wife answered again, ha ha, and I told her it was "work" calling for Hugh. Her voice betrayed the fact that she didn't believe me. I heard her say to him, her voice oozing with sarcasm, "It's your *girlfriend*." He protested, "She's *not* my girlfriend!" before taking the receiver.

"Yeah?"

"Hello to you, too, Hugh."

"What do you want?"

"You're not in trouble with the missus, are you?"

"Just tell me what you want."

"Okay. On December 1st, stay away from the warehouse.

Especially that night."

"Uh, is that when the, uh, business plan you mentioned goes into effect?"

"Yes."

"Thanks for letting me know."

"Either I or someone will be in touch with you afterward to get your statements. You'll be protected, so don't worry. You've been a big help, Hugh."

"Uh, okay."

"Stay out of trouble, you hear?"

"Sure."

We hung up. After that, I called Leo and Christina's house. There was no answer. I tried again the next day, and again on Thanksgiving. I'm hoping someone will be home this week, or else I'll have to reschedule the date.

However, I did reach Paulie DeAngelo using the number Hugh gave me. I was almost surprised it worked. Some flunky answered the phone and said, "Talk to me."

"Hello, stranger," I said in my sultry Marilyn Monroe imitation.

"Who the hell is this?"

"It's the Black Stiletto and I'd like to speak to Paulie. Is he there?"

"*Who?*"

"You heard me. I think your boss will want to talk to me." The guy put down the phone, and I waited nearly a minute before Paulie picked it up.

"Hello?"

"Paulie DeAngelo?"

"Yeah?"

"This is the Black Stiletto."

"That's what Luca said. How do I know it's you?"

"You'll just have to believe me."

"Well, if it's really you, I'd like to break your neck, Black Stiletto. You killed my sister."

"No, I didn't. That wasn't me, and I can prove it."

"What are you talking about?"

"Someone was impersonating me on New Year's Eve. She dressed up as the Black Stiletto and killed Maria and stole her diamond necklace. Then the same person robbed the Sandstone Casino in Las Vegas. *And* she killed Sal Casazza too. None of those Black Stilettos were the real deal."

There was silence at the other end.

"Paulie?"

"Yeah, I'm here. If she wasn't you, then who was she?"

"Someone you know. She and an assistant. You and your father trust them."

"You're talking mighty big, lady. Who are they?"

"Paulie, I can't tell you now, you'd just go off and kill them. But I'll deliver them to you safe and sound with the proof."

"Are you crazy, lady?"

"No. You have to believe me. Don't you want to avenge your sister?"

"Sure, but how are you going to prove this to me?"

"Do you know the warehouse that's being used to make counterfeit money? The building called A-1 Outriggers?"

"Yeah?"

"Be there at eight o'clock, Sunday night, December 1st. Bring some of your men. I'll be there with the proof, inside the building. Don't be late; I need you to arrive *exactly* at eight."

"This is a bunch of crap. You're setting me up."

"You're on the outs with your father, aren't you? How would you like to deliver your sister's killer to him, and also prove to him that you were right about someone you detest? A fellow by the name of Kelly?"

"I'm listening."

"That would smooth things between the two of you, wouldn't it?"

Silence again. Then—"This better not be a bunch of crap."

"It's not. Just don't say anything to your father or anyone else about this before then. You have *my* word I'll come through with this. Can I have *your* word you'll keep it to yourself?"

He thought about it. "Sure. But this better not be—"

"—a bunch of crap, I know. I'll call again just before the 1st to confirm."

Then I hung up.

Martin's crying about something, gotta run...

NOVEMBER 29, 1962

I finally got hold of both Leo and Christina.

On the evening of the 27th, I reached Christina at home. When she answered, I asked, "How's the nose?"

It took a second for her to realize who I was, and then she shouted, *"You bitch! I'm going to kill you!"*

"I bet you say that to all the Black Stilettos."

She drew her voice down and spoke with a growl. "You coward. For months I've challenged you to meet me in person. That last fight we had—I wasn't prepared. You cheated."

"How did I cheat? It seemed pretty fair and square to me."

She unleashed a torrent of four-letter words at me. When she was done, all I said was, "That was very unladylike, Christina. But I tell you what. I'll meet you. We can 'settle our differences,' as you put it last time. And bring Leo too, I'd like him to be referee."

"We don't need a goddamned referee!"

"Listen, Christina. You'll get your chance to get at me. But I want you to wear your Black Stiletto costume."

"What? Why?"

"I want to fight you Stiletto-to-Stiletto, so to speak. You caused me a lot of trouble by impersonating me. Let's end this the same way."

"Fine. It's goddamned *weird*, but if that's what you want..."

"And another thing. It will be in that empty warehouse. A-1 Outriggers. Nine forty-five on the night of December 1st. You don't have plans that night, do you?"

"Wait a minute. What are you doing? Are you setting me up?"

"Only to get your butt kicked. And, I know, I know, you want to break my knees. So, are you going to meet me there or not?"

"I'll be there."

"If you're not in costume, I'm leaving."

"Why nine forty-five?"

"You ask too many questions. Would you rather meet at nine thirty? Nine o'clock?"

"Nine forty-five is fine!"

"Good. See you then."

And I hung up. I didn't reach Leo until yesterday. When I asked where he'd been, he replied that he was out of town over Thanksgiving and had just returned to LA.

"Where did you go? Europe again?"

I felt him tense up. "How do you know I went to Europe?"

"I know things, Leo. I know everything about you. And I've decided, once and for all, that I'm ready to meet again. What do you say?"

"Well, sure."

"Have you spoken to your sister?"

"Yeah. She says you two are finally going to have it out. But it sounds fishy. Why the empty warehouse? I think you're setting us up."

"I'm not. And I want you there. You can watch me kick her rear end to Timbuktu. Then afterward, you and I can mosey on off into the sunset and you can have your way with me. Maybe I'll even take off my mask."

"You're bullshitting me. I don't buy it."

"I want you, Leo. And I want you to have *me*."

I could sense his male ego expanding.

"And if Christina wins?"

"Then you probably wouldn't want to kiss me. My lips might be all busted up."

"You'll probably be *dead*."

"That too. But here's another incentive. How about if the winner gets to keep the diamond?"

That got him. I knew then that he and his sister would be willing to risk me "setting them up" for a chance to get the diamond.

"You'll bring it?" he asked. "So we can have it if you, uh, die? Which is what's going to happen."

"You sound very confident. It will be there, Leo, you can count on it." I repeated the date, time, and place.

"I don't like it."

"Look, Leo, it's *your* turf. It'll be quiet and out of the public eye. We'll have the entire empty warehouse for our arena. What could be better?"

"All right. We'll be there."

"One other thing, Leo. You two better be alone. If I detect that you've brought anyone else with you, I'll leave and take the diamond with me."

He agreed.

I'm convinced that if I hadn't done all that taunting and teasing on the phone since the summer, I never would have convinced Christina and Leo to meet me. Christina was so full of hatred for me that she probably would have met me in the middle of crowded Hollywood Boulevard! I worked them up to such a frenzy that they weren't thinking rationally. Just for a chance to get at me.

I can't wait.

DECEMBER 1, 1962

Dear diary, everything is in place for tonight. I called Paulie and confirmed that the show was on.

Rosa will stay at the house to watch Martin while Barry and I go to the warehouse. We're taking Barry's car. Once we're there, we'll split up. He'll coordinate with the cops, while I do my thing. One thing I needed was a portable tape recorder, which Barry was able to procure fairly easily. He showed me how to set it up and work it. Nothing to it, as long as the batteries held out.

There are butterflies in my stomach. I'm sure I can beat Christina, but there's always the chance that she and Leo will try something sneaky. I'm going to be extra careful before I reveal myself. I want to make sure they have no backup hit men with them, and also confirm that Christina's not going to just take out a gun and shoot me. Yes, it's a risky thing I'm doing, but it must be done. I need to finally end this thing.

Now it's down to timing. Everyone has to be in the right place at the right time.

In a little bit, I'll dress in my outfit, put the Chinese jewel box and diamond in my backpack, kiss Martin good night, and Barry and I will drive down the mountain.

Wish me luck, dear diary!

39
Martin
THE PRESENT

Maggie and I had dinner at the cabin, and then I fed Mom, sitting beside her bed and spoon-feeding her a nutritional smoothie. She had trouble chewing some solid foods, such as steak, but chicken and soft vegetables weren't a problem. Smoothies were a favorite; that she'd consume in its entirety. Everything else she just nibbled at, leaving more than half the meal in the bowl or plate. It was no wonder she'd become so thin. All that great muscle tone she used to have was gone.

So sad.

I spoke to Gina a while ago. It was unbelievable what she had accomplished in Odessa! She'd met my cousin! Gina certainly had more chutzpah than me. I think I would have been too intimidated to try and find my mom's kin after so long. Perhaps, after Mom is gone, I'll be able to go to Odessa and meet them.

Gina was making progress on the case, but I really got after her for snatching the Stiletto costume. She was suitably sorry, and I admonished her to make sure nothing happened to it. But I couldn't stay mad long. Again, she got after *me* for not finishing the last diary, so I promised I'd try to get through it tonight and tomorrow.

It was too nice of an evening not to be outside, so Maggie and I sat in a couple of lawn chairs in front the house, facing Lake Shore Drive and the lake beyond it, and watched the sky as the sun fell behind us. Mom was already asleep, but we kept the door open so we could hear her if she made any noise. Trees along Lake Shore Drive blocked most of the view of the water from our lawn, but we could see part of it. Cars went past every now and then. The air was cool, but winter was on its way out. In Chicago we rarely had much of a spring or fall, so we embraced the fleeting instances; I liked to joke that we had only two seasons—winter and construction.

"This feels good," Maggie said.

"Yeah, it does."

She clasped my hand. "You doing all right, Martin?"

"As best as I can. The meds help. I'm worried though. Gina's down in Texas. There's a madman looking for us. My mom might die any day. It's hard to relax, but I'm so glad you're here with me, Maggie. I mean it."

"I'm glad too."

"It *is* nice here. We could fix this place up, maybe use it more?"

"I'd like that."

"It could be our little love nest away from home."

She laughed, and then I looked at her. The question popped out of nowhere. I had no idea it was coming, and I hadn't planned it.

"Will you marry me?"

Her expression changed from amusement to something I could only describe as *awe*. Her eyes became moist and her lips parted in a spectacularly sensual way that I'd never seen before. "Really?" she whispered.

"Yeah. Will you?" Three seconds went by. Eight seconds. Twelve. "Take all the time you want to think about it," I said with a chuckle.

"Of course I will, Martin. Yes. Yes, I will."

Then I kissed that sexy mouth and we held each other, even though it was awkward doing so sitting in two separate lawn chairs. I had a feeling we were both going to get lucky when we went to bed.

The special moment, however, was interrupted by a car's headlights. The vehicle didn't move past the house like all the others, but instead slowed and then turned into the cabin's driveway. It was a black, official-looking sedan. The lights went out when the driver shut off the engine.

For a second I tensed up, and then Detective Scott emerged and walked toward us.

"Good evening," he said.

"Hello, Detective," my bride-to-be answered.

"Nice night." He stood near us on the lawn. "I think summer just might be around the corner."

"I was just about to say it was getting too cool to sit outside," Maggie commented.

"What can we do for you, Detective?" I asked.

"How's Mrs. Talbot doing?"

"She's fine. She's inside, asleep."

He nodded, but then said, "I spoke to Ms. Hawkins. She's worried that your mother might not be receiving the best care out here."

"Virginia? She was just here," I said. "She's going to come and help every other day."

"Detective," Maggie said, "as Judy Talbot's doctor, I assure you that she's receiving the same good care here that she would get at Woodlands."

"Mm," Scott muttered. "Well, I guess no crime's being committed. The director of the nursing home's not too happy about it."

"That's my concern, Detective," she said.

"So was there anything in particular you wanted?" I asked.

"Rather than calling your cell—which you don't always answer promptly—I thought I'd come pay you a visit and make sure everything's okay. And I wanted to tell you in person that we think we know who our suspect is."

"Is that so?" I stood. "Why don't we go inside where we can all sit?"

He followed Maggie and me into the house, and we sat in the little living room around the coffee table. Maggie asked him if he wanted coffee or anything, but he declined.

Scott spoke. "We processed fingerprints at Thomas Avery's

office, and they matched some sets found at your house, and I don't mean yours. When we put them through the national database, we got a hit. They belong to a man named Haines, Dallas Haines. He's from Texas. He served thirteen-and-a-half years in prison for manslaughter from the late eighties to the New Millennium—he was sentenced for fifteen but got out on parole. Apparently, he's a very dangerous person, and we're doing everything we can to find him."

"Do you think he's still in town?"

"That I don't know." He opened the folder and showed us a mug shot of the guy. The man had a broken nose and the coldest eyes I'd ever seen. Not someone I'd want to bump into in a dark alley. "This picture is twenty years old," Scott said. "So put a little more gray hair and wrinkles on him, and you might have an idea what he looks like now. Does he look familiar?"

"Never seen him before."

"Me neither," Maggie answered.

"The receptionist at Woodlands—"

"Marissa?"

"—yes, I'll have to run this by her tomorrow and see if it's the same guy that pulled a gun on her." Scott looked at me. "Then I'll show it to your partner, Mr. Wegel. If they both concur this was the man, then I'm afraid we have to assume he's still looking for you."

"Well, gee, that's *wonderful* news," I muttered as my anxiety level shot up a notch.

Then he stood. "Is there anything I can do for you in the meantime?"

"Post some armed guards outside?"

"I can give you the name of a good firm that hires out security men if you want."

I looked at Maggie and she shrugged. "Okay."

He took out his notebook and thumbed through it. Maggie wrote down the name and number. "They're expensive, but good," he said.

After that, Scott said he'd be in touch, and then he left. It was now full dark outside. We closed and locked the door, and then I turned to embrace my fiancée. "Did that visit destroy the mood?"

"Not for me," Maggie answered. "Shall we get ready for bed?"

"Sure."

We started to move to the bedroom, but a knock on the door stopped us.

"Shit. What did he forget?" I let Maggie go, went to the door, and opened it.

The man standing there was not Detective Scott.

I recognized him as an older version of the guy in the mug shot, and he pointed a gun right at me.

"Hi," he said in a gravelly drawl. "My name's Dallas. Can I come in?"

40
Judy's Diary
1962

Everything has gone to hell, dear diary. My hand is shaking as I write this and I'm not sure it's very legible.

I'm in a fleabag motel outside of Phoenix, Arizona. The Desert Inn. It's an apt name, too, for it's surrounded by flat, dreary desert. Kind of reminds me of Odessa, which is where Martin and I are heading.

We're on the run.

I suppose I should back up and try to put everything down as I remember it. I'm very upset, though, so there's no telling how my memory will play tricks on me.

Barry is dead. My friend, my lover, my companion—Barry Gorman, you were a brave and kind individual. You took me in when I needed help. You saved my life and you nursed me back to health. You became a father to Martin for a few short months. I suppose I should have told you I loved you, but I never did. It wouldn't have been the truth, but I was, and still am, extremely fond of you. You were a saint. Lord knows you did some bad things in the past and went to prison for it, but you were good to me and Martin. You had a benevolent, loving soul. I am so sorry that I brought this upon you. It seems that everywhere I go there's death.

And it's the Black Stiletto's fault.

On the evening of December 1st, Barry drove the Buick into the city to the Wholesale District. We circled the block where the A-1 Outriggers warehouse sat and didn't see any signs of early arrivals. I suppose it was possible that Leo and Christina might show up early to set a trap of some kind, but from the way things looked on the exterior, that wasn't the case. Barry parked right across the street. It was 7:30. No one was in sight, and the sun had just disappeared.

He walked around the corner to Alameda to an ad hoc command center that the police had set up in a bodega. There, he would meet with a guy named Captain Frank, who was in charge of the ten-man police force we were provided. I thought we'd need more, but ten was all we could get.

While he did that, I walked across the street to the front of the warehouse, used my lock pick to get inside, and turned on the lights. The key Hugh gave me fit in the little panel lock that was near the loading door controls. I pushed the button and—*voilà*—the trap section of the floor opened. The opposite edge from the loading dock began to drop, and I could see the rung ladder on the side wall leading to the basement floor. I quickly climbed down and turned on the lights there too. Sure enough, the place contained a printing machine, large skids of paper, a fridge, tables and chairs, even a few cots. The floor section that dropped was now angled such that it was a ramp; machinery or whatever could be rolled up to the ground floor. It was a pretty ingenious setup, I must say, although the place smelled like the locker room at the gym, and with more chemicals added. I couldn't see how anyone could stand working down there for any length of time.

I climbed up the ramp to the ground floor and checked my watch. The next thing I did was open the loading dock door. A cool breeze flooded the warehouse and it felt good. Even though it was December, the weather was still pretty nice. If I'd been in New York, there probably would be snow on the ground!

Paulie and four of his goons arrived right on time. They appeared in the back, on the loading dock, with guns in hand. I raised my arms and said I wasn't armed.

"Where's this guilty Black Stiletto?" he asked.

"Not here yet. She and her accomplice will be here at nine forty-five."

"Nine forty-five? Then what the hell are we here *now* for?"

"It's part of the plan, and if you'll put your guns down, I'll explain it to you."

"I should shoot you now," he said. "My father sure would be happy if I brought him your mask."

"Then you wouldn't be handing over the real killer," I answered. "Put your guns away, please, and I'll tell you the plan. Oh, and you're going to have to move your cars and park somewhere down the street. No one can know you're here."

Paulie nodded at his men and they holstered their weapons. "All right, talk."

So I did.

A little over an hour later, the trapdoor in the floor was back in place, but I kept the loading dock door open. Lights full on. Then I set up the portable boxing ring, the equipment I borrowed from Luis. It was easy. The ropes extended 14 feet on all sides. Not bad. When I was done, the "ring" sat on the front half of the floor, away from the loading dock and the trap section.

Then I sat outside the ring and waited.

Relax. Breathe.

Timing was everything.

Relax. Breathe.

I must have drifted off into a trance of some kind, for the sound of Leo's voice brought me back to reality.

"Maybe we should just shoot her now."

I opened my eyes and there they were, standing on the loading dock. Leo had a gun. Christina was dressed as the Black Stiletto, and she held a pistol too.

"Black Stilettos use knives, Christina," I said. "Put that away."

"Where's my diamond?" Leo asked.

"Come inside." They didn't move. "Look, if you shoot me, you'll never get the diamond, will you? Put those things away and come in." The siblings looked at each other and, finally, he nodded. She tucked her pistol in her belt, while he shoved his in a shoulder holster under his jacket.

"Nuh-uh," I said. "Christina, give Leo your gun to hold."

She grimaced and gave it to him. He stuck it in his waist. Once I felt safe, I opened my backpack and pulled out the Chinese box. I shook it so he'd hear the diamond rattling against the felt interior. "Recognize it, Leo?"

His eyes grew wide. I swear he salivated when he saw it.

"It's going to stay in my backpack until we're done," I said as I replaced the box and zipped up. "I promise to hand it over if Christina wins."

"Or, if you're dead, we'll just take it," Christina said.

They stood right on top of the trapdoor, and I didn't want them there. "Come over here." I pointed to the west wall, and said, "Leo, why don't you stand—or sit on the floor if you want—over there." I indicated the portable boxing ring. "How do you like it? Christina and I can use this space to 'settle our differences.' "

"You expect me to fight you there?" she asked.

"You're the one who accused me of cheating last time. No, Christina, it's going to be fair and square. Hand-to-hand combat. No weapons. Is that all right with you?"

She scoffed. "Whatever. You're dead, bitch. Remember what I told you? I'm going to break your kneecaps. You're going to beg me to shoot you."

I checked my watch. 9:52.

"Let's get started," I said, and then I ducked between the two ropes on one side of the ring and stood in a corner. Christina did the same and faced me from the opposite one.

"Do we have a bell to ring?" Leo asked, and then laughed.

"Shut up, Leo," Christina snapped. "There are no rounds."

"She's right, Leo," I said. "No rounds. We start and we fight until it's done."

And with that, Christina emitted her signature banshee yell and ran toward me. She didn't even wait for someone to say, "One, two, three, go." I must say it was very strange for a person that looked like the Black Stiletto to be attacking me. I thought I was looking in a mirror. My outfit, of course, was made of better material and was constructed more sturdily. Hers consisted of cheap cloth. I think it might have been one of those Halloween costumes that went on sale a year or two ago. She didn't have her long brown hair tucked underneath the mask—it hung down her neck and shoulders. It was a strange look for a Black Stiletto.

I was prepared for her assault. With a *harai-te*—sweeping block—I cleared the space between us by knocking her blows out of the way, and then kept avoiding her attacks with a series of *sukui-uke*—scooping blocks, which catch the punches with my open hand or fist. This threw Christina off balance, allowing me to deliver several *tsuki-te*—hand attacks—that took her by surprise. With regular fists, I struck her upper body and face with a rapid rhythm. It forced her to retreat.

"Get her, Christina!" Leo shouted.

I needed to get her to talk. "Does putting on that costume give you a sense of power, Christina?" I asked her between breaths.

"Enough to send you to hell!" she replied. She came at me again. Once again, I was impressed with her technique, even though it was undisciplined and wildly uneven. She managed to land a blow on the left side of my face, but I reciprocated with an *uraken*—back fist—punch to her chin. I followed that with a standard left jab. My fighting system has always combined elements of boxing, *karate*, and *wushu*. No one fights like me, and it's one of the reasons why I can usually master my opponents.

Christina backed up and danced around the ring. I let her do so—she would tire out quicker. I stayed in place but in a defensive stance, ready to accept whatever offensive she launched next.

"Come on, Christina!" her brother urged.

"Why did you kill Sal Casazza, Christina?" I asked. "What was he to you?"

"I couldn't stand the fat slob," she spat. "And his job should have been Leo's, not that rat Paulie." Then she jumped toward my waist to tackle me—and she succeeded. We fell to the hard floor and rolled. She ended up on top and started punching me repeatedly. I did my best to block her blows, but my right arm was trapped under her left leg. I took the punishment and it hurt, dear diary, the girl was strong. I struggled to break free, but she had me down.

"That's it, Christina! Yeah!" Leo was beside himself.

Then I remembered her broken nose. It hadn't been that long since I had damaged that sensitive area of her face, so I formed an *ippon-ken*—single-point fist—by bending my middle finger so that it protruded beyond the rest of my knuckles to form a striking point—and I aimed for the center of her mask.

Wham. I felt her nose give way again.

She cried out and jerked away, stunned. I used the reprieve to buck her off of me. I got to my feet and she was still reclined on the floor. Blood poured from beneath the bottom front of her mask.

I should have kicked her in the head right then and finished it, but I still needed to get her confession. Instead, I showed some mercy and backed off.

"Come on, Christina, get up!" Leo urged.

"Yeah, Christina, it can't be over this soon," I taunted. "Hey, I want to know something. Why did you blame that Sandstone Casino heist on me? Was that necessary?"

She looked at me and cursed, and I was surprised by how quickly she managed to stand. She wiped the blood off her mouth and flung it toward me. Yuck. "Better you than me," she said.

"Wow, you really did it? I'm impressed."

"So what?" she snapped, and then a glint of steel caught my eye. There was a knife in her hand. I don't know where on her body she'd had it hidden, but she had just improved her odds. She lunged at me fast, blade forward, but my quick reflexes went into play and I sidestepped her.

"Now who's cheating, Christina? No weapons, remember?" I panted.

She answered with a string of expletives as she advanced, swinging the knife back and forth. It was my turn to dance around the ring, unfortunately, on the retreat. Then she got me against the ropes. There was nowhere to go, unless I slipped out of the ring. I was prepared to do that to prevent getting sliced, but I also didn't want to give her the satisfaction of thinking she had the upper hand. So I attempted an unbalanced *mae-geri*—front kick—which merely glanced her swinging arm. No good. She inched forward—the blade would make contact any second. Her mistake, though, was that her swinging motion was predictable—she didn't vary the position of the arc. This allowed me to perform a *kakae-te*—trapping block—which meant I grasped her arm, pulled, and locked it under my own arm, and then let her have it in the nose again with my free fist.

She yelped and dropped the knife. I kicked it out of the ring.

"You're beaten, Christina," I said between my teeth. "Admit it. You killed Maria Kelly, didn't you! *You* stole her diamond!"

"So what! She didn't deserve my brother!" With that, she attacked again, but she was so full of rage, pain, and madness that her blows were all over the place. I blocked most of them, but a few landed on my face and chest. I drew back and performed a perfect *yoko-geri* side kick and slammed my boot into her chest, right in the sternum. I had to be careful I didn't break it. She went down on all fours, the breath knocked out of her. I couldn't help myself—I went around behind her, grabbed the hair streaming down from under the hood, and pulled her head back.

With my face right in hers, I snarled, "I want to hear you say it. You killed Maria!"

Blood covered Christina's mouth and teeth. Her eyes stared into mine through the mask holes, and I swear, dear diary, I'd never glimpsed such hatred in the soul of a person.

The woman actually started to laugh.

"Who do you think killed her, bitch?" she croaked. "Of course I did it. Just like I'm going to kill *you*."

"No," Leo said. "I'm going to do it."

I raised my head and saw that he was pointing his gun at me. With a split-second response, I released Christina and leapt to the side as he pulled the trigger. The gunshot echoed loudly in the empty warehouse. I hit the floor and rolled, but I knew there was no place to take cover. It was what I was afraid would happen—that Leo would simply pull out a weapon and shoot me in the middle of the fight.

But before he could fire again, the rumble of the building's machinery filled the air. The trap section of the floor near the loading dock began to drop. Naturally, it surprised both Leo and Christina.

It's about time! I thought.

Paulie and his goons ran up the floor/ramp from the basement, turned, and pointed weapons at all of us. It was an impressive sight, I must say. They were framed dramatically by the stage-like rectangle of the open loading dock door and the back parking lot beyond it.

"I got you, Kelly, you son of a bitch," Paulie said. "Drop the gun."

Leo was shocked and flustered at first. There were three weapons trained on him. The other one was aimed at me and Christina.

"I heard everything your sister said down below through that speaker system you set up, and we got it on a tape recorder too," Paulie continued. "You and your sister are going to have a talk with my father. Drop the gun and come along with us. Now, Kelly." Then he looked at me, and said, "You too, Stiletto."

That wasn't in the plan. I had no intention of going anywhere with those guys.

Leo kept his handgun trained on me and came up with the best lie he could muster. "Look, Paulie, it's the real Stiletto, we got her, you and me, this was my plan all along, to lure her here so that you could capture her. Christina was lying, Paulie, that bitch was torturing my sister and made her say those things. Let's kill the real Stiletto and move on."

"No, Kelly. Now drop the gun or we start shooting."

"Then shoot." And then Leo did something I *really* didn't expect. I never thought this would happen. Leo *shot* Paulie. Hit him right in the chest. It was a damned good shot. *Immediately*, Paulie's four goons started shooting at Leo! Leo fired back at them as he *ran toward them*. The idiots working for Paulie were lousy shots—they couldn't hit him at all. The racket in the warehouse—the overpowering cacophony of the gunshots echoing in the building—was painful to all of us.

Christina growled like a *tiger*, I swear, and she yelled, "*You* did this!" And she attacked me again. It took my attention off what was happening to Leo. Paulie had fallen down the ramp and rolled into the basement. I was pretty sure he was dead. It seemed to me though that Leo was intentionally running for the open section of the floor.

Several hard power punches in a row brought me back to my opponent, but a particularly vicious blow rattled my head and I found myself falling. I hit the floor hard and for a moment I thought I was going to black out. It was as if I was underwater. For a split second I even thought I'd been shot again!

Then Christina kicked me. Repeatedly. I had to curl into a fetal position and take it because I was too dazed.

I do remember thinking, *Is it ten o'clock yet? Or am I going to die before—*

The police arrived. Two patrol cars with flashing lights and sudden, blaring sirens pulled up behind the warehouse, visible through the loading dock. At the same time, several officers positioned themselves behind the vehicles, guns aimed at the men in the building. Because there were gunshots being fired anyway, the police must have thought they had no choice but to shoot too. Paulie's men turned their attention to the cops and started shooting at them, but I think you know, dear diary, how that turned out. They dropped like rats into the basement. I didn't see Leo, so I assumed he had *jumped* down there when the gunfight began.

The front door also burst open, and four armed officers positioned themselves outside, ready for any attempt of escape.

Christina kept kicking me. I knew I had to stop her before she seriously damaged my kidneys or spine. I struggled for the presence of mind and the amount of strength needed to twist out of my position and use my legs to defend myself. I remembered to *breathe* and then I performed the maneuver. As I rolled onto all fours, I contorted my body so that my rear end pointed at Christina, and then I kicked out—like a *horse*—and hit her really hard on her right kneecap. Oh, my gosh, I heard the snap. Christina screamed bloody murder, and fell to the floor.

By then, the shooting had stopped.

Exhausted and in pain, I stood and looked down at my opponent. She was writhing in agony. "*That's* what a busted knee feels like, *bitch*," I said.

Several cops ran down the ramp, ready to clean up anyone left alive in the basement. Others moved inside around the pit and toward us, weapons aimed.

A senior officer told me to raise my hands. Was he kidding?

"Excuse me?" I asked.

"Get your hands up."

"Why don't you call for an ambulance? This woman is hurt. And her brother, Leo, is down there. He's the one you want! And you'll find a tape recorder down there that has Christina Kelly's confession of the murders of Maria Kelly and Sal Casazza."

I climbed out of the portable ring, ignoring the order.

"Stop, Stiletto, I have orders to arrest you!" the man said to my back.

So I stopped and turned to him. "Aren't we on the same side?"

"Not anymore," he said.

One of the cops from the basement ascended the ramp far enough to address the guy holding a gun to me. "They're all dead, Captain."

I thought, *What?* Had Leo been hit? I could have sworn I'd seen him running *unharmed* toward the floor opening, his gun blazing—cowboy-style—at Paulie's men.

Then we heard the ambulances and possibly more cops. They'd be at the warehouse in less than a minute.

"Let's go, Stiletto. Hands up," the captain ordered.

Dear diary, I did the only thing I could think to do. It was instinct. I bolted toward the loading dock.

"Halt!" I heard him shout behind me.

I ran, built up momentum, and then I performed a broad jump just like I learned to do in track when I was a kid in school. I leaped across the open pit farther, I think, than I've ever jumped before, just as a couple of cops fired their weapons at me. They missed. I hit the angled ramp near its top and immediately scampered over the loading dock. From there, I propelled myself onto the top of one of the police cars, ran across it, and hopped down to the parking lot. Before the police knew what I'd done, I was already running around the side of the building to the street and toward Barry's Buick, which was still parked where he'd left it. Thank goodness he was behind the wheel. He pulled out of the space, I got in the passenger seat, and we took off. The cops didn't chase us.

"They tried to arrest me!" I said.

"I know, and I'm sorry. Captain Frank let me know before they went in. McKesson wanted you arrested along with the others. I didn't know, Judy, and I didn't know how I could warn you."

"I believe you, but geez!" I looked back. "Why aren't they after us?"

"Well, I think the captain is an admirer of yours. He said he had to make the attempt to arrest you, but that if you got away, he wouldn't pursue."

"They know *you* though. What if they come to your house?"

"Our house, you mean?"

"Yeah," I answered.

"They won't."

"What makes you so sure?"

He had successfully driven out of the Wholesale District, and we were now heading north to canyon land. Ignoring my question, he looked at me, and asked, "Judy, are you hurt?"

"I'm sure I'll have bruises everywhere and my back sure took a pounding. I'll probably pee blood."

"Don't say that. Do you think you need a doctor? Should I call Abernathy?"

"No. Let's go home. I want to see Martin."

So, we did, but I pulled off my bloody outfit in the garage before going into the house. Barry went inside to pay Rosa and escort her to his car so he could take her home without her seeing me. After they left, I went in the house and found Martin sound asleep in his crib. He looked so cute and happy and content.

I took a quick shower and then dressed in my gym clothing because I was too electrified to go to sleep. I wanted to wait for Barry to return so we could talk about everything that happened. My outfit was still in the garage, so I went out to retrieve it. Back inside, I washed the dried blood off the leather and laid everything out on the bed in mine and Martin's room. Then I sat with Martin. A familiar odor drifted toward me, so I got up to change Martin's diaper. Sure enough, he'd made a bit of a mess. I cleaned up his bottom and left him in the crib with no pants on as I went to put the dirty diaper in a hamper we keep out back, ready for laundry. Then I heard the tires of Barry's car crunch the gravel in front of the cabin. The front door opened and he called, "Judy? Someone's coming. A car followed me up the hill."

I joined Barry and stood in the open doorway with him. Two blinding headlights were approaching, but that's all I could see. I didn't know whether to hide, to quickly dress as the Black Stiletto, or what.

"Stay here and close the door," Barry said as he started walking across the gravel to meet the car as it approached. I did as I was told and went to look out the window—and as soon as I did, I saw that it was Leo's Karmann Ghia that had pulled up behind Barry's car.

In horror, I watched Leo get out of the car, aim his gun, and shoot Barry, right in front of our house.

41
Leo
THE PAST

I reacted the only way I knew how.

The goddamned bitch set a trap for Christina and me. I knew she was planning something fishy, but I had to go through with it and see what the hell was going on. I wanted my diamond back. All that teasing the Stiletto did on the phone—it turned out that was all for show. There was no way she was actually going to *sleep* with me! How could I have been so stupid as to fall for her tricks? I was actually beginning to trust her.

As soon as Paulie and his crew opened the trapdoor and came up from the basement, I knew I was in deep shit. He had heard everything my loud-mouthed sister said during the fight. Me and my ingenious speaker system.

So I did what I had to do. I killed Paulie and made a run for it. It was a miracle that Paulie's crew didn't hit me when they shot at me. I leaped into the pit and fell hard on the basement floor. Hurt my ankle, but it wasn't terrible. I quickly went to the west wall, flicked the switch behind the refrigerator, and the panel I installed opened to reveal the tunnel that was an underground connection to the building next door. Once I was inside the passage, I shut the panel, and groped my way in the dark to the staircase at the other end.

Kelly Warehousing owned that building too. I leased it to a shipping firm, and they couldn't care less if there was a tunnel that led to A-1 Outriggers. I'd never used it before. Originally I thought it might come in handy someday in case any of my *men* had to escape quickly. It's ironic that it's *me* that had to use it.

It was a good thing Christina and I took separate cars. Her Corvette was stuck in the back of the warehouse. I parked my Karmann Ghia behind the building next door. It was a safety precaution, and I was glad I did it.

Now Christina was in the hands of the cops and probably at the hospital. *Damn! Damn! Damn!* My sister was probably going to die. Once Vince DeAngelo found out it was Christina who killed his daughter, her life won't be worth a penny. She wouldn't even be safe in prison. DeAngelo would find a way to get to her.

The front of A-1 Outriggers was visible through a window. I hid in the building and watched what was going on next door. The cops and ambulances arrived and blocked a good part of the street—and then I saw the Black Stiletto run out of the parking lot. There was a Buick Electra across the street—it pulled out of a space, and she got in the passenger seat.

Without thinking, I ran outside and got into my car. I drove out the alley and ended up on Alameda. Which way did the Buick go? Heads or tails? I gambled and went north. I didn't want to speed and get stopped, but I pushed the gas pedal as much as I could risk.

Unbelievable. I caught up with the Buick as it veered toward Hollywood. Maybe my luck had changed.

All I could think about was how I was going to make the Black Stiletto pay for what she'd done. Hell, she beat up my sister and probably destroyed her kneecap. She ruined my counterfeiting business and now all my stuff would be confiscated. The cops would learn I was behind the operation and an accessory to Maria's killing. But worst of all, DeAngelo was going to know I betrayed him.

I was a dead man. Nothing else mattered. The least I could do was get revenge on the woman who caused it all. So I followed the Buick up into North Hollywood, and finally onto Laurel Canyon Boulevard. They headed into the Hollywood Hills. It figured that the Black Stiletto lived like a hermit on a mountain. The area was starting to become an enclave for movie stars, so it wouldn't be the boondocks much longer.

A traffic light turned red before I could cross an intersection, and the Buick went on. I would have run the light, but a cop car was behind me. Damn. I waited. Eventually it turned green and I moved on. I had to keep my speed down because the goddamned policeman kept tailing me. Did he have my license number and description of the car? Were the cops looking for me? The Buick disappeared around bends and curves up ahead. At Kirkwood, the cop thankfully pulled off the road and into the parking lot of a country store. I went on and then floored it. The road was treacherous, winding up and down. The Buick was nowhere in sight. There were other dirt roads leading off Laurel Canyon Boulevard here and there—the Buick could have pulled off onto one of them.

Where the hell did it go?

I started punching the steering wheel and cursing as loud as my throat could take it. I was so mad and crazed and scared. I wasn't thinking rationally. Believe it or not, I considered taking my Browning Hi Power semiautomatic and pointing it at my temple. One squeeze of the trigger and all my troubles would be over. The cops wouldn't get me, and I'd deny DeAngelo the pleasure of taking me out. I'd belong to God—or the Devil.

The only problem with that scenario was that I'd be dead, and I was rather fond of being alive.

I had to get out of town. No question about it. I had to leave LA and go someplace where DeAngelo and his tentacles couldn't reach me.

But first I had a score to settle.

If I could only find that goddamned Buick!

After ten minutes of aimless driving, I turned around and went back. Eyeing the various dirt-road turnoffs, I considered trying them, one by one, to see where they led. What the hell. I turned right into one and followed it up a steep hill. My headlights were the only thing that illuminated the dangerous road. When I got to the top of the cliff, there was a fancy house with a gate around it. Looked like a movie star's place. I didn't see the Buick. Wrong road.

I went back to Laurel Canyon Boulevard. I was so frustrated and angry that tears were streaming down my face. I didn't know what to do. Go home? Maybe I'd have time to collect some things before getting the hell out of Dodge. It would take a few hours before DeAngelo heard about what happened at the warehouse.

Geez, first his daughter, and then his son. If DeAngelo caught me, I was in for a world of pain.

Forget the Black Stiletto. Pretend I never had that goddamned diamond. Get out of town *now*. There, I made the decision.

As I passed Kingwood and the store, I saw that the patrol car was gone. A pair of headlights was behind me and I was afraid they might belong to the police vehicle, so I kept my speed down. Eventually, though, the car passed me—and wouldn't you know it?

It was the Buick!

There was a God!

I let it get ahead of me for a ways, and then I stayed on its tail. The car didn't go too far before turning onto a road where there were a few houses. It stopped in front of a small place. I pulled over, cut my lights, and watched. The Buick was maybe forty feet away.

A man was at the wheel. It was too dark, he was too far away, and it was a different car, but I thought he might be the guy that picked up the Stiletto in front of my home after I shot her. It was difficult to say for sure. However, the woman who got out of the passenger side and started walking up to the house was a small Mexican woman! *What?*

Was I mistaken? Did I have the wrong car?

The woman waved at the driver and went inside the house. The Buick pulled away, turned around, and headed back to Laurel Canyon.

Just to make sure, I followed it. This time, I stayed close. I didn't care if the driver knew I was behind him. I wasn't going to let it out of my sight.

He turned off onto one of the dirt roads that wound up a mountain. Once again, it was a perilous route with no illumination and no safety guardrails. Going more than thirty miles an hour would have been extremely hazardous.

It took maybe ten minutes, but eventually we made it to the top. The Buick stopped in front of a small, quaint cabin. I thought I could see a second structure—a shed or garage—around the side and in the back.

I pulled up and stopped, but kept my headlights aimed at the front of the house so I could see. The guy got out of the Buick—and I was *sure* it was the same guy that helped the Stiletto that night at my house. Bingo! He went to the door and opened it. I got out of the car with my Browning in hand. The man stepped inside the cabin for a moment, and then he appeared with a woman. She stood beside him in the doorway, but she wasn't wearing a Black Stiletto costume. She looked familiar. The man started walking toward me. I think he asked, "Can I help you?" but I'm not so sure.

I pointed the gun and fired. He went down.

The woman shrieked and ran to him. I walked forward and then stopped cold when I saw her face up close.

No.

It couldn't be.

She was Judy. Judy Cooper. My Judy.

Oh my God.

Judy was the Black Stiletto!

42
Gina
THE PRESENT

Right on cue, my cell phone rang. Even though I was in shock, I grabbed it from my purse and glanced at the screen. I didn't recognize the number, but it was a Texas area code.

"H-hello?"

It was a woman's voice. Older. Stern. Husky and deep. "You've probably discovered the surprise we left at your hotel room. Am I right?"

My body trembled and I couldn't speak evenly. "Who is this?" I whispered.

"I'm Mrs. Ricky Bartlett. And I have your costume."

"What do you want?"

"I'm inviting you to come and get it. You know where the Bartlett Ranch is?"

"Yes."

"I'll be expecting you within the hour. Hurry up, it's nearly my bedtime."

Then she hung up.

Wow. I was shaking.

The first thing I did was call Mr. McCambridge. No answer. Got his voice mail, so I asked him to call me back as soon as he could. Then I phoned Dad. *Again*, no answer. He was probably preoccupied with Grandma. It was too early for him to be in bed, unless he was exhausted from being a caregiver.

At least Josh answered his cell when I called *him*.

"Hey, honey. Have you left Texas yet?" he asked, way too cheerily for the moment.

"No. Listen, you know how you've always told me to take risks with my ability and test myself?"

"Yeah?"

"I'm about to do just that."

Pause. "Gina, what's going on?"

"I can't tell you yet."

Pause. "I also told you that you shouldn't take those risks unless I'm there too."

"I can handle it."

"Gina, not only am I your trainer and Krav Maga instructor, I'm your boyfriend. I don't want you to do something foolish and get hurt."

I prickled a little at that. "You think I would do something foolish?"

"No, I didn't mean it that way. You know what I mean."

"I don't have time to argue with you, Josh, I have to go. Just tell Mr. Page that I'm going to prove I'm the right girl for the job."

"Gina—"

"I'll call you later. Wish me luck."

"Gina!"

"I love you. Bye!"

Then I hung up and ignored his return call.

The ranch was located about fifteen minutes southwest out of Odessa, on the highway toward a town called Monahans. It wasn't far from a state park that consisted of nothing but sand dunes. I'd read someplace that it was where Odessans went when they wanted to go to the "beach," except there was no water. Weird.

My GPS directed me to the correct exit, for there was no

signage marking the ranch's location. I drove over a cattle guard
past barbed-wire fencing that stretched parallel to the highway for
what seemed like miles. Then it was a dirt road that led to another
big metal gate and barbed-wire fence. My headlights revealed an
old, faded, curved wooden sign—"Bartlett Ranch," it proclaimed,
although the paint on the entire right side had worn off so that it
read, "Bartle—Ranc" A dark SUV was parked on the other side
of the gate; but as soon as I pulled up, a man got out of it and
waved at me.

Ralph McCambridge.

I lowered my window. "I didn't expect to find you here, Mr.
McCambridge," I said, trying not to let my nervousness show.

"Follow me, Miss Talbot," he said. "When the gate opens just
come on through. Wait for me to drive ahead of you. Otherwise
you might get hurt."

Whoa. Whatever friendliness he had at our Starbucks meeting
was completely missing. My headlights illuminated him as he got
back in his SUV and drove a few feet forward. The gate automatically opened, so I went through and tailed him along a winding
dirt road until we came to a large, dark structure. I wished it was
daylight so I could see it better. There were other small buildings
on the property as well; one was a barn shape.

I pulled my rental onto a paved area near the front of the house,
beside McCambridge's SUV and a pickup truck. He stood next to his
vehicle and waited for me to get out of the car. It was pretty dark.
A few outdoor lamps illuminated a walkway to the front door, and
there was some glow emanating from the windows. Otherwise, the
stars and moon in the clear night sky provided the only glimmer of
light on the flat, black landscape. It was pretty scary.

"What's going on, Mr. McCambridge?" I asked him.

"Mrs. B. wants to talk to you."

"Do you work for her?"

"For sixteen years now."

"So you were working for her while we talked at the coffee shop?"

"Nah, that was my morning off." I could detect a wicked grin in the moonlight.

"Was it you that broke into my hotel room?"

He shrugged. "I just follow orders, Miss Talbot. Mrs. B. pays me a lot better than the county did when I was sheriff. Now, if you would, please turn around and place your hands on the back of your vehicle. I have to frisk you."

"*What?*"

"Please." It was a command, not a request. There wasn't much I could do about it. I did as I was told.

I was wearing jeans, a t-shirt, and tennis shoes. Bra and panties underneath. "I don't have any weapons, if that's what you're thinking," I said. I'd been frisked twice before in New York, but then there had been no lingering pressure on my breasts and between my legs. Old pervert.

"Let's go," he said, after he'd had his fill—or *feel*, I should say.

We moved up the bricked path to the door. He opened it, and as soon as we were inside, the pungent sweet smell of scented candles overwhelmed me. In fact, the hallway leading to the rest of the house was lined with lit votives. There must have been twenty.

"What's with the candles?" I asked.

"Mrs. B. likes candles," McCambridge answered. He said it in a way that indicated he wasn't too fond of the smell either. "Just go on into the parlor, straight ahead."

The man stayed behind me as I entered a large room that was also illuminated by candlelight. Tall candlesticks on wrought iron floor stands dominated the space, and I felt like I was in some kind of church. An archway, decorated with drapes on both sides, led to other parts of the house. The furniture was old and looked like it came out of an old western TV show. Some pieces were covered in sheets. A gigantic stuffed longhorn steer's head overlooked the room from a wall. The effect was terribly bizarre. It might have been a leftover set from *The Texas Chainsaw Massacre*.

"I'm going to have to ask you for your cell phone," McCambridge said.

"I don't think so," I answered with as much indignation as I could.

"You don't have a choice, young lady." He held out his hand. "Don't make me take it from you."

Geez. I reached in my purse, grabbed the phone, and handed it over. He opened the back, removed the battery, pocketed it, and gave the device back to me. Did he think I was going to record a conversation? "I'll give it back when you leave," he said. "Now have a seat. Mrs. B. will be with you in a minute. Can I get you something to drink?"

"No, thanks." He left me alone, so I sat in a hard, oak chair. I was extremely nervous, but I tried to concentrate on everything I'd learned from Josh. If push came to shove, I knew I could fight my way out of the place. I didn't care if McCambridge was bigger and stronger than me. I could take him. As for Mrs. B—

She was a fairly tall and very thin woman with long, white hair and dressed in a simple black housedress. She walked into the room through the archway. She used a cane and moved unsteadily, as if her legs were made of toothpicks and she had to be extremely careful. In her other hand was a shotgun. McCambridge had said she was seventy-nine years old, and she looked it; and yet from peering into her cold, dark eyes, I detected that there was a malevolence deep within her that was as ancient as time.

"So this is the Black Stiletto's granddaughter," she said in the same husky voice I'd heard on the phone. I was frozen in my chair and couldn't move or speak. "I suppose you resemble her. You see, I knew your grandmother, and she knew me, a long time ago, when my name was Christina Kelly."

43
Judy's Diary
1962

I ran to Barry after screaming his name. He fell on the gravel right in front of his car. Leo stood next to his Karmann Ghia, gun in hand and pointed at me. I knelt to examine Barry—he was still alive, his eyes exhibiting distress. I could tell he wasn't going to make it in time for an ambulance to arrive all the way out there. Even with Leo pointing a gun at me, I considered picking Barry up, running to my car, and attempting to take him to the hospital myself.

"Judy?" Leo's voice was full of shock and surprise and anger.

"We have to get him to the hospital," I said, not necessarily to Leo.

"*You're* the Black Stiletto," he said, walking nearer. "Of course, it all makes sense now. Why didn't I see it? I'm a goddamned idiot."

I said to Barry, "Hang in there, I'm taking you—" But Barry grabbed my arm and managed to shake his head.

"Too late," he whispered. "Skipper—he'll help you."

"Barry—"

"I love you."

Those were his last words, dear diary. I heard and felt the breath go out of him. His eyes remained open, so I closed them. I wanted to cry. I wanted to scream to the heavens. But Leo Kelly was standing in front of me with a gun aimed at my head, still muttering about what a lying, deceitful girl I was.

"And I want my goddamned diamond back," he said. "*Now,* Judy!"

I looked up at him and could barely control my venom. "Leo Kelly, you are a monster."

Then he remembered. "Wait! Where's my son?"

It felt as if I was moving in slow motion as I stood. My entire consciousness focused on that horrible man, a murderer, a cheat, a thief, and God knows what else. He backed up a little, the gun still aimed at me. My original plan of him being arrested along with his sister had gone out the window, so I had to take care of him myself. The father of my child.

"Leo, you will never see him." I began walking toward Leo.

"Stay back, Judy. Is he inside? I'm going to kill you for what you've done, Judy, I swear!" He raised the gun slightly higher. My extremely agitated senses anticipated his squeezing the trigger, and that's when I used the next split second to leap forward and perform a body block. The impact was enough to throw off his aim when his finger eventually pulled the trigger. The round went wildly off to his right and the sound of the gunshot was lost in the night sky. He didn't drop the weapon, though, so I stepped back before he could recover, and I delivered a *mae-geri*—front kick—to his arm. The pistol went flying into the darkness, out of the wash of the headlight beams.

Leo saw the punch coming. His eyes grew wide and his mouth formed that *oh* expression that forms on anyone who knows they're about to get hit in the face. I let him have it, and he fell to the ground and lay on his back, his body dramatically lit by the car beams.

I couldn't kill him, of course. I sure wanted to, but I knew I couldn't. I had to call the police. But then a thousand scenarios went through my head. The time had come for me to disappear. I couldn't be discovered at Barry's house; my Stiletto identity would be compromised. So I decided to tie up Leo, pack to leave, and *then* call the cops. When they were on their way, I'd take Martin in my car somewhere. I'd have to act quickly.

So I turned around and went back in the house. Martin was crying.

I went in the room to get my rope off the Stiletto belt. Martin's pacifier had fallen out of the crib, so I picked it up and stuck it in his mouth. He immediately quieted, wiggling in the crib without a diaper on. That could wait.

I went back outside with the rope and my heart stopped for a second. The headlights still illuminated Barry's body, but Leo was gone.

"Leo!" I snapped. "Where are you?" I dropped the rope and rushed to the area where his pistol had flung, but I didn't see it. He hadn't gone in the front door, so I figured he was around the side of the house. I didn't care if he might be armed, I had to find him. I hurried around the cabin all the way to the back, but he wasn't there.

The back door was open.

Frantic, I bolted inside and went straight to the bedroom.

Leo stood by the crib, holding Martin against his chest with one arm, and pointing the pistol at the baby's head with his other hand. The poor boy was frightened and crying.

"Put him down, Leo!"

"Give me the diamond or I'll shoot him!"

"Leo, I swear!"

It's kind of funny now when I think of it, but Martin saved the day. *He started peeing on Leo!* As soon as Leo felt the warm liquid penetrating his shirt, he reacted as if he was holding a poisonous snake. He *threw* Martin at me! Oh my God, if I hadn't caught him… but I did. I snatched him in midair, and a stream of urine was still blasting out of his little penis.

"Goddamn you!" Leo shouted. He pointed the gun at me and I *knew* he was going to shoot. But I was within kicking distance, and I resorted to the old trick Soichiro taught me—*there are no rules in a real fight.*

I kicked Leo in the groin.

The noise he made was more of an enraged *gasp* than a cry of pain, but the maneuver worked. He released the weapon and fell to his knees. His hands went to his crotch and his face grimaced in agony. Leo then rolled to the floor and writhed while I placed Martin back in the crib. He had stopped crying and was actually smiling at me. "Good job!" I whispered to him, ha ha, and I stuck the pacifier in his mouth. Then I turned to Leo and said, "I have to tie you up now." But darn it, I'd dropped the rope outside in front. Just like the *first* time I left Leo alone and prostrate, I really thought he'd be down for the amount of time it would take me to run and fetch it. So I picked up his pistol and left the room. It took me maybe all of ten seconds, but as I headed back, I saw Leo stagger out the back door. Alarmed, I quickly checked the crib—Martin was there and seemingly happy. I took an extra two seconds to grab the flashlight from my belt on the bed.

We had an outdoor bulb—not very strong—in back of the cabin, where the grill and patio furniture sat. I flicked the light on and looked out the door. No sign of Leo, of course. I had his gun in my hand, so I opened a drawer in the kitchen and placed the weapon in there. I didn't want to take the chance of him getting hold of it again. Since the combat was down to hand-to-hand, I felt more comfortable without it.

I stood in the open door, listened, and looked. The naked bulb wasn't much help, but I could see all the way to the cliff, near where the steps to the target range were. I carefully stepped outside, my senses on red alert for any movement or sound. Had he gone back to his car to flee? I rejected that notion—Leo was far too desperate for that diamond, and he wanted to kill me and Martin just to be an evil bastard. He was out in the darkness somewhere, and he wanted me to come find him. Fine.

The flashlight helped, especially on the sides of the house. I didn't find him. His car was still in front with the beams on. Then I went through the front door, veered by the bedroom, and checked that Martin was still in the crib. I thought Leo might try to snatch him again by luring me outside. Best to hide Martin. I picked him up, with pacifier but still no jammy bottoms, and took him into the kitchen. Looking back, I can't believe I did this, it was insane, but at the time I was frantic and angry; I wanted to hurt that man, but I was also in shock and saddened by what I'd seen happen to Barry right in front of me. We had a pot in the pantry that was big enough for a Thanksgiving turkey. It was a terrible thing to do, but it was necessary. I placed Martin in the pot and put the lid on it. He started wailing, and I don't blame him. I put the pot back in the pantry, and shut the door, and *then* realized he might not be able to breathe. So I reached in and reset the lid askew, allowing air inside. I told myself it was only temporary and I'd be right back. If anything, the ruse would delay Leo long enough for me to catch him in the act of looking for the baby. Forgive me, Martin!

Time was crucial, so I rushed out the back with the flashlight on. I hadn't checked the garage before, so I did. My car was safe and sound and he hadn't punctured the tires. No sign of Leo.

Then I went out toward the cliff. I swung the beam of my light back and forth. I gazed down at the target range. The figures on the targets looked very creepy at night. I turned to go and—

Wham—Leo slammed into me. I didn't sense him coming. I was too emotionally frazzled, I think. He had a big rock in his hand and tried to pummel me with it. We wrestled on our feet for several seconds. For a man who'd recently been kicked in the balls, he was showing a tremendous amount of strength. Then I recalled him telling me that he'd been something of a street fighter growing up. Despite his small stature, he could defend himself. I dropped the flashlight and employed *karate* blocks to keep the rock from connecting, although he managed to get through twice and bash my shoulder. I wasn't wearing my leather jacket, so it really hurt. It was also strange being the Black Stiletto without my outfit or mask on.

A *kake-te*—hooking block—made him drop the stone. I followed it with a *seiken* attack, in which I let him have it with my fists. He held up, though, and he kept pushing me backward with his own offensive maneuvers. We whaled on each other, dear diary, fighting in the dim light next to a precarious drop into a canyon. I realized the man wanted to push me off the cliff.

He managed to pick up the rock again and come at me while swinging it with both hands. It's much more difficult to block that kind of an attack, and I tried several *uke-te*—hand blocks—all the while unwillingly inching back toward the brink. Leo was getting wilder and increasingly reckless with the swinging, which made him more dangerous. I couldn't get an opening to attack. Backing up a little more, my heel felt the edge of the cliff. Then I had an idea. I stood tall and said, "Hit me, Leo!" He swung with all his might from his right to left—and as he did so I quickly ducked under his swinging arms and dived past his side. I never touched him, but the momentum of the swing and not hitting its target, combined with his weight, caused Leo to soar forward and fall into the abyss. He yelled and I heard an ugly thump some ways below. I grabbed my flashlight and pointed it down there, but I didn't see him. He had to be dead, I thought. I took a few more seconds pointing the light into the canyon.

"Leo?" I called.

Silence.

Dear diary, I think Leo Kelly is dead.

It didn't mean I could relax. The plan was still in effect. The first thing I did was rescue poor Martin, who was bawling inside that awful pot. I held him to me, and as motherly as I could, I gave him kisses and loving. "There, there, Mommy's here," I kept saying. Finally, he quieted down. I put a diaper on him and fed him a bottle of Similac. Then I started packing. All the while I kept thinking about Barry's body lying in front of the house, but it was best if the police found him that way.

There was very little money left. I had a little over six hundred dollars. That wouldn't go far, but I had the diamond.

I loaded everything I owned into my Futura. I even got my records and record player in. The crib wouldn't fit, though. Martin would stay in the baby seat I'd bought for the car. It's a bucket-like thing that hooks over the front seat and has a toy steering wheel on it. Martin enjoys riding in it. Someday they're going to have to invent car seats for babies that are much more protective.

The next to last thing I did at the cabin was phone the police. I told them it was the Black Stiletto and reported that Leo Kelly had shot Barry Gorman and that Leo's body was somewhere down in the canyon. Perhaps they'd have better luck looking for it in daylight. I gave them Barry's address and hung up. The last thing I did was remove Leo's gun from the drawer and place it outside near Barry's body.

I put Martin in the car seat, backed out of the garage, and drove down the mountain. Passing the cops as they came up the road was not desirable, so I may have gone a little too fast—but I made it to the bottom and found my way to Laurel Canyon Boulevard.

The only place I could go was Odessa, Texas. That's where Skipper Gorman lives. Barry told me to go to him for help, and besides, Skipper would want to know about his brother getting killed and he was the only one who could fence the diamond.

I stopped at a 24-hour gas station and filled up. Inside I bought some road maps, food, and water to take on the trip. Once I was set, dear diary, I drove out of Los Angeles, probably never to return. We hit Arizona around the time the sun came up. I was dead tired and way too much in shock from what had happened at the house to be driving so long. Outside of Phoenix, I decided to stop at the Desert Inn.

And here we are. Mother and child.

Fugitives.

44
Judy's Diary
1962

DECEMBER 4, 1962

Martin and I are in Hobbs, New Mexico. I've taken my time driving across the country. We've made several stops along the way. I want to make sure we're not being followed. I don't know if DeAngelo's people would know who I am, but just in case—it's best to be careful.

So far we've been in places like Safford, Arizona, and in New Mexico—Las Cruces, Alamogordo, and Artesia. I decided to kill a day in Artesia because I was so weak and exhausted. Caring for Martin, grieving for Barry, and being not just a little traumatized by the possibility that I killed the father of my son, has made a tough couple of days for me. Now, though, I don't know for sure if Leo is dead.

The *Los Angeles Times* had news yesterday. The Black Stiletto was credited in busting a counterfeit racket in the Wholesale District. Paulie DeAngelo, son of reputed mobster, Vincent, was found dead at the scene, along with several other gangsters. Police Captain Brad Frank praised the Stiletto for her help in solving the case. Apparently there were some other big arrests in connection with the operation, and the cops expected more. The police were "still looking" for Leo Kelly, who was said to be the mastermind behind the business.

He was wanted for questioning and was a suspect for more serious crimes. That makes me nervous. Why didn't they find him in the canyon? Did he survive? Is he looking for me? Christina was under arrest on a number of charges—including the murders of Maria Kelly and Sal Casazza. She's currently in the hospital, under police guard. Vince DeAngelo was arrested in Las Vegas, and I read this morning that he's been indicted and faces racketeering charges, counterfeiting, and illegal arms sales. He's out on bail, but I doubt the judges and lawyers he had in his pocket are going to do him much good now. The FBI is building a big case against him that spreads beyond California. Good. Apparently, all that work Barry and I did is now paying off.

There was nothing in the paper about Barry, though. I have to assume the police made it to his house and found him. And what happened to Leo? Maybe in a day or two I'll know more. By then I should be in Odessa. Skipper might have heard something. He's Barry's next-of-kin, so I imagine the cops would contact him.

Martin seems to be taking the road trip in stride. Dealing with dirty diapers on a road trip is a bit challenging. I bought a plastic pail with a tight lid that I keep them in until I can get to a Laundromat. As long as he has his pacifier, gets his diapers changed, and is fed his bottle when he wants it, he's pretty happy. I bought him a little springy toy that fastens to his car seat. It has a bunny rabbit on it, and he can bounce it up and down and knock it back and forth. He laughs when he plays with it, and that's music to my ears.

Tomorrow I imagine we'll be in my old hometown.

And that's going to be very strange.

DECEMBER 6, 1962

A lot has happened in two days. First of all, Martin and I are in Odessa! We're staying at the Sahara Motel on 2nd Street. It's nice enough. These types of motels are all the same.

From Hobbs I drove into Texas and went through Seminole,

Andrews, and, finally, hit Odessa yesterday morning. Coming in on Andrews Highway didn't produce any possibilities for places to stay. I kept going until I got to 2nd Street, downtown. I remembered this area was close to Whitaker and 5th St., where I grew up with my mom and two brothers. That house doesn't exist anymore. I learned that during my last trip to Odessa in 1958. I want to see my brothers. Frankie worked at a hardware store on 8th Street the last time I was in town. John was in the army. I wonder if he still is.

Odessa doesn't look like it's changed much. Downtown is the same. Colored Town is still south of the railroad tracks. The air smells like petroleum. I saw a bunch of oil wells on the highway driving in, so I guess that's still the big business in West Texas. The men I've seen dress like cowboys or oil field roughnecks, and the women just look like small-town girls. It feels like it's still the 1950s here. I suppose it takes a while for a town like Odessa to catch up with the big cities, if it ever does.

The Sahara Motel appeared to be the most inviting of the joints on 2nd—it has a colorful sign with a palm tree on it, and I guess that reminds me a little of the good things that were in LA. After a wonderful bath, I fed Martin and looked in the phone book for Frankie. I found one Frank Cooper on Beechwood Street, but I didn't call him. Not yet. I have to prepare myself mentally and emotionally for that reunion. There were several John Coopers, so I don't know which one is my brother, if any of them are. Then I looked up Skipper Gorman. There were several Gormans, but no "Skipper." I guess Skipper is a nickname. I don't think Barry ever told me Skipper's real name. Then I remembered that Skipper is some kind of investment banker. Finally, I found a "Gorman Financial Services" in the yellow pages. The office is downtown. I picked up the phone and called. When a man answered, I said, "Hello, I'm looking for Skipper Gorman."

"You found him. How can I help you?"

"Uh, my name is Judy C—Talbot." Being back in Odessa almost made me forget I'd changed my name! "I knew your brother Barry in LA."

"Judy! My God, I've been expecting you to call, but I had no idea if you would or not."

"You know who I am?"

"Barry told me all about you, dear. Are you all right? Where are you?"

"I'm fine. I'm in a motel in town. My…me and my son."

"That's right, Barry said you have a baby boy. How is he?"

"Good. Listen—do you . . . do you know about Barry?"

"Yeah, I do." His voice dropped in pitch. "I've been talking to the police in LA. They haven't caught the guy who did it."

"Leo Kelly?"

"Apparently, he's in hiding or on the run."

So he's still alive, dear diary. My heart sank when I heard him say that.

"Listen, can we meet?" I asked.

"Absolutely. Like I said, I've been hoping I'd hear from you. We have a lot to talk about. And don't worry—any friend of Barry's is a friend of mine. You can trust me."

"I believe it." I confirmed his office address, and said I'd be there soon.

Skipper's office is on Texas Avenue, near the Ector, a movie theater I remember going to when I was little. I saw Walt Disney's *Peter Pan* there, among other things. Down the block is what looks like a fairly new movie theater, the Scott. It wasn't there the last time I was in Odessa. Gorman Financial is its own little building that looks like a house, so I parked in front and carried Martin inside.

I'd forgotten that Skipper is in a wheelchair. I remember now that Barry said he'd been shot by Vince DeAngelo. I gathered by the layout of the little building that Skipper lived there as well. Barry also said his brother was four years younger than him, but Skipper appears older. He's heavier, for one thing, and his face has a weathered look that Barry didn't have. I can see the resemblance, though, especially in the eyes and mouth. My good-guy, bad-guy instinct kicked in, and at first I wasn't sure about him. He smiled and greeted me nicely, but there wasn't much warmth. I didn't get any danger signals though. Perhaps he was grieving for his brother. Now that I've known him for a day, I think he just has a harder edge than Barry.

I put Martin on the carpeted floor to play. He's not crawling yet, he just wiggles around on his tummy. Skipper looked around for an old set of toy blocks that he said his kids used to own, but he found a rattle that looked like it had seen better days. I washed it off real good and let Martin have it. That thrilled him! I asked Skipper about his family, and he said he hasn't seen them for years. He's divorced, and his ex-wife and two kids—now in their teens—live in Florida. Maybe that's where a lot of the sadness I detect in Skipper comes from.

He made coffee—I offered to do it, but he wouldn't let me—and we sat and talked. "How much did Barry tell you about me?" I asked.

"Enough to know you're in trouble, that you need help disappearing, and you have a valuable diamond you want to fence," he said. He leaned forward and spoke softly. "I also think I know who you are."

That surprised me. "What do you mean?" I asked.

"You're the Black Stiletto." He waited for a reaction. "Aren't you?"

"How do you know that?"

"Educated guess? I knew Barry was working with the Black Stiletto. And I knew a woman named Judy Talbot lived with him and that he was madly in love with her. I put two and two together."

That made me blush, and it also saddened me.

"Can you keep a secret?" I asked him.

"Yes."

I looked him in the eyes and detected no avarice, no hidden agenda, and no deceit. "Okay. You're right, I'm the Stiletto," I said with a sigh and a smile.

He smiled and then a spark of joy appeared in his face. He held out his hand and said, "Then I'm really happy to meet you. You're a very courageous young woman. You're very pretty too."

I shook his hand and blushed again. "No wonder my brother loved you."

"Thank you. I . . . I loved him too. He was very good to me."

"Can you tell me what happened?"

So I told him the whole story, dear diary. I related how I met Barry at Boardner's and how we became partners. I outlined our battles against DeAngelo, Casazza, and Leo and Christina Kelly. And I explained as best I could about what happened to Barry at his house.

Skipper nodded. "That fills in some gaps in the tale the police told me," he said. "At first I was going to fly out there and bring his body back here to bury. Then I decided to just have him cremated there. I didn't think I could bear to see him. They're going to send me the ashes. I hope you understand." He looked away, and tears welled in his eyes.

"I do." I put a hand on his for a moment.

"You know, the cops didn't find Leo."

"That's what I've read. Do you know anything?"

He shook his head. "I have a few contacts in the LA area, and I know some people here that aren't exactly on the right side of the law. I've got inquiries out. Would Leo have any reason to suspect that you're here?"

"Not that I know of. He didn't even know about Barry until the other night."

Skipper nodded again. "Well, hopefully we'll know about it if he shows up. I have—friends—here that he probably knows."

"Would that be Ricky Bartlett?" I asked.

He shot me a look. "Do you know Ricky?"

"Never met him, but I've seen him. I know who he is."

"Very powerful man in this town."

"You're friends?"

"I wouldn't call us friends. We know each other. I've done some business for him. Financial business. We won't talk about that."

I waved him off. "I know all about Barry's past. And yours. I understand."

He shook his head. "Then you know why I'm glad Vincent DeAngelo is in trouble. They better convict that son of a bitch—excuse my language, I'm sorry—"

"That's okay, I totally agree with you!"

Skipper laughed slightly. "I just hope the evidence is strong enough to nail him."

"I hope so too."

We talked some more about Barry and our adventures in LA. Skipper told me about Odessa and how dull it is. I mentioned my brothers. Skipper doesn't know them, but he offered to see if he could find them. I said I think I knew where Frankie was, and as soon as I got up the nerve, I was going to call him.

Then we spoke about my plans for the future. I said I was short on money and that I needed to sell the diamond as soon as possible.

"I'm going to need to get it appraised, Judy," Skipper said. "You'll have to trust me with it."

I thought about that for a moment, but I figured there was nothing else I could do. I'd brought the Chinese box with me, so I gave the whole thing, along with the gold key, to him. When he saw the gem, his eyes bugged out like a cartoon character! "Holy Mother of God," he said. I explained that I'd promised Barry to give him half of the proceeds, so I would happily give Skipper that share. "We'll see what we can fetch for it," he said. "It won't be what it's worth. We have to be very careful. News can't get out that it's for sale except in very discreet circles."

"I understand."

Then I told him I wanted to live somewhere safe with Martin. I wasn't going to be the Black Stiletto anymore. And I didn't want anyone from my past to find me.

Skipper knew about Martin's fake birth certificate and my name change. He asked if we had Social Security numbers. My old one was no good, so he promised to arrange to get both me and Martin new ones. He had shady connections, just like his brother!

Then he said, "Judy, I have a cousin up in Illinois. His name is Thomas Avery and he lives in a suburb of Chicago called Arlington Heights. He's helped Barry and me in the past with 'witness protection.' "

"What's that?"

"It's when we help place someone who doesn't want to be found. The government does it with trial witnesses who might be in danger from the mob or whatever. I can help you. Thomas can help you. How do you feel about living in the Chicago area?"

I shrugged. "I've never been there."

Then Skipper *stood* and limped to a safe in the wall behind his desk. He twirled the combination, opened it, put the Chinese box inside.

"You can walk!" I said, stupidly.

"Sure, but it's painful. I stay in the chair most of the time, but I'm supposed to walk a little every day. I can drive too. I go out. You hungry? Want to go out to one of Odessa's finest barbecue restaurants?"

Dear diary, that sounded wonderful, so I took him up on it. So last night I drove him—and Martin—to Johnny's Barbeque on Grant and 10th Street. It wasn't a "fancy" restaurant. In fact, it was kind of a hole in the wall, but the food was fantastic. I hadn't tasted Texas barbecue in a long time.

This morning, I debated whether or not to call Frankie. I'm just not ready to answer the inevitable questions. So, instead, I spent the time catching up here in the diary, and making funny faces at Martin, ha ha.

45
Martin
THE PRESENT

My brain ceased to function. My stomach was in my throat. "Why don't you stand aside and let me in," Haines said. It was an order, not a request. On automatic pilot, I moved back and he strode into the cabin. I heard Maggie gasp behind me. Haines shut the door and gestured with the gun. "Move back, Mr. Talbot. Why don't you and the missus sit on the couch there, and we'll have a little talk."

Incongruously, I said, "We're not married yet."

"What?"

"You said 'missus'—we're not...never mind." I sat with Maggie and held hands. The terror of being tied up in that hotel room in New York returned in full force. I never thought I'd ever be as scared as I was then. I was wrong. Maggie squeezed my hand and I knew she was just as afraid as me.

Haines took a seat, the coffee table between us. He pushed my briefcase out of the way and put his cowboy boots on the table and stretched out in the chair as if he was just making himself at home. The gun was still pointed at us, of course.

"Well, ain't this cozy? Nice quiet place you have here, hidden from the rest of the world. You thought you were safe, didn't you?" We didn't answer. "That cop from Arlington Heights. He was easy to follow. I knew he'd lead me to you sooner or later. I just waited for him to leave, and now, here I am."

Thank you, Detective Scott, I thought.

"So where's the Black Stiletto? She's here, ain't she?"

Maggie answered, "She's asleep. And she's dying. So why don't you just leave? It's going to be over for her in days."

He raised his eyebrows. "Well, that's too bad, ain't it? Okay, folks, this is how it's going to be. I'm going to ask you some questions, and depending on how you answer them, I decide whether the Stiletto lives those extra few days or not."

"You killed Thomas Avery," I spat. "And Janie. They were innocents in all this."

"Your man Avery was no innocent. The secretary, well, okay, maybe she was, but what can I say? She was in the wrong place at the wrong time."

"At least tell us who you work for," I said. "Are you part of Bartlett Supply Company too?"

"Me? Nah. That was a long time ago. I worked there when I was a kid. But I do work for Mrs. B. Uh, Mrs. Bartlett. So did Bernie and Stark. We were sort of a team. And they were friends of mine. And you and your kid fucked 'em up."

"They tried to kill us!" I blurted. Not only was I scared, but I was suddenly very angry. How *dare* this guy come into our private residence and make threats! Not that I was going to be able to do anything about it, but—

"Too bad they didn't succeed," Haines said.

"Why are you doing this?" Maggie asked. "What's it all about?"

Haines nodded at me. "Your mother—the Black Stiletto—and my employer, Mrs. B., knew each other back in Los Angeles in the sixties. Her name was Christina Kelly then."

Holy shit. It all made sense. Now I knew we were really in trouble.

"Mrs. B. has been looking for the Black Stiletto ever since she got out of jail in 1975. Your mother put her there. Served thirteen years and got out on parole, thanks to some very good lawyers Ricky

Bartlett hired. They got married soon after that and she moved to Texas. Then Ricky died and Mrs. B. sort of runs things now. And she wants some payback."

"Christina Kelly was a murderer and a thief and . . . and . . . a *terrible person!*" I blubbered.

Haines gestured with the gun. "Watch it. You're talking about someone who's near and dear to me."

"Look, Mr. Haines," I said, "my mother has Alzheimer's and she's in the last stages. She doesn't know where she is and can barely function. She can't walk without assistance. She can't eat without our help. She can't *go to the bathroom* without aid. For God's sake, leave her alone."

Haines sat forward. "Let me tell you how this works, Mr. Talbot. Back in 1962, the Black Stiletto stole a very valuable diamond from Mrs. B. At the time it was worth around three million. Now it's probably worth between eight and twelve, maybe more. Your mother also stole over a million dollars from Mrs. B.'s husband. Then she ran off and disappeared. Both Ricky and Christina spent years looking for her, and then after Ricky died, Christina continued searching for decades. It was pure luck that you happened to be in New York when Bernie and Stark were investigating that crazy broad that claimed she was the Stiletto. And then you were stupid enough to send that private dick down to Odessa."

"Bill Ryan," Maggie said.

"Yeah, him. He started asking questions, and they were the kinds of questions that made Mrs. B. sit up and take notice. What with you and your daughter being involved in that incident in New York, and Ryan revealing that he was working for you, it made sense that Martin Talbot had something to do with the real Black Stiletto." Haines sat back in his chair. "You've been found out, sir. The jig is up. You have to come clean now. Mrs. B. wants her *nephew* to make things right."

That was a low blow, and the killer knew it. He grinned at my reaction.

"Did you kill Bill Ryan?" Maggie asked.

"Never mind that. Let's just say Mrs. B. pays me to fix things. Like I'm doing now. So. I'm going to ask you nicely first. Where is the diamond, and what happened to the one point twenty-five million that was taken from Ricky Bartlett?"

"I don't know what you're talking about," I said. Would he be able to tell I was lying through my teeth?

"Bullshit."

"I don't know anything about a diamond or that money! And my mother won't either. She doesn't even know her name anymore. Or mine. She can barely speak."

Haines rolled his eyes and grinned. "Right. Okay, Plan B." He reached into a pocket and removed a cell phone. He punched a speed-dial button, waited, and then spoke. "It's me. I'm here with Mr. Talbot and his missus. His mother is in the other room." Pause. "Uh-huh." Pause. "Right." Then he switched off, put away the phone, and said, "At this moment, your daughter—what's her name?—Gerri?—"

"Gina."

"Gina is at the Bartlett Ranch outside of Odessa, face-to-face with Mrs. B. Now maybe you don't still have the diamond and that money, but unless you tell us what *happened* to it all, my friends in Texas are going to kill your little girl."

"No!" I started to jump up, but Maggie held me back.

"Don't make any sudden moves like that, Mr. Talbot; I have a very itchy trigger finger. Sometimes I react without thinking, you know? Just sit there quietly and talk to me. If Mrs. B. doesn't get a phone call from me by—" He looked at his watch again. "—ten o'clock, your kid is as good as dead. And then, well, I'll make another attempt at getting the truth out of you by making you or your missus here suffer. Finally, my last order of business is to go in the bedroom and put the Black Stiletto out of her misery. If you ask me, it'll be a blessing."

"Fuck you," I muttered. I was near tears.

He rolled his eyes again. "Whatever you say, tough guy." Suddenly, he pointed the gun at the ceiling and *fired*! The blast was incredibly loud and it scared the holy crap out of us. Maggie shrieked, and I jumped out of my skin. *Christ*!

This was a sadistic brute, no question about it. The bastard enjoyed watching our terror. He laughed and lit a cigarette with his free left hand. Then he gestured with the gun again, and said, "I'm waiting."

It was exactly 9:50. I had ten minutes to figure out what to do.

46
Judy's Diary
1962

DECEMBER 8, 1962

Yesterday Martin and I stayed at the motel. We went out only for me to get food to eat in our room. I had a lot of laundry to do, too, especially dirty diapers! There was a Laundromat not far from the Sahara. But, to tell the truth, I was a little scared to venture any farther. All day I had the feeling that trouble was coming, it just wasn't in town yet. I didn't know how long it would take Skipper to get the diamond appraised by a fence, but thank goodness he called my room last night to say he had news.

This morning we met Skipper at Antler's Coffee Shop, farther west on 2nd Street. Skipper was already there, in his wheelchair at a table. It's a fairly new place that's become popular. At one point the owner walked through, and Skipper said, "Hey there, Mr. Green." Green waved and said hello. Skipper is obviously known about town. We put Martin in a high chair. He was a polite gentleman and didn't make any fuss the whole time. Since I'd already fed him, he was content with his pacifier and looking at the people.

"Okay, my guy was real impressed with your diamond. He can get you one point twenty-five million for it," Skipper told me in a low voice after some initial chitchat. Dear diary, I gulped so hard that I nearly swallowed my tongue! I actually started coughing and had to drink some water. Then he said, "It's probably worth more than that, but considering the, uh, private nature of the piece and the difficulty of finding buyers who'll keep their mouths shut, we have to take the best we can get."

"That's pretty good, don't you think?" I can't *imagine* having that much money.

"Yes, I do," he said. "And, Judy, I'm only going to take fifty grand from you. That money is yours, not mine or even Barry's."

"Don't be silly. I promised Barry half the proceeds," I argued.

"No. I won't do it if you insist on this. I mean it, Judy." We went back and forth until I had to give in. Then he said, "There's one hitch."

"What?"

"It's going to take a couple of weeks to get the money."

"*Two weeks!* That's not good," I said. "Martin and I need to get out of here, Skipper. If he's really still alive, I just know Leo will track me down sooner rather than later."

"I understand. Let me see what I can do. Try to sit tight for at least a couple of days, all right?"

There wasn't much choice. "Okay."

"You wanted to see your brothers, right? It'll give you some time to catch up."

I still hadn't called Frankie. "You're right."

He then took an envelope out of his jacket. Inside were two new Social Security cards in mine and Martin's names, and the gold key to the Chinese jewel box. "The box is in my safe at the office, and I suggest you keep it there for the time being. I thought you should hold on to the key."

"Good idea, thanks." I put the key in my purse, and was startled to see the gun Barry gave me, plain as can be! I keep forgetting I stuck it in there. I quickly snapped the purse closed. Odessa still has some Wild West qualities about it, but I didn't want to get caught with an illegal handgun.

So, it looks like I'm going to get a million dollars, dear diary. I hope Skipper is really fine with taking only $50,000. I guess that's a lot of money too.

We were nearly done, and then someone walked in the coffee shop that I recognized—none other than Ricky Bartlett. Tall, blond, and handsome. There were a couple of burly men with him. He also said hello to the owner and to several other patrons at tables as he walked past. Then he saw Skipper and *came over*! I about died.

"Morning, Skipper," he said, friendly like.

"Hey, Ricky, how are you?" Skipper shook his hand. Bartlett looked at me and Martin.

"Oh, this is Nancy, my cousin from Dallas. That's her son, Leroy," Skipper explained.

I retained my composure as Bartlett reached to shake my hand, and say, "Pleased to meet you, Nancy. How do you like our town so far?"

Stupidly, I said the first thing I thought of. "Dallas is bigger than Odessa."

He and Skipper shared a laugh, and Bartlett said, "Yes, that's true." Then he squeezed Skipper's shoulder and said, "You'll be getting what we talked about in the next day or so, all right?"

"Oh, sure, Ricky, I'll be looking out for it, thanks," Skipper replied.

Bartlett then went and sat at another table with his buddies—bodyguards more like it.

"Nancy? *Leroy*?" I whispered to Skipper.

He chuckled. "Just popped in my head. I thought it best that he didn't know your real names."

"Tell me more about him."

"You heard of the Bartlett Ranch?"

"That's where he lives, right?"

"Yeah, it's a huge spread outside of town, on the way to Monahans."

"He has a family?"

"No, he's single. He has a lot of girlfriends, though, from what I hear."

Ricky Bartlett was a pretty good-looking man, as far as cowboy criminals went. I guess he's about thirty or so.

"Inherited the ranch from his father, of course," Skipper continued.

"And he's with the Dixie Mafia?" I asked.

Skipper's eyes widened and said, "Shhhh, Jesus, Judy, not so loud."

I put my hand over my mouth. "Sorry!" I didn't think anyone heard me, but I'm glad he warned me. "Maybe we should talk about this somewhere else."

He kept his voice down. "No, it's okay. He's far enough away. But yes, he's pretty powerful in what you said. We don't really call it that. I guess some folks do. I know he's associated with what Leo Kelly was doing in LA. And he's been doing business with Vince DeAngelo and Sal Casazza."

"There was a big arrest in New Mexico with the Heathens, that motorcycle club that—"

"I know who they are," Skipper said. "Yeah, and it was Ricky that *allegedly* took a big financial hit on that."

"He didn't seem to know me, so that's a good thing."

"Would Leo contact him about you?"

"I don't know. If DeAngelo wants Leo dead, I don't know if Bartlett would rat on him or help him."

"Leo is damaged goods, Judy. I doubt Bartlett would want anything to do with him now." He leaned in, and said. "I'm doing some, uh, investing for Ricky Bartlett. I've helped him in the past. Like I said, Judy, I do some shady things too."

"What do you do, exactly?"

"He gives me money and I invest it for him. I deposit it in a bank somewhere, usually Zurich."

"What's wrong with that?"

"Let's say it's income he doesn't want the government to know about." Skipper shrugged. "It's a living, Judy."

"That's what he was talking about?"

"Yeah."

"How much is he giving you?"

"I don't know yet. A lot."

"Millions?"

"Could be."

"And it's all from illegal activity?"

"I imagine so. But he's squeaky clean as far as the local cops are concerned. The Feds, though, that's another story. He's been keeping his nose clean lately because of what happened in LA. He's part of DeAngelo's network, and it's possible the FBI will follow the money trails that went back and forth."

Wow. Bartlett should be in jail along with DeAngelo.

"Bartlett lives by himself?"

"He's got men there. And the occasional girls that might be visiting for a while and are then replaced."

"I see."

My Stiletto instincts actually gave me a buzz. I wondered what Bartlett's ranch looked like and if it might be possible for me to do him some harm while I was in Odessa. It would be a very risky thing to do, but I see him as part of the same well of villains from which Leo and DeAngelo emerged.

I felt safer today, so after breakfast Martin and I went to Sherwood Park to look at the prairie dogs. I took our stroller and we went around to the various structures you could climb on and watched older kids laughing and playing. Another mother with a baby said to me, "Some day our kids will be big enough to do that." Martin is now asleep in his stroller, and I'm sitting on a bench in the park writing in the diary.

I think after dinner tonight I'll try to give Frankie a call.

DECEMBER 9, 1962

Martin and I saw Frankie today, and it didn't go well. I found out my brother John is dead. I left Frankie's house in tears. I feel better now, but I wanted to get it all down on paper.

It started pleasantly enough. I went over to his home on Beechwood this afternoon, after they got home from church and had lunch. His modest brick house is in the expanding east side of town, on a quiet street with many other brick houses. My brother thinks the city will spread a great deal farther east over the next decade. There are two large high schools in town for the white kids to accommodate the growing population. A "colored high school" is across the tracks. That element of Odessa sure makes me uncomfortable.

Frankie—he's now 28 years old—has a family. His wife is Sarah, a pretty little thing who is very shy but nice. They have a 2-year-old daughter named Angela who is very cute. I was introduced to her as "Aunt Judy," a term I couldn't quite get used to! Angela was very interested in Martin. I had to carry him around most of the time I was there except when I could put him in Angela's crib. Sarah left to take Angela to play with a friend, so Frankie and I were alone.

He hasn't changed much. The glass eye looks the same. He said he owns his own hardware store now, and it's located on the east side of town. I liked his house. It looked like what I imagined a middle-class, small-town family home would be. There were three bedrooms, one of which was a guest room. Frankie asked where I was staying and I told him, but he didn't offer the room to me. I didn't expect him to anyway. In the living room, I spotted an antique chime wall clock that looked very familiar.

"Is that from our old house?" I asked.

"Yeah. I think it's the only thing that survived from then."

"It still works?"

"It's in great condition. And it's worth something—it's a genuine Westminster that plays the classic chime—dee da dum daaa, da dee da dummm."

"I remember! And isn't there something odd about it?"

He opened the front to reveal the intricate workings and the pendulum. "It's special. During Prohibition, our grandfather, or whoever had it then, built a false back, where you could store booze!" I had a vague memory of that. "Look here." He showed me the hidden catch inside the main chassis, flicked it, and the whole thing opened like a door, revealing an empty bin-like space against the wall. Gosh, I haven't thought about it in a long time. I took it for granted when it was in our crummy house where I grew up. It's old—turn-of-the-century old—and it was handed down in my mom's family. I guess Frankie got it after she died.

"So that's the only thing left from our mother?"

He nodded.

"Is John still in the army?"

Frankie looked at me with a hurt expression on his face.

"What?" I asked.

"You don't know."

"Know what?"

"John's dead." My mouth dropped open but I couldn't force out any sound. Although it's been a long time since I saw John, I felt a small dagger pierce my heart. "What happened?" I whispered.

"Helicopter accident. A *training* accident. On the base. Here in the United States! The army called it a 'tragic accident.' Jesus, Judy, it happened two years ago, the same year Angela was born."

"*Two years?* And I didn't know?"

And that started it. Frankie laid into me. I guess I deserved it.

"I *wanted* you to know. I wanted you to be at his funeral. They sent him back here and there was a military funeral with the flag over his coffin. How was I supposed to contact you, Judy? You left last time without giving me any clue how to reach you. You had my phone number, but you never called *me*. You ran away from home and we worried about you for years, then you showed up unexpectedly—when was that, 1958?—and I saw you for ten minutes and then you vanished again. My *sister*. For God's sake, Judy, you're family. Why don't you want to be in contact?"

Because it's too painful. That's what I told him. He knew about Douglas raping me, and he understood why I'd have bad memories of the time when he was living under our roof. He didn't see how or why that alone could spoil the entire emotional impression of my childhood in Odessa. I told him it did, and that I was sorry.

After a long awkward pause, he said, "Well, John's buried at Ector County Cemetery, where Mom is, in case you want to pay your respects." The sarcasm in his voice was painful to me. "Do you still live in New York?"

"No. I've been living in LA," I told him. "Now I'm looking for another place to live for Martin and me."

I felt like I was about to cry. What Frankie had said really hurt.

He narrowed his eyes at me. "Are you in some kind of trouble?"

"No. Forget it. I'd better go."

Frankie didn't stop me.

47
Leo
THE PAST

The drop into the canyon knocked me out, but not for long. I don't remember the impact, but I must have slid down the side of the cliff. I had scrapes and cuts all over my body, and my clothes were torn. When I woke up, I was draped over a prickly sagebrush or tree or something. It had broken my fall, otherwise I'd probably be dead. While my first sensation was a hell of a lot of pain, I noticed a flashlight beam sweeping across the rocks and ground around me. I heard Judy up above call, "Leo?" I stayed still and silent. The beam never swept over me.

I managed to climb off the branches and perch on a rock. It was pitch-dark, but I could see the night sky above my head. The edge of the cliff was maybe thirty feet up. I knew I had to get out of there. The bitch would call the cops and I wanted to be long gone by then. So I started to climb. It was really tough going. My entire body ached, but miraculously I didn't think anything was broken. I was bleeding from various cuts. My shirt was soaked in sweat and blood.

When I reached halfway, there was a more-or-less flat ledge where I could rest. I must have passed out again there, for I woke up when I heard the sound of a car. Shaking the cobwebs from my brain, I unzipped and took a badly needed piss and then started to climb again. The sound of tires on gravel lessened. Just a little farther—

Well, I made it. I climbed over the edge of that goddamned cliff and crawled toward the house. Finally, I got to my feet and staggered inside. Judy wasn't there, and neither was the kid. Then I went outside—my Karmann Ghia was still in front with the headlights shining at the open door. The guy I shot was still lying on the gravel. My gun was on the ground, so I picked it up and pocketed it. I knelt beside the guy and searched his pockets—found a wallet and opened it. His name was Barry Gorman. His business card said he was an investigator, but it didn't look like he was a professional one. I went over to the car and shut off the lights, and then I went back inside. There wasn't much time.

The police would be there soon. Was there anything in the cabin that would provide a clue as to where Judy went? I did a quick search of a bedroom that was probably hers—the one with the crib in it. Nothing. So I went to the other bedroom—surely it was Gorman's, it looked like a man's room—and I saw some framed photos on a dresser. One was a picture of Judy with Gorman. They looked happy. I couldn't tell where it was taken. I took it out of the frame and stuck it in my pocket. Another photo showed Gorman with another man who was in a wheelchair. Gorman was younger in the picture, but there was a resemblance between the two men. Probably brothers. I took the photo out of the frame and saw, written on the back, "Barry and Skipper, Odessa, Texas, 1959."

Odessa.

Judy was from Odessa. She'd told me that when we first started dating. What a coincidence. Ricky Bartlett was in Odessa. He was my partner now.

Could she have possibly gone to Odessa? Did she know Gorman's brother?

It was a lead, but that's all it was. There was nothing else, so I was determined to follow it. I shoved that photo in my pocket too, and then ran out to my car. I drove like crazy down the mountain—and wouldn't you know it, as soon as I turned on to Laurel Canyon Boulevard, three cop cars with lights flashing and sirens squealing shot past me going the other way. I held my breath. I'm sure the police were looking for my Karmann Ghia, but I watched them turn on the mountain road in my rearview mirror.

I was safe. I guess they were too intent on getting up to that house on the hill and weren't paying attention to my car. It was a liability, though, and I had to get rid of it.

I couldn't go home. The cops were likely watching it. So I thought of Boone and went to his place in Hollywood. I was tempted to drive by my house—it was only a couple of blocks away—but I dared not. When I got to Boone's apartment building, I saw my Lincoln Continental at the curb. That was just what I needed. I parked illegally, jumped out of the car, and ran to Boone's apartment door—and found it ajar.

"Boone?" I called. There was a radio playing in his bedroom. I drew my Browning, stepped inside, and slowly walked through his living room to the hallway. The bedroom door was closed. I knocked. "Boone?" Nothing. I opened the door—the lights were off, so I flicked them on.

Boone had been executed in his bed. He was on his stomach, and someone had shot him in the back of the head.

That had to be DeAngelo's team.

Which meant they were looking for *me*. Poor Boone couldn't tell them where I was.

Frantic, I grabbed Boone's discarded trousers and searched his pockets. The keys to the Lincoln were there, and so was his wallet. I took all the money—one hundred and twenty-four dollars—and fled. I got in the Lincoln and drove away. Luckily, there was a full tank of gas, which was enough to get me into Arizona. With the cash I took from Boone, I had a little over three hundred dollars on me. Not very much.

That didn't matter. My life did. It was a minor miracle that Boone's apartment wasn't being watched. Maybe they figured I wasn't stupid enough to go to his place. Wherever I went, though, I was a dead man. Even giving myself up to the cops wasn't an option. DeAngelo could have me murdered in prison. No, I had to disappear and find another identity and life somewhere else.

But first, I had a score to settle with one Judy Cooper. The Black Stiletto.

Maybe driving to Odessa was a bad idea. Would she be fool enough to go there? It was possible. At any rate, Ricky would surely help me out. He could front me some money and help me get set up in another part of the country.

As I left LA behind and got on Highway 60 toward Phoenix, all I could think of was how I was going to murder Judy and her goddamned kid. Or maybe I'd take him. I could raise him as my son. That was an idea.

When I stopped to get gas, the teenager at the filling station looked at me like I was a monster. Of course, I resembled one. I told him I'd been in a fight. I went to the men's room and, sure enough, the guy staring back in the mirror was not me. My face had all kinds of cuts and bruises. Blood had dried and painted my skin—I looked like an Indian. My suit was in tatters. I was a mess. I felt like crap too. It was morning and I hadn't slept. I probably wouldn't sleep until Judy Cooper was history.

I did my best to wash off and clean up, but then I said screw it and decided to find a motel. I was pushing myself too hard. I needed to eat and sleep. So after I paid for the gas, I asked the kid where the nearest motel was. I didn't even know what town I was in. Turned out to be some shithole called Quartzsite, Arizona.

The motel was called "Motel"—how original—but it was clean and it had a shower. I cleaned up, got in bed, and was immediately asleep.

It was night when I woke up. I was confused as to what day it was, but I didn't care. The clock said it was 2:43. I looked outside and it was black. I considered getting in the car and driving on, but I wanted new clothes. I wasn't about to put back on the torn suit. My skin and face weren't as bad, although I looked like someone was using me as a dart board.

I decided to wait until morning.

I made it to Odessa after a journey that took a lot longer than I'd planned. For one thing, the Lincoln got a flat tire when I reached New Mexico. I was in the middle of the goddamned desert—and wouldn't you know it—there was no spare in the trunk. What was Boone thinking? No spare tire? I'd fire him if he wasn't dead. At least it wasn't too hot, being December and all.

The last thing I wanted was for the highway patrol to come by. For all I knew, my name and face was on every Most Wanted list in the country. I tried waving down passing cars for over an hour, and then a pickup stopped. A Mexican was at the wheel. He only spoke Spanish, but he asked if I needed help. How about that? He took me into the next town so I could buy a tire, and then he even brought me back to my car. I gave him twenty bucks and he even helped me change the tire.

When I got to Artesia, the engine overheated. I stopped at a filling station and the guy said I needed a new *carburetor*. And it was going to take some time. He promised to have it done the next day.

So it was motel time again. At least I had a chance to buy some clothes. After taking care of that and the carburetor, I'd be broke.

Finally, four days after I left LA, I arrived in West Texas. I went straight to the Bartlett Ranch, where I've visited before. Maybe I should have called Ricky first, but I'd wasted so much time already. The thing was I didn't know if Ricky was going to welcome me like a friend or shoot me and deliver my head to DeAngelo.

Bartlett's spread was outside of Odessa and it was huge. It was surrounded by barbed wire because he owned cattle and horses. His front was an oil field supply company that his father started. The guy was richer than sin. I sometimes wondered why he got into the crime business since his legitimate ones did so well. His father was also a big shot in the Dixie Mafia before he was, well, bumped off. There were rumors that Ricky was behind the hit. I knew nothing about Ricky's mother, she was long gone.

I pulled up to the gate. A shiny, freshly painted, carved, wooden sign proudly stated that I'd arrived at the Bartlett Ranch. There wasn't much security. I guess Ricky didn't think he needed it. All I had to do was get out of the car, open the gate, get back in the car, drive through, get out of the car, close the gate, and get back in the car. Maybe all that effort discouraged anyone who might want to sneak up on the house and kill Ricky. That and all his armed men he kept around him.

After going through the gate, I drove on a dirt road nearly a mile to the sprawling ranch house. There were other buildings on the property too—a barn, smokehouse, and I don't know what else. Bartlett lived in a fancy mansion. He was the Vincent DeAngelo of West Texas. He didn't have a swimming pool though. Since Odessa was pretty much a flat, hot desert, the first thing I would have built was a pool.

Two men met me at the house. They were dressed like cowboys and wore six-shooters on their belts. Was that a standard uniform at the Bartlett Ranch? It was how Ricky always dressed too, only without the guns. I rolled down my window and told them my name and that I was there to see Ricky. One guy said, "Hold on," and went into the house while the other guy babysat me. After a few minutes, the first guy came back and said, "Ricky will see you."

I smelled barbecue when I walked in. Looking at my watch, I saw that it was nearly dinnertime. My stomach growled, but I was too nervous to think about food. I waited in a large parlor that was filled with cowboy paraphernalia. There was a longhorn steer's head mounted on the wall. A cabinet full of old rifles from the 1800s stood beneath it. Most of the furniture was made of leather, the kind you'd see on saddles.

"Leo Kelly, you old cattle rustler, what a pleasant surprise!"

Ricky walked in, as tall as the Lone Ranger, and shook my hand. That was a relief. He didn't pull his gun and shoot me.

"Hello, Ricky," I said. "I hope you don't mind me dropping in like this."

"Not at all, but I wish you'd told me you were coming. You couldn't call?"

"It's been a little hectic lately."

He winked at me. "That's what I've heard." He jerked his head to follow him. "Let's go get a beer. You hungry? Milton's got a few slabs of ribs on the grill, and there's plenty to go around."

"That'd be great, Ricky, thanks."

So I had several beers and stuffed myself with barbecue while sitting around a huge table in the dining room with Ricky and his crew. The meal took a while, and after some delicious cherry cobbler, Ricky finally said, "Leo, let's go in my office and have a chat. That's obviously why you came to see me, right?"

"Yeah. Thanks, Ricky. Wonderful meal."

I followed him through a hallway and into a lavish private office that was full of cowboy stuff too. There was a buffalo head mounted on the wall behind Ricky's big wooden desk. He sat and gestured to a leather-covered comfy chair for me.

The first words out of his mouth were, "Leo, did you know I'm supposed to kill you?"

"Uh, no."

"I am. DeAngelo sent the word out. Nationwide. Find Leo Kelly and skin him alive."

Suddenly I didn't feel so good. Those ribs weren't agreeing with me.

He held up his hands. "Relax, Leo. We're friends. We're in business together. Or we were. I have no allegiance to Vincent DeAngelo, who's probably going to jail. Did you know?"

"No, I didn't!" I hadn't read any papers since I left LA. I had no idea what was going on, and I said so.

"Well, your counterfeiting operation is completely dismantled. They've arrested everyone. They brought Vince in for questioning and ended up putting him under arrest. He's out on bail. In the meantime, he wants your hide, Leo."

"I was afraid of that. Look, I—"

"No need to explain. You had an opportunity to run, so you took it. I understand."

I couldn't tell if he was being sarcastic or not. "Do you know anything about Christina?"

Ricky made a sour face. "Yeah. That's the part that bugs me the most. You know your sister and me, well, we were getting a little sweet on each other."

"I know that. That's why we're in business together."

"*Were*, Leo. We ain't in business together anymore. That's finished."

"All right."

"Christina is in jail. Well, she's in the hospital, but she's been charged with murder and robbery. So tell me—was she the *real* Black Stiletto or was she just impersonating her?"

"Christ, she was just impersonating her. I kept telling her to get rid of that goddamned costume."

He laughed. "She's something else, your sister. I like a girl with that kind of fire. But I imagine she'll go to prison. For a long time too. Her knee is pretty bad. It's a question whether she'll walk again."

"I'm…I'm really sorry to hear that."

"Yeah." He looked at me a long time, and then asked, "So why did you drive all this way to see me? You thought I'd give you *sanctuary?*"

"Not at all. I'm looking for someone. A girl. Actually, she's the mother of my son."

"What? Since when did you have a wife?"

"She's not my wife. She's my ex-girlfriend." I decided not to mention that she was the real Black Stiletto. If I did, *he* would want to catch her too, and I wanted the bitch all to myself.

"Why would I know where she is?"

"She's from Odessa. I think she might have come here recently. Just a hunch. I'm pretty sure she has family here. Her name is Judy Cooper." I pulled out the photo of Judy and Gorman together and handed it to him. "That's her."

Ricky furrowed his brow as he studied it. "She does look familiar," he said. "So does he. Who's the guy?"

"His name is Barry Gorman. He worked for the cops in LA."

"Gorman. Yeah, now I know where I've seen her. I know Barry Gorman, and I know his brother, Skipper Gorman. Skipper lives here in Odessa. I saw her just the other day at Antler's with him. She had a kid with her too. She didn't say her name was Judy, though. I think he called her Nancy."

I couldn't believe my luck! "Really? She's here?"

"She was the other day. Maybe Skipper knows where she is."

"Do you know where I can find him?"

"I do. He's my investment counselor. I just gave him a big chunk of money to deposit for me." Ricky thumbed through a box of index cards, pulled one, and wrote an address on a piece of paper. "Here it is. Don't hurt him, though. Like I said, he's doing some work for me."

"No problem, Ricky. Thanks a lot. I owe you."

"More than you know. You all right otherwise? You have money?"

It was too tempting not to respond. "I'm broke, Ricky."

He reached into his back pocket, tugged out his wallet, and counted five twenties. "Here you go, Leo."

"Wow, thanks, Ricky. I'll pay you back. I swear."

"I know."

I put the money away, stood up to leave, and held out my hand. Then he said, "Leo, you have until noon tomorrow afternoon to get your business with this woman done."

"Why?"

"Because you're Christina's brother and I'm giving you a chance. A head start, so to speak."

"What do you mean?"

"Like I said, I'm supposed to kill you. Vince has offered a pretty nice reward too. I want that reward. But being the nice guy that I am, I'm giving you 'til noon."

I backed toward the door. "And if I'm gone by noon?"

"Then you better find a good place to run to, because I'm not the only one who'll be after you."

"Ricky," I pleaded, "you don't mean it. We're friends. You and my sister—"

He raised his voice and stood. "Your sister's in jail because of you! Paulie DeAngelo is dead because of you! I've lost a lot of money because of you! Now get the hell out of my sight before I change my mind and drill you right here and now!"

I took his advice and left. I drove away from the ranch like a bat out of hell.

It wouldn't be hard to find Skipper Gorman. And despite what I said to Ricky, I was prepared to murder anyone who stood in my way in finding Judy Cooper.

And if I died in the process, so be it.

48
Judy's Diary
1962

I'm back at the motel after a wonderful day. I'm now richer beyond my dreams and I've reconciled with my brother.

This morning Skipper called the motel and said I should come see him. So, after lunch, Martin and I went to his office home. I've come to trust and like him a lot more than I did at first. Skipper has opened up to me, and I now see a lot of Barry in him, too. I really miss Barry. I think about him every day.

We set Martin up on the floor with the old rattle again, and that kept him happy while the adults talked.

Skipper pointed to an old battered suitcase sitting on the coffee table. He told me to open it. When I did, I saw that it was filled entirely with stacks of bills—$20s, $50s, and $100s. I'm sure my eyes popped out of my head.

"Oh my gosh, what is this?" I asked.

"Well, Judy, that's yours."

"What?"

"That's one million, two hundred thousand dollars stuffed in that suitcase. I already removed my fifty thousand, so everything there is yours. It's heavy, can you lift it? We might need to put it in two suitcases, but I don't have another one to give you."

"Wait a minute," I said, "I thought it was going to take two weeks to sell the diamond."

"It will. Let's just say I'm borrowing this money to give you now, and I'll repay it when I sell the diamond in two weeks," he said.

That sounded fishy, so I gave him a look. "Whose money is this?"

A devilish grin appeared on his face, and he said, "It's Ricky Bartlett's."

"Skipper! I can't take his money!"

"Sure you can. Like I said, it's a loan. He won't know about it. He dropped all that here last night—plus more—so I took out the one point twenty-five to let you have for now. You said you wanted to leave town as fast as possible, so now you can. You can take the dough, and leave today if you like."

"Aren't you supposed to do something with it?"

He shrugged. "I will, but that doesn't have to happen today or tomorrow. If it happens in two weeks, that's all right. Ricky will never know."

"What if something goes wrong and you don't sell the diamond?"

"That won't happen. I've already received a hundred thousand down payment—nonrefundable—if the sale doesn't go through."

"Wow." I started touching all that money and suddenly felt overwhelmed.

Skipper handed me an envelope. "In there is my cousin Thomas's information in Illinois. He knows you're coming. He'll help you safely invest your money so that it'll last you, gosh, maybe your whole life. You won't have to work again, Judy."

"I don't believe it."

"If you follow Thomas's advice and do what he says, you can believe it. He'll also help you find a place to live. You might have to move around a few times at first while we make sure no one's after you. Eventually, though, you'll get to settle down and start a new life as Judy and Martin Talbot."

That sounded wonderful. Then an idea struck me. "Skipper, I want to give some of my money to my brother Frankie."

He thought that was a nice idea, but he suggested that I wait until I got it all set up in a bank in Illinois, and then I could send Frankie a check. It might be too suspicious if I handed my brother a wad of cash. On reflection, I agreed. He took down Frankie's name, address, and phone number to have on hand in case he needed it.

I closed the suitcase and tried to lift it. It wasn't too bad. I wouldn't want to carry it farther than to the trunk of my car though! I leaned over and gave Skipper a big hug and kiss. "This is so incredible! Thank you, Skipper. Thank you so much!"

"You're welcome," he said. "Good luck to you. I hope I'll see you again sometime."

Dear diary, I hauled the heavy suitcase out and put it in the car. Then I came back, picked up Martin, and said goodbye to Skipper once more.

Back at the motel, the office had a message for me from Frankie. It said to call him, so I did. On the phone, he said he was happy that I hadn't left town yet and that he needed to speak to me. I told him to come to the motel while I packed up.

When he arrived, he had a sheepish look on his face. The first words out of his mouth were, "I'm sorry."

"What about?"

"For what I said. Judy, you're my sister, and I love you. I want you and Martin to come stay with us. I want you to be part of our family."

That touched me so much I started crying. We hugged each other and it was almost as if I'd never left home. "Frankie, I was going to leave in the morning. We're getting out of town. I need to."

"Why?"

"Frankie, I'm just not the same girl I was when you knew me. I've—grown up. I've changed. I'm a big city girl now. I've done . . . some things . . . that you might not understand."

"Try me."

I shook my head. I really didn't want him to know about the Stiletto. "I can't."

"Have you broken the law somewhere? You're obviously running from someone or something. Let me help you."

"I'm fine, Frankie, especially now." Then I thought—I'd been in Odessa for a few days, what would one more hurt? The feeling of imminent danger that I had when I first arrived had dissipated. Perhaps it was safe to stay a while longer, go see my mom's and John's graves, and be with my brother and his family. So I told him I'd spend the day with him tomorrow if he could take off work. Frankie said he'd be happy to do so; there was an assistant manager who could mind the store while he was gone.

So I'm putting off leaving Odessa for one more day. Tomorrow I'll spend with *family*.

49
Gina
The Present

"Do you know who I am?" Mrs. B. asked. "Have you heard of Christina Kelly?"

I didn't want her to know about Grandma's diaries. "No, I don't think so," I said.

The woman hobbled to the couch, which was one of the pieces of furniture covered by a sheet, and slowly lowered herself to a sitting position. She leaned the shotgun barrel down next to her right leg and kept her hand on the receiver, above the trigger. I recalled from Grandma's diary that the woman was good with firearms. "Well, I won't bore you with the history. Just know that your grandmother caused me a great deal of suffering. She killed my brother. That was her biggest sin. She also destroyed my right kneecap and left me a cripple for years. I can't tell you what agony that was. I went to a prison hospital where the care, well, wasn't too good. It was 1962 and they didn't have the kind of treatments to fix a fractured kneecap like they do now."

I knew that a busted knee was one of the worst pains imaginable. That bone was a prime target in Krav Maga—if you disabled an opponent by smashing the kneecap, then you've won the fight.

"I see you squirming," the woman said. "Yes, it hurt. Shall I describe it in detail for you? That way, you might understand why I *hate* your grandmother so much, and why she deserves to die a slow and painful death."

Mrs. B. smiled, and I could see that at one time she was probably a very beautiful woman. Now, though, she just looked like an exotic witch, what with the long white hair and bony frame.

"Imagine the kneecap fractured into two pieces," she continued. "Some bone fragments were lodged in the knee joint. The severe trauma also ruptured and tore the tendons and ligaments that support the knee. Back then the only thing they could do was surgically wire the kneecap together. First, they drilled holes in the pieces to attach the wires, which were then twisted to tighten the fit. The wires went around the patella and pulled the pieces together."

Oh my God, I really *was* fidgeting at the description. I could practically feel it in my own knee as she described it.

"The bone fragments had to be removed, and the torn tendons were repaired surgically. I had to wear a cast for two months. By then, I was in Frontera. The California Institute for Women, in Chino. At my trial, I faced two counts of first-degree murder and a few for armed robbery. I was convicted of only one count, and the charge was lessened to second-degree murder. The prosecutors just didn't have enough evidence to convict me of the other charges. I was sentenced to twenty years, but I got out in 1975, thanks to my former husband's team of lawyers."

Despite my discomfort and worry that I was in a very dangerous situation, her story fascinated me.

"Anyway," she said, "once the cast came off, that knee was incredibly stiff. My leg muscles had atrophied. I couldn't walk. They didn't have much in the way of rehab in prison. I was in misery for a long, long time. I had to rebuild the muscles. It was a slow, painful process. Finally, a year later, I was able to walk again with a cane. It wasn't until 1979, after I had married my husband and moved to Texas, that I had a knee replacement. *Then*, after months of excruciating rehab, I could walk without a cane. It was only in the last fifteen years that my old age has forced me to use a cane again. But I will *never, ever* forget the agony the Black Stiletto caused me."

"I'm sorry to hear that," I said. I really was. However, I knew from Grandma's fourth diary that she suspected it was Christina Kelly who impersonated the Stiletto and murdered Maria Kelly.

Mrs. B. added, "If it hadn't been for Ricky Bartlett, I probably would have been killed in prison. Do you know who Vincent DeAngelo was?"

"Yes."

"There were several attempts on my life while I was in jail. He had his fingers everywhere, even in prison. But DeAngelo was indicted in '64, and he ended up going to jail too, in '66. He died there in '69. The hits on my life perished with him."

Why was she telling me all this? It seemed she just wanted to talk, to unload a lot of her shit on me because it had been building inside her for years. There wasn't much else I could do but sit there, listen, nod, and make faces of concern. Eventually, I figured, she would tell me what she wanted, and I could get back Grandma's costume.

"I'm not boring you, am I?" the old woman asked. She didn't say it politely. It was spoken in the same way a snake might ask if it was in my way.

"No, ma'am, I'm actually learning quite a lot," I answered truthfully.

"Well, are you aware that your grandmother *stole* a valuable diamond from me and my brother? It's worth millions. Do you know where it is?"

She must have been talking about Maria Kelly's diamond necklace. "I don't know what you're talking about," I answered truthfully. Was there more about it in the fifth diary?

"Liar." The woman curled her lips in a silent snarl at me. "Your grandmother also stole a great deal of money from my late husband. A million and a quarter dollars, to be precise. Just ran off with it. We've been looking—" A cell phone ring interrupted her. "Excuse me." She reached in the pocket of her housedress, removed the device, and answered it. "Yes?" Her eyes watched me as she listened. "Good. I take it there were no problems?" Pause. "Very well, proceed. Give them until ten o'clock on the dot. I'll await your call."

She hung up and replaced the phone in her pocket. "That was my man in Illinois. He's sitting with your father and his lady friend."

"What?"

"If they don't tell him what happened to the diamond and the money in the next ten minutes, I'm afraid we'll have to hurt you."

I immediately stood, ready to bolt out of the place. There was no way *she* could catch me, but—

"Stay right where you are, Miss Talbot," McCambridge's voice boomed from behind. I sensed that his gun was aimed at my back. I stood still and slowly raised my hands.

"If my dad gets hurt—" I wasn't in much of a position to make a threat, but I said it anyway.

The harpy spoke again. "Young lady, tonight, using very painful methods, my man will get rid of the three people in that cabin. He's very good at that, and he's been instructed to leave your grandmother for last."

My anger rose, but I tried to control it as I said, "Mrs. Bartlett, you are very wrong. My grandmother is dying of Alzheimer's. Even if what you say is true, that she did take that diamond and money, she must have had a good reason. She was the one on the right side of the law—you and your brother weren't. I think you're just an old, angry, bitter woman who's at the end of your life. My grandmother was—is—a good person, helpful, kind, and very independent in her thoughts and actions. Now please call your 'man,' if that's what he is, which I doubt, seeing that he would harm a helpless, dying woman and an innocent man and his companion, and tell him to back off. And then give me back the Stiletto costume. I'll leave quietly and promise to never say a word about our meeting."

Christina Bartlett started laughing. She pushed herself off the couch and stood, leaning on her cane, and then she picked up the shotgun and pointed it at me. "You silly little bitch, you're just like Judy Cooper. What were you thinking, coming to Odessa, like this? What did you expect to find?" She cocked her head a little and looked me up and down. "And what were you doing with the costume?

Did you think you were going to dress up as the Black Stiletto and come fight me again?" Her body shook as she laughed some more. I was afraid she'd accidentally pull the trigger. Then she stopped, studied me, and said, "I do think it will fit you."

"What?"

"The costume. You *should* put it on. I want you to. What sweet vengeance it will be. I almost hope my man doesn't call back. Slaughtering the bitch's granddaughter while the girl is dressed as the Stiletto will taste so, so delicious. Don't move. I'll be right back."

She turned and hobbled out of the room. What was I going to do? The woman was mad, absolutely crazy bonkers, evil, witch-fucking mad. I twisted my head and looked at McCambridge, who indeed still had his gun trained on me.

"Don't try anything," he said.

"Are you insane too? Why do you work for her? The money can't be *that* good. She's crazy, don't you see that?"

He shrugged. "I've known Christina a long time. She's a little eccentric. So what? Oh, and the money is that good, so shut up."

After a moment, Mrs. B. returned carrying a paper grocery bag stuffed with the Stiletto costume. She emptied the contents on the coffee table. Everything was there—the jacket, trousers, boots, gloves, mask, belt, and accessories, and the stiletto and sheath. She removed the knife, though, and placed it in her housedress pocket. "I don't think you should have this," she said. "It's sharp and you might cut yourself." She laughed at her "joke." "Okay, my dear, get dressed."

"No," I said. "You're out of your mind."

"We can make you do it, you know."

"Then make me. I'm not going to fulfill some stupid fantasy of yours."

She glared at me and then shrugged her shoulders. "Fine. I'll call my man back and tell him to kill your grandmother now and hold the phone up to her so you can hear her scream. I'm sure she remembers how to scream. Pain is pain, Alzheimer's or not."

"*All right!*" I shouted. "I'll do it! Jesus! You're a fucking *freak!*"

The woman's eyes burned red. It was as if the fires of hell had erupted inside her body and were visible through those dark, menacing pupils. She picked up the shotgun and aimed it at me.

As humiliating as it was, I did it. I removed my t-shirt, jeans, and sandals, revealing myself in my underwear in front of the awful woman and that creep, McCambridge, who, I was certain, enjoyed the little show. I then put on the Black Stiletto costume—excuse me, the Black Stiletto *outfit*, as my grandma insisted on calling it. The trousers fit, but the bottom hems were a little long—my grandma was slightly taller than me when she was my age. The jacket was perfect. The mask I'd already tried—I knew how to bunch up my hair and push it under the hood. The gloves and belt were next.

"Go ahead and strap on the knife sheath," Mrs. B. ordered. "Your leg doesn't look right without it."

Fine. I did as instructed, and then stood there, on display, as the Black Stiletto.

The gradual change that came over the woman's face was palpable. I truly believed her sick mind transported itself back to another time and place. Her eyes grew wide and her mouth formed an *O*, as if she was gazing upon the real thing. At that moment, Christina Bartlett lost her sense of reality, for her breathing became rapid, she became visibly agitated, and she cried out with glee—

"Finally. After all these years. I found you."

"Now what, lady?" I asked. I felt very self-conscious.

"At last, I finally found you! I always said I'd break *your* kneecaps, and I will, I surely will!"

Holy shit, she really was going bonkers.

"*Ralph*! Let's take Judy to the barn. I don't want to get blood all over my parlor."

Judy? I was right. The woman had gone off the deep end.

I twisted my head back to McCambridge. From the expression on *his* face, I could tell that he was more than a little disturbed by the turn of events. Nevertheless, he gestured with the gun and said, "Let's go."

50
Judy's Diary
1962

DECEMBER 13, 1962

It's morning and I'm in Abilene, Texas, at a motel. Terrible things have happened, dear diary. Oh my God, I don't know how I can live with myself. Martin and I are on our way to Illinois, and I'm frightened and saddened and I hate the fact that I ever became the Black Stiletto. My alter ego has caused so much pain and now death.

On the 11th, Martin and I visited my mother's and John's graves at the cemetery, which was sobering and depressing. I told Martin that his grandmother and uncle were buried there, but of course he just goo-goo'd and slobbered as I held him. We didn't stay long—I just couldn't. Then we spent all day with Frankie and his family. It was cold and overcast, so we couldn't have a picnic outside. We ended up just eating a lot and playing with Angela. Sarah took a picture of Frankie, Martin, and me with her camera. I wish I had a copy of it. Oh gosh, I can't help the tears as I write this.

Well, Martin became a little fussy, and I figured out he missed that old rattle. We left it at Skipper's. I also realized that I still had the gold key to the Chinese jewel box. Skipper would need that to open the box when it came time to sell the diamond. He had the diamond and the box in his safe. So, I called Skipper. He said he was going to be out all day, but if I wanted to come by in the morning before I left town, he'd be there.

That night, after a lovely visit, I promised Frankie I'd be in touch once I was settled, and to expect a "gift" from me in the near future. I wouldn't elaborate. I said goodbye to Sarah and my beautiful niece, Angela, and hugged and kissed Frankie goodbye.

Little did I know—

Martin and I went back to the Sahara Inn to sleep. Yesterday morning, I checked out, packed everything, and planned to run by Skipper's place on my way out of Odessa. When I got there, I pulled Martin out of his car seat and went to the door. Skipper didn't answer my knock—but the door was open. I felt a sudden rush of apprehension; my old instincts indicated something was very wrong.

"Skipper?" I called. No answer. I pushed the door open and went in.

Oh God, dear diary, Skipper was dead. He was on the floor and his wheelchair was turned over. I quickly covered Martin's eyes— although he was so young I don't think it registered. I took him back out to the car and sat him in the seat, but I left the door open. "I'll be right back, honey," I told him. He started to cry, but I had to go back in for a moment.

What could have happened? Who did this?

Upon further examination of Skipper, I saw that he'd been tortured. There was a hammer on the floor and its head was bloody. Skipper's hands were broken, mashed, and in a mess. Oh my Lord, I felt so terrible.

Then my eyes went to the safe behind his desk—and it was wide open. I rushed over and saw that the Chinese box was missing.

I went to his desk and called the police. And as I was talking to the dispatcher, I saw a notepad on which Skipper had written my brother's name, address, and phone number. *Frank Cooper.*

Oh heavens, they were in trouble. I knew it. Whoever killed Skipper probably went to Frankie's house, no doubt looking for me.

Leo. It had to be him.

I rushed back outside—with the rattle, which I found on the floor where we'd left it—and that calmed down Martin. I probably should have waited for the police to arrive, but I had to get to Frankie's as soon as possible. It was clear on the other side of town. Besides, the questions I would have to answer might be too much. I'd have to explain to the cops who I was, what was stolen from the safe, and so on. Best they handled it on their own.

On the drive over, I felt absolutely terrible. First Barry and then his brother Skipper. They had died because of me. If I hadn't entered their lives, they'd still be alive. And what was I going to find at Frankie's house?

Sure enough, a Lincoln Continental was parked in front of the home on Beechwood. I recognized it as Boone's car, the one Leo used for business purposes. I grabbed my purse, took Martin out of his seat, and went to the door. I rang the doorbell. After a moment, I heard movement and low voices. Frankie answered. He face was ashen. He held the door open for me.

"Frankie?"

"Come in, Judy."

I walked in, and there was Leo, holding a gun at us.

"Leo!" I snapped. "You've gone too far this time!" Of course, it was only bravado, considering the situation. He looked absolutely crazed, as if he'd been charged with electricity. His hands shook and his eyes were red. I knew the man would be totally unpredictable, so I had to be very careful.

"*There's* my son," he said, and a smile played on his lips.

"*He's* Martin's father?" Frankie blurted.

"*Shut up!*" Leo barked. "Bring him here, Judy."

"No, Leo." Martin started to cry. He sensed the tension in the air.

"All right, everybody come in the living room and sit down." He pointed the gun at Frankie. "Or the brother gets it. And no funny stuff, Judy. You keep your distance."

I had no choice but to comply. Martin clung to me and I held him in my lap as I sat on the sofa. Leo sat in a chair opposite us, and Frankie sat on a chair next to the antique wall clock.

"Where're Sarah and Angela?" I asked.

"Angela had an earache and they went to the doctor," Frankie said. He looked at the clock. "I'm afraid they'll be back in an hour. I was about to go to work when *he* showed up."

"Shut up!" Leo commanded.

Oh God, I thought, *please get us out of this*.

"Judy," Leo said. "I've gone to a lot of trouble to find you."

"Leo, can't you just leave? Can't you forget about us? Please?"

He shouted, causing Martin to cry louder. "No! You goddamned bitch, do you realize what you've *done*? The Black Stiletto! You're the goddamned Black Stiletto!"

Frankie looked back and forth at us. "What?"

"Be quiet, Frankie," I said.

"That's right, *Frankie*, your sister is the legendary Black Stiletto. And you know what she did to me? First of all, she stole a very precious diamond from me. You have the gold key, Judy, so hand it over. *Now*." He kept the gun trained on me and held out his other hand.

"You'd really shoot me and your child, Leo?" I asked.

"Shut up! The *key*."

I reached into my purse and was surprised once again that my Smith & Wesson was still there, loaded and ready. I kept forgetting about it, but I was sure glad it was there. Could I risk it? I had to distract him somehow.

"All right, Leo, I assume you have the box and the diamond."

"Right here in my pocket."

I noticed the bulge in his jacket. So I pulled out my keys, removed the gold one, and *tossed* it to him. It landed on the carpet at his feet. I thought I'd reach for the gun when he averted his eyes to pick up the key. But he didn't move. He kept watching me and the baby. I set the purse on the sofa, directly by my right side, where I could reach it easily.

"What did you name him?"

"I'm not telling you."

"What's his name?"

It was no use. "Martin."

Leo tried it out. "Martin. Martin Kelly. I like it."

Then I slipped up. "It's Martin Talbot. He'll never be Martin Kelly."
I winced. I hadn't meant to tell Leo our new last name, although it
was possible that he already knew it from Skipper.

"We'll see about that. Maybe Martin would like to come live
with me in Florida. Or Europe. Wherever we can go to be safe."

"You wouldn't dare take him," I said with venom.

"Aren't you going to say, 'over my dead body'? 'Cause that's
probably how I'll do it."

My heart was pounding. I kept telling myself to *think, think, think*!
I had to keep him talking. "You killed Barry and Skipper," I said.

"Oh, too bad. Were they friends of yours?"

Ignoring his cruel words, I said, "I understand there's a contract
out on you, Leo. You know it won't take long for DeAngelo to find
you, no matter where you go."

Leo addressed Frankie, but kept the gun on me. "You know
what else your sister did? She ruined my business. She ruined me.
She broke my sister's kneecap and now Christina's going to prison."

"She's a murderer and deserves it, just like you," I said.

"You'll pay for it, Judy. Why don't you put Martin on the floor?"

He was going to shoot me as soon as I did. I didn't want Martin
hurt, so I did. The poor boy started to cry and reach for me; it was
a good thing he couldn't crawl or stand yet. His helplessness actually saved his life and kept him out of harm's way.

Then Leo aimed at my chest and said, "Judy, you broke my heart.
See you in hell." Without taking my eyes off of him, I shot my hand
toward the purse. I grasped the grip of the gun—but *Frankie* jumped
out of his chair and attacked Leo!

"No!" I shouted, but Frankie had already knocked Leo off the
chair. The gun discharged and the round hit the wall behind me.
I pulled out my gun, stood, and aimed it at the two figures now

grappling on the carpet. "Frankie, get off of him!" I yelled, but Leo's gun went off again. Frankie jerked and gasped.

"NO! Frankie!"

Leo rolled Frankie off and pointed the gun at me—but I squeezed the trigger first. The bullet went through the bastard's forehead. My practice in Barry's canyon paid off. Leo dropped his weapon and immediately went limp.

"Frankie, Frankie," I cried as I knelt beside my brother. He was barely alive. "I'll call for an ambulance!" But then I heard car doors slam outside in front. Had Sarah and Angela returned already? I couldn't let them walk in on this scene! Frankie whispered, "Run."

I stood and looked out the window. *Oh, no*—it was a fancy black car, and Ricky Bartlett and the same two men I saw him with at the coffee shop got out of it.

Ricky Bartlett! Could I hold them off? Would I be able to shoot all three of them?

Dear diary, I had the presence of mind, right then and there, to squat by Leo, reach into his jacket pocket, and grab the Chinese box. I shook it—heard the diamond rattle inside—and, not knowing what else to do, I went to the antique wall clock and opened it. I felt for the latch and revealed the hidden compartment. I stuck the jewel box inside, shut the clock, picked up the gold key from the floor, went to the sofa, shoved my gun and the key into my purse, and resumed my place on the floor beside my brother. By then, Bartlett and the men were inside, guns drawn. Frankie was gone. Calling an ambulance wouldn't have helped. I picked up Martin and held him, trying to comfort his cries.

Bartlett took a moment to examine the situation. "Let me guess," he said. "Leo tried to take the baby, and your brother tried to stop him. They shot each other."

That sounded as good as anything I could make up. I didn't know what Bartlett knew about me, so I nodded. "Yes." Tears poured down my face.

Bartlett nodded to his two men. "Search him." They got down and went through Leo's pockets and pulled out everything.

"It's not here, boss," one said.

Bartlett replied, "Go search his car, both of you. I'll handle her." The two men put away their weapons and went outside. Bartlett looked at me, and asked, "So that's Leo's kid, huh?" I didn't answer. "So is your name Nancy or Judy?"

"Judy."

"Judy Cooper, right?"

He didn't know my new last name. "Yeah."

"When Leo told me you had family in Odessa, I looked up some public records. I knew your brother. He ran a nice hardware store. That's how we found you just now." I didn't say anything. "So, Judy Cooper, do you know anything about a diamond Leo and his sister stole from Maria DeAngelo?"

I shook my head.

"You sure? I talked to Vince DeAngelo this morning. He told me all about it. Said Leo and Christina killed Maria and took her diamond necklace, and it's worth *a lot.*"

"I haven't spoken to Leo in months before today."

"Would Skipper Gorman know anything about it? Should I go talk to him?"

Oh, my gosh, I thought, he wasn't aware that Skipper was dead. It suddenly dawned on me that Skipper wouldn't be "investing" Bartlett's money, and the man didn't know it was missing. Yet.

"Why would he?" I asked and shrugged as I wiped the tears off my face.

Bartlett held out his hand. "Hand me your purse."

"What?"

"I'm just looking for the diamond. Covering all the bases. Hand it over."

So, I did. I sure was glad I'd hid the jewel box in the clock! The man rummaged through it, took nothing, and handed it back.

"I don't know anything about a diamond or money," I said.

Bartlett sat in a chair and looked at us. "So what am I going to do with you?"

"Let us go?" I meekly suggested.

He was quiet for a moment. Then he surprised me. "Yeah. Okay. Get out of here. Take the kid. I'll handle this. I'll get rid of Leo's body. I'm afraid I can't do anything about your brother though. The police will have to find him and piece together what happened. You know, a robbery gone wrong."

I nodded. I felt so bad for Sarah and Angela. But I knew I had to get out of there before Bartlett figured out I really did know something about the diamond and that I had over a million dollars of his money. So I stood with Martin in my arms, dear diary, and said, "Thank you." Then I walked out the door. Bartlett stuck his head out and told his men to let me go. Had any of the neighbors heard the gunshots? No one was outside, except for some kids playing down the block a ways. And they were playing with cap guns! The real firearms probably blended in with those!

I got in the Futura and drove away. I got on Highway 80 and headed toward Midland. Martin soon fell asleep and I started bawling. I felt immense guilt about Frankie and his family. Was I crazy to walk away? Should I have done something to Bartlett?

The more I thought about it, though, the more I realized I'd done the smart thing. *Martin's* life was more important. If I'd stayed and tried to do something, I would have dug a hole so deep I couldn't have crawled out. Frankie's murder would be a mystery for the police and would become a cold case. I knew that someday in the future I will have to come back and get the diamond out of the hiding place. I just hope no one finds it before I do! Although, if Sarah discovers it, I guess that will be yet another puzzle for her to solve, but a very nice one. Frankie said she didn't know about the trick compartment in the clock, so who knows what will happen?

Bartlett will soon find out his money is gone. Will he figure out that *I* took it? Probably. He seems like an intelligent guy. So the sooner I get to Illinois and "disappear," the better. Above all, I want Martin to grow up safe.

Do I feel bad about killing my son's father? I don't know. Maybe a little. He was a very bad man. I'm still determined that Martin will never know who his father really was while he's growing up.

Now we're about to check out of the motel in Abilene and drive on. The future is very murky, but I know one thing—I don't think I'll ever be the Black Stiletto again.

51
Martin
THE PRESENT

"You have eight more minutes," Haines announced.

Maggie and I sat there like dunces, not saying a word. Eventually, Haines sighed, removed his feet from the coffee table, and stood. He slowly walked around the room with the gun still in his hand and stopped behind the couch. The bastard put his free hand on Maggie's hair and stroked it. I felt her wince.

"This could all be over if you'd just tell me where that diamond is and what happened to the money," he said to me. "Are you going to be brave for your woman here, and cough up what I want to know? Or are you going to be a worm and a coward and let her down? Are you going sit there like a toadstool while I do *this?*"

He abruptly pulled Maggie's hair and jerked her head back hard. She shrieked and I hollered, "Hey!" but I was incapable of action. Poor Maggie closed her eyes and whimpered as he held her head in that position. I couldn't just sit there like a *toadstool*. I finally got to my feet, feebly pushed on Haines, and shouted, "Leave her alone!" He released her and shoved me away as if I was a bug. The man was strong. I tripped backward over the coffee table and fell on the floor.

Maggie got up to attend to me. "Martin, are you hurt?"

"Only my pride," I grumbled. "I'm sorry. Are you okay?"

Haines laughed. He strode around from behind the couch and resumed his place in front of the chair. "Lady, get your worm off the floor and sit him down where he won't get hurt," he said. That smarted even more than the shove. We both stood and resumed sitting on the couch. My heart was beating so rapidly I thought it would burst out of my chest. The anxiety level was hovering in the red Danger Zone. Tears formed in my eyes. Maggie took my hand.

"Oh, look, I made the worm cry," Haines said. He sat again and put his feet back on the coffee table. Noting his watch, he proclaimed that we had six minutes left.

"Don't listen to him, Martin," Maggie whispered.

We heard my mom moan in the other room. Maggie and I looked at each other. One of us needed to go in there. Haines narrowed his eyes and gazed toward the little hall that led to the two bedrooms.

"Is that the Black Stiletto making all that noise? She sounds like a sick cow," he said.

That made my anger overtake my fear, so I said with all the bravado I could muster, "One of these days, Mr. Haines, you, too, will be old and maybe you'll have Alzheimer's."

He chuckled. "Old, yeah. I'm certainly going to outlive her and you two. Now, are we going to start talking about that diamond and money? Time's a-wasting."

"I must go see to her," Maggie said. "Please."

Haines thought about that and again removed his feet from the coffee table. In doing so, he knocked my briefcase on the floor. "All right. Let's all go see the Black Stiletto." He stood but kept the pistol on us.

My briefcase. My mom's Smith & Wesson was inside of it. Was it possible...?

The man jerked his head toward the hall. "I'll follow you. Don't forget, I can blow holes in both of you in one stinking second."

Maggie and I shared a glance and she nodded. We got up and went to Mom's room, where she lay in bed. Her eyes were closed, but her head rocked slowly back and forth. The low moan indicated something was wrong, but I didn't have a clue what it was.

"Judy?" Maggie said to her. She placed her palm on Mom's

forehead and stopped the rocking. Mom's eyes fluttered open and she looked at us. Haines stayed in the doorway, so she didn't see him. "What's wrong, Judy? Are you thirsty?" Maggie reached for the cup of water and straw on the nightstand and offered it to my mother. With the straw in her mouth, Mom took a little bit of liquid.

"How pathetic," Haines said. "So this is the Black Stiletto. What a joke."

I wanted to kill the guy. The son of a bitch had to die. How was I going to do it? *Could* I do it? It was something I thought I never in a million years could consider. The idea was preposterous. Martin Talbot—the *nebbish* accountant with an anxiety disorder and the courage of a doormat—a killer?

Leaning over my mother, I got her attention by speaking softly. "Mom? It's me, your son, Martin." Her eyes locked on mine. "Hey, guess what, Mom. I'm going to prove to the world that I really am the son of the Black Stiletto." She blinked but didn't freak out like she used to do whenever I mentioned her alter-ego. Then she blinked again. Was she giving me permission? Giving me the green light? I brought my face closer and kissed her cheek. "It's going to be all right, Mom."

Then I turned and addressed the intruder. "All right, Mr. Haines. I'll give you the diamond. It's in there." I nodded toward the living room. "I'd like Maggie to stay in here with my mother, though."

Maggie was confused. "What? Martin?"

I looked at my fiancée and answered, "It's okay, Maggie. We have to do what the man says, otherwise they'll hurt Gina and us."

"Martin, he'll kill us anyway. And you don—"

"I have to take the man at his word," I interrupted. "I'm going to give him the diamond. It is mine, and you don't have any say about it." I moved toward the door. "Follow me, Mr. Haines." There was even some surprise written on *his* face.

We both went into the hall. I locked eyes with Maggie as I started to close the bedroom door. Her expression silently demanded, *What the hell are you doing?* "Just wait here, Maggie," I said for Haines's benefit.

"Please. Comfort Mom." I didn't let her protest—I shut the door and led Haines back into the living room.

"I'm afraid I can't do anything about the missing money, Mr. Haines," I told him. "Mom used that all up. It's what we lived on. But I can give you the diamond. It's brought nothing but trouble."

I picked up my briefcase from the floor, set it on the coffee table, and knelt in front of it. The only thing I had to do was rotate the two combination locks on either side of the latches. Haines stood at the other end of the coffee table, his back to the fireplace and his gun still aimed at me.

"Please, Mr. Haines. Do you have to point the gun? It makes me very nervous. I feel like I might throw up, and that'll be really gross."

"You weak little shit," Haines said. He lowered his arm, but the gun remained in his hand. "Just open the goddamned case, worm."

"Okay, okay."

I slid the correct numbers in place and unlatched the briefcase. I opened it so that the top blocked his view of the contents, which faced me. Then I faked surprise. "Where the…oh, no, I thought I put it in here!" I grasped the Smith & Wesson firmly in my hand before lifting it out of the case.

Haines started toward me. *"What do you mean?"*

I raised my arm and squeezed the trigger.

The loud recoil scared the holy hell out of me and practically jerked my wrist and hand off. The round hit Haines square in the chest. Time stood still for a couple of seconds, and then a red inkblot spread on his shirt just left of his sternum. His eyes grew wide with astonishment. He staggered and lifted his arm to shoot me. I leapt to the side as his gun went off, missing me by a mile. By then, his legs had lost their ability to hold his weight. The man crashed onto the coffee table where I had earlier, and then he slid to the floor.

Maggie rushed out of the bedroom. *"Martin!"* She beheld the scene in front of her; her hand went to her mouth to stifle a scream.

"I'm all right!" I said. "I'm all right!" I still held the gun. "Check him. Is he dead?"

She hurried over and placed her fingers on his neck to check his pulse. "Yes. Martin, he's dead. You killed him!"

I managed to stand and gaze at the man lying on the floor like a ragdoll. "Who's the worm *now*, asshole?" I spat.

After a moment, I placed the gun back in my briefcase and locked it inside. Maggie and I stared at each other for a moment—and then we collided in an intense embrace. "Oh my God, Maggie," I said repeatedly.

"Christ, Martin!" she said. "You crazy fool, I love you!"

It was only then that the enormity of what I'd done hit me. I fainted.

I remembered coming to on the floor. Apparently, I was out only for a few seconds. Maggie was kneeling over me, lightly slapping my face.

"Martin? Martin? Oh, there you are. Oh, Martin, are you all right? Did you hit your head when you fell?"

Nothing hurt. "I don't think so."

I tried to sit up but she pushed me back. "No, wait a minute before you get up. I'm calling the police. Stay here." She stood and found her purse.

"Call Detective Scott," I said. "He'll know what to do." I told her where his card was, and she phoned him while I took some meds!

I felt fine twenty minutes later, but the house was a scene of pandemonium. The street was full of cops, an ambulance, a fire truck, and every neighbor within ten blocks. Detective Scott somehow found a way to take charge, even though it wasn't his jurisdiction. I'd already tried to call Gina, but got her voice mail. I told Scott what was going on in Odessa, so he got on the radio to alert the local police there.

"Don't worry, Mr. Talbot," he said, "we'll make sure your daughter is safe."

I hoped so. We were awfully late sending help.

Maggie decided it was best to take Mom back to Woodlands that night. Calls were made, strings were pulled, and an ambulance took Mom and Maggie to the nursing home in the middle of the night. I repeated my story several times to Scott and other policemen, and I promised to appear in person at the precinct to make a detailed statement during daylight hours. The words "Black Stiletto" were never mentioned. There was a lot of sitting around and waiting, so I picked up Mom's fifth diary and continued reading while men—uniformed and not—went back and forth, in and out. I nearly made it to the end of the book. Boy, did I learn some things.

Finally, Detective Scott took me aside and said that the Odessa police and sheriff's department had gone to the Bartlett Ranch and found it burning to the ground. He didn't have all the details, but there was no sign of my daughter. I continued to call her cell but just got voice mail. Of course, I freaked out and demanded that he find out more. Scott suggested I go home—to Maggie's—and wait for news.

Damn.

52
Gina
The Present

I had to think fast. All of my training in Krav Maga was at my disposal. Josh always said I'd advanced faster than any pupil he'd ever taught, but I was still a novice. I'd been practicing the discipline for less than a year. But I knew a few things. There was no way I was letting McCambridge and that crazy bitch march me outside and into a barn.

The concept behind Krav Maga was to instinctively make defensive moves and deliver attacks without thinking about them. *Retzev.* I knew to use my entire body by pivoting at the hips and striking through my target. I knew it was important to breathe. And I knew to aim for vulnerable targets.

We hadn't left the parlor yet. Christina Bartlett stood several feet away, the shotgun still aimed at me. A coffee table and footstool sat between us. McCambridge, though, was two feet behind me, between two iron candleholder stands. His gun remained pointed at my back.

"I said 'let's go,' " he repeated.

And so it began. Instead of my grandmother leaping into action as the Black Stiletto, it was me. That thought alone was empowering.

First, I closed the short distance between me and the old man by taking a step back. Then I used my head to lead my body while my hips generated power to deliver a short, compact strike to McCambridge's neck with my right elbow. I brought my wrist into my body with my forearm parallel to the ground. As I turned, I opened up with my right leg by stepping to the rear to build momentum and force in the arm. As the elbow propelled back, I pivoted my rear in the same direction, increasing the strength of the strike. The hard knob of the elbow connected with the soft tissue under McCambridge's chin, and there was an ugly snapping sound.

I didn't stop there. Josh had taught me to follow through with at least one or two more attacks to make sure my opponent was disabled. I continued to swivel my body so that I faced the man. Before he could react to the pain and damage my first blow inflicted, I delivered an uppercut elbow strike with my left arm, which was perfect for attacking someone taller than me. I bent my knees slightly to generate power from my lower body, which allowed my hips to explode through the target. I pivoted my front leg inward, straightened my knees, brought my striking arm close to my ear for proper follow-through, and thrust my elbow upward. Again, I hit McCambridge's exposed throat.

A knee to the groin was automatic.

By then, the man had been incapacitated—his brain just hadn't realized it yet. It had taken three seconds at most. The gun in his right hand still pointed at me, but he hadn't been able to send the command to his finger to squeeze the trigger. I grabbed his right wrist with my left hand and then quickly brought my right elbow down hard on his forearm—breaking it. The gun fell to the floor. His impulse to scream was hampered by the crushed larynx. Instead, he made horrid choking sounds and collapsed to his knees.

I had the presence of mind to whirl around and face Mrs. Bartlett, who was lifting the shotgun and screaming, *"No!"* I leaped to the side as the deafening blast shook the room. The shot pellets missed me entirely as I dropped to the floor and rolled, but they sprayed McCambridge and most of the parlor furniture in our vicinity. The explosion knocked over one of the candle stands too. The crazy woman had perforated her own employee, although I was pretty sure he'd have choked to death from the injuries I'd wreaked on him.

I heard her slide the pump on the gun, effectively cocking it to fire another shell, so I bolted forward, hovering close to the floor. The most practical way out was for me to duck through the draped archway *behind* the woman, although I had no idea where it would take me. It was a better plan than retreating, for her second shot covered the entrance.

"Hold still, damn you!" she hollered. "Wha—?"

My maneuver confused her and she was too slow to turn around. Once I was through the arch, I found myself in a corridor that led two ways—to the left was a larger, open room, while to the right the hall went on toward closed doors—bedrooms, maybe? I went left.

It was a rustic, huge living room that adjoined a spacious kitchen. A dining room could be seen through an archway on the other side of the space, and a utility room was next to the kitchen. More old western-like furniture and candle stands were the dominant decorative theme. A sliding glass door on the opposite wall opened to the outdoors, which I figured was the back of the house. That's where I headed, hoping the woman hadn't employed more gunmen at the ranch. When I made it to the door, Mrs. Bartlett appeared in the living room, expertly reloading the shotgun with shells. There was no time to unlock the latch and slide open the door before she raised the gun and fired across the room, so I performed a sideways leap toward the kitchen. The blast shattered the glass and made a mess of some shelves stocked with knickknacks and chinaware. Everything crashed to the floor.

I landed hard on my left side, crawled until I reach a food-prep stand in the middle of the kitchen, and then got to my feet. The crazy woman was shouting at me, treading across the living room in pursuit. Mrs. Bartlett wasn't using her cane, so her steps were very wobbly. She spied me in the kitchen, stopped, and raised the gun—but her balance was off; she wavered and dropped the shotgun to prevent toppling, but it was too late. To catch her fall, her left hand caught the nearest object—a candle stand—but her weight and momentum were too much for her to control. She went down hard, and took the stand with her. The lit candles landed just beneath decorative drapes that outlined the archway—and they caught fire.

She cried out in pain. The woman was old; falls can be serious for the aged. Mrs. Bartlett might have broken a hip. I didn't care about her or the fire, I just wanted out of that place. I moved back to the sliding glass door. The shattered hole was too jagged for me to slip through, so I unlatched the lock, slid open the door, and ran outside.

I found myself on a large brick patio with an outdoor grill and a variety of lawn furniture. Beyond that, the barn was to my left and another small building was to my right. As I ran to the side of the house and to the front, where my car was, I heard Mrs. Bartlett scream. I tried to block it out, but when I reached my car, the smoke alarms had gone off and now accompanied her shrieks. They were so loud I thought they might be audible for miles.

Nevertheless, I got in the driver's seat. The safety of my car was a huge relief. My heart was pounding and I took a moment to catch my breath. Then I reached for the keys to start the car and—

Shit! My purse was still in the damned parlor! The keys were in it, along with my driver's license, money, credit cards, well, all that was unimportant, but I needed those keys.

When I got out of the car, I suddenly remembered I was still dressed as the Black Stiletto. It was a totally bizarre sensation.

I burst through the front door and rushed inside. Oh my God, the fallen candles had also set stuff on fire in the parlor. The place was *ablaze*! Wincing from the smoke, I went in, quickly found my purse, and moved to run out the front to fresh air.

Mrs. Bartlett's screams halted me.

Damn, I couldn't leave her to burn to death. No matter what she'd done to my Grandma, or to me, the woman deserved better than that.

Silently cursing some more, I avoided a wall of fire and darted through the archway and into the living room. The flames on the drapes were raging. Portions of burning fabric had dropped to a rug and set *it* on fire. The situation had become quite serious. Christina Bartlett was helpless on the floor, very near the broiling carpet. I jumped over the blaze and knelt beside her. Christ, a side of her housedress was smoking, so I grabbed a cushion from a nearby chair to smother the flames around her.

Seeing the terror on her face was unforgettable, but I thought her reaction might be more from the face of the Black Stiletto looking down at her rather than the fire.

"I'll get you out of here," I said. Despite the possibility of broken bones in her frail body, I cradled the old woman in my arms and picked her up. Her arm and much of her side had been burned. She screamed in pain.

I carried her quickly across a barrier of flames toward the back door I'd left open. The fresh air hit us like a wall, and it was such a relief. I had to stop and lay her on a patio recliner in order to catch my breath, but the coughs came loud and hard. She also wheezed and coughed and groaned. After my strength returned, I dragged the recliner, with her on it, away from harm's way, about thirty yards toward one of the other little buildings on the property.

Much to my shock, there was a woman standing in front of it.

She was Hispanic, wore a nightgown, looked to be in her forties or so, and was scared to death.

"Who are you?" I asked, probably a little too aggressively. Her appearance had startled me.

She was too frightened to speak. It was the costume. She was looking at the Black Stiletto.

"It's all right. I'm the Black Stiletto," I said. "I saved Mrs. Bartlett from the fire. Did you call the fire department?"

She didn't answer.

"You need to call the fire department. What's your name?" Finally—"Marisol."

"Do you work here?"

She nodded. "I'm the cook. And maid."

I gestured to the little building. "You live there?"

She nodded again.

"Well, look. I have to go. Call the fire department and take care of Mrs. Bartlett." I turned toward the ranch house—the place was indeed burning down. "I'm afraid I couldn't do anything for Mr. McCambridge."

I took a few more seconds to look down at the broken woman once known as Christina Kelly. She was still breathing, but I thought it doubtful she would survive the fall and burns. Then I remembered—I reached into her housedress pocket, took the stiletto, and sheathed it on my leg.

Once I was in my car, driving back to Odessa, I realized I was still wearing the mask. I tugged it off. I wanted to call Dad, but I needed a battery for my phone. My speed was off the charts, so I forced myself to slow down and breathe. Several police cars, an ambulance, and two fire trucks passed me on the highway into town, headed in the opposite direction toward the ranch.

At the hotel I changed clothes. I'd have to forget about what I'd worn and left at the ranch. A nearby twenty-four-hour convenience store sold batteries for the phone, and I saw that Dad had left several frantic messages. When I called him, he was at Maggie's, and boy, was he glad to hear from me. I filled him in on what had happened, and he told me *his* story. Jesus, I was so proud of him. I can't believe he stepped up to the plate the way he did. I told him I loved him and he repeated the words to me.

Then he said, "Gina, you need to get back here soon. Your grandma is dying. When they got back to the nursing home, she took a turn for the worse. Honey, Maggie thinks it might happen in the next forty-eight hours."

"Oh, no!"

"Yeah."

I had an open ticket so I said I'd try to get home that very day, but it was the middle of the night. I was sore and my energy was depleted; I needed to shower and try to sleep a few hours.

"Listen, Gina, there's something you need to do before you go to the airport," Dad said.

"What's that?"

"Go by Angela's house."

He told me where the diamond was hidden.

I woke up in my hotel bed around nine o'clock, later than I'd intended, after some fitful hours of sleep. My dreams weren't pleasant; all I remembered, though, was that I was really *hot* and couldn't find an air conditioner! A cup of coffee would help clear the cobwebs. Before I dressed, I got online and made my flight arrangements. I'd get back to Chicago late afternoon. It was the best I could get—there weren't that many daily flights operating from Midland-Odessa.

To save time, I ate breakfast at McDonald's, and then I drove to Angela's house. I didn't know how I was going to accomplish what I was about to do, so I figured I'd just tell her the truth about the diamond. If I really find it, I resolved that Angela should have some of the money it brings in. Dad would be okay with that, I'm sure.

But no one was home. I rang the doorbell and knocked several times.

Damn. What to do?

I sat in my car to think about it, and then an idea struck me. I got out, opened the trunk, got my suitcase, and pulled out Grandma's outfit. A little pouch was attached to the belt. As I expected, a ring of thin metal rods was in there, so I took them to the front door of the house. I'd never used lock picks before. I didn't know how. But I started trying the freaking things, one by one, in the keyhole. I twisted and poked and pulled and rattled them, certain that I'd fail.

And then the door opened!

Whoa, I thought. I looked up and down the neighborhood to make sure no one saw me, and then I went inside.

The antique clock on the wall was tick-tocking away. Dad had tried to explain how to find the secret compartment over the phone, but I was flying by the seat of my pants. I opened the front and reached inside to feel around in the back—which *was* set farther out from the wall than it appeared. I found a latch and flicked it. Something snapped. The entire clock housing pivoted open on a hinge. I looked in the slot in back, and sure enough—there was an ornate jewel box with Chinese markings on it.

I shook it and heard something rattle inside.

Oh my God.

My family was going to be rich.

53
Judy's Diary
1962

December 18, 1962

Martin and I are in Arlington Heights, Illinois. It's a sleepy little suburb of Chicago. I haven't seen the big city yet. Apparently the suburbs around Chicago are expanding at a rapid rate. All of the surrounding towns, or "villages," sort of run into each other—there's Palatine and Wheeling and Rolling Meadows and Northbrook and so on. A lot of the housing is either pretty old or quite new. We're at a hotel right now, but we should be moving into an apartment before the New Year. At first I didn't think I could stand to live in such a quiet, unexciting place, but Thomas convinced me that it would be the safest thing I could do.

Thomas Avery is Barry and Skipper's cousin. He's younger than I expected, he's not quite 30. He's a lawyer who handles all kinds of stuff, but mostly estate planning and financial issues. How he has the knowledge to work around the system to help me integrate into society as "Judy Talbot" is beyond me. I guess he took lessons from his cousins, ha ha. He's not married, and actually he's a very nice-looking man. I like him. Martin has taken to him as well. To Martin, I call him "Uncle Thomas." I think Thomas and I will become very good friends.

Our trip to Illinois was uneventful. Let's see, after Abilene we drove through Wichita Falls, and then entered Oklahoma. In that state we drove through Lawton, Oklahoma City, and Tulsa. That was all pretty boring. Missouri was next, and we went through Springfield and stayed a day in St. Louis. I liked that city. Illinois was next, and most of the state was flat and prairie-like—we went through another town called Springfield, where Abraham Lincoln lived, and finally made it to Arlington Heights, which is northwest of Chicago. Pretty soon Thomas said he'd take Martin and me into the city and show us around.

Thomas took my 1.2 million dollars and will set up what he calls a "trust" that I'll be able to draw on. He'll take a commission each year for acting as my lawyer. The money will be deposited through underground channels to an offshore account. I don't really understand how it works, but as long as Thomas can do it and it's not illegal, then I'm good with that. I've set up regular checking and savings accounts at the First Arlington National Bank, which is located not too far from Thomas's office, at Campbell and Dunton. He's fixing it so I'll receive $2500 a month for forty years. That means I won't have to work! He said that as time goes on, $2500 a month might not be worth as much as it is now, especially when I'm older. But we'll worry about that when the time comes.

He's going to help me find a place to live and we have our eyes on an apartment in the same general area. He, too, suggested that Martin and I move around a lot for the first few years and not settle permanently until we know it's safe. From what he's managed to find out, I'm *not* safe. Ricky Bartlett is looking for me. Apparently, he discovered that his money is missing. And, by now, Vincent DeAngelo must know that Leo didn't have the diamond. Thomas believes that these guys aren't stupid. They're going to figure out that "Judy Cooper" took the money *and* the diamond.

For now, though, the diamond is safe back in Odessa. I don't know when I'll be able to go back and get it, but I'm not going to worry about it. I'm pretty much set for life without it. The money will support us. At least I still have the gold key, so no one can open that darned Chinese box without me.

I asked Thomas if Bartlett or DeAngelo will find out about *him*, since he's related to Barry and Skipper. Thomas isn't concerned. He told me—in confidence—that Thomas Avery isn't *his* real name either! I guess that explains why he knows so much about clandestine money matters. He must have done something in his past that necessitated his "disappearing" from wherever he was before. I asked him what it was, and he replied that it was best I didn't know and to forget about it.

My, my, dear diary, you never know who you're going to meet.

I've arranged to anonymously send Frankie's widow $100,000. That should help them. The news out of Odessa is that Frank Cooper was killed by an unknown assailant in his home, and the police have no leads. I feel bad about that, but if the truth came out it would open up a can of worms.

I just hope Bartlett or DeAngelo—or anyone else—doesn't put it together that Judy Cooper was the Black Stiletto. I don't think Leo had the chance to tell his sister. Hopefully, the secret died with him. Thomas knows, and I trust him.

As time goes on, I'm pretty sure I'll be able to resist the urge to put on the outfit. I don't want to get rid of it, though. Right now, all of my equipment is in a safe storage facility.

Maybe one day I can open a Black Stiletto museum, ha ha.

54
Martin
THE PRESENT

After Gina was back, we all looked online for news coming out of Odessa. It was a pretty big story there. The Bartlett Ranch house had burned down. Former sheriff Ralph McCambridge, an employee at the ranch for years, died in the fire, although there was evidence that he'd been shot by the matriarch of the Bartlett Supply Company empire, Mrs. Christina Bartlett. The seventy-nine-year-old woman was seriously injured, but she had been rescued by a mysterious woman in a "costume." The cook and maid at the ranch, Marisol Espinoza, claimed the savior was "the Black Stiletto," but Ms. Espinoza was said to have been "hysterical" when the authorities arrived on the scene. The investigation was still underway. Unfortunately, Mrs. Bartlett was unable to speak and succumbed to her injuries and second-degree burns in the hospital, nine hours after the incident. A spokesman said she would be remembered for running the Bartlett business with an iron hand after the death of her husband, Ricky Bartlett, who also died, coincidentally, in a fire in 1983.

When I read the bit about the Black Stiletto, I really wanted to scold Gina for what she'd done, but I never said a word. Yes, it was a little strange that she had dressed up in my mom's costume in order to settle a very old score of my mother's, but deep down I was proud of my daughter.

Within twenty-four hours of the awful events in Texas and in Pleasant Prairie, Wisconsin, we had all moved back to our respective homes in Illinois and resumed business as usual. Gina was at my house, and Maggie and I were at hers. Mom was back in her room at Woodlands. Detective Scott was still baffled by it all, and he knew there was a connection between the violence that had occurred in the two states on the same night. He was also pretty sure we knew more than we were telling him. We weren't going to enlighten him. We'd all agreed to play dumb so that he would think that whatever Mrs. Bartlett's beef was with my mother, the secret would die with both women.

The diamond was more magnificent than I imagined. Maggie, Gina, and I talked about what we were going to do with it. Maggie said it would be nice if we knew more about the gem's origin and where it originally came from. It used to be owned by *someone* before Leo Kelly and his sister stole it from that bank in LA and gave it to Vincent DeAngelo. But we weren't going to worry about it. I talked to Sam Wegel about finding a fence who could sell it, and he said he "knew people." Everyone agreed that Angela Sandlin and her family would share in the proceeds, which would be in the millions.

It's what my mother would have wanted.

Mom held out for four more days. The three of us—Gina, Maggie, and I—gathered in Mom's room at the nursing home after Virginia, the hospice caretaker, called to say that the end was imminent. Maggie, as Mom's doctor, had little to do with my mother anymore. Everything was now in the hands of hospice, because what was about to happen was inevitable. The important thing was to make sure Mom was comfortable and without pain. Maggie joined us as part of the family, of course. We had told Gina our news for a wedding in the future, and my daughter was overjoyed and very happy for us. I wished I could tell Mom. She would have been glad for me too. When Carol and I got divorced, Mom took it hard. She always wanted me to love my life and was disappointed that the marriage didn't work out. It was too bad Maggie never knew Mom prior to the Alzheimer's. I think they would have liked each other a lot. My mom did take great joy in being Gina's grandmother. For so many years, the two of them were like two peas in a pod, to use a cliché. They were so much alike, and for years I subconsciously refused to acknowledge it. Now it was all very clear.

Virginia left us alone with Mom except for occasional stop-ins to check on her patient. She'd given Mom a sedative, and my mother had slipped into a deep sleep earlier in the day—almost like a coma, except she could breathe on her own—and that was a sure sign she had only hours to go. Her breaths came rapidly and steadily, almost as if she was exercising. Her eyes were closed and her mouth was slightly open. Her chest rose up and down in sync with the breathing. There was nothing we could do but wait.

It was surprisingly somber-less in the room. All three of us tried our best to bring levity to the situation by discussing Gina's crazy life in New York and recounting stories about my mother and me. I recalled one morning shortly after we'd moved into the house in Arlington Heights. I was about eight or nine. I was in the kitchen and heard a rhythmic pounding noise coming from the basement, so I went down to see what it was. Mom was whaling on a punching bag that she had affixed to the ceiling. That was a surprise. I asked her what she was doing, and she replied, "Beating up bad guys." It seemed to me she was joking, and we both laughed. I was into comic books at the time, so I could relate. If I'd only known.

Gina put an Elvis CD in the portable player we kept in Mom's room. Some people might have thought the music was inappropriate, but we kept the volume down so that Mom's favorite singer was comfortably in the background. It helped us stay positive and not become morose. Again, Mom would have wanted it that way.

Time went by, and I asked Gina, "Was that Josh you were talking to this morning?"

"Yeah."

"You were on a long time."

"I know. There's some stuff going on back home we had to talk about."

"Good? Bad?"

"Oh, definitely good. In fact, Josh gave me the green light to tell you guys a little about what's been going on."

That got my attention. "What do you mean?"

"The Krav Maga and all that. Listen," my daughter said, "what I'm about to tell you has to remain a secret. I can tell you, and I'll tell Mom and Ross, but after that you've got to keep quiet."

"Geez, Gina, what are you talking about?"

"I have a job. A new job. It pays a lot of money."

"Really?" Maggie and I looked at each other. "Doing what?"

"Working for the government."

That answer was not what I expected at all. "What? How?"

"Dad, do you remember when you were in New York and you visited Josh's studio?"

"Yeah?"

"You met a guy there, a man wearing a suit, who was watching me."

"Yeah, I do remember. What was his name? Payne?"

"Mr. Page. Frederick Page. He works for, well, the government. I can't really say. He was recruiting me."

"What?"

Maggie started to chuckle. "What's so funny?" I asked her.

"Don't look so surprised," she answered. "Your daughter has already proven she's capable of extraordinary things."

I turned back to Gina. "What do you mean, exactly, working for the government?"

"Dad, I can't tell you too much. They're putting together a team. Think of us as *special* Special Ops. I've been asked to join and continue my training near DC."

"What, you're going to be a *soldier*?" I was sure my eyes were popping out.

"No, not really. Well, sort of. I'll be on classified missions and stuff. Dad, it was an honor to be chosen. They looked at hundreds of candidates. After what happened in Texas, they decided I was right for the job."

"My God, Gina, will it be dangerous?" She grinned and shook her head as if I'd said something stupid. I didn't care. I wanted to hear her reply. "Well?"

She raised her eyebrows, and said, "I hope so."

"Congratulations, Gina," Maggie said. She got up from her chair and the two of them met in the middle of the room to embrace. I was too stunned to move.

"You going to give me your blessing, Dad?" Gina asked me.

I had no choice, did I? With a heavy sigh, I stood and hugged my daughter.

She was simply amazing in so many ways.

"Oh, and guess what," she said.

"What?"

"We get to pick code names. Take a wild guess what mine is."

I looked at her. "Not—"

"Yep. The Black Stiletto."

I didn't know what to say. Tears came to both our eyes and we held each other again.

At that moment, Mom's breathing changed. Now it sounded like she was having trouble. The three of us moved to her bed. I sat in the chair beside Mom and took her hand. Maggie pressed the call button to send for Virginia.

"Mom?" I didn't expect her to respond, of course, but I hoped, in some way, she could hear me. "It's me, Martin. It's going to be all right, Mom. We got the diamond. Your secret is safe for now. Gina and I are here, and Maggie too. We're with you."

The erratic breathing went on. Virginia came in to take a look. She listened to Mom and said, "Her body's shutting down. It won't be long now." She gave us an encouraging smile and then left us alone.

More tears welled in my eyes and I choked up trying to comment, "After waiting all day, this is kind of sudden."

Maggie stood beside me and put her arm around my shoulders. I continued to hold Mom's hand.

"I love you, Grandma," Gina said. "I hope you can hear me."

"Thank you, Mom." It was difficult to speak. "Thank you for the sacrifices you made to protect me." The salty drops ran down my cheeks. I couldn't help it. "I love you so much."

And then the breathing just stopped.

It was over.

No one said anything or moved for several seconds.

Silently, I stood straight and held out my arms. Maggie and Gina joined me, and we clutched each other in a tight, supportive embrace.

Then, I leaned over and kissed my mother's cheek for the last time.

55
Judy's Diary
1962

DECEMBER 31, 1962

So here it is, New Year's Eve again.

Although we're in a strange town where I know only one person, and there won't be any parties or celebrations to attend tonight, I'm confident this will be a *much* better New Year's than the last one!

We moved in to our new apartment over the weekend. It's located on Euclid Avenue and is very close to "downtown" Arlington Heights, if you can call it that. I don't know how long we'll stay here; we may be moving to a different town next year.

It's snowing. Gosh, I haven't seen snow since I left New York. It's very pretty outside. We didn't have a White Christmas, but it was cold and wintery. Thomas said the winters in Illinois can be brutal. That may take some getting used to.

Martin had his first Christmas, but of course he's still too young to know what was going on. He got some presents from me—toys, clothes, and a little indoor swing that he loves. Thomas got me a *mink fur coat* to help combat the cold! I told him that was way too expensive, but he winked at me and said he has "connections" and got it for a song. Still, I felt funny receiving such a nice gift from him. Actually, I think he's a little sweet on me.

Wow, tomorrow it will be 1963. I can't believe it's been nearly eleven years since I left Texas and ran away to New York. What a decade! I think I can honestly say that during the last *five* years—my Black Stiletto years—I experienced more *life*—and death—than most people do in sixty. I lived hard and fast. I am grateful for that, and I will always treasure my time as the Stiletto. I'm proud of what I accomplished. The other women I see everywhere seem so compliant and unassertive. It's a man's world, and all the other women go along with it. Will that ever change? I think so. I have a feeling the next ten or twenty years will see massive transformations in our society. At least it's my wish that will happen.

The pain of some of the Stiletto memories, though, is going to be hard to shake, especially those of the past month—the deaths of my brother Frankie, of Barry and Skipper. These will haunt me until my dying days.

That's why I'm retiring the mask.

Still, I wonder if the world will remember the Black Stiletto, or if she will fade into obscurity and be just a curiosity from the late 1950s and early '60s. Who knows? I just hope history is kind to my legacy. There are still some who say I was a criminal and should have been behind bars. For my part, I believe I did some good. At least I keep telling myself that.

I just looked back at the first diary I wrote in 1958. On the first page, I mentioned hearing Elvis's song, "Hard Headed Woman." Even then I said the song could have been written about me. I think it's true now more than ever, although I don't particularly think I'm a "thorn in the side of man"—or maybe I am, ha ha! For kicks, I put on the record and sang along to it. Martin laughed and bounced in his swing and shook his rattle. He's going to be crawling soon, I know it. He'll be four months old in January—*oops*, I mean *three* months old, ha ha. Sorry, Martin.

Will he ever see these diaries? Maybe, when I'm old and dying, I'll let him read them and he'll find out all about who his crazy mother really was. For now, though, I will keep them under lock and key, along with my outfit and other "souvenirs" I've kept from my

Stiletto days. I'm hiding *all* the memories and will try my hardest not to think of them again. I have a dream that someday Martin and I will live permanently in a house somewhere—probably here—and I'll have a secret room built. I'll keep all the Stiletto stuff there for safekeeping. I'm sure Thomas can help make that wish a reality. Then, after I've departed this earth, maybe Martin can sell it all and make a fortune, ha ha. Fat chance that it will be worth anything!

It's going to be difficult adjusting to my new life. Living quietly and not attracting attention will be a challenge for me. After all, I'm a big city girl and crave excitement. I'll have to find other ways to entertain myself.

Pretty soon, when I know it's safe, I'll write to Freddie and Lucy in New York and let them know where I am. I believe I won't keep a diary anymore. I'm done writing my "life story," because I'm pretty sure the rest of it will be uneventful, and that's on purpose. Instead, I'll read a lot, continue to work out and exercise, see movies, play records, and raise Martin.

Martin, Martin, Martin—he's such a cute kid. I love him like crazy. I've done all this for *him*, dear diary. I'm saying goodbye to the Black Stiletto and devoting the rest of my years to the ordinary because of my little boy. She was a part of my existence that I can now put to rest because Martin is my life from now on. The important thing is to protect him.

So from this day forth I'll just live like everyone else. I'll be plain, ordinary Judy Talbot.

I think I can be happy with that.

So long, dear diary. It was lovely knowing you.

Happy New Year!

ABOUT THE AUTHOR

Raymond Benson is the author of over thirty books and previously penned *The Black Stiletto* (2011), *The Black Stiletto: Black & White* (2012), *The Black Stiletto: Stars & Stripes* (2013), and *The Black Stiletto: Secrets & Lies* (2014).

Between 1996 and 2002, he was commissioned by the James Bond literary copyright holders to take over writing the 007 novels. In total, he penned and published worldwide six original 007 novels, three film novelizations, and three short stories. An anthology of his 007 work, *The Union Trilogy*, was published in the fall of 2008, and a second anthology, *Choice of Weapons*, appeared summer 2010. The six original titles are now available for Kindle. His book *The James Bond Bedside Companion*, an encyclopedic work on the 007 phenomenon, was first published in 1984 and was nominated for an Edgar Allan Poe Award by Mystery Writers of America for Best Biographical/Critical Work.

Raymond recently co-edited, with Jeffery Deaver, the anthology *Ice Cold: Tales of Intrigue from the Cold War*. Using the pseudonym "David Michaels," Raymond is also the author of the *New York Times* best-selling books Tom Clancy's *Splinter Cell* and its sequel Tom Clancy's *Splinter Cell: Operation Barracuda*. Raymond's original suspense novels include *Evil Hours*, *Face Blind*, *Sweetie's Diamonds* (which won the Readers' Choice Award for Best Thriller of 2006 at the Love is Murder Conference for Authors, Readers and Publishers), *Torment*, and *Artifact of Evil*. *A Hard Day's Death*, the first in a series of "rock 'n' roll thrillers," was published in 2008, and its sequel, the Shamus Award-nominated *Dark Side of the Morgue*, was published in 2009. Other recent works include novelizations of the popular videogames, *Metal Gear Solid* and its sequel, *Metal Gear Solid 2: Sons of*

Liberty, *Homefront: The Voice of Freedom*, co-written with John Milius, and *HITMAN: DAMNATION*.

The author has taught courses in film genres and history at New York's New School for Social Research; Harper College in Palatine, Illinois; College of DuPage in Glen Ellyn, Illinois; and currently presents Film Studies lectures with *Daily Herald* movie critic Dann Gire. Raymond has been honored in Naoshima, Japan, with the erection of a permanent museum dedicated to one of his novels, and he is also an ambassador for Japan's Kagawa Prefecture. Raymond is an active member of International Thriller Writers Inc., Mystery Writers of America, the International Association of Media Tie-In Writers, a full member of ASCAP, and served on the board of directors of The Ian Fleming Foundation for sixteen years. He is based in the Chicago area.

www.raymondbenson.com
www.theblackstiletto.net

DATE DUE			